Carl GOES LONDON

Who is Carl?

Carl Goes is named after an old friend with wanderlust who died too young. Carl was an avid collector of travel guides from the 1800s, a time in which a global standard for travel books was set.

Our friend Carl had only debts when he passed away, so everything he owned had to be sold at auction. We decided to pool our money and buy back everything we knew he loved — some antique paintings, family jewellery, and of course, his beloved travel book collection. Remarkably, when the antique traders in the room realised we were the friends and family of our dear friend, they stopped bidding, helping us save everything we could.

We wanted to pay tribute to our friend Carl by creating a modern-day series of books encapsulating a new type of travel, where work, play, creativity and curiosity combine. Capturing the spirit of the man *Carl Goes* is named after, our guides are for all the curious and creative folks on the planet. We hope Carl would be proud.

Foreword

Welcome to *Carl Goes London*, a book that brings the local voices of Londoners to our curious and creative travellers. *Carl Goes London* is a lifestyle accompaniment. Many of our fans read our books from cover to cover before they travel to a destination, as an immersive experience before they even arrive. They dip their toe in and out while they're in a city, taking inspiration from our interviewees and our recommendations, before veering off and crafting their own adventures. Unlike most other books out there, we've cut out the middle men in our production process and have written and published the book within the same year. We think all of these things make *Carl Goes* a little different from other city guides, but we'll let you decide for yourselves.

Our readers are urban nomads and inquisitive entrepreneurs, but despite their love of tech, they find the tactile experience of a book to be a luxurious rarity amid the clutter of all the gadgets and apps out there. *Carl Goes London* is for intrepid city breakers and seasoned globetrotters. It's for enterprising business executives and spirited start-up owners. And it's for everyone working in or interested in a broad spectrum of creative industries, motivated to slot in with the locals during their London visit.

The feeling in London at the moment is one of courageous creativity. Long known as a corporate and costly global centre, London's ecosystem is increasingly supportive of smaller scale ventures and tech start-up innovation. Thanks to enterprising government initiatives, East London Tech City is thriving and there are more than 5,000 active start-ups working across London. Although the expense of London can be frustrating for locals at times, London's wealth is positive in the business scene, as start-ups have access to rich consumers, influential businesses, a strong funding landscape and an established city system — London has the largest city ecosystem in Europe, after all.

Despite the strong business ethos in the city, London has a quirky social vibe. Londoners love nothing more than to discover the latest pop-up restaurant on a rooftop or speakeasy-style bar in a basement. They dress up for themed events, from post-war dances to outdoor screenings of iconic films. The industrial chic style is all the rage and the trendiest shops and businesses just love to operate out of old shipping containers. And although the sheer scale of the city can be mind-boggling, there are plenty of pockets where village-like charm and strong local identities reign supreme. Ever since the London 2012 Olympics and William and Kate's royal wedding, London has been permeated with a healthy dose of national pride too.

Londoners utterly embrace the internationalism, multiculturalism and vibrancy of their city and there's a gleam of true pride in the eyes of locals when they say this makes London a city like no other. The global thinking and business outlook is another element making the city ripe for business success, while visitors to the city and those coming to work for a while quickly feel at home.

Through *Carl Goes London*, we want you to become a citizen of London for the timebeing. That's why we haven't created a directory of museums and landmarks, sightseeing tours and tourist hotspots. Instead, we let city residents describe their city in their own words. We tell you about co-working spaces and networking events, we handpick eateries and hotels with finesse and flair, and we give you inspiration for getting lost in the city, so you can discover London on your own terms, in your own time.

Sascha Mengerink, Publisher
Sasha Arms, Editor

The locals

No-one knows London like the people who live there, whether they've lived in the city for a lifetime, or moved there and discovered everything for themselves. Throughout *Carl Goes London*, we bring you interviews with some well-known and well-connected Londoners, who have shared their London experiences and best bits of the city especially for you.

Emyr Thomas
page 20
Concierge and luxury business founder Emyr has lived in London for more than a decade. He left a corporate career in the City to set up his own business, Bon Vivant, recommending the best of London's offerings to his impressive client list. When he's not working, he spends his time checking out all of London's newest restaurant and hotel openings, getting fit at Barry's Bootcamp and exploring London on foot.
Our favourite London tip from Emyr: Join The Hospital Club for networking and socialising with creative types and business owners in London.

Roberto Revilla
page 40
Fashion designer and bespoke tailor Roberto Revilla is a born and bred Londoner. He spends his time in the offices of media professionals, in the homes of up-and-coming entrepreneurs and in the hotel rooms of high-flying international clients, who are all looking for Roberto's sought-after tailoring skills. When he's not working, Roberto enjoys spending time in his north-west London home with his wife and pets.
Our favourite London tip from Roberto: Listen to the songs of Londoners Nerina Pallot and Lily Allen to get a feel for the city.

Nathalie Rozencwajg
page 90
Architect Nathalie divides her time between London and Paris, and is best known for the multiple award-winning Town Hall Hotel in east London, where she added a contemporary extension to a historical building, creating an iconic London landmark. She's been commended as Architects' Journal's Emerging Woman Architect of the Year and named by The Guardian as one of ten women to watch in architecture. When she's not working, Nathalie enjoys finding some peace and quiet in London's green spaces.
Our favourite London tip from Nathalie: Check out the aviary and penguin pool at London Zoo — it's a top piece of design in the city.

Graham Hollick
page 114
Creative director Graham started his career in trend forecasting with Li Edelkoort. He now leads on interiors trend forecasting for WGSN, works in magazine styling and art direction, and has his own collection of ethical textiles, produced in collaboration with artisans in Nepal and India. When he's not working, Graham spends his time vintage shopping and roaming around London on his scooter.
Our favourite London tip from Graham: Check out Tom Dixon's 'scent of London' candle to experience an uncannily accurate London smell.

Lee Thornley
page **140**
This design entrepreneur and founder of Bert & May specialises in the reclamation and production of tiles and wood. Before this, Lee built a boutique hotel in Spain, named as one of Tatler's top 101 hotels in the world. Commuting between Yorkshire and London, Lee lives on a 'Bert & May Space' in the form of a barge on the canal outside his office during the week. When he's not working, Lee rummages in antique shops and sates his foodie cravings.
Our favourite London tip from Lee: Visit the climbing wall in Mile End for an adrenalin rush.

Jess Williamson
page **162**
Californian start-up guru Jess is a director at the Techstars accelerator and development programme. After living in Chicago, Edinburgh and Cambridge, she now considers herself a converted Londoner. A contagiously enthusiastic member of the UK's start-up community, Jess is an avid adventurer in her spare time, wandering aimlessly in different parts of the city until she finds places she likes.
Our favourite London tip from Jess: Don't feel a social pressure to have an answer when someone asks where you're going. Just head out the door and see where you end up.

Alice Hodge and Ellen Parr
page **194**
This duo run The Art of Dining events: immersive dining and theatrical pop-up experiences at unusual locations across London. Alice, a set designer, and Ellen, a Moro-trained chef, scour the city for the perfect venues for their themed events, and have hosted everything from Tudor feasts in grand dining halls to kitsch seventies-era dinners. When they're not working, they tend a vegetable patch, scour the city for quirky props, and swim al fresco in Hampstead.
Our favourite London tip from Alice and Ellen: Get baked goods from The Dusty Knuckle — a bakery in a shipping container helping ex-gang kids get jobs.

Marama Corlett
page **222**
Maltese actress Marama has starred in various high-profile TV series and films including Desert Dancer alongside Freida Pinto and Maleficent with Angelina Jolie. She's also been in London theatre productions including The Crucible at The Old Vic and The Children's Hour alongside Keira Knightley. When she's not working, she loves preparing for casting calls in Soho and going to afternoon showings in the cinema.
Our favourite London tip from Marama: Maison Bertaux and Cotton Café are Soho gems undiscovered by tourists.

Contents

Essentials

Work

Live

Getting away and getting lost

London's DNA

A visual tour of the London identity.

1. The cycling sidekick
2. Sitting outside as soon as it's not raining
3. Canalside life
4. The latest sandwich trends — this week: hot salt beef
5. Tube escalator etiquette: stand to the right, walk on the left
6. Comfy commuter shoes
7. Splashes of colour brightening up grey days
8. A city under constant construction
9. Too many tourists
10. Too many people
11. Iconic black cabs
12. Basements...
13. ...and rooftops — wherever there's space!
14. The Tate, and many other free museums and galleries
15. The River Thames
16. A love affair with Indian food
17. The scotch egg obsession
18. Short trousers / exposed ankles
19. The social conscience of Londoners
20. Coffee, laptop...what more do you need?
21. Speakeasy style
22. Getting around quickly
23. Quirky pastimes
24. Humorous signage
25. Eclectic fashions
26. Embracing internationalism
27. Street markets
28. Street food and food markets
29. London loves sub-cultures
30. Vintage and old-is-new style
31. Public transport
32. Busking and street performers
33. Traditional British foods: fish and chip Fridays, Sunday roasts, and pie, mash and eels any day of the week
34. Handmade culture
35. Pop-ups
36. Queuing
37. Bridges
38. Famous people and blue plaques
39. Outdoor fitness
40. Pavement beers

14

15

16

17

18

CHIVES
No.1 Woburn Walk

Skinny people are easier to kidnap. Stay safe! Drink Full fat Coffee Then you can run fast or buy Coca-Cola

WOODSEER ST. E.I.

AIRSTREAM CAFÉ

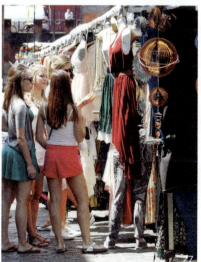

3 days in London

Soak up the vibe of a few different London neighbourhoods and join the locals in the eateries and bars they adore during three thrilling days in the city.

Day one

Take the advice of Londoners and get a sense of London from above ground instead of taking the London Underground, or 'Tube' as Londoners say. The number 23 bus travels from Liverpool Street to Westbourne Grove, and goes past some of London's iconic landmarks such as St. Paul's Cathedral, Nelson's Column and Marble Arch. Not only will this journey give you a feeling of London from east to west, you'll be travelling alongside real Londoners going about their everyday business. After arriving in this west London locality, take a stroll along Golborne Road to grab a coffee and some pastéis de nata at one of the Portuguese eateries, peruse the vintage wares of the market and take in the Ernö Goldfinger designed Trellick Tower, a cult London landmark. Walk along Portobello Road afterwards for the iconic vintage market and a slice of Notting Hill life.

Head back into central London for a street food lunch at Exmouth Market (p56), a locally revered spot by London foodies. Check out the Museum of the Order of St. John (p56) nearby afterwards — a lesser known spot on London's museum scene offering an insight into London's long and important history. Then visit the Guildhall (p57) and enjoy the grandiose courtyard, before tracking down The Old Doctor Butler's Head pub (p57) squirrelled away along a centuries-old alleyway for an afternoon drink.

As late afternoon approaches, make your way over to the tallest building in Europe: The Shard (p58). Go to the faux grass clad viewing platform at the top or simply admire its height from the shadows below, before going to The Scoop (p58) — the sunken amphitheatre by London's riverside with a year round calendar of free events. Take your pick of one of London's many foodie gems for dinner. If you want to stay in the London Bridge area, make a reservation at The Rooftop Café, unexpectedly hidden away in a co-working space, or enjoy the sun splashed flavours of Arabica near Borough Market (p191). For a nightcap, make your way to the speakeasy basement bar at the Mayor of Scaredy Cat Town (p192), or join a laid back post-work crowd at the Provence-inspired Baranis (p193).

Day two

If you're curious about London's co-working and start-up scene, spend your second day in east London, in and around the Tech City start-up hub near Old Street. Start off with a visit to Google Campus (p156) and even hire a desk there at one of the co-working spaces (p127) located inside. There's a vibrant calendar of activities going on, giving you the chance to experience the buzz of London's creative and start-up community. Later on, visit the café/workspace and 'social experiment' Ziferblat (p78), where you only pay for the time you spend there. Follow up with lunch at Merchants Tavern (p138), an east London stalwart for entrepreneurial business meetings. Do a little early afternoon shopping at BOXPARK (p210), a series of shipping containers in trendy Shoreditch that play host to some of the latest inventions from creative London start-ups. Follow this up with a browse of the stalls at the relatively newly regenerated Spitalfields Market (p210). Carry on to Hackney as the afternoon goes on to take in the locally loved Broadway Market (p77), then admire the architectural magnificence of the Town Hall Hotel (p216) before popping inside for a drink in The Corner Room.

For dinner, go to the affectionately known 'Pho Mile' on Kingsland Road for a low-key Vietnamese dinner at Viet Grill (p183) or anywhere else that takes your fancy. Carry on to one of London's arts or cultural institutions such as the Barbican Centre (p56) or the Southbank Centre (p60) for an evening performance. If you're looking for a nightcap afterwards, try BrewDog Shoreditch (p192) or its basement speakeasy for London crafted beers, or pay a visit to one of design guru Graham Hollick's favourites: Hand of Glory (p124).

Day three

Relax a little on your final day in London and enjoy some of the wide open spaces the city is famed for. Start off in the leafy north London locality of Hampstead (p64) with a coffee in the pavement seating area of Ginger & White (p187) followed by a stroll around Hampstead Heath (p64); make your way to Parliament Hill for views over London. Follow this up with a visit to Abbey Park Cemetery for a wander around this overgrown Victorian resting place and a quiet slice of London's history.

As you pass through the centre of town from north to south, stop for lunch at NOPI (p179) by celebrated chef Yotam Ottolenghi, or visit chef Ellen Parr's favourite restaurant Bao (p180), for a delicious and quick steamed bun. Once you're south of the river, head over to Tooting Bec Lido (p72) for a quick dip — it's one of the largest outdoor swimming pools in the UK. Pay a visit to Brixton for the locally revered Brixton Village filled with small eateries and quirky shops, and POP Brixton (p191), where start-ups are being given a foot on the business rung inside this venue made of shipping containers. Squeeze in an early evening summertime drink at Frank's Campari Bar (p192), a Peckham bar on the roof of a multi-storey car park with unexpectedly brilliant views of London.

Do something a little different in the evening, and go to a themed pop-up dinner by The Art of Dining (p190), or find out if any Secret Cinema (www.secretcinema. org) events are on. Secret Cinema takes over a London space for a few days and creates a themed carnival atmosphere on a massive scale relating to the film it airs on a big screen. Think fancy dress and being transported into another reality.

Three weeks in London

Explore the central cityscape by foot, dip your toe into London's start-up scene
and explore localities in London neighbourhoods far and wide.

Week one

Get a feeling of what makes London tick during your first week in the city by
sticking to central areas and taking in historic landmarks combined with quiet side
streets. Londoners agree the best way to do this is on foot. The Jubilee Walkway
(www.tfl.gov.uk/modes/walking/jubilee-walkway), divided into five loops, is a
15 mile route that takes in the key London icons and locally loved pockets of
life. Spend your first five days walking a different loop, pausing to veer off in
interesting-looking directions as the mood takes you. By the end of the week,
you'll be surprised by the history you've been able to take in, as well as the feeling
of the streets and the local life you've been able to absorb. The art-minded should
take one of London's many art trails too, such as The Line (theline.org).

Intersperse your meanderings by foot with some of London's more centrally
located cultural and social offerings. Visit the Royal Academy of the Arts (p59) one
afternoon then dine in the restaurant after closing time for an exclusive out-of-
hours feeling. Take in a dance performance at the internationally-famed Sadler's
Wells (p56), watch an independent film at the Prince Charles Cinema (p60) or
watch a play in the Sam Wanamaker Playhouse, a candlelit attachment to the
Shakespeare Globe (www.shakespearesglobe.com). Dip into the variety of London's
dining scene, from champagne and hotdogs at Bubbledogs (p182) to the foodie-
favourite eateries along Bermondsey Street.

Week two

It might be time to buckle down and do some work during your second week in
London and there's no better place to do it than from a desk at a co-working space
in Tech City near Old Street. The branch of TechHub (p127) at the Google Campus
is a great option if you want to make the most of the networking opportunities
available there. This week is all about experiencing the entrepreneurial and start-
up culture of east London, so make the most of the events going on. Check out
what other business related events are happening in London during the week too.

In your spare time, get out and about and explore London's design and creative culture further by visiting Chelsea Harbour Design Centre (p58) and perusing the antiques shops such as Labour & Wait on Redchurch Street (p150). Find creative inspiration at the Fashion and Textile Museum (p58) or the Victoria & Albert Museum . Enjoy evenings rubbing shoulders with entrepreneurs and start-up owners at private clubs such as The Hospital Club (p156), in quirky restaurants such as Beach Blanket Babylon (BBB) Shoreditch (p78) and at artsy evening events such as Fitzrovia Lates (p56), First Thursdays (p150) and The Society Club (p60) for literary buffs.

Week three

After exploring central London areas and start-up hubs in London, spend your final week getting out into neighbourhoods further away from the city centre. In north London, visit The Wellcome Collection (p206) — described as a museum for the curious, visit The Pavilion Café (p65) tucked away in Highgate Woods and dine at The Seagrass restaurant (p183) in an old marketside pie and mash shop. In south London, pick up some craft beer, hot sauce or vinyl in the quirky Hop Burns & Black shop (p71), have a drink, free toast and shisha in Café Cairo (p70), and take in a performance at Theatre503 (www.theatre503.com), hailed for its focus on new writing. Alternatively, hunt down a production by Opera Settecento (www.operasettecento.com), an organisation that sources 'lost' opera seria from the 18th century.

In east London, have a traditional British breakfast at the greasy spoon E. Pellicci (p186), watch opera performances on big screens in Canary Wharf (p76) and visit the Meantime Brewing Company (p76) for some locally brewed beer in Greenwich. In west London, get lost in Holland Park (p85), participate in Bogan Bingo (p82) — the retro comedy bingo show, and take in the Little Venice waterways with a coffee at Café Laville (p84) with its perfect vantage point by the water.

Three months in London

Spend three months living the London life based from different localities of the city,
to experience the identity and charm of the city's neighbourhoods.

Month one
Spend your first month in London living and working in a central spot to help you
get your bearings in all directions. Stay in a design hotel like CitizenM (p215) or
find a room in a house share to get acquainted with some Londoners and their way
of life. The Soho Collective (p134) is an ideal place to rent a desk for a month in the
centre of London's action.

This first month is all about living life to the maximum in the centre of the city
alongside London's locals. In Soho, spend your time ducking in and out of shops
and eateries, such as Maison Bertaux (p235) for tea and cake, Neal's Yard for
holistic and health shops and La Bodega Negra (p234) for Mexican food via an
entrance that looks like a sex shop. Radiating further out of this locality, enjoy the
quaintness of Lamb's Conduit Street and Shepherd Market (p59), find peaceful
moments in some of the city centre's many garden squares, and take in the
changing architecture in the city, from the 'Inside-Outside' Lloyd's Building (p57)
to the art deco Michelin House (p57).

Spend evenings with like-minded Londoners, whether at one of the city's many
Meetup events (p156) or at the weekly Silicon Drinkabout for start-up workers.
Share a table with eleven other Londoners at UNA (p64) in the St. Pancras Clock
Tower or at a supper club such as the one run by MsMarmitelover (p190) out of her
home. By the end of your first month, you'll have met plenty of locals and found
out about their favourite things to do in the city.

Month two
Immerse yourself in the creative and start-up world in London during your second
month by living and working in the east of the city. Stay in the playful but design-
conscious Ace Hotel (p215) in Shoreditch or rent a room in a creative house share.
Rent a desk for the month at one of the many co-working spaces in the area such
as Shoreditch Works (p134).

If you've got a business idea or want to broaden your career horizons, this is the
time to do it. Join a start-up bootcamp run by start-up founders or visit co-working
spaces to develop business ideas alongside well-known entrepreneurs. Network
at every opportunity, whether it's at the more formal Institute of Directors events
or low-key Meetups such as MiniBar (p156). Keep yourself informed of the city's
calendar of conferences (p158) and specialist events like Social Media Week and

the Business Startup Show. Enjoy the one-of-a-kind downtime in the east of the city too by visiting the canalside art gallery café — The Proud Archivist (p77), the Dalston Roof Park (p77) for supper clubs and film screenings, and Hurwundeki (p78) for a Korean café and hair salon rolled into one.

Month three

Move to the quieter neighbourhood of Hampstead (p64) for your final month to get a more village-like perspective on London. Find an apartment to rent for a month for that homely feeling while you decide if London's a place you may want to stay in even longer. For work, there are plenty of cutesy cafés ripe for sitting with a laptop and a coffee, or hire a desk for a month in the Hampstead Design Hub (p134).

When you're not working, enjoy the rhythms of everyday life in north London, using Hampstead as a base. Go for strolls on the country-esque Hampstead Heath (p64) and observe (or join) the ardent swimmers enjoying the open air Hampstead Heath ponds. Explore the area's affinity with the arts at Keats House (p65), or venture a little closer to the centre of town by joining the celebrity set at Primrose Hill (p64). Music and vintage lovers should head over to Stoke Newington (p66) for the stringed instruments at Bridgewood & Neitzert (p66) and an eclectic range of throwback furniture at the Cobbled Yard (p66). For food, venture over to Harringay's Green Lanes for the best Turkish in town in restaurants like Gökyüzü (p183), or go to The Clissold Arms (p189) in East Finchley for pub food, themed evenings and a proud history (The Kinks played their first gig there in the 1960s).

By the end of month three, you'll have lived and breathed the London life in different contexts, from the bustle of the city centre and the entrepreneurial drive of Tech City, to the peaceful lifestyles of the London outskirts. If you decide to stay in the city for longer, you may have a tough time deciding which corner of the city is the perfect one for you.

We're lucky enough to live in a city that's at the forefront of changing trends and styles.

Photo: Emyr Thomas

Emyr Thomas
Concierge and
luxury travel business founder

Introduce yourself.
I run a company called Bon Vivant, which is a concierge and luxury travel company that essentially helps individuals and corporate clients run their lives. It involves anything from planning holidays, booking restaurants and securing tickets to events, to helping people with everyday questions they may have and arranging corporate events and hospitality.

How long have you been living in London?
Since 2002; I'm from south Wales originally.

Tell us about your background and how that led to your company being formed?
I moved to London straight after university to train with a big city firm as an accountant. I thought I was going to the City of London to make my millions, but I did it for six years and found the reality was very different; I hated it! I decided I had to find a job where I enjoyed going to work every day, although I didn't really know what. I loved visiting hotels and restaurants and knew I wanted to work with them in some capacity, but I didn't necessarily want to work in them. I had a good knowledge of London restaurants, bars, clubs and hotels. In my existing job, clients or colleagues would ask me to make recommendations all the time, like finding a suitable restaurant in Mayfair to take clients, or a bar in the City that would be good for a group. Mostly I had a good idea of the perfect place to recommend; if I didn't know, I'd be inspired to do some research to find out more about the options available. The more I did it, the more I enjoyed it. It was as if I was doing the role of a concierge already and so I decided to try to make it a career. I knew of some larger concierge companies and I thought I could try to get a job with them, but I didn't really want to start from scratch at the bottom. With my business background, I thought I'd try to do it myself, and a year and a half later, Bon Vivant was in operation.

How has Bon Vivant evolved since those early days?
It's still a small company because the whole point is that we offer a really personal service. Each client gets one person they deal with directly for all requests, so from their point of view, they get a really personal service and from our point of view, we really get to know the client well. We get

to know how to tailor each recommendation to that person in specific scenarios. Although we still focus on London, we do a lot more travel now, helping make arrangements for clients travelling to different countries for business or pleasure. Our travel business is growing day by day so it's an exciting time for the company.

What is it about London that makes a concierge company successful?

It's a mixture of being based in a big enough city, a wealthy enough city and having a volume of services that warrant people needing a steer on where to go and what to do. My job wouldn't really work without these factors. We're facilitators: we have the clients, we know the venues and we bring them together through our recommendations. Some of our clients are eating out five times a week and they're travelling abroad several times a month. They're entertaining their clients, they need access to events and they have busy social lives.

What does it take to be a concierge in London?

When I'm hiring someone for Bon Vivant, I don't tend to search for someone who's been a concierge before, because a lot of what we do is about having a knowledge of the city we live in. The thirst for knowledge is the most important thing. A lot of my job is about going out most days to try new places, to eat in new restaurants, to have a drink somewhere different. It's a great life, but it can also get tiresome, so our concierges need to love that lifestyle and want to seek out the best of the best for our clients.

What kind of people use concierge services in the city?

It varies, but our clients are typically in their mid-30s to mid-50s. They're people who are busy, such as senior professionals, small business owners or people in the public eye, of whom we have a few. They're the classically cash-rich time-poor Londoners, but they're not necessarily millionaires. They're people who earn good money and want to know they're spending it wisely in the right places. It's not only high earners, but people who are new to London and want someone to advise them; we've even had a couple of teachers as clients before.

What's the most bizarre request you've had?

We don't really get too many extreme requests as I'd say our clients are pretty normal people. I did receive one strange request from someone who wasn't a client, who wanted us to arrange for them to go to the theatre with Prince Albert of Monaco. When I said that wasn't a service we offered, they said that Prince Andrew would do! Again, I had to politely say that wasn't a service we offered.

Do entrepreneurs like yourself experience the city differently from other Londoners?

There's very much a crossover between my work and my own time and I like to think my clients are relying on my personal experiences. I probably experience the city differently from other Londoners because I'm always looking out for things not only that I want to do, but that my clients would like too. I'm always looking out for a new art gallery that's opening, or what's on at the opera, or a new play, a new restaurant... I have to be interested in everything because I know the tastes of my clients and want to make proactive as well as reactive recommendations. I look at the city through a million different eyes.

What's your favourite place to work in the city?

The Hospital Club, because it's where I used to work back when I first set up my company. It was convenient as it's about a 20 minute walk from home, and now it's about halfway between home and the office. It's got a great working environment but it's not stuffy. You can come in a suit, but most people are wearing jeans and a jacket. There's such a good mix of people that you could come and work in your slacks or you could get dressed up and go for a meeting. The social elements of the club help new business owners have a cut-off time from work. Up until about 18:00 everyone's sitting around with their laptops, but then it changes into more of an evening vibe. It's almost like having someone tell you that it's evening time, so it's time to pack up and go, or get a drink in. I really like it.

What would you suggest business travellers should do to unwind during an evening in London?

My fall-back is always a nice bar and a restaurant; there are so many in London to recommend. Unless they're coming in from New York or Paris or a city where there's an equivalent restaurant and bar scene, just being in a London bar or restaurant gives an amazing buzz. The design is really cool and sitting there and taking it all in is just something to behold, not to mention the food and drinks themselves. We find some travellers are amazed that places in London are super busy even on a Monday or Tuesday, and not just on a Friday or Saturday like in smaller cities.

Where is your personal favourite for a business meal and drink in the evening?

I've been raving about Fera at Claridge's recently: it's definitely one of my all-time best meals. Some clients of mine emailed me after they went to tell me it was outstanding. You don't often get feedback from clients unless something goes wrong, so to have a good comment from a client means it must be good. I also love the two bars at the Connaught Hotel, called the Connaught and the Coburg. If someone's going to Mayfair for business, those are the places to go.

Which neighbourhood do you live in and what is it like?
I live in Clerkenwell. It's quite urban and industrial with a lot of loft conversions. Unfortunately it doesn't have much green space, but it feels quite cool without trying too hard to be cool. It has that kind of relaxed, friendly vibe and it's not typically a family place, so it's not overrun with buggies at the weekend. It has a really good food and restaurant scene. I'm a big fan of walking around London and Clerkenwell is a 20 minute walk from the City of London, a 25 minute walk from Soho and a 40 minute walk from Mayfair. So you're smack bang in the middle of everything and being able to walk pretty much anywhere centrally within 45 minutes is a huge draw.

What's your favourite place to eat out in Clerkenwell?
There's a great tapas bar called Morito. It's on Exmouth Market and I live just a few minutes from there. It's amazing. It's a tiny place and it holds about 30 people maximum. It's always rammed full, but the tapas is probably the best I've ever had, including in Spain. It's brilliant.

Where do you go shopping?
I love Lamb's Conduit Street for menswear. It's not too far from home for me and it has some really nice, independent boutiques. I also love Liberty; it's a department store that feels quite cool and quirky.

How do you keep up with the new openings happening in London?
One thing we do for our clients is a monthly summary of new openings of bars, restaurants and hotels. The number of new things that are opening on a weekly basis is just incredible. You simply cannot get bored in London, and thankfully it's my job to go and try these things and to find the best to recommend to others. While I'm sure I'd like the odd day where I can just watch TV, that's rare because there's always something new to explore. I think the downside is that you often forget the more established places in London. There are restaurants, for example, that have been open for a few years that are still firm favourites like Dean Street Townhouse, Scott's or The Wolseley. It can become a habit to jump onto what's new all the time.

What is the current trend in London?
A recent trend in London is high-end specialised exercise classes. Whether it's spinning classes or my personal favourite, Barry's Bootcamp — a gruelling indoor bootcamp favoured by celebrities in LA — this trend is here to stay.

It sounds like you love the buzz of the city. Is there ever a time you want to get away from it all and is there a particular place you go?
I love going to Waterloo Bridge. For me, it's the bridge where you can stand and see the best view of London in all directions. You can see all the landmarks all the way down past St Paul's to the City, Canary Wharf,

the Houses of Parliament and the London Eye. You can really take in
the beauty of the city and the buildings; get it on a clear day and it's just
spectacular. If I ever feel down I can take a quick walk there and in a few
minutes I can just be looking at that view and everything's right again.

Do you have a favourite chill-out place in London?

I rarely get a chance to relax! I love going to Primrose Hill. That's a really
nice place to get away, although it can get packed up there during the
warmer months as Londoners use every available green space to make the
most of the sun!

What would your perfect day in London involve?

I'd walk around the centre of town; I just love walking around the city and
along the river. I would have some spa treatments at the Corinthia Hotel,
as they have an amazing spa there. Then I would go to my favourite hotel,
The Connaught, and have drinks in the bar. If I was very lucky, I might get
to stay in their penthouse, which I've stayed in before and it's fantastic.
Then I'd go out for dinner, but there are so many good places to choose
from...actually I might try and do a few dinners in one night!

How would you advise visitors to London to become citizens of the city for the duration of their stay?

My biggest bugbear is that some visitors tend to visit the places they
hear most of. You see the queues outside Madame Tussauds, you see the
hoards at the Hard Rock Café and Leicester Square, and then you'll see
people only eating in the chain restaurants. Then they might go home
and complain that London has terrible restaurants. You literally just have
to delve 100 yards away from the landmarks and you've got a world that's
completely different to that. I'd advise people to do a little bit of research
before travelling or just walk around and see where Londoners seem to be
spending their time.

Visitors should also realise the city, in the centre especially, is much smaller
than you think and it's completely accessible by foot. The Tube from
Covent Garden to Leicester Square might take 15 minutes by the time you
get in and out of the stations, whereas it's a 5 minute walk. You get to see
far more of London by foot compared to getting the Tube from A to B and
ticking off landmarks.

What's your top tip for people-watching in London?

Hotel lobbies. If you sit in the Claridge's lobby, for example, you'll see
all walks of life. You see the guests, the people coming in to use the
restaurants and bars, and the staff; everyone is interacting together
and it's fascinating.

Is there anything you'd change about London?
Less traffic would help!

Where do you like to go for a meal out?
It's funny, I spend my life advising other people and I sometimes forget where I actually like to go myself! For fine dining, I love Marcus Wareing at The Berkeley. Cecconi's is great for a weekend brunch, Dean Street Townhouse for a Soho night out and Hakkasan for high-end Chinese. I went to a great Peruvian restaurant recently called Pachamama in Marylebone; that's really good.

Where do you like to have a casual drink or a classy cocktail?
My new favourite bar is the Fumoir at Claridge's — it's dark, seductive and so sexy in there. For a more casual drink, you may find me at Riding House Café, which is right next to the office, or in one of the many excellent gastropubs in Clerkenwell near home.

Do you go out to see live music?
I don't see a huge deal, but I've been to a few concerts in The Roundhouse in Camden, which have been really good. I've seen some more modern musicians at the Royal Albert Hall; that's a really good venue and people don't always realise there's more than just classical music on offer. I've seen a few musicians at Bloomsbury Ballroom, which is a great venue too.

What's your hot tip for cultural pursuits in London?
You've got all the classics like the Tate Modern and National Portrait Gallery, but a really great smaller museum is called the Sir John Soane's Museum. It's on Lincoln's Inn Fields just behind Holborn and it's just an old house filled with artefacts and old discoveries. It's really really interesting. There are always queues outside and they only let a few people in at a time so they get a cosier experience.

Is there anything that surprises you about London?
With such a diverse population and a rapidly changing city in terms of areas developing and new shops, bars and restaurants opening, I'd be very surprised if anything surprised me about London. We're lucky enough to live in a city that's at the forefront of changing trends and styles that we create as opposed to follow.

What is London's best quality?
The people. There's such a diverse mix and it's rare to have so many different cultures, attitudes, shapes and sizes living harmoniously with each other. Of all the various pockets and cultures we have in the city, from east London and Soho to Mayfair and Chinatown, and all the other neighbourhoods; it's really diverse and I think that gives London a real sense of balance.

Photo: Emyr Thomas

Emyr's London

Places to visit

Barry's Bootcamp
163 Euston Road, London NW1 2BH
+44 (0)207 387 7001
london@barrysbootcamp.com
www.barrysbootcamp.com
Rail/Tube: Euston

Bloomsbury Ballroom
Victoria House, Bloomsbury
Square WC1B 4DA
+44 (0)207 242 0002
enquiries@
thebloomsburyballroom.com
www.thebloomsburyballroom.com
Tube: Holborn

Corinthia Hotel – ESPA Life spa
Whitehall Place SW1A 2BD
+44 (0)207 321 3050
espalife.london@corinthia.com
www.espalifeatcorinthia.com
Tube: Embankment

Lamb's Conduit Street
Tube: Russell Square

Liberty
Regent Street W1B 5AH
+44 (0)207 734 1234
www.liberty.co.uk
Tube: Oxford Circus

National Portrait Gallery
St. Martin's Place WC2H 0HE
+44 (0)207 306 0055
www.npg.org.uk
Tube: Charing Cross or Leicester
Square
Rail: Charing Cross

Primrose Hill
Tube: Chalk Farm or Camden
Town

Royal Albert Hall
Kensington Gore SW7 2AP
+44 (0)207 589 8212
www.royalalberthall.com
Tube: Knightsbridge, South
Kensington or High Street
Kensington

Sir John Soane's Museum
13 Lincoln's Inn Fields WC2A 3BP
+44 (0)207 405 2107
www.soane.org
Tube: Holborn

Tate Modern
Bankside SE1 9TG
+44 (0)207 887 8888
visiting.modern@tate.org.uk
www.tate.org.uk/visit/tate-modern
Rail/Tube: London Bridge

The Hospital Club
Royal Opera House, 24 Endell
Street WC2H 9HQ
+44 (0)207 170 9100
reception@thehospitalclub.com
www.thehospitalclub.com
Tube: Covent Garden

The Roundhouse
Chalk Farm Road NW1 8EH
+44 (0)300 678 9222
www.roundhouse.org.uk
Tube: Chalk Farm
Waterloo Bridge
Rail/Tube: Waterloo

Bars and restaurants

Cecconi's
5a Burlington Gardens W1S 3EP
+44 (0)207 434 1500
www.cecconis.co.uk
Tube: Piccadilly Circus

Dean Street Townhouse
69 - 71 Dean Street W1D 3SE
+44 (0)207 434 1775
www.deanstreettownhouse.com
Tube: Leicester Square

Fera & Fumoir at Claridge's
49 Brook Street W1K 4HR
+44 (0)207 107 8888
reservations@feraatclaridges.
co.uk
www.feraatclaridges.co.uk
Tube: Bond Street

Hakkasan
17 Bruton Street W1J 6QB
+44 (0)207 907 1888
mayfairreservation@hakkasan.
com
www.hakkasan.com
Tube: Piccadilly Circus

Marcus Wareing at The Berkeley
Wilton Place SW1X 7RL
+44 (0)207 235 1200
www.marcus-wareing.com
Tube: Knightsbridge

Morito
32 Exmouth Market EC1R 4QE
+44 (0)207 278 7007
info@morito.co.uk
www.morito.co.uk
Rail/Tube: Farringdon

Pachamama
18 Thayer Street W1U 3JY
+44 (0)207 935 9393
www.pachamamalondon.com
Tube: Bond Street

Riding House Café
43-51 Great Titchfield Street
W1W 7PQ
+44 (0)207 927 0840
info@ridinghousecafe.co.uk
www.ridinghousecafe.co.uk
Tube: Oxford Circus

Scott's
20 Mount Street, Mayfair W1K 2HE
+44 (0)207 495 7309
www.scotts-restaurant.com
Tube: Bond Street or Green Park

The Connaught – Connaught and Coburg bars
Carlos Place, Mayfair W1K 2AL
+44 (0)207 499 7070
www.the-connaught.co.uk/
mayfair-restaurants-bars
Tube: Bond Street or Green Park

The Square
6-10 Bruton Street W1J 6PU
+44 (0)207 495 7100
reception@squarerestaurant.com
www.squarerestaurant.com
Tube: Green Park

The Wolseley
160 Piccadilly W1J 9EB
+44 (0)207 499 6996
info@thewolseley.com
www.thewolseley.com
Tube: Green Park

Find out more about Emyr Thomas and Bon Vivant at www.bonvivant.co.uk or on Twitter @BonVivantLiving

chapter 1

Essentials

*London's neighbourhoods, how to get there
and how to get around.*

Facts and figures

Need to know
Currency
Pound sterling (£)

Customs
Visit the gov.uk website for more information: www.gov.uk/uk-border-control

Electricity
230 volts, 50 Hz; Type G plug with three rectangular pins

Geographical location
51.5072° N, 0.1275° W

Language
English

Local time
Greenwich Mean Time Zone (UTC+00:00)

Postal code areas
E, EC, N, NW, SE, SW, W, WC

Tax
20% value-added tax (VAT) is added to most items for sale in England. Non-residents are able to claim a tax refund on eligible items. Visit the gov.uk website for more information: www.gov.uk/tax-on-shopping

Telephone country code
+44

Telephone area code
0207 in inner London; 0208 in outer London

Tipping
It is customary to add 10-15% of the value of the bill as a tip when eating out. Some restaurants add on this service charge automatically, although you are not obliged to pay it.

Visas
Not required by EU nationals visiting for tourism or work. Some other nationalities may require a visa when visiting for tourism purposes. Other nationalities hoping to work will need to apply for a visa and work permit. Use gov.uk's online tool to find out more about visa requirements: www.gov.uk/check-uk-visa

Important phone numbers
Police, ambulance or fire brigade (emergencies): 999
Police (non-emergency): 101

Currency exchange
Major credit cards such as VISA and MasterCard are widely accepted. Smaller shops and restaurants tend to accept credit cards too, although they may add a small fee to the transaction. ATMs can be found across the city. Bureaux de change are also plentiful and many of London's Post Offices have a travel money counter.

Etiquette
Acceptable behaviour in London mostly revolves around general politeness. Say 'please', 'thank you' and 'sorry' at the appropriate times and take your proper place in a queue when there is one, and you'll generally be fine.

Some bars, clubs and higher-end restaurants have a dress code, which will typically mean 'proper' shoes (not trainers), no jeans and a shirt with a collar for men. Men should always have a tie handy too. Many pubs do not have waiting staff on the floor, so expect to go up to the bar to place your orders for food and drinks. If you're invited to dinner in a family's home, it's customary to bring a bottle of wine, and perhaps some flowers or a box of chocolates too.

When greeting people, men will tend to shake hands and women will give a brief hug and/or a single kiss on the cheek.

When travelling on public transport, a set of unwritten rules kick into play that must be observed if not to incur the wrath of the London commuter. On escalators going up and down to the Tube (London Underground), stand to the right to allow people in a hurry to walk up or down the left-hand side. The same rule applies when walking between different Tube lines: walk slowly on the right, walk fast on the left. Make sure you let passengers off a Tube or train first before boarding. It's generally expected you'll give up your seat to those less able to stand; pregnant women wear "baby on board" badges to make it clear they're expecting. Have your ticket ready well in advance of approaching the ticket barriers when exiting a Tube or train station as not to cause human congestion behind you.

Useful websites
Visit London:
www.visitlondon.com
Visit Britain:
www.visitbritain.com
Daily Secret:
uk.dailysecret.com/london

Population: 8.6 million; foreign nationals = 2.8 million Size of city: 1,572km^2 **Population density: 5,354 people per km^2** Total length of Tube network: 402km **Amount of green space: 173km^2** Number of allotments rented to Londoners for growing fruit and vegetables: 30,000 **Length of the River Thames: 346km** Tallest building: The Shard, 309 metres **Number of rooms in the Houses of Parliament: 1,000** Number of journeys made on London's public transport network every day: 24 million **Number of languages spoken in communities across London: more than 300** Number of museums: 240 **Number of music performances per week: 621** Number of listed (protected) buildings: 40,000 **Longest tennis match at Wimbledon: 11 hours and 5 minutes** Number of public lidos and outdoor swimming pools: 14 **Number of visitors to the Tate Modern per year: 4.7 million**

Getting there

By air

London has six international airports serving the city: Heathrow, Gatwick, Stansted, Luton, City and Southend. Between them, the airports handle around 134 million passengers per year. Most of these airports are on the periphery of the city with good transport links leading into the city centre.

Heathrow (LHR)

London Heathrow is the largest of London's airports, with its five terminals located 32km to the west of London. While short haul flights do also fly into Heathrow, this airport is London's hub for long haul flights, with many of the world's globally recognised airlines flying in here.
www.heathrowairport.com

Travelling to London city centre:

Tube

Heathrow Airport is in zone 6 at the end of the Piccadilly line of the London Underground. This is one of the cheaper ways to reach any central London destination. Buy a single ticket from the ticket kiosk for around £6, or if you'll be travelling by public transport throughout your stay, buy an Oyster card for £3, as fares via this tap-in tap-out system are cheaper. If you have a contactless debit or credit card, or Apple Pay, you can simply tap this at the ticket barriers to be charged directly to your card. The travel time into central London takes around 35 minutes and Tubes run between around 5:00 and midnight.

Train

The Heathrow Express is the fastest way to reach central London, with trains departing every 15 minutes to London Paddington between around 5:00 and 23:30. The journey takes just 15 minutes, but costs a pricey £21.50 one-way.
www.heathrowexpress.com

The Heathrow Connect service is a slower stopping train service going into London Paddington. Trains run every 30 minutes between around 5:00 and 23:30 and take 25 minutes to reach Paddington, but the fare is closer to £10.

Trains depart from Heathrow Central Station, which is walking distance from terminals 1,2,3 and 5, or a free shuttle bus journey from terminal 4.

Bus

Travelling into central London by local bus is the cheapest option, although you will need to change onto different bus lines a few times to reach most central London locations. At night, the very convenient N9 bus runs all the way from Heathrow and stops at major central London locations such as Trafalgar Square, Charing Cross and Aldwych. It runs from 23:30 to 6:30.

Coach

National Express is the main coach provider running services from Heathrow Airport to central London terminals. National Express coaches depart from all of Heathrow's terminals and Heathrow Central Bus Station; there is a regular service throughout the day. Tickets cost as little as £6 one way; book online in advance

to secure a place at the best price. The journey into central London takes around two hours.
www.nationalexpress.com

Taxi

Fully licensed London taxis, or 'black cabs' stop in taxi ranks outside all of Heathrow's terminals. Fares are on the meter and cost approximately £45 to £70 to get into central London, with the journey taking around an hour, depending on traffic.

Booking a taxi in advance via a minicab firm can be a little cheaper, and the drivers will meet you in the arrivals hall. Online services such as minicabit and greentomatocars allow you to compare prices between different minicab companies.
www.minicabit.com
www.greentomatocars.com

Gatwick (LGW)

London Gatwick is the second busiest of London's airports with two terminals: North and South. It's located in West Sussex, 47km south of central London. Long haul airlines fly into Gatwick, as well as short haul and budget airlines such as easyJet, Flybe and Monarch.
www.gatwickairport.com

Travelling to London city centre

Train

This is the fastest and most convenient way of travelling into central London. The quickest service is the Gatwick Express, a non-stop service from Gatwick to London Victoria taking just 30 minutes. Trains depart every 15 minutes between around 4:30 and 1:30. The fare

is approximately £20 one-way, although this price is discounted if you buy online in advance.
www.gatwickexpress.com

There are a number of slower stopping train services into London that are a little cheaper than the Gatwick Express and run to a similar schedule. The journey time into London on these trains is around 50 minutes.

Gatwick train station is in the airport's South terminal; there's a free shuttle bus to the station if you fly into the North terminal.

Coach

This is the cheapest transport option from Gatwick to central London. easyBus is the lowest budget option, operating minibuses to London Victoria, Waterloo and Earl's Court. The journey time is around an hour and fares cost between £2 and £6, depending on the time of day you want to travel. Book online in advance to secure a space on a bus at the best price.
www.easybus.co.uk

National Express also runs a number of coach services into central London, with fares costing as little as £5 one way. Book in advance online to secure your place at the best price.
www.nationalexpress.com

Taxi

Fully licensed London taxis, or 'black cabs' stop in taxi ranks outside both of Gatwick's terminals. Fares are on the meter and cost approximately £50 to £80 to get into central London, with the journey taking just over an hour, depending on traffic.

Booking a taxi in advance via a minicab firm can be a little cheaper, and the drivers will meet you in the arrivals hall. Gatwick's website has a fare finder tool to help you book a minicab.
taxis.gatwickairport.com

Stansted (STN)

London's third busiest airport is located in Essex, 48km north-east of central London. The majority of flights into Stansted are short-haul from budget airlines, such as Ryanair and easyJet.
www.stanstedairport.com

Travelling to London city centre:

Train

The fastest but most expensive way of travelling into central London, the Stansted Express runs every 15 minutes and takes 45 minutes to get into London's Liverpool Street station. The fare costs around £20 one way, although cheaper fares can be available when booking online in advance. The train station is on the level below the terminal building.
www.stanstedexpress.com

Coach

Travelling by coach into central London is the cheapest option and there are a number of coach providers serving the airport. The cheapest is easyBus, with minibus services running to Baker Street or Old Street in just over an hour. Fares typically cost between £2 and £6; book online in advance to secure a seat at the best rate.
www.easybus.co.uk

Terravision, National Rail and Green Line also run services into central London locations

with fares starting from around £6 one-way.
www.terravision.eu
www.nationalexpress.com
www.greenline.co.uk

Stansted's bus station is just outside the airport's terminal building.

Taxi

24x7 Stansted Airport Taxis is the airport's taxi provider. Book a taxi from the reservation desk in the international arrival concourse or phone them from the courtesy phone in the domestic baggage reclaim area. Alternatively, email or phone them in advance before you travel. The fare into London costs around £100 and takes approximately an hour.
www.24x7stansted.com

You could alternatively use an online taxi comparison service such as Airport Pickups London to compare prices from local minicab firms.
www.airport-pickups-london.com

Luton (LTN)

London's fourth largest airport is located 56km north of central London in Bedfordshire. A number of short-haul budget airlines fly into Luton, including easyJet, Monarch and Wizz Air.
www.london-luton.co.uk

Travelling to London city centre:

Train

Rail services from Luton Airport Parkway station run frequently between 5:00 and midnight, with journey times of 30 to 40 minutes to either St Pancras International or Blackfriars in central London. A single ticket costs around

£14. The train station is a ten minute shuttle bus journey from the airport and costs £1.60. This cost can be included in the price of the train ticket if you buy a train ticket from inside the airport, or specify 'Luton Airport' rather than 'Luton Airport Parkway' when buying tickets in advance online through a provider such as thetrainline.com.

Coach

Travelling by coach into central London is the cheapest option and there are a number of coach providers serving the airport. The cheapest is easyBus, with minibus services running to Victoria or Liverpool Street in around an hour. Fares typically cost between £2 and £6; book online in advance to secure a seat at the best rate.
www.easybus.co.uk

Terravision, National Rail and Green Line also run services into central London locations with fares starting from around £10 one-way.
www.terravision.eu
www.nationalexpress.com
www.greenline.co.uk

Taxi

Fully licensed London taxis, or 'black cabs' stop in the taxi rank outside Luton Airport. Fares are on the meter and cost approximately £60 to £90 to get into central London, with the journey taking just over an hour, depending on traffic.

Luton Airport's website also lists some local minicab companies who may be able to offer a cheaper fare. Book in advance and they'll meet you in the arrivals hall.
london-luton.co.uk/en/airport

City (LCY)

The closest airport to central London, London City Airport can be found in the area of London that was previously the city docks. A couple of kilometres to Canary Wharf and just 11km to the City of London, this is the favoured airport for people flying in on business. Given the proximity to central London, there are restrictions on the number of flights that can come in and out, so flights tend to be more expensive to this airport.
www.londoncityairport.com

Travelling to London city centre:

Docklands Light Railway (DLR)

London City Airport has a DLR station in zone 3 of London's transport zones, running services that link directly to London's Tube network. A single fare to anywhere within zones 1-3 costs just under £5, or less if you buy a touch-in touch-out Oyster card. The journey time to most central London destinations takes around 20 minutes and services run from around 5:00 to midnight.

Taxi

Fully licensed London taxis, or 'black cabs' stop in the taxi rank outside the airport. Fares are on the meter and the cost is approximately £25 to get into the City of London, with the journey taking half an hour or less, depending on traffic.

Southend (SEN)

This small London airport is 67km from the centre of London in the county of Essex. London Southend Airport recently expanded its operations to receive more flights from Europe, with budget airlines such as easyJet and Flybe flying there.

Travelling to London city centre:

Train

The train station is a short walk from the arrivals hall opposite the terminal. Up to eight services run per hour during peak times, with trains going to Liverpool Street or Stratford, and journey times of just over 45 minutes. Single fares cost around £15 off-peak and services run between approximately 6:30 and 23:00.

Taxi

Andrews Airport Cars is Southend Airport's taxi partner and it's possible to book a taxi when you arrive at the airport, or online in advance. Fares cost around £100 into central London.
www.southendairporttaxis.com

Car hire at airports

All London's airports have car hire kiosks that are typically manned between 7:00 and 23:00. Book in advance with your car hire provider of choice before you travel for the best prices, or compare the prices of different car hire providers via a website such as Rhino Car Hire.
www.rhinocarhire.com

To plan a journey from London's airports using any of London's public transport options, visit **www.tfl.gov.uk/plan-a-journey**

By train

It is possible to travel by train to London from numerous European cities thanks to the Eurostar and the Channel Tunnel connecting the UK to France and subsequently the rest of Europe. It's possible to travel directly to London from Paris or Brussels via Eurostar trains, with fares of as little as £69 return. The journey from Paris takes between two and three hours and from Brussels it takes two hours. For those wishing to travel to London by train from elsewhere in Europe or further afield, it's possible to plan a journey across Europe to London using different rail providers on websites such as Seat 61.

www.eurostar.com
www.seat61.com

By coach

Multiple coach providers run services from an array of mostly European cities to London. Providers include Megabus, OUIBUS and GoEuro. Fares can be cheap, but journey times long.

www.megabus.com
www.ouibus.com
www.goeuro.co.uk

Getting around

Public transport

The Tube (London Underground), train and bus are the most commonly used modes of public transport in London. Run by Transport for London (TfL), many journeys will involve a combination of these transport types.

The London area is divided into six main zones when it comes to the public transport system. Zone 1 covers central London and zone 6 is in the London suburbs. Travel fares vary depending on which zones you travel in, as well as the time of travel, since it's more expensive to travel at peak times (6:30 to 9:29 and 16:00 to 18:59 Monday to Friday). Pick up a free Tube map from any London Underground station to see the exact locations of the travel zones.

If you're planning to travel by public transport a lot while in London, there are two ticket options that will give better value for money than buying single tickets:
Travelcards: Available for a day, a week, a month or a year, you can get travelcards that are valid in just the zones you will travel in. You can get off peak or anytime travelcards and they're valid on multiple modes of public transport in London and give you a third off the price of riverboat services.
Visitor Oyster cards: These touch-in touch out cards cost £3 and can be topped up with credit so you only pay for the journeys you make on public transport. It's possible to order one in advance of your trip to London with credit

pre-added so you're ready to get on public transport as soon as you arrive in London. In London, Oyster credit can be topped up at Tube and train stations, and at many local newsagents. If you have a contactless debit or credit card, or Apple Pay, you can use it in the same way as an Oyster card. Simply tap this at the ticket barriers to be charged directly to your card. Visit: visitorshop.tfl.gov.uk

Tube
The Tube, or underground, is one of the most popular modes of transport in London and you're never too far from a Tube station. There are 13 main Tube lines on the underground network, which have different names and are colour coded to make it clear where to interchange for different lines. The Tube system is more than 100 years old so there is a constant programme of upgrade work going on, which can cause some stations to close for months at a time, and can cause planned service closures on the weekends. Check the TfL website for planned engineering works and for live information on service disruption. Tubes typically run from 5:00 to midnight, and as of Autumn/Winter 2015, most parts of the Piccadilly, Northern, Jubilee, Victoria and Central lines run all night on Fridays and Saturdays.

Bus
London's iconic red buses have an extensive network throughout the city, and this is a great way to see more of London while you travel. Most are 'talking buses', where the location of the next stop is announced over a speaker system and on visual displays. There are

numerous night buses, whose bus numbers are preceded with the letter 'N', that only run at night, making all parts of London easily accessible whatever the time of day. London buses no longer accept cash payments, so make sure you have a topped-up Oyster card or Travelcard before you board.

Train
Trains in London tend to connect areas outside of London to central railway hubs in the city centre. London's major railway stations include Waterloo, Charing Cross, Victoria, Euston, King's Cross and Paddington. Oyster cards and travelcards are only available up to the edge of zone 6, so if you're travelling further afield you'll need to purchase an additional ticket.

River bus
There are several river bus piers along central areas of the River Thames connecting destinations on either side of the river. Journey times are comparable to other modes of transport and it can be a more scenic way to get from A to B.

Emirates Air Line
This cable car connecting the Royal Docks and North Greenwich is part of the London transport system and offers cool views over London. Open during daylight hours, the journey across takes around 10 minutes.

Taxi
London taxis are easy to spot from the distinctive black design of the Hackney Carriages and taxi lights on the roof. If a taxi is available, the 'taxi' sign above the vehicle is lit with an orange light. It's standard practice

to wave your arm in order to hail a taxi down. Alternatively, most major rail stations and transport hubs have a taxi rank nearby. Fares are on the meter, so the total fare depends on how far you're travelling and how heavy the traffic is, although typically a ten or fifteen minute journey will cost around £10.

Minicabs cannot be hailed down and can only be pre-booked; there are kiosks and small minicab shops throughout the city. Since these taxis are private saloon cars, it can be easy for non-licensed minicabs to pose as licensed minicab drivers. Exercise caution and only take black cabs if you're unsure.

Alternatively, use your Uber app!

Cycling
Londoners love cycling. Although there can be heavy traffic, more cycle lanes and cycle 'superhighways' have been built in recent years to improve safety. The city has a cycle scheme with bicycles sitting in docking stations at points across the city. Follow the on-screen instructions at the docking stations to hire a bike (you'll need a credit card too) and use the release code to free one of the bicycles. The cost of hiring a bicycle for 24 hours is just £2. The TfL website helps you find a bicycle docking station near you and also has information about cycle paths, cycle superhighways and recommended routes and maps.
www.londontransport.co.uk/modes/cycling

London Bike Rental
For those who prefer snazzier bikes than the ones available via the city's cycle scheme, London Bike Rental has a range of bicycle models available to hire per day or per week. Prices start from £10 for a day or £45 for a week, rising to £175 per week for deluxe models.
www.onyourbike.com/london-bike-rental

The London Bicycle Tour Company
This company runs cycling tours in London, some in different languages, exploring everywhere from the West End to Hampton Court. They also have bicycles available to hire, with hire periods of one day to three weeks. Basic models cost £20 for a day or £95 for three weeks. There are also mountain bikes, carbon framed bikes and tandem bikes available to hire. The folding bikes are useful for those who may want to travel with the bike on public transport, as bicycles are banned from most public transport modes during peak times. Many trains also have restrictions on which carriages will allow bicycles during non-peak times.
www.londonbicycle.com

By car
Few visitors to London choose to drive due to parking restrictions and heavy traffic. There is also a congestion charge of £11.50 per day for driving in the central London charging zone from Monday to Friday, 7:00 to 18:00. The congestion charge must be paid online on or before the day of driving in London, otherwise cameras will log the car's registration number and generate an automatic fine. London streets have signposts stating what the parking restrictions are. Some allow no parking whatsoever, some allow only residents with permits to park and others have a pay meter on the street. Check the signage carefully before parking. To identify a car park in advance, try consulting a website such as Parkopedia.
congestioncharging.tfl.gov.uk
www.parkopedia.co.uk

Car hire is also available across London as well as at the airports. Visit the website of your preferred car hire provider to find the nearest office in London, or compare prices using a website such as TravelSupermarket or Kayak.
www.travelsupermarket.com/c/cheap-car-hire/uk/london
www.kayak.co.uk/cars

To plan a journey using any of London's public transport options, visit:
www.tfl.gov.uk/plan-a-journey
www.londontransport.co.uk/maps
The Citymapper app is widely used:
www.citymapper.com

London is probably the best place to be doing this type of work.

Roberto Revilla
Fashion designer

Introduce yourself.
I'm a London-born menswear designer and bespoke tailor. I've lived in London my whole life —38 years and counting — and I currently live in north-west London, in a town called Mill Hill.

How would your friends sum you up in a tweet?
I actually asked a friend this question and he said: "Classy and elegant James Bond type whose drink of choice is a vintage port." I'm not sure if he was being sarcastic, but it sounds pretty accurate!

Tell us about your work.
I'm constantly on the move — our tailoring service is highly personal and I look after a huge number of successful gentlemen who rely on me to save them time and hassle. I visit a large number of our clients at their offices, homes, and even the hotel rooms of international clients travelling into London. I help them by creating bespoke suits, shirts and smart casual wear that reflect their personalities and individual styles.

Tailors in London have a long and prestigious history. What's it like to be a modern day tailor in the city?
It's always busy, but London is probably the best place to be doing this type of work. There is always something happening in London; you just have to look around to see signs of progress.

What are your clients like?
Our clients range from high-level executives, to highly ambitious young gentlemen on their way to great success. I also work with a number of television and media personalities. Most of our customers are London-based, but we have a growing number of international clients, from places as far flung as Hong Kong, the Bahamas, the Middle East and the US, as well as Europe.

What's the fashion scene like in London and how does it differ from other cities and countries?
The first word that springs to mind is eclectic. I don't think you'll find as many mixes of styles and personal interpretation anywhere else, because we have the highest mix of cultures from all over the world within the capital. We are a real international melting pot and this comes across in what you see on the street.

How would you describe the London style?

In terms of suits, there has been a move towards simple, crisp and sharp designs. London used to be known as the city of the pinstripe suit, but there has been a big move away from that look in the years since the global economic crisis. Men moved more towards plain colours for suits, shirts and ties to appear more 'austere' and in doing so, found that it was a much easier way to dress since one didn't have to think so much about what went with what.

As far as the broader London style goes, I think we are generally regarded as being quite a smartly dressed city, but you only have to walk through any part of town to see that there is no general London style. If anything, I would describe the London style as the ability and freedom of individuals to express themselves in the way they wish, with no fear of judgement. We are an all-embracing city, and that's why we have designers from all corners of the world descending on our city and choosing to base themselves there.

How do people working in fashion experience the city differently from other Londoners?

We are always looking for inspiration in everything around us. Not just people, but in architecture and spaces too. So we tend to look up, down and around us more often than perhaps the average Londoner might do.

Where's your favourite place to work in London?

I'm lucky to be in and out of so many different buildings all over London each day, so I don't really have one favourite place to work. But one of my favourite buildings is the News Building next to The Shard. The view is just amazing from the top floor; you can see out across the whole city and every single important and famous landmark is spread out in front of you. It feels like you have the world at your feet; it's very inspiring.

Where do you find inspiration in London?

I find inspiration all around; one of the benefits of travelling everywhere by bike or scooter means you see so much that you might not normally spot from a car, bus or train. However, my favourite and most inspirational places have to be our parks, particularly Hampstead Heath, Primrose Hill, Regent's Park and Hyde Park. These oases of calm right in the city centre are incredible places to be, whether it's just to enjoy nature or to people-watch. You can let your mind wander and break away from the hustle and bustle of city life beyond the park boundaries for a little while.

What are your future plans?

I'm so busy dealing with and living in the present I haven't had much time lately to focus on the future! But we recently launched a new denim collaboration with the US jeans brand Blue Delta, which is really exciting. I am also in talks to partner with a new ladies tailoring brand, so we can provide a service to the many women who keep asking if I can take care of them. We have been working hard behind the scenes on the online identity for Roberto Revilla London, as well as the online store, so it's exciting to see where we can take that heading into the future. Other than that, I really want to focus more on the home front to spend more time with my wife and our Cavachon puppy, Emily, plus our cats Jessie and Frankie. As our house is newly built, it needs a lot of work to make it a home, so that's a nice project for the next year or two.

Tell us about the neighbourhood you work in.

The West End is a fantastic place to work in, especially when you travel around frequently like I do. It's always busy and full of people no matter the time of day or night. And there is always somewhere to eat, shop, relax and socialise. I'm not sure there's anywhere else like it!

What's the vibe like in the neighbourhood you live in?

Mill Hill is a great escape from the bustle of London's city centre; it's really green and I love walking our dog around there. We have at least three golf courses in the area — although I don't play, I like the scenery they provide. It's a pretty friendly place; even though it's a big town, it feels quite familiar and people are generally approachable.

Are there any other areas of London you feel a close connection to?

Although I live in north London, I grew up in south London, so that's always a special place for me. It has changed so much over the years, for the better, and nowadays there's a wide and varied choice of amazing bars and restaurants. I love the trendy bars in places like Clapham, the new food culture that has appeared in Bermondsey and the eclectic mix you find in Brixton. If you have time to explore, there are so many little gems you can find.

What's your favourite place to eat out in your neighbourhood?

For great food, The Rising Sun in Mill Hill is a must. It's a pub and Italian restaurant run by the Delnevo family. Super-friendly, dog-friendly — which is very important for us — and the menu Chef Roberto has created is amazing. My favourite dish there is the veal with spaghetti carbonara; it's very filling but just divine. The Adam and Eve is also a fantastic venue with theme nights, good food and a great local atmosphere. It's also dog friendly and we try to get in there at least once a week.

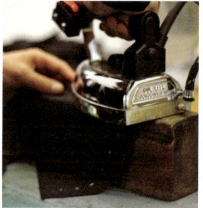

What are your top restaurants in the city as a whole?

In London, you're really spoiled for choice when it comes to good food and restaurants. For fine dining some of my favourites are Corrigan's Mayfair and Marcus Wareing's restaurants. There are too many to choose from. For more down-to-earth food, Negozio Classica in Primrose Hill is a must for good Italian food done simply and well. Ibérica on Great Portland Street is great for Spanish tapas, Maguro in Maida Vale is perfect for Japanese sushi, and for steak, it has to be Beast near Oxford Street. For Indian food, I either head straight for Southall — sometimes called Little India — or Queensbury. Hands down, the best curry can be found in either of those two places. My number one in Queensbury has to be The Regency Club, which I've frequented for years.

Where do you like to go for a drink?

The bars of most of the five star hotels in town are excellent, but in particular I like the bar in the Hilton Park Lane. It's called Galvin at Windows and offers excellent views of the city. The rooftop bar at the Mondrian Hotel on South Bank, called Rumpus Room, is also excellent, with views across the city and over St Paul's Cathedral. Hawksmoor's bars at either their Air Street or Spitalfields branches are amazing, with bang-on cocktails; I love Shaky Pete's Ginger Brew. The Zetter Townhouse in Clerkenwell is another cocktail haven, while Oscar, the bar at the Charlotte Street Hotel, is always worth a visit.

Where do you go shopping?

I used to shop in the West End a lot, though not so much anymore as I don't really have as much time for doing that these days. Anything I can find online is far more convenient. That said, when I do get time, I love Regent Street and the surrounding area in the West End, which always seems to cater for everything I need. It has the Apple Store, Barbour, and Oliver Sweeney — my shoemaker of choice. My wife is a big fan of Karen Millen, who has a flagship store in the area. We also have fantastic shopping centres in London. Westfield London in White City is amazing and you literally have everything there under one roof. You could spend a whole day there and I'm sure many people do, although that's not something that has ever appealed to me. When I go shopping, I tend to know what I want, so it's a strategic strike in and out, nice and quickly!

Where do you like to soak up culture in London?

For seeing and interacting with London's people, any park and most local pubs will do. I don't find it hard to get into conversations with strangers in most places! We have a great number of markets in London, some of which have existed for years — Camden, Covent Garden, Leather Lane, Berwick Street and Portobello. There are so many and they're so varied. London also has the greatest number of free museums and galleries. I especially like The National Gallery, the Victoria & Albert Museum, Tate Modern, the Natural History Museum and the British Museum. There is so much going on in the city.

Do you like live music?

We love live music and try to get to as many gigs as we can. We don't live too far from Wembley Stadium and Arena, which are both fantastic venues to see the bigger stars and bands. The O2 in Greenwich isn't bad either, although I find the acoustics in that venue a bit difficult to deal with sometimes. There's a large number of smaller venues that are fantastic too. Union Chapel on Upper Street in Islington is a particular favourite, and we've seen some amazing artists perform there over the years. The Scala in King's Cross is another fantastic venue.

What would your perfect day in London entail?

No work would be a must! It would start with a lazy brunch in Queen's Park, followed by a mooch around Portobello Road. Following that, we'd have afternoon tea at the Winter Garden in The Landmark London hotel, preceding a short cab ride to the West End to take in a show. Charlie and the Chocolate Factory is a must! The day would finish with dinner at the most romantic restaurant in London, Clos Maggiore in Covent Garden. A midnight stroll through Covent Garden and Piccadilly is one of the loveliest things to do with your partner before going home, full and content!

What music do you associate with the city?

Anything by a British artist, but I particularly think of London when I hear anything by The Clash, Madness and more recently, Lily Allen, who we used to live quite close to and she's therefore very dear to us. Nerina Pallot is another local artist we've followed for a long time; she lives in Camden and anytime I hear one of her songs, London springs to mind. The soundtracks to Lock, Stock and Two Smoking Barrels and Snatch also remind me of London, and they're two of my favourite London-based films.

What smell do you associate with London?

If I'm away from London and I smell freshly baked bread, it takes me right back home, as it's a smell I come across on my early run through town at 6.30. And the smell of prawn crackers always remind me of Chinatown.

What's the most bizarre thing you've seen in London?

Recently there were around 100 sculptures of the British animated character, Shaun the Sheep, that popped up in Covent Garden. We came out of the theatre one night and they were just all over Covent Garden square. It was amazing and something magical. Things like that are just so London!

Where do you go to get away from it all?

Home House in Portman Square is my favourite place to escape to. It's a private members' club that we joined a couple of years ago and although we don't get down there much these days, I always have my membership card with me as it's like a 'get out of jail free card'. I know when things get too much and I need to hide and recharge, I can dive in there and it's like a home from home.

What is London's best quality?

London's best quality is its diversity. People, food, culture, entertainment, architecture — name one thing and I bet you can find hundreds if not thousands of variations on that thing in the city. It's one of the most diverse cities in the world.

Is there anything you would change about London if you could?

The road works. The problem with a city in a constant state of change and progress is that things have to be dug up, or torn down and re-built. So there are always roadworks and building sites somewhere. As much as cranes on the horizon signify progress to me, they also signify a traffic jam somewhere too!

What's the current trend in London?

There are a few; some are getting a bit irritating. I'm not sure they are confined to just London, as the advent of social media means the world has just become a much smaller place. As a result, things spread globally more quickly. This selfie-stick thing is getting quite a bore now; it's taken personal interaction between strangers out of the equation. I still prefer to hand my camera to someone and ask them to take a picture. The selfie-stick is murdering social interaction!

How would you advise visitors of London to blend in and become 'citizens' of the city for the duration of their stay?

Stop using selfie-sticks! Previously tourists used to walk around with a camera wrapped around their necks; now they carry selfie-sticks around. I'm stuck on the selfie-stick thing now, ha ha!

The easiest and simplest thing to do is to throw all caution and reservation out the window and embrace being in the greatest city in the world. The great thing about London is that you don't have to act or dress a certain way to blend in; being a Londoner is about being true to yourself. Do everything, try everything, embrace everything. You'll be just fine.

<u>Where are good places to 'get lost' in London?</u>
I think most visitors get lost in London anyway, but if I had to choose, I'd drag you back to the West End first of all, then send you to get lost around Soho and Chinatown. Portobello Road and Notting Hill are also great places to get lost. There is so much to discover and find in those places on a small scale; you'll never want to be found.

Roberto's London

Places to visit

Apple Store
235 Regent Street W1B 2EL
+44 (0)207 153 9000
www.apple.com/uk/retail/
regentstreet/
Tube: Oxford Circus

Barbour
73-77 Regent Street W1B 4EF
+44 (0)207 434 0880
info@thehighlandstore.com
www.barbour.com/shop/barbour-
partner-store-regent-street
Tube: Oxford Circus

Berwick Street Market
Berwick Street W1
www.berwickstreetlondon.co.uk/
market
Tube: Tottenham Court Road

British Museum
Great Russell Street WC1B 3DG
+44 (0)207 323 8299
information@britishmuseum.org
www.britishmuseum.org
Tube: Goodge Street

Camden Market
56-56 Camden Lock Place NW1
8AF
+44 (0)203 763 9999
support@camdenmarket.com
www.camdenmarket.com
Tube: Camden Town

Chinatown
Gerrard Street W1D
www.chinatownlondon.org
Tube: Leicester Square

Covent Garden Market
Covent Garden WC2E
Tube: Covent Garden

Hampstead Heath
Rail: Hampstead Heath
Tube: Hampstead

Home House
20 Portman Square W1H 6LW
+44 (0)207 670 2000

www.homehouse.co.uk
Tube: Marble Arch

Hyde Park
Tube: Hyde Park Corner,
Knightsbridge, Lancaster Gate or
Queensway

Karen Millen
247 Regent Street W1B 2EW
+44 (0)207 629 1901
www.karenmillen.com
Tube: Oxford Circus

Leather Lane Market
Leather Lane EC4
Tube: Chancery Lane

Natural History Museum
Cromwell Road SW7 5BD
+44 (0)207 942 5000
www.nhm.ac.uk
Tube: South Kensington

Oliver Sweeney
5 Conduit Street W1S 2XD
+44 (0)207 491 9126
westend@oliversweeney.com
www.oliversweeney.com
Tube: Oxford Circus

Portobello Market
Portobello Road W11 2DY
www.portobelloroad.co.uk
Tube: Ladbroke Grove

Primrose Hill
Tube: Chalk Farm or Camden
Town

Regent's Park
Tube: Regent's Park, Great
Portland Street, Baker Street or
Mornington Crescent

Soho
W1S
Tube: Oxford Circus, Piccadilly
Circus or Tottenham Court Road

Tate Modern
Bankside SE1 9TG
+44 (0)207 887 8888
visiting.modern@tate.org.uk
www.tate.org.uk/visit/tate-
modern
Rail/Tube: London Bridge

The National Gallery
Trafalgar Square WC2N 5DN
+44 (0)207 747 2885
information@ng-london.org.uk
www.nationalgallery.org.uk
Rail/Tube: Charing Cross

The News Building
3 London Bridge Street SE1 9SG
Rail/Tube: London Bridge
Book meeting rooms at www.
regus.co.uk

The O2
Peninsula Square SE10 0DX
+44 (0)208 463 2000
www.theo2.co.uk
Tube: North Greenwich

The Scala
275 Pentonville Road N1 9NL
+44 (0)207 833 2022
www.scala.co.uk
Rail/Tube: King's Cross

The Victoria & Albert
Museum (V&A)
Cromwell Road SW7 2RL
+44 (0)207 942 2000
contact@vam.ac.uk
www.vam.ac.uk
Tube: South Kensington

Union Chapel
Compton Terrace N1 2UN
+44 (0)207 226 1686
events@unionchapel.org.uk
www.unionchapel.org.uk
Rail/Tube: Highbury & Islington

Wembley Stadium and
Arena
Arena Square, Engineers Way
HA9 0AA
+44 (0)208 782 5566
customerservices@ssearena.co.uk
www.ssearena.co.uk
Rail: Wembley Stadium
Tube: Wembley Park

Westfield London
Ariel Way W12 7GF
+44 (0)207 061 1400
uk.westfield.com/london
Rail/Tube: Shepherd's Bush

Eating and drinking

Beast
3 Chapel Place W1G 0BG
+44 (0)207 495 1816
reservations@beastrestaurant.co.uk
www.beastrestaurant.co.uk
Tube: Bond Street

Clos Maggiore
33 King Street WC2E 8JD
+44 (0)207 379 9696
enquiries@closmaggiore.com
www.closmaggiore.com
Tube: Covent Garden

Corrigan's Mayfair
28 Upper Grosvenor Street W1K 7EH
+44 (0)20 7499 9943
reservations@corrigansmayfair.com
www.corrigansmayfair.co.uk
Tube: Marble Arch

Galvin at Windows
London Hilton, 22 Park Lane W1K 1BE
+44 (0)207 208 4021
reservations@galvinatwindows.com
www.galvinatwindows.com
Tube: Hyde Park Corner

Hawksmoor
www.thehawksmoor.com

5a Air Street W1J 0AD
+44 (0)207 406 3980
airstreet@thehawksmoor.com
Tube: Piccadilly Circus

157a Commercial Street E1 6BJ
+44 (0)207 426 4850
spitalfields@thehawksmoor.com
Rail: Shoreditch High Street

Ibérica Marylebone
195 Great Portland Street W1W 5PS
T. +44 (0) 207 148 1615
reception.marylebone@
ibericarestaurants.com
www.ibericarestaurants.com
Tube: Great Portland Street

Little India/Southall
Southall UB12
Rail: Southall

Oscar
Charlotte Street Hotel, 15-17
Charlotte Street W1T 1RJ
+44 (0)207 980 1007
www.firmdalehotels.com
Tube: Goodge Street

Maguro
5 Lanark Place W9 1BT
+44 (0)207 289 4353
www.maguro-restaurant.com
Tube: Warwick Avenue

Marcus Wareing
marcuswareingrestaurants.co.uk

Rumpus Room
Mondrian Hotel, 20 Upper
Ground SE1 9PD
+44 (0)20 3747 1000
www.morganshotelgroup.com/
mondrian/mondrian-london
Tube: Southwark

Negozio Classica
154 Regent's Park Road NW1 2XN
+44 (0)207 483 4492
info@negozioclassica.co.uk
www.facebook.com/
negozioclassica
Tube: Chalk Farm

The Adam and Eve
The Ridgeway NW7 1RL
+44 (0)208 959 1553
info@adamandevemillhill.co.uk
www.adamandevemillhill.co.uk
Tube: Mill Hill East

The Regency Club
19-21 Queensbury Station Parade
HA8 5NR
+44 (0)208 952 6300
info@regencyclub.co.uk
www.regencyclub.co.uk
Tube: Queensbury

The Rising Sun
137 Marsh Lane NW7 4EY
+44 (0)208 959 1357
www.therisingsunmillhill.co.uk
Rail: Mill Hill Broadway

The Zetter Townhouse Clerkenwell — cocktail lounge
49-50 St John's Square EC1V 4JJ
+44 (0)207 324 4567
www.thezettertownhouse.com/
clerkenwell/bar
Rail/Tube: Farringdon

Winter Garden
The Landmark London, 222
Marylebone Road NW1 6JQ
+44 (0)207 631 8000
www.landmarklondon.co.uk
Rail/Tube: Marylebone

Read more about
Roberto Revilla at
www.robertorevillalondon.com
or on Twitter
@ItsBobbyRevilla

Luton

Jealous Gall

Hampstead Heath ●

WEST

LONDON

The Hospital C

CENT

BY

Dock Kitchen ●
Habanera ●

Chelsea Harbour
Design Centre ●
Holland Park ●

● Lillie Road

Le Bureau

Flotsam & Jetsam ●

Heathrow

LONDON

The Bedfo

SO

Gatwick

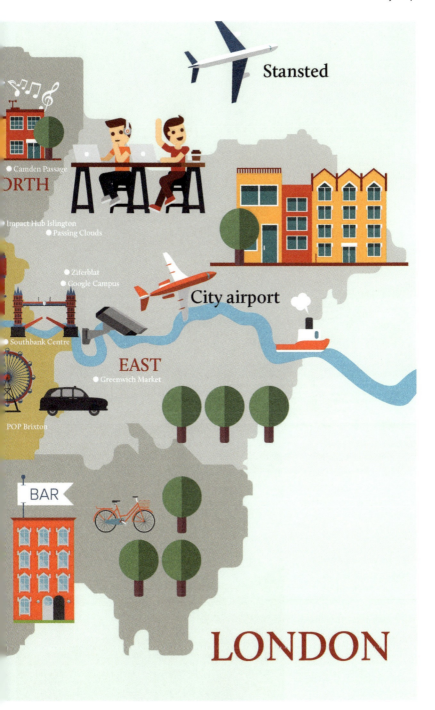

Stansted

Camden Passage

NORTH

Impact Hub Islington
Passing Clouds

Ziferblat
Google Campus

City airport

Southbank Centre

EAST

Greenwich Market

POP Brixton

BAR

LONDON

Central London

The central areas of London are filled with the world renowned historical and cultural landmarks of the city. Blended in are leafy residential neighbourhoods with townhouses and apartments charging some of the highest rents in the city. Brimful with galleries, museums, theatres and restaurants, central London is all about being in the middle of the action in the city's famed streets.

A work day in Central London:

Morning

OpenCoffee Meetup
Join this entrepreneurial coffee morning every Thursday. Page 156.

Chelsea Harbour Design Centre
A bright space for a casual business meeting, check out the interiors retailers afterwards. Page 58. Rail: Imperial Wharf

Fashion and Textile Museum
Get some creative inspiration from this bright Bermondsey Street museum. Page 58. Rail/Tube: London Bridge

Afternoon

Oblix
Try out this slick restaurant ideal for business lunches in Europe's tallest building, The Shard. Page 138. Tube: London Bridge.

The Wallace Collection
Be inspired by the décorative arts collection in this townhouse museum. Page 58. Tube: Bond Street

The Soho Collective
Grab a desk at this central co-working space loved by designers and creatives. Page 134. Tube: Covent Garden

Evening

The Hospital Club
Pop along to this members club that turns social in the evening. Page 156. Tube: Covent Garden.

Dabbous
This Michelin-star restaurant with an industrial chic interior is ideal for business dinners. Page 138. Tube: Goodge Street

Barbican Centre
Treat your business contacts to a vibrant concert at this arts venue. Page 56. Tube: Barbican

A day of play in Central London:

Morning

Southbank Centre
Enjoy a morning coffee at this cultural hub on the Thames. Page 60. Rail/Tube: Waterloo

Shepherd Market
Experience a throwback to Victorian times by wandering around this Mayfair ode to the past. Page 84. Tube: Green Park

Jewel Tower
Soak up some of Westminster's history at this 650 year old tower. Page 61. Tube: Westminster

Afternoon

Exmouth Market
Sample some of London's best street food for lunch. Page 56. Rail/Tube: Farringdon

King's Road
Browse in the boutiques along one of Chelsea's best-loved roads. Page 57. Tube: Sloane Square

The Old Doctor Butler's Head
Partake in an afternoon beverage in this old alleyway boozer. Page 57. Tube: Bank

Evening

Royal Academy of the Arts (RA)
Check out the art before enjoying the dining room after hours. Page 59. Tube: Green Park

Soho Theatre
Experience some of London's newest comedy or cabaret talent. Page 60. Tube: Tottenham Court Road

BYOC
Bring bottles of spirits and be wowed by mixologists in this speakeasy Page 192. Tube: Leicester Square

Central London neighbourhoods:

Barbican and Clerkenwell

This locally loved neighbourhood has an artsy atmosphere and a charming, low-key vibe despite the relatively central location. Barbican in particular has a history in performing arts. William Shakespeare lived in the area in the 16th century and today, the locality is home to renowned art, dance and music venues. Clerkenwell is a hip area loved by city professionals. With award-winning foodie credentials and a penchant for shabby chic gastropubs, this fashionable neighbourhood has a fun mix of residents and local workers.

Where the locals recommend:

Barbican Centre

This centre for the arts plays host to London's most innovative projects, from immersive art installations and cinema to classical concerts and creative learning opportunities.
Silk Street EC2Y 8DS
+44 (0)207 638 4141
tickets@barbican.org.uk
www.barbican.org.uk
Tube: Barbican

Exmouth Market

This foodie haven has artisanal food stalls perfect for lunch Monday to Friday, and a selection of cosy restaurants with big reputations, such as Moro and Paesan, ideal for the evening.
Exmouth Market EC1R 4QL
www.exmouth-market.com
Rail/Tube: Farringdon

Leather Lane

Just around the corner from London's diamond district, Hatton Garden, is Leather Lane with its bric-a-brac market and street food vendors.
Leather Lane EC1N 7TJ
Tube: Chancery Lane

Sadler's Wells

A world-famous centre for international dance, Sadler's Wells hosts an exciting calendar of dance performances.
Rosebery Avenue EC1R 4TN
+44 (0)844 412 4300
reception@sadlerswells.com
www.sadlerswells.com
Tube: Angel

The Museum of the Order of St John

One of London's hidden museums, this historical spot centres on the story of the Order of St John and St John's Gate, which dates back to the 1500s.
St John's Gate, St John's Lane EC1M 4DA
+44 (0)207 324 4005
museum@sja.org.uk
www.museumstjohn.org.uk
Rail/Tube: Farringdon

Bloomsbury and Fitzrovia

The literary and academic centres of London, both Bloomsbury and Fitzrovia have cultural kudos in the intellectual world. Home to London's major academic institutions, students and professors stalk the streets lined with Georgian townhouses and garden squares. With a smattering of stalwart pubs and speakeasies, Bloomsbury and Fitzrovia are iconic London locales to spend some time.

Where the locals recommend:

Grant Museum of Zoology

This museum owned by University College London (UCL) is home to tens of thousands of animal specimens, skeletons and a vibrant events calendar.
Rockefeller Building, University College London, 21 University Street WC1E 6DE
+44 (0)203 108 2052
www.ucl.ac.uk/museums/zoology
Tube: Euston Square

Fitzrovia Lates

On the last Thursday of every month, galleries stay open to 9pm and artists lead thought-provoking discussions.
twitter.com/fitzrovialates

Fitzroy Square

This peaceful haven is one of London's Georgian squares and is surrounded by the homes of notable Londoners past and present: find out who they are by reading the blue plaques affixed to the building facades.
Fitzroy Square W1T
Tube: Warren Street

Café Le Cordon Bleu

This patisserie and café just a stone's throw from the British Museum is the first European café from the internationally famed culinary school, and it takes you right back to 1950s Paris.
Pied Bull Yard, 15 Bloomsbury Square WC1A 2LS
www.cordonbleu.edu/london/cafelecordonbleu
Tube: Holborn

Sicilian Avenue

This pedestrianised avenue dates back to 1910 and brings a little southern Italian old-world charm to London. It's ideal for a casual wander and a pit-stop at one of the Mediterranean eateries.
Sicilian Avenue WC1A 2QH
Tube: Holborn

City of London

The internationally-renowned financial centre of London centres on the City of London, referred to by many as 'the City'. As well as being one of Europe's major economic powerhouses, it's also home to some of the most historically relevant buildings in London, including St Paul's Cathedral. Brimful with the suited and booted during the week, the City takes on an almost eerie quiet during the weekends, making this a great time to explore without the crowds.

Where the locals recommend:

Guildhall

The ceremonial and administrative centre of the City of London also allows members of the public into the gallery's permanent collection and the Roman amphitheatre free of charge. The expansive courtyard at the front of the building is ideal for an al fresco packed lunch. Listen out for the musical sound of rehearsals from the Guildhall School of Music and Drama.
Guildhall Yard (off Gresham Street) EC2V 5AE
www.cityoflondon.gov.uk
Tube: Bank

The Old Doctor Butler's Head

Squirrelled away along an old City alleyway, this pub is easy to miss. It's a traditional boozer, but you feel like you're in on a secret when you find it.
2 Masons Avenue EC2V 5BT
+44 (0)207 606 3504
www.shepherdneame.co.uk/pubs/moorgate/old-doctor-butlers-head
Tube: Bank

Lloyd's building

Also known as the 'Inside-Outside' building, this is the first building to have its lifts and staircases built on the outside of the building to save space. It was also the youngest building to be given a Grade 1 listed status.
1 Lime Street EC3M 7HA
Rail: Fenchurch Street

Leadenhall Market

This covered market dates back to the 14th century. The interior feels like London from another era, with its Victorian glass roof and cobbled streets. It's a popular spot for food, drinks and window shopping.
Leadenhall Market EC3V 1LT
+44 (0)207 332 1523
www.cityoflondon.gov.uk
Tube: Monument

Mansion House

This is the official residence of the Lord Mayor of London and it's possible to have a guided tour just once a week, on Tuesday afternoons. Once a year is the Lord Mayor's Show, which involves a 7,000 person strong procession.
The Mansion House EC4N 8BH
+44 (0)207 626 2500
www.cityoflondon.gov.uk
www.lordmayorsshow.london
Tube: Bank

Knightsbridge and Chelsea

Another well-to-do part of London, Knightsbridge in particular is known for its ritzy restaurants and swanky boutiques, of which the Harrods department store is the epitome, and a destination in its own right. Chelsea blends boutiques and art galleries effortlessly, and the crowd is less corporate than in other parts of town. Previously London's bohemian quarter, Chelsea has always been popular with those in the arts, and continues to be a popular home for wealthy public figures today. A huge stretch of the River Thames is incorporated into the Chelsea area, bringing a relaxed riverside life into the mix too.

Where the locals recommend:

Chelsea Physic Gardens

This walled garden dates back to the 1600s when apprentices used it to study the medicinal properties of plants. It's a secret world inside London and can be found along the leafy Royal Hospital Road.
66 Royal Hospital Road SW3 4HS
+44 (0)207 352 5646
enquiries@chelseaphysicgarden.co.uk
www.chelseaphysicgarden.co.uk
Tube: Sloane Square

King's Road

Chelsea's beating heart, the King's Road stretches for miles. Start at Sloane Square and continue walking south west to catch a glimpse of the boutiques, café culture and changing architecture.
King's Road
Tube: Sloane Square

The Saatchi Gallery

This modern art gallery in the impressive facade of the Duke of York's Headquarters shows work from unseen local artists and an eclectic mix of international artists.
Duke of York's HQ, King's Road SW3 4RY
www.saatchigallery.com
Tube: Sloane Square

Michelin House

The UK HQ and tyre depot for Michelin tyres opened in 1911 and it's still a treat today

to visit the exuberant art deco building. It's now home to the restaurant, Bibendum, named after Michelin's tyre-like mascot.
81 Fulham Road SW3 6RD
+44 (0)207 581 5817
reservations@bibendum.co.uk
www.bibendum.co.uk
Tube: South Kensington

Chelsea Harbour Design Centre

A mecca for those in the interiors and design worlds, Chelsea Harbour Design Centre (open Monday to Friday) has three glass domes over its galleria, dozens of showrooms of interiors brands, a bookshop stocked with design titles and a couple of bright and airy cafés. The centre also hosts The Design Club, the private members' club for design professionals.
Chelsea Harbour, Lots Road SW10 0XE
+44(0)207 225 9166
concierge.desk@dcch.co.uk
www.dcch.co.uk
Rail: Imperial Wharf

London Bridge and Bermondsey

There's been a bridge in the London Bridge area since AD50, making this one of many mind-bogglingly historically relevant spots in the city. The area has a modern claim to fame now too, as it's home to the tallest building in Europe: The Shard. Foodies also flock here for Borough Market and other delectable food offerings in the area. Bermondsey has a shabby chic reputation following the renovation of the area's wharves. Bars, boutiques and vintage antiques markets are the order of the day here, with some unusual cultural offerings attracting Londoners and visitors alike.

Where the locals recommend:

Bermondsey Street

This quiet London street has had a recent foodie awakening, with restaurants such as Casse-Croûte, Zucca and Restaurant Story on the top of every food-lover's list.
Bermondsey Street SE1
Rail/Tube: London Bridge

Fashion and Textile Museum

This bright museum in a converted warehouse is dedicated to all things fashion and design. An inspiring spot for anyone who works in London's creative industries, the museum also runs workshops to help people learn and improve their textiling skills.
83 Bermondsey Street SE1 3XF
+44 (0)207 407 8664
info@ftmlondon.org
www.ftmlondon.org
Rail/Tube: London Bridge

Bermondsey Antiques Market

This vintage antiques market runs in Bermondsey Square every Friday morning. Find everything from china and cutlery to hulking furniture.
Bermondsey Square SE1 3UN
www.bermondseysquare.net/bermondsey-antiques-market
Tube: Bermondsey

The Scoop

This outdoor sunken amphitheatre by London's riverside has a year-round calendar of free events, from theatre and fringe to opera and dance.
2a More London Riverside SE1 2DB
+44 (0)207 403 4866
enquiries@morelondonestates.co.uk
www.morelondon.com
Rail/Tube: London Bridge

The Shard

As Europe's tallest building and one of the newest additions to London's skyline, taking in the view from the top of The Shard is a must. Digital telescopes help you discover London a little better, while the viewing platform at the top has faux grass and deckchairs: perfect for supping champagne and enjoying new heights.
The View From the Shard, Railway Approach SE1
+44 (0)844 499 7111
enquiries@theviewfromtheshard.com
www.theviewfromtheshard.com
Rail/Tube: London Bridge

Marylebone and Paddington

Marylebone retains a village-like feeling despite being in such a central location. Boutiques, pavement cafés, artisan food purveyors and farmers' markets create a country-in-the-city feeling with a sense of local pride. Paddington is Marylebone's more bustling neighbour, centring on the transport hub of Paddington Station. Paddington is no less refined, however, with independent markets and European-inspired cafés found in every nook and cranny.

Where the locals recommend:

The Wallace Collection

This museum of décorative arts is found inside a London townhouse. The courtyard plays host to a stunning French brasserie style restaurant, ideal for a hidden-away moonlit dining experience.
Hertford House, Manchester Square W1U 3BN
+44 (0)207 563 9500
reservations@thewallacerestaurant.com
www.wallacecollection.org
Tube: Bond Street

The Button Queen
This quirky shop is every vintage craft-lover's dream. Buy buttons of any description and era, or simply visit for inspiration.
76 Marylebone Lane W1U 2PR
+44 (0)207 935 1505
information@thebuttonqueen.co.uk
www.thebuttonqueen.co.uk
Tube: Bond Street

Paul Rothe & Son
This perfectly villagey delicatessen has been run by the Rothe family for generations. It's now a café too and a quintessentially English spot to spend some time.
35 Marylebone Lane W1U 2NN
+44 (0)207 935 6783
paulrotheandsondelicatessen.co.uk
Tube: Bond Street

Connaught Village
A locality full of boutiques and highly acclaimed restaurants, Connaught Village has a luxuriant, laidback feeling.
Connaught Street W2 2AY
www.connaught-village.co.uk
Tube: Marble Arch

Wigmore Hall
This lesser known music venue is said to have near-perfect acoustics. The focus is on chamber music and the hall plays host to hundreds of events every year, including radio broadcasts.
36 Wigmore Street W1U 2BP
+44 (0)207 258 8200
boxoffice@wigmore-hall.org.uk
www.wigmore-hall.org.uk
Tube: Bond Street

Mayfair and Belgravia
This luxurious corner of London is home to the city's grandest architecture and the refined residences of the super-rich. The amenities in this neighbourhood match the decadence of its reputation, with wine bars and high-end restaurants making for discerning nights out. Mayfair in particular is perfectly placed in between Soho and the swathes of open space in Hyde Park, making it a location for the best of fun and relaxation in the city.

Where the locals recommend:

Shepherd Market
The square and piazza here date back to the 1700s; it has a distinct throwback feeling to London from a different era, with Victorian pubs and quaint boutiques lining the streets.
Shepherd Market W1J 7QU
www.shepherdmarket.co.uk
Tube: Green Park

Fortnum & Mason's
One of London's most revered and luxurious department stores, Fortnum & Mason's is a treasure trove worth exploring and a slice of London history, since it was established as a humble grocery store in 1707.
181 Piccadilly W1A 1ER
+44 (0)207 734 8040
www.fortnumandmason.com
Tube: Piccadilly Circus

Burlington Arcade
A covered shopping street with luxuriously branded boutiques, Burlington Arcade is a plush and picturesque place to window-shop. It's a stone's throw from Jermyn Street too, famous for its tailors and men's fashions.
51 Piccadilly W1J 0QJ
+44 (0)207 493 1764
www.burlington-arcade.co.uk
Tube: Green Park

Royal Academy of the Arts (RA)
The RA is a grand enough venue as it is, but dine in The RA Grand Café by Peyton and Byrne in the evening and you'll soak up the exclusivity of being an after-hours guest. The Keeper's Garden, through the Shenkman Bar on the lower ground level, is another secret London spot.
Burlington House W1J 0BD
+44 (0)207 300 5608
restaurant@royalacademy.org.uk
www.royalacademy.org.uk
Tube: Green Park

Belgrave Square
Many foreign embassies are found around this garden-like 19th century square, while many statues of historically important figures adorn the greenery. The hushed feeling of the square makes it a quiet London spot for a walk.
Belgrave Square SW1X
Tube: Hyde Park Corner

Soho and Covent Garden
Embracing the fun side of London's personality, the Soho area of London stretches as far as the bustling Oxford Street for shopping, Piccadilly Circus basking in the glow of its neon signs, and Leicester Square with its famous cinemas where film premieres are a regular occurrence. Previously known for the sex industry, there's still a smidgen of the sordid peppered around the area, but for the most part it's a fashionable corner of London where late-night European style cafés, nightlife and quirky shops collide. Also home to theatreland and its trailblazing West End shows, Chinatown's eateries and the cobbled streets and street performers of neighbouring Covent Garden, this part of town is a whirlwind force to be reckoned with.

Where the locals recommend:

Prince Charles Cinema

A cinema with a loyal following, films vary from arthouse and cult classics to the latest releases. Beware of the rumoured ghost on the upper levels!
7 Leicester Place WC2H 7BY
+44 (0)207 494 3654
www.princecharlescinema.com
Tube: Leicester Square

Soho Theatre

This theatre hosts comedy, cabaret, new theatre productions and writers events (it's also home to a writers' centre to support new writers).
21 Dean Street W1D 3NE
+44 (0)207 478 0100
www.sohotheatre.com
Tube: Tottenham Court Road

The Society Club

A haven for literature buffs by day, in the evening The Society Club turns into a literary members' club with a calendar of events, from film night and poetry evenings to book launches and talks by authors.
12 Ingestre Place W1F 0JF
+44 (0)207 437 1433
www.thesocietyclub.com
Tube: Piccadilly Circus

National Portrait Gallery

This gallery hosts portraits of historically important and famous British people. It first opened in the 1850s, making it the first portrait gallery in the world. Many creative types find great inspiration here.
St. Martin's Place WC2H 0HE
+44 (0)207 306 0055
www.npg.org.uk
Tube: Charing Cross or Leicester Square
Rail: Charing Cross

Neal's Yard

This small Covent Garden alley offers a quaint and colourful respite from the bustle of the area's shopping streets and piazza. There are several health food and natural remedy shops here.
Neal's Yard WC2H 9DP
Tube: Covent Garden

Waterloo and South Bank

The location of another of London's famed bridges, Waterloo is known for its large rail terminus and its smattering of cultural offerings. The South Bank marks a two mile riverside stretch from the London Eye to Tower Bridge and is a hive of activity, from the cultural activities of the Southbank Centre and the beating heart of London's skateboarding community, to the daily second hand and antique book market, and eateries with indoor and outdoor seating. There's never a dull moment here.

Where the locals recommend:

The Old Vic

This iconic London theatre has a long history and outstanding reputation, with productions that sell out quickly.
The Cut SE1 8NB
+44 (0)844 871 7628
www.oldvictheatre.com
Rail/Tube: Waterloo

Udderbelly Festival

An annual spring-summer festival housed inside a temporary upside-down inflatable cow on the banks of the Thames, go to the Udderbelly for comedy and entertaining circus shows.
Belvedere Road Coach Park SE1 8XX
+44 (0)844 545 8282
www.udderbelly.co.uk
Rail/Tube: Waterloo

Ev

This hidden-away Turkish restaurant, bar and café is housed inside the railway arches behind a small community garden. The architecture is dramatic and the interior has a jovial atmosphere. There's even a little outside space which is perfectly tranquil for summertime drinks.
The Arches 97-99 Isabella Street, London SE1 8DD
020 7620 6191
www.tasrestaurants.co.uk
Rail/Tube: Waterloo

Tate Modern

This world famous modern art gallery housed inside a former power station on the Thames is known for big-idea installations and awe-inspiring spaces.
Bankside SE1 9TG
+44 (0)207 887 8888
visiting.modern@tate.org.uk
www.tate.org.uk/visit/tate-modern
Rail: Blackfriars

Southbank Centre

A hub of life and activity along the South Bank, there's always a show or a tea dance going on inside. It's also a fab place for a coffee — head up to the balcony on the fifth floor for a little fresh air.
Belvedere Road SE1 8XX
+44 (0)207 960 4200
customer@southbankcentre.co.uk
www.southbankcentre.co.uk
Rail/Tube: Waterloo

Westminster

London's political centre, Westminster boasts an array of impressive historic buildings that have been home to centuries of political decision-making. There's a corporate atmosphere here, with business attire and weighty briefcases the uniform of choice for the local workers. On their way to meetings of the highest political importance, the suited and booted dodge the groups of tourists who flock to the area to see the Houses of Parliament and Big Ben, the Prime Minister's residence at 10 Downing Street, the Horse Guards Parade, Westminster Abbey and Buckingham Palace.

Where the locals recommend:

Victoria Street and Abingdon Street

Soak up the historical and political importance of Westminster by taking a stroll along these two streets, which allows you to take in Westminster Abbey and the Houses of Parliament. Duck into Victoria Tower Gardens to rest and reflect on your surroundings.
Victoria Street and Abingdon Street SW1P 3JY
Tube: Westminster

Strutton Ground Market

This weekday market serves food, coffee and interesting trinkets — it's much loved by local office workers in an area that has relatively few food and shopping options.
Strutton Ground SW1P 2HY
Tube: St James's Park

Bannatyne Spa Millbank

Found inside a regal-looking office building, this gym and spa is a favourite with the local government workers. Treat yourself to a day spa and get a slice of Westminster leisure time — there are two jacuzzis and a small pool among other facilities. Pop next door for a coffee and quick bite in EAT and sit in the airy indoor-outdoor courtyard.
4 Millbank SW1P 3JA
+44 (0)844 248 3777
www.bannatyne.co.uk/spa/millbank
Tube: Westminster

Jewel Tower

This lesser known Westminster site dates back 650 years and was previously known as the King's Privy Wardrobe. It's a quiet corner of a bustling area.
Abingdon Street SW1P 3JX
+44 (0)370 333 1181
www.english-heritage.org.uk/visit/places/jewel-tower
Tube: Westminster

Churchill War Rooms

As the wartime bunker that sheltered Churchill and his government during the Blitz, this is an insight into a secret wartime history.
Clive Steps, King Charles Street SW1A 2AQ
+44 (0)207 930 6961
www.iwm.org.uk/visits/churchill-war-rooms
Tube: Westminster

North London

The conversation — 'North or South London: which is better?' — is a common one to be heard between Londoners. The more spacious north London has chocolate-box villages that feel a little more rural than their southern counterparts, and there are a lot more hills. Various north London pockets are favoured by those in the public eye, and spontaneous and liberal north Londoners have a history of championing ethical causes. Embracing a European-style café culture, trendy bars and a celebrated music scene, north London is elegant and gutsy.

A work day in north London

Morning

The Breakfast Club
Start the day as you mean to go on with a hearty breakfast at the Angel branch of this 80s retro spot. Page 179. Tube: Angel

Impact Hub Islington
Get a desk at this co-working space with an original skylit warehouse interior. Page 131. Tube: Angel

Cass Art
Stop in at this store revered by London's creative community. Page 213. Tube: Angel

Afternoon

The Albion
Take your business contacts to this traditional Islington pub for lunch. Page 189. Rail: Caledonian Road & Barnsbury

Wellcome Collection
Have a look around this museum for the curious and grab a coffee in the airy café while catching up on emails. Page 206. Tube: Euston Square

British Library
Grab a desk and spend a few hours working on your laptop in this enriching environment. Page 135. Rail/Tube: King's Cross

Evening

Jealous Gallery
Stop by this gallery before is closes at 18:00 to peruse the urban art. Page 65. Tube: Highgate

UNA
Impress your business contacts by treating them to a meal at this St Pancras Clock Tower pop-up project. Page 64. Rail/Tube: King's Cross

Hand of Glory
Finish off the evening with a drink at this trendy countrified Dalston pub — another example of London's inherent creativity. Page 124. Rail: Rectory Road

A day of play in north London

Morning

Ginger & White
Start the morning with a coffee at this European style pavement café. Page 187. Tube: Hampstead

Goldfinger House
Check out the previous architect's home said to be far ahead of its time in design terms. Page 64. Rail: Hampstead Heath

Hampstead Heath
Explore the vast expanse of the greenery, ponds and woodland and enjoy London's skyline from Parliament Hill. Page 64. Rail: Hampstead Heath

Afternoon

Camino
Stop for a treat-filled tapas lunch in this Spanish eatery squirrelled away in a courtyard. Page 180. Rail/Tube: King's Cross

Camden Passage
Search for antiques and quirky gifts along this pedestrianised street. Page 65. Tube: Angel

Abbey Park Cemetery
Lesser known than Highgate Cemetery, this overgrown Victorian space has a peaceful otherworldly feel. Rail: Stoke Newington

Evening

The Seagrass
Have dinner at this marketside pie and mash shop that converts into an evening restaurant. Page 183. Tube: Angel

Camden Lock
Have a stroll along the canalside here during long summer evenings. Page 64. Tube: Camden Town

The Forge
Enjoy some drinks at this classy venue and take in some world music. Page 63. Tube: Camden Town

North London neighbourhoods:

Camden and King's Cross

A haven for sub-cultures and one of London's musical heartlands, Camden is unlike anywhere else in the city. From goth to punk and everywhere in between, piercings, studs and retro band t-shirts reign supreme. Neighbouring King's Cross is reinventing itself from a grubby nondescript transport hub to a decent-looking creative centre. International cuisine, food and the modern plaza in front of the station make it a destination now as well as a transit route.

Where the locals recommend:

British Library

The UK's national library and the largest library in the world, visit the British Library for an insight into books and maps. The imposing building of brutalist architecture has a concourse with a café ideal for a lunchtime pit stop.
96 Euston Road NW1 2DB
+44 (0)330 333 1144
Customer-Services@bl.uk
www.bl.uk
Rail/Tube: King's Cross

The Forge

This Camden music venue and bar isn't as grungy as Camden's other musical locations. With an events calendar of world music and literary gatherings, together with great value food and drinks, this is a vibrant place to sit back and relax while enjoying the show.
3-7 Delancey Street NW1 7NL
+44 (0)207 383 7808
contact@forgevenue.org
www.forgevenue.org
Tube: Camden Town

Camden Lock

After checking out the market and food stalls at Camden Lock, take a walk along the canal towards Little Venice. It's about a two hour walk and you get to see a changing area of London and experience canalside life.
Camden Lock NW1 8AB
Tube: Camden Town

UNA

Argentinian chef Martin Milesi hosts the UNA culinary project in the St Pancras Clock Tower. It's a pop-up project where 12 diners sit around the table and are treated to Milesi's gastronomic journey around Latin America.
St Pancras Chambers N1C 4QP
www.grubclub.com/una
Rail/Tube: King's Cross

Wellcome Collection

A 'free destination for the incurably curious', this museum displays medical artefacts and artworks relating to medicine. The huge airy café is an uplifting place for a caffeine break too.
183 Euston Road NW1 2BE
info@wellcomecollection.org
www.wellcomecollection.org
Tube: Euston Square

Hampstead

Coined as an urban village, Hampstead has been a popular place to visit for centuries. Writers, poets and artists find inspiration in the village and on the 800 acre Hampstead Heath; Keats, Constable and George Orwell — and many more — had an affinity with the area. Boutiques, pavement cafés and charming homes of historical importance are the order of the day in Hampstead. Near South Hampstead, discover St John's Wood, the famed Lord's Cricket Ground and the celebrity haunts of Primrose Hill and Belsize Park.

Where the locals recommend:

Hampstead Heath

It really is possible to lose yourself in this huge expanse of ancient woodland and grassy open space. There are even ponds for swimming — something London's al fresco swimming fanatics love to do whatever the weather. Parliament Hill also offers outstanding views of London's skyline.
South End Road NW3 2QD
Rail: Hampstead Heath

Goldfinger House

This National Trust property doesn't look like much from the outside, but is hailed as an architectural and design triumph that was well ahead of its time when it was conceptualised by architect Ernö Goldfinger in 1939. It remained his home until he died in 1987 and has been maintained ever since with his original furniture and possessions. Even more extraordinarily, Goldfinger was a poor Hungarian immigrant when he first built it, although he went on to become a wealthy and successful architect.
2 Willow Road NW3 1TH
+44 (0)207 435 6166
2willowroad@nationaltrust.org.uk
www.nationaltrust.org.uk/2-willow-road
Rail: Hampstead Heath

Primrose Hill

The hill itself is found in the northern part of Regent's Park and offers stunning views of London's skyline. Primrose Hill is also the name of the nearby neighbourhood, filled with small independently run restaurants and boutiques. It's a popular place for London's public figures to live and hang out.

Primrose Hill Road NW3 3AA
Tube: Chalk Farm

Freud Museum

The London home of the father of psychoanalysis Sigmund Freud after he escaped from the Nazis in Vienna, the Freud Museum offers an insight into his work and a peek at his consulting room.

20 Maresfield Gardens NW3 5SX
+44 (0)207 435 2002
www.freud.org.uk
Tube: Finchley Road

Keats House

The home of John Keats for a couple of years, he wrote Ode to a Nightingale in the garden. It's a reminiscent place in a residential Hampstead area.

10 Keats Grove NW3 2RR
+44 (0)207 332 3868
www.cityoflondon.gov.uk
Rail: Hampstead Heath

Highgate and Crouch End

A leafy north east London locality, Highgate is one of the most expensive neighbourhoods in the city. Known for its green spaces and high-brow village-like feeling, this is a distinguished part of town that feels a little countrified. Neighbouring Crouch End has a similar kind of charm and is favoured by free-spirited and family-orientated Londoners.

Where the locals recommend:

Highgate Cemetery

This Victorian cemetery is the resting place of many influential figures of history, including Karl Marx, George Eliot and Michael Faraday. It's a popular place for those who

like a reflective wander.

Swain's Lane N6 6PJ
+44 (0)208 340 1834
info@highgate-cemetery.org
www.highgatecemetery.org
Tube: Archway

Pavilion Café

The old cricket pavilion amid the ancient woodland of Highgate Woods is now home to a café, ideal for winter warming soups, and tea and cake in the outdoor seating area.

Highgate Woods, Muswell Hill Road N10 3JN
+44 (0)208 444 4777
Tube: Highgate

Painted Black

This retro vintage clothes shop sells fashions from around the 1930s onwards and miscellaneous trinkets for the home.

22 Veryan Court Park Road N8 8JR
+44 (0)207 341 76161
www.paintedblack.co.uk
Tube: Highgate

Jacksons Lane

A venue that plays host to London's most cutting edge theatre, performance art and comedy, Jacksons Lane is at the vanguard of London's dramatics.

269a Archway Road N6 5AA
+44 (0)208 341 4421
admin@jacksonslane.org.uk
www.jacksonslane.org.uk
Tube: Highgate

Jealous Gallery

The Crouch End branch of this screenprint studio and gallery is filled with contemporary urban art. There are regular exhibitions and limited edition prints available on fine art paper.

27 Park Road N8 8TE
+44 (0)208 347 7688
info@jealousgallery.com
www.jealousgallery.com
Tube: Highgate

Islington and Canonbury

This vibrant and urban north London neighbourhood is loved by those who worship the north London feeling, and comes with the added bonus of super proximity to the centre of town. Café culture, gastropubs, boutiques and a stylish veneer form the backdrop to the way of life in this area, with townhouses, chic flats and smatterings of garden squares and parks thrown in for good measure. It's a high-end but unpretentious part of London.

Where the locals recommend:

Camden Passage

A warren of pedestrianised streets in Angel, Camden Passage is home to antiques stalls and shops, cute cafés and bright design-led shops.

Camden Passage N1 8EA
camdenpassageislington.co.uk
Tube: Angel

Almeida Theatre

This theatre puts on a range of classic and new plays, with the particularly successful ones often transferring to the West End. The theatre also runs partnerships with local schools to give children opportunities in the arts.

Almeida Street N1 1TA
+44 (0)207 359 4404
boxoffice@almeida.co.uk
www.almeida.co.uk
Rail: Essex Road

Citroën Garage

This abandoned car garage tucked away off Upper Street plays host to occasional pop-up restaurants. It's a quirky spot for an evening out; check the Just Opened London website for details of forthcoming pop-ups.

The Garage, 133b Upper Street N1 1QP
www.justopenedlondon.com
Rail: Essex Road

Estorick Collection
A small gallery of Italian art in a Georgian townhouse, the majority of the art was the private collection of American author Eric Estorick.
39a Canonbury Square London N1 2AN
+44 (0)207 704 9522
www.estorickcollection.com
Rail/Tube: Highbury & Islington

Worker's Café
This greasy spoon contrasts starkly with the shiny Islington boutiques that surround it, which makes it all the more loved by locals. Pop in for a British fry-up or staple ham, egg and chips lunch. With a cup of builder's tea, naturally.
172 Upper Street N1 1RG
+44 (0)207 226 3973
www.workersislington.co.uk
Rail/Tube: Highbury & Islington

Stoke Newington
This neighbourhood known as 'Stokey' by local residents has a strong local spirit, with many independently run businesses in the area. Life revolves around Church Street here, with a cacophony of bars and pubs interspersed with vintage stores and quirky fashion labels.

Where the locals recommend:

Clissold Park
A previous 18th century country estate, Clissold Park is a peaceful park that regularly hosts festivals and special events. The mansion at the epicentre is now the swanky home to the park's café.
Stoke Newington Church Street N16 9HJ
Tube: Arsenal

Castle Climbing Centre
Every indoor climber's dream, this huge climbing centre is found inside an old Victorian pumping station and offers 450 routes and 90 roped lines.
Green Lanes N4 2HA
+44 (0)208 211 7000
info@castle-climbing.co.uk
www.castle-climbing.co.uk
Rail: Finsbury Park

Abney Park Cemetery
This overgrown Victorian cemetery is lesser known than Highgate Cemetery, and has a similar mystical feeling. There's a crumbling Gothic chapel in the middle of the grounds and a monument to the many local victims of the Blitz.
South Lodge, Abney Park, Stoke Newington High Street N16 0LH
+44 (0)207 275 7557
info@abneypark.org
www.abneypark.org
Rail: Stoke Newington

Bridgewood & Neitzert
The place to go in Stokey for string music lovers, this duo sell violins, violas, cellos and double basses. Supremely knowledgeable, they can also make lutes, violas and baroque violins.
146 Stoke Newington Church Street N16 0JU
+44 (0)207 249 9398
violinsbn@btclick.com
www.londonviolins.com
Rail: Stoke Newington

Cobbled Yard
This vintage furniture store inside an old Victorian stable offers an eclectic range of throwback goods big and small.
1 Bouverie Road N16 0AH
+44 (0)208 809 5286
info@cobbled-yard.co.uk
www.cobbled-yard.co.uk
Rail: Stoke Newington

Have a stroll along the canalside at the Camden Lock during long summer evenings

South London

The great debate of whether north or south London is better doesn't bother south Londoners too much. Enjoying a riverside life due to the huge stretch of the river running by, south Londoners enjoy a flatter and greener existence. It's a little more compact down south, but space is used well in the locality, with squirrelled away rooftop bars and artsy enclaves. Small neighbourhood hubs enjoy a great sense of community and feeling of shared identity.

A work day in south London

Morning

Battersea Arts Centre
Check out this historical building with free Wi-Fi in the atmospheric café. Page 70.
Rail: Clapham Junction

Pump House Gallery
Grab some inspiration from this Battersea Park art gallery. Page 70. Rail: Battersea Park

POP Brixton
Visit the latest start-ups being given a helping hand by this shipping containered venue.
Page 191. Rail/Tube: Brixton

Afternoon

No32 The Old Town
Have a business meeting over a craft beer on the rooftop of this Clapham classic. Page 151.
Tube: Clapham Common

Le Bureau
Use a desk at this classy co-working space with designer furniture and bean to cappuccino coffee machines. Page 132. Rail: Queenstown Road

Pullens Yards
Drop into an open workhouse event in this creative community. Page 72.
Tube: Kennington

Evening

The Wine Tasting Shop
Treat your business associates to a wine tasting session. Page73. Rail/Tube: Balham

Brunswick House
Dine at this classy restaurant alongside quirky architectural salvage. Page 72.
Rail/Tube: Vauxhall

CLF Art Café
Track down an inspiring performance to watch at this much loved community arts centre. Page 71. Rail: Peckham Rye

A day of play in south London

Morning

Flotsam & Jetsam
Enjoy an eclectic brunch boutique style in Wandsworth Common. Page 187.
Rail: Wandsworth Common

Tooting Bec Lido
Take a dip at one of the largest outdoor swimming pools in the UK. Page 72.
Rail: Streatham

Bean & Hop
Have a specialist coffee or a craft beer at this continental-style café. Page 71. Rail: Earlsfield

Afternoon

Brixton Village
Grab some lunch at one of the small eateries in this trendy hub. Page 70. Rail/Tube: Brixton

Clapham Picturehouse
Take in an arthouse film with some tea and cake. Page 70. Tube: Clapham Common

Hop Burns & Black
Pick up some craft beer, hot sauce or vinyl in this off-the-wall shop. Page 71.
Rail: East Dulwich

Evening

Frank's Campari Bar
Enjoy a drink and small plates at this quirky bar atop a multi-storey car park. Page 192.
Rail: Peckham Rye

Café Cairo
Have a drink, free toast and shisha in the Middle-East-meets-disco bar. Page 70.
Tube: Clapham North

The Bedford
Watch some comedy at this pub's award-winning Banana Cabaret. Page 73.
Rail/Tube: Balham

South London neighbourhoods:

Battersea and Clapham

Spotted from afar by its iconic power station, Battersea is a riverside neighbourhood with swathes of apartment-dwellers and lovers of local neighbourhood eateries. Fun-loving Clapham has some locally loved nightlife along the High Street and around Clapham Junction train station, but there are also pockets of peace and quiet, with villagey localities, sweet shopping areas like Northcote Road, and the thriving Clapham Common.

Where the locals recommend:

Abbeville Village

Centring on Abbeville Road, this locality has a quaint village-like feeling and is one of the most sought-after locations in Clapham. Think trinkety shops, pavement cafés and picture-perfect pubs.
Abbeville Road SW4 9LA
Tube: Clapham South

Pump House Gallery

Found within Battersea Park, this contemporary art gallery is inside a renovated building that used to supply water to the park's lakes. Exhibitions range from photography to performance arts.
Battersea Park SW11 4NJ
+44 (0)208 871 7572
info@pumphousegallery.org.uk
www.pumphousegallery.org.uk
Rail: Battersea Park

Clapham Picturehouse

This cinema shows a combination of mainstream and arthouse films; the café is a destination in its own right too, with tea, cake and wine to enjoy before, after or during the screening. Wander around the artisan food market on the pedestrianised pavement out the front if you have a little extra time.
76 Venn Street SW4 0AT
+44 (0)871 902 5727
www.picturehouses.co.uk/cinema/Clapham_Picturehouse
Tube: Clapham Common

Battersea Arts Centre

This Grade II listed building is a performing arts space and a community hub. Check out the calendar of events, enjoy the feeling of history and chill out in the on-site Scratch Bar, which also has free WiFi.
Lavender Hill SW11 5TN
+44 (0)207 223 2223
boxoffice@bac.org.uk
www.bac.org.uk
Rail: Clapham Junction

Clapham Old Town

This area on the edge of Clapham Common has a range of boutiques and restaurants and is a quieter part of the neighbourhood to meander. Pop in for a drink in The Sun, a much-loved pub in the area, or try out the independently-run No 32 The Old Town, which has a roof terrace.
Clapham Old Town SW4 0LB
Tube: Clapham Common

Brixton

This neighbourhood has reinvented itself to become south London's artistic centre. Cultural diversity and creativity blend in Brixton, resulting in vibrant market food offerings, quirky shops and a thriving music scene spread across an array of highly-regarded venues from the Brixton Academy to Hootananny. A hotbed for new ideas against a proudly gritty backdrop, the energy on Brixton's streets is palpable.

Where the locals recommend:

Brixton Village

A destination for fun-loving foodies on a budget, Brixton Village Market is found inside a renovated arcade, and is now home to small cafés, eateries and a few shops. Eat your way around the world and enjoy the palpable buzz of the locals having a great time.
Market Row, Coldharbour Lane SW9 8LB
+44 (0)207 274 2990
info@brixtonmarket.net
brixtonmarket.net/brixton-village
Rail/Tube: Brixton

Electric Avenue

Sung about by Eddy Grant, Electric Avenue is famous for being the first market street to be lit by electricity. Today the street forms part of Brixton Market and is a spirited road to wander along to get a feeling of Brixton life.
Electric Avenue SW9 8JP
Rail/Tube: Brixton

Brixton Jamm

A little further away from Brixton's main drag is this music venue that hosts London's up-and-coming music talent and after-parties.
261 Brixton Road SW9 6LH
+44 (0)207 274 5537
info@brixtonjamm.org
www.brixtonjamm.org
Tube: Stockwell

Café Cairo

This eccentric spot between Clapham and Brixton is an evening-only café and late night bar, with a Middle-East-meets-disco style décor. Wonderfully vibrant and not-too-hipster, patrons can help themselves to free toast, play chess by the fire and enjoy the shisha pipes in the shisha garden.
88 Landor Road SW9 9PE
0207 207 0926
info@cafecairo.co.uk
www.cafecairo.co.uk
Tube: Clapham North

The Beer Hive
This brewery co-operative helps small, local breweries create their beers. The Beer Hive also has a quirky calendar of events, such as 'board game Sundays'.
Arch 283 Belinda Road, off Coldharbour Lane SW9 7DT
www.beerhive.london
Rail: Loughborough Junction

Dulwich and Peckham
A well-to-do part of south London, Dulwich is characterised by mansion houses and chestnut tree lined avenues. Dulwich Village is the beating heart of the neighbourhood: a designated conservation area with its rural idyll feeling, boutiques and café culture. Peckham doesn't have as picturesque a history as Dulwich, but recent gentrification has made it a sought-after place for Londoners to live. An influx of artists gives it a creative edge, while international gastronomic offerings, from the Balkan Peckham Bazaar to the south Indian Ganapati, keep foodie appetites sated.

Where the locals recommend:

Bellenden Road
This road with a community feeling is a haven for independent shops, from vintage fashion retailers and doggie salons to artisan chocolatiers and butchers.
Bellenden Road SE15
Rail: Peckham Rye

Horniman Museum
This slightly offbeat museum is an ode to anthropology and natural history, with a large collection of stuffed animals and stunning landscaped gardens with lovely London views.

100 London Rd SE23 3PQ
+44 (0)208 699 1872
www.horniman.ac.uk
Rail: Forest Hill

Hop Burns & Black
This shop brings together what it calls three of the world's biggest obsessions: beer, hot sauce and vinyl records. Find hundreds of these products painstakingly sourced from across the world.
38 East Dulwich Road SE22 9AX
+44 (0)207 450 0284
info@hopburnsblack.co.uk
www.hopburnsblack.co.uk
Rail: East Dulwich

Dulwich Farmers' Market
Held on the last Sunday of the month, foodies flock here to buy some of the best ingredients and artisanal concoctions. It's located on the grounds of the historic Dulwich College, so it's also an opportunity to enjoy the regal primped and preened surroundings.
Dulwich College, Dulwich Common SE21 7LD
Rail: West Dulwich

CLF Art Café
Inside this old warehouse space is the centre of the locality's nightlife. The CLF Art Café hosts music, theatre, art and comedy events, as well as film screenings on the roof.
Block A Bussey Building, 133 Rye Lane SE15 4ST
020 7732 5275
info@clfartcafe.org
www.clfartcafe.org
Rail: Peckham Rye

Earlsfield, Southfields and Wimbledon
An increasingly popular area for south Londoners to live, people are clocking onto the fact Earlsfield has great transport links into the centre of town. As a result, things are getting a little trendier in the area, albeit in a very low-key way, with quirky cafés and innovative restaurants opening up. The area between Southfields and Wimbledon is best known for the tennis championships that take place every summer. There's still a thriving tennis community the rest of the year too, and these areas maintain an elegant aura of suburban-village-life.

Where the locals recommend:

Wimbledon Park
Ideal for the athletically-minded, go to Wimbledon Park to play some tennis, use the athletics track or play some crazy golf. There's also a lake and watersports centre, beach volleyball courts and a pavilion café.
Home Park Road SW19 7HS
Tube: Wimbledon Park

Bean & Hop
Bringing a little continental culture to Earlsfield, Bean & Hop is all about local craft beer and specialist coffee. Served alongside fresh bread and pastries, this is a great place to kick back and relax.
424-426 Garratt Lane SW18 4HN
+44 (0)207 998 6584
beanandhop@outlook.com
www.beanandhop.co.uk
Rail: Earlsfield

The Alexandra
This pub in the centre of Wimbledon stretches in all directions, meaning there are plenty of nooks and crannies to explore. The part-covered, patio-heated roof terrace is a particular favourite, with its bright beachy feel.
33 Wimbledon Hill Road SW19 7NE
+44 (0)208 947 7691
Alexandra@youngs.co.uk
www.alexandrawimbledon.com
Rail/Tube: Wimbledon

Wimbledon Village

Up the hill from Wimbledon town is the village, with its countrified pubs, independent shops and proximity to the rugged Wimbledon Common. Wander in any direction to get a feel for the polished village surroundings.

High Street Wimbledon SW19 5DX

Rail/Tube: Wimbledon

The Park Tavern

This Southfields pub in a restored 19th century coaching inn is loved by locals for a quiet pint, especially in the quirky garden during the warmer months. There are also regular events, such as quiz nights and burger evenings.

212 Marton Road SW18 5SW

+44 (0)208 488 8855

info@park-tavern.com

www.park-tavern.com

Tube: Southfields

Kennington and Camberwell

An inner London enclave with brick houses and Georgian architecture, Kennington is a stone's throw from central London and is a residential hub for young professionals. Camberwell is a more artsy part of town, with several galleries and the Camberwell College of Arts attracting young creative minds.

Where the locals recommend:

The Cinema Museum

A must-visit for film buffs, discover a host of memorabilia and artefacts from throughout the history of cinema. There's also a vibrant events calendar of talks, screenings and bazaars.

2 Dugard Way (off Renfrew Road) SE11 4TH

+44 (0)207 840 2200

info@cinemamuseum.org.uk

www.cinemamuseum.org.uk

Tube: Elephant & Castle

Beefeater Gin Distillery

Home of London's famous gin brand, the Beefeater Gin Distillery is found inside a previous military pickle factory. Take a tour through the distillery and sample some of the gin products.

20 Montford Place SE11 5DE

+44 (0)207 587 0034

info@beefeaterdistillery.com

www.beefeaterdistillery.com

Tube: Oval

South London Gallery

This public-funded contemporary art gallery has a fast-paced events calendar of exhibitions, film screenings and talks. The No67 café is popular with the locals too.

65-67 Peckham Road SE5 8UH

+44 (0)207 703 6120

mail@southlondongallery.org

www.southlondongallery.org

Rail: Peckham Rye

Brunswick House

Staying true to its roots as an architectural salvage yard in a wrecked Georgian mansion, Brunswick House is now a restaurant, café and bar. The décor is made from the architectural salvage and is all for sale, so the backdrop is constantly changing.

30 Wandsworth Road SW8 2LG

+44 (0)207 720 2926

info@brunswickhouse.co

www.brunswickhouse.co

Rail/Tube: Vauxhall

Pullens Yards

A mix of designer-creatives live in these good-looking live-work spaces that date back to the 1800s. They host a range of open workhouse events throughout the year giving people a chance to glimpse into the artists' work.

Peacock Yard SE17 3LH

+44 (0)207 701 2422

secretary@pullensyards.co.uk

www.pullensyards.co.uk

Tube: Kennington

Tooting, Balham and Wandsworth Common

A leafy south-west London locality, the area around Wandsworth is characterised by sweeping residential streets with imperious Victorian townhouses and a laidback café culture. This is interspersed with huge green commons and small villagey centres with many independent shops and boutiques. Furthest to the south of this area is the recently revived Tooting, a haven of well-priced family-run curry-houses and hipster bars, frequented by artsy locals and a fun-loving medical crowd from the nearby St George's Hospital. Balham is a thriving but laidback hub, with the independent shops of Hildreth Street and the chilled out bars, pubs and original cafés.

Where the locals recommend:

Tooting Bec Lido

One of the longest outdoor swimming pools in the UK at more than 90 metres, Tooting Bec Lido first opened in the early 1900s. The colourful changing cabins along the side give it a nostalgic feeling. It also attracts the occasional film crew: Brad Pitt's boxing pool scene in the film Snatch was filmed there.

Tooting Bec Road SW16 1RU

+44 (0)208 871 7198

www.placesforpeopleleisure.org/centres/tooting-bec-lido

Rail: Streatham

Tram and Social

A bar in a converted tram shed, the shabby-chic décor and regular live music events make this a chilled-out midweek drinking spot or weekend party venue.

46-48 Mitcham Road, SW17 9NA

+44 (0)208 767 0278

tootingtram@anticlondon.com

www.tootingtramandsocial.co.uk

Tube: Tooting Broadway

The Bedford

An epicentre of Balham's community, The Bedford has a long and colourful history, from early gigs by The Clash and U2 to an impromptu courtroom. Today it's most renowned for its award-winning Banana Cabaret comedy shows in the amazing Globe Theatre at the centre of the premises.

Rail/Tube: Balham

Wandsworth Common

This beautiful rugged common serving an exclusive south London locale just calls out for a stroll. Walk past the duck ponds, stop for a coffee in the Skylark Café and have a go on the pull-up bars or other exercise equipment if you're feeling particularly energetic.

Rail: Wandsworth Common

The Wine Tasting Shop

With a fresh selection of wines daily, this is the place to buy a bottle as well as stop in and sample the range while nibbling on cheese and charcuterie platters. There's also a calendar of events and some pavement seating for the warmer months.

18 Hildreth Street SW12 9RQ
+44 (0)208 616 8658
www.thewinetastingshop.co.uk
Rail/Tube: Balham

East

The beating heart of London's start-up scene, east London is trendy, creative and constantly on the cusp of the globe's latest innovations. There's also a sense of old London in the east, with reminders of London's traditional and hard-working East End community. There's a little grittiness in this neck of the woods and some remarkable graffiti adorning the walls of old warehouses. If anything, this feeling of authenticity inspires the creative locals and makes them feel part of a real community. Things get a little leafier down towards the south east, with vast green waterside spaces.

A work day in east London

Morning

Ziferblat
Pay only for your time in this social experiment café-workspace. Page 78.
Rail/Tube: Old Street

Whitecross Village
Be inspired by the art installations in this locality with a big community spirit. Page 77.
Rail/Tube: Old Street

BOXPARK
Check out the latest inventions and creations from the start-up scene at this shipping container shopping strip. Page 210.
Rail: Shoreditch High Street

Afternoon

Merchants Tavern
Have a business lunch in this Tech City stalwart for entrepreneurial meetings. Page 138. Rail/Tube: Old Street

TechHub
Head over to one of TechHub's three east London co-working spaces for some desk time. Page 127.

The Proud Archivist
Enjoy some inspirational downtime in this canalside art gallery café. Page 77.
Rail: Haggerston

Evening

Beach Blanket Babylon (BBB) Shoreditch
Impress design conscious business contacts with a meal in this bohemian chic restaurant.
Page 78. Rail: Shoreditch High Street

Google Campus
Head over to this Tech City hub for inspiring networking events. Page 156.
Rail/Tube: Old Street

The Nightjar
Rub shoulders with Tech City's workers and listen to live jazz in this innovative cocktail bar. Page 192. Rail/Tube: Old Street

A day of play in east London

Morning

E Pellicci
Start the day at this greasy spoon for a breakfast fry-up. Page 186.
Tube: Bethnal Green

Greenwich Market
Find original designs and vintage goods in this villagey market. Page 210.
Rail: Cutty Sark

Greenwich Foot Tunnel
Walk 370 metres under the Thames to the Isle of Dogs and enjoy this civil engineering feat. Page 76. Rail: Cutty Sark

Afternoon

Lady Dinah's Cat Emporium
Play with the resident cats while you eat a light lunch or afternoon tea. Page 187. Rail: Shoreditch High Street

Broadway Market
Visit this hip market for vintage finds, artisanal food and a good dose of people watching. Page 124. Rail London Fields

Passing Clouds
Check out the events calendar of this alternative community and cultural venue.
Page 77. Rail: Haggerston

Evening

Rough Trade East
Unearth music talent in this vinyl music store. Page 213. Tube: Aldgate East

Dalston Roof Park
Check out a supper club or another event in this hip rooftop hangout. Page 77. Rail: Dalston Junction

BrewDog Shoreditch
Try out the beers from this London brewer, or head to the speakeasy downstairs for beer cocktails. Page 192.
Rail: Shoreditch High Street

East London neighbourhoods:

Canary Wharf and the Isle of Dogs

This financial centre peppered with a handful of high rise towers owned by banks is a city slicker stomping ground with a modern edge. While corporations, shiny offices and bars spilling out with the suited and booted reign supreme around Canary Wharf, big business isn't the only string to this neighbourhood's bow. The Isle of Dogs was originally the city's docklands. The area went through a period of great decline before reinventing itself; now it's a place where Londoners embrace the maritime feeling and can almost guarantee a River Thames view from their flats. Summertime street food and shopping by the dockside make it a good-looking place to hang out.

Where the locals recommend:

Summer Screens

Sit outdoors in Canada Square Park during the summer months to watch everything from the Wimbledon Tennis Championships to live opera from the Royal Opera House on the big screen.
Canada Square Park E14 5AX
www.canarywharf.com/arts-events/events
Tube: Canary Wharf

Canary Wharf Ice Rink

During the winter months, head over to the ice rink that pops up in the area every year and enjoy skating amid the skyscrapers.
Canada Square Park E14 5AB
info@icerinkcanarywharf.co.uk
www.icerinkcanarywharf.co.uk
Tube: Canary Wharf

Docklands Sailing and Watersports Centre

Making the most of the neighbourhood's water, this centre runs sessions and courses for those who want to go sailing, kayaking, windsurfing or power boating.
235a Westferry Road E14 3QS
+44 (0)207 537 2626
info@dswc.org
www.dswc.org
Rail: Crossharbour

Mudchute Park and Farm

This surprisingly huge park on the Isle of Dogs feels like a rural island wilderness. The 32 acres is home to a working farm with pigs to alpacas, stables and wide open spaces for a quiet ramble.
Pier Street E14 3HP
+44 (0)207 515 5901
info@mudchute.org
www.mudchute.org
Rail: Mudchute

Greenwich Foot Tunnel

At the southern tip of the Isle of Dogs is the foot tunnel enabling you to walk under the river to the heart of Greenwich. It's mostly commuters who use the 370 metre long tunnel, so visiting the tunnel is an insight into an underground London world, as well as a civil engineering triumph.
Greenwich Foot Tunnel SE10 9HT
Rail: Island Gardens or Cutty Sark

Greenwich

Marrying maritime history with rustic traditions, Greenwich has a truly individual London feeling. Famous for its responsibility for global timekeeping revolving around 'Greenwich Mean Time (GMT)', the locality is steeped in history, yet there's a mellow vibe keeping the area fun-loving and low-key too. The market has a country fair feeling, while the riverside parks and walkways mark some of the most chilled-out River Thames hangouts in the city. Cutesy eateries and traditional pubs complete the picture of this south east London haven.

Where the locals recommend:

Greenwich Park

Previously Henry VIII's hunting reserve, Greenwich Park is home to a hilly open green space, ancient woodland, the National Maritime Museum and of course, the Royal Observatory, where you can stand on the prime meridian itself.
Greenwich Park SE10 8QY
www.royalparks.org.uk/parks/greenwich-park
Rail: Greenwich

Meantime Brewing Company

This local Greenwich brewery produces beers that have become popular across London and further afield. Head over there for a beer in the bar or a brewery tour.
Lawrence Trading Estate, Blackwall Lane SE10 0AR
+44 (0)208 293 1111
www.meantimebrewing.com
Rail: Westcombe Park

The Brasserie @ The National Maritime Museum

Perched up high in the prestigious museum building, this restaurant is ideal for a classy lunch next to good looking views of the greenery of Greenwich.
National Maritime Museum, King William Walk SE10 9NF
+44 (0)208 305 0445
reservations@brasseriegreenwich.co.uk
www.brasseriegreenwich.co.uk
Rail: Cutty Sark

Craft London Café

The café on the ground floor of this café/restaurant/bar is famed for its on-site roasted coffee and the Peninsula Garden outside.

Peninsula Square, Greenwich Peninsula SE10 0SQ
+44 (0)208 465 5910
hello@craft-london.co.uk
www.craft-london.co.uk
Tube: North Greenwich

The Fan Museum

This quirky museum looks into the history and art of fan making. Go for a little creative inspiration followed by afternoon tea in the orangery.

12 Crooms Hill SE10 8ER
+44 (0)208 305 1441
www.thefanmuseum.org.uk
Rail: Cutty Sark

Haggerston, Hackney and Dalston

These east London locales blend edgy cool with artistic influence. With a combination of graffiti and cool apartments, waterside life along Regent's Canal and offbeat artsy cafés, the feeling is somewhere between trendy and edgy. Regardless, innovation and creativity are a way of life in these localities that retain the old East End spirit.

Where the locals recommend:

Lauriston Village

This Victoria Park locality has a bohemian feeling, as a cool mix of independent shops keep a sense of community spirit. Visit Loafing Café for artisan cakes, The Workshop for clay crafts and buy fresh meat to cook at home for dinner from W. Wells.

Lauriston Road E9 7HA
Rail: London Fields

The Proud Archivist

This café, bar, restaurant and art gallery is right on the edge of the canal. The bright library-esque interior makes it an inspiring place for a coffee or some time with the laptop, while the events calendar has a mixture of comedy nights and workshops for start-up entrepreneurs.

2-10 Hertford Road N1 5ET
+44 (0)203 598 2626
info@theproudarchivist.co.uk
www.theproudarchivist.co.uk
Rail: Haggerston

Passing Clouds

This cultural project and progressive music venue runs a range of community events, from conscious hip hop and self development workshops to film screenings and live jazz music. Food is 100% vegetarian and drinks are ethically sourced through local and fair trade initiatives.

1 Richmond Road E8 4AA
+44 (0)207 241 4889
we@passingclouds.org
www.passingclouds.org
Rail: Haggerston

Broadway Market

You can't visit this area without paying Broadway Market a visit. Buy antiques, artisan food and locally made crafts, then stop off at one of the cafés for a good session of people-watching.

Broadway Market E8 4QJ
www.broadwaymarket.co.uk
Rail: London Fields

Dalston Roof Park

This summertime spot is filled with faux grass and deck chairs and hosts parties, film screenings and supper clubs.

Print House, 18 Ashwin Street E8 3DL
www.bootstrapcompany.co.uk
Rail: Dalston Junction

Shoreditch and Old Street

London's creative and start-up centre is brimming with entrepreneurs, creatives and those who like to keep ahead of the trends. There's a feeling of gritty cool and it's a place where trendsters are compelled to see and be seen. Old warehouses have become galleries, while every other business in some way contributes to the success of Tech City. Whether you're a hipster or not, this neighbourhood genuinely captures the imagination. Aiming high is a way of life here, as is making dreams come true.

Where the locals recommend:

Whitecross Village

The street party on Whitecross Street every July is an important date in the diary for London creatives. During the rest of the year, the daily market sells widely revered street food among other things, while the art galleries and installations keep the feeling on the street fresh.

Whitecross Street EC1Y 8NA
Rail/Tube: Old Street

Columbia Road

Every Sunday this street becomes a jungle during the immense flower market. The strong feeling of neighbourhood continues during the rest of the week in the independently run eateries, interiors shops and vintage treasure troves.

Columbia Road E2 7RG
Rail: Hoxton

Ziferblat

An 'adult tree house' and social experiment, Ziferblat wants to create a community of people who use the space to create something interesting. Tea, coffee and snacks are free in this Russian café; instead you pay for the time you spend there (a cost of 5p per minute). It's a kind of social micro-tenancy for the duration of your visit; you keep track of time by picking up an alarm clock when you enter.

388 Old Street EC1V 9LT
+44 (0)7984 693 440
ziferblat.london@gmail.com
london.ziferblat.net
Rail/Tube: Old Street

Hurwundeki

A Korean café and hair salon rolled into one, this is an original place to go for a cut and a coffee and pastry. The Korean food is MSG-free and is crafted with house-made soy and chilli sauces.

Arch 298, Cambridge Heath Road E2 9HA
+44 (0)207 749 0638
www.hurwundeki.com
Rail: Cambridge Heath

Beach Blanket Babylon (BBB) Shoreditch

Found inside a building with an ominously black facade, BBB Shoreditch describes itself as a lifestyle club without the membership. The interior is far from plain, with its feeling of bohemian decadence with a Parisian aura. It's ideal for a drink in the champagne lounge or a meal surrounded by finery.

9-23 Bethnal Green Road E1 6LA
+44 (0)207 749 3540
reservations@beachblanket.co.uk
www.beachblanket.co.uk
Rail: Shoreditch High Street

West

The generally affluent west London is a favoured stomping ground of media moguls, literary types and people in the public eye. Small community hubs offer a vibrant, postcard-perfect street life, while sweeping residential streets filled with Victorian and Georgian townhouses and cobbled mewses indicate a well-to-do way of life. West London feels greener than other parts of town, with quiet parks, public spaces and a predilection for a verdant frontage on grand homes. A less polished side to west London does exist, in charmingly chaotic markets and the odd building of brutalist architecture.

A work day in west London

Morning

Lillie Road
Window shop for antiques over a coffee and pastry along this traditional street. Page 82. Tube: West Brompton

William Morris Society and Museum
View the work of this Victorian artist and designer in his former riverside home. Page 83. Tube: Ravenscourt Park

Museum of Brands, Packaging & Advertising
Get some creative inspiration by looking at brand and packaging designs through the ages. Page 84. Tube: Ladbroke Grove

Afternoon

Dock Kitchen and Tom Dixon Shop
Have a business lunch in this converted wharf overlooking the Grand Union Canal, followed by a browse of the latest designs in the shop below. Page 84.
Rail/Tube: Kensal Green

ClubRoom Paddington
Work at a desk in this plush co-working space inside a building from the 1800s. Page 134. Rail/Tube: Paddington

Serpentine Galleries
Have a late afternoon browse in these Hyde Park art galleries. Page 83.
Tube: High Street Kensington

Evening

Kensington Roof Gardens
Impress business associates with dinner and a drink on this 1.5 acre rooftop haven. Page 83. Tube: High Street Kensington

Friday Late
Hear new ideas at art and design themed evenings at the Victoria and Albert (V&A) Museum on the last Friday of the month. Page 83. Tube: South Kensington

Blue Anchor
Finish the night with a drink overlooking the Grade II listed Hammersmith Bridge. Page 83. Tube: Hammersmith

A day of play in west London

Morning

Habanera
This Mexican eatery with locally sourced ingredients does a great weekday breakfast or weekend brunch. Page 179. Tube: Shepherd's Market

Shepherd's Bush Market
Soak up the vibrant feeling of this historical market with a modern twist. Page 84. Tube: Shepherd's Bush Market

Holland Park
Get lost in this jungle-like green space. Page 85. Tube: Holland Park

Afternoon

Geales
This fish and chip restaurant dates back to 1939 and does a great value two course lunch. Page 180. Tube: Notting Hill Gate

Golborne Road
Experience the spirited market, Portuguese cafés and the cult landmark: the Trellick Tower. Page 84. Tube: Westbourne Park

Warrington Village
After checking out Little Venice, soak up the community charm in the streets nearby. Page 84. Tube: Warwick Avenue

Evening

Kateh
Try this Persian restaurant in an elegant neighbourhood with a delectable menu. Page 183. Tube: Warwick Avenue

Bogan Bingo
Partake in this retro comedy bingo show with a penchant for eighties fashions. Page 82. Tube: Fulham Broadway

Princess Victoria
Have a drink in this pub inside a restored Victorian Gin Palace, with walled herb garden and Cuban cigars. Page 189. Tube: Shepherd's Bush

West London neighbourhoods:

Fulham and Putney

With a pristine appearance and serene residential roads, Fulham is an affluent area much sought-after for its proximity to other upscale neighbourhoods in the area. Immaculately kept, classical looking homes adorned with verdant trellises are found along sweeping streets, while neighbourhood parks, cafés and organic greengrocers form hubs for local life. Just across the river, Putney has a bustling centre of pubs, bars and restaurants and a spirited riverside life.

Where the locals recommend:

Fulham Palace

One of the lesser known of London's palaces, Fulham Palace was the previous residence of the Bishop of London. Some of the buildings date back to the 15th century and together with the extensive gardens and riverside Bishop's Park next door, this is a fabulous place to spend one chill-out time.
Bishop's Avenue SW6 6EA
+44 (0)207 736 3233
admin@fulhampalace.org
www.fulhampalace.org
Tube: Putney Bridge

Lillie Road

Wandering along this cute but buzzy road gives a real sense of Fulham life, as you pass boutiques, pubs, filming and photography studios and the many antique shops Lillie Road is well-known for.
Lillie Road SW6
www.lillieroad.co.uk
Rail/Tube: West Brompton

Amuse Bouche

This champagne bar is known for serving bubbly at affordable prices. There's an extensive list of classic champagne producers, with several available by the glass.
51 Parsons Green SW6 4JA
+44 (0)207 371 8517
info@abcb.co.uk
www.abcb.co.uk
Tube: Parsons Green

Bogan Bingo

This retro comedy bingo show involves music and fashions from the eighties and nineties and general mayhem — all while bingo numbers are being called.
The Slug at Fulham, 490 Fulham Road SW6 5NH
info@boganbingo.co.uk
www.boganbingo.co.uk
Tube: Fulham Broadway

Half Moon Putney

A pub and music venue that's been famous since the sixties, the Half Moon has something going on most nights of the week, from music performances to stand-up comedy.
93 Lower Richmond Road SW15 1EU
+44 (0)208 780 9383
halfmoon@geronimo-inns.co.uk
www.geronimo-inns.co.uk/london-the-half-moon
Rail: Putney

Hammersmith and Chiswick

Known as being a centre for entertainment in west London, Hammersmith has an urban hub with multinational HQs juxtaposed with an idyllic riverside life. From the music shows in the art deco Hammersmith Apollo to the sweeping beauty of neighbouring Ravenscourt Park, Hammersmith blends fun with outdoor freedom. Further west, leafy Chiswick enjoys an enviable location in a meander of the River Thames. Filled with open green spaces, small community centres and verdurous residential streets, Chiswick has a charming feeling. For those who fancy a hop across the water to the opposite side of the Thames, Barnes is a country-style village much-loved by Londoners looking for a break from the city.

Where the locals recommend:

Lyric Hammersmith

This hub for creative and performing arts has been thriving since its 2015 makeover. The original Victorian theatre plays host to many thought-provoking theatre performances, while elsewhere on the site there are rehearsal spaces, dance studios, editing suites, a film studio and a bar, café and roof garden.
Lyric Square, King Street W6 0QL
+44 (0)208 741 6850
tickets@lyric.co.uk
www.lyric.co.uk
Tube: Hammersmith

Potli

This bright Indian restaurant has the aura of an upscale bazaar, with vivid colours, market-style hessian sacks and the odd idiosyncratic picture hanging. The food is truly marvellous, with classic curries, pillowy breads and vibrant Indian wines.
319-321 King Street W6 9NH
+44 (0)208 741 4328
info@potli.co.uk
www.potli.co.uk
Tube: Ravenscourt Park

William Morris Society and Museum

This society is based in William Morris's previous home on the banks of the Thames and aims to make the work of the Victorian artist and designer better known. The small museum is open on Thursday and Sunday afternoons.

Kelmscott House, 26 Upper Mall W6 9TA
+44 (0)208 741 3735
info@williammorrissociety.org.uk
www.williammorrissociety.org.uk
Tube: Ravenscourt Park

Blue Anchor

This family-run riverside pub next to the Grade II listed Hammersmith Bridge is revered by locals, who love to spill out onto the Thames-side path with a lunchtime or post-work beer.

13 Lower Mall W6 9DJ
+44 (0)208 748 5774
manager@blueanchorlondon.com
www.blueanchorlondon.com
Tube: Hammersmith

Fuller's Griffin Brewery

The historical home of the British beer brand, Fuller's has been brewing beer at this location for 160 years. It's ideal for soaking up some of London's brewing history after a walk along the nearby stretch of the Thames.

Chiswick Lane South W4 2QB
+44 (0)208 996 2085
fullers@fullers.co.uk
www.fullers.co.uk/brewery
Tube: Stamford Brook

Kensington and Earls Court

The monarchical locality of Kensington is filled with majestic airs and graces, combined with modern conveniences, warm locals and an international spirit. The regal feeling comes naturally in Kensington, given the area is home to Kensington Palace and old opulent buildings that are home to London's most prestigious museums. Nevertheless, a year-round summertime feeling pervades, with leisurely strolls around shops and lazy afternoons spent at pavement cafés a necessity for Kensingtonites. Earls Court has a less glistening and more metropolitan centre, and is best known for hosting immense trade shows and the pristine Georgian townhouses hidden away from the main drag.

Where the locals recommend:

Kensington Roof Gardens

The most famous rooftop in London, these gardens on top of a Kensington High Street building span a whopping 1.5 acres. Flamingos, bridges and waterways pock the pristine gardens. It's a place to dress up and enjoy a drink, meal or one of the special events regularly hosted there.

99 Kensington High Street W8 5SA
+44 (0)207 937 7994
www.virginlimitededition.com/the-roof-gardens
Tube: High Street Kensington

Friday Late

Held in the Victoria and Albert Museum (V&A) on the last Friday of each month is a themed art and design event with installations, music and a bar.

Victoria and Albert Museum (V&A), Cromwell Road SW7 2RL
+44 (0)207 942 2000
www.vam.ac.uk/content/articles/f/friday-late
Tube: South Kensington

Serpentine Galleries

Found in the middle of Hyde Park, the Serpentine Gallery and the Zaha Hadid designed Serpentine Sackler Gallery are housed inside a former tea pavilion and former gunpowder store respectively. The galleries host works from emerging and established artists.

Kensington Gardens W2 3XA
+44 (0)207 402 6075
information@serpentinegalleries.org
www.serpentinegalleries.org
Tube: High Street Kensington

Kensington Church Street

This road connecting Kensington to Notting Hill is well known for its fine art and antique shops.

Kensington Church Street W8 7LN
Tube: High Street Kensington

Evans and Peel Detective Agency

This speakeasy is found in a part of town where innovative nightlife is otherwise scarce. There's an element of faux-detective role play involved to get through the door before being permitted to enter the shadowy bar for cocktails and smoked American food.

310c Earls Court Road SW5 9BA
www.evansandpeel.com
Tube: Earls Court

Maida Vale and Kensal Green

The pretty residential neighbourhood of Maida Vale is best known for the waterways of the various canals converging here, earning it the title of 'Little Venice'. Enjoying the brightly coloured narrowboats and supping coffee or cocktails in the waterside cafés is what life's all about, and it feels far away from London's hectic

city centre. Kensal Green has a bit of a grittier reputation with a more animated feeling on the streets. Yet the sense of boutique charm and canalside life continues, making it a disheveled and carefree place to be. Design firms and TV production companies love to call the area home.
Where the locals recommend:

Warrington Village
This area between Maida Vale and Warwick Avenue has a small community charisma with a distinct creative focus. Check out Clifton Nurseries, Amoul for coffee and Pipa London for hip fashions.
Warrington Crescent and Formosa Street W9 2QA
Tube: Warwick Avenue

Paradise by Way of Kensal Green
This goth-infused bar and restaurant comes complete with velvet drapes and oversized chandeliers. The locally-sourced food comes highly raved about, while events from cabaret to cult film nights are locally loved.
19 Kilburn Lane W10 4AE
+44 (0)208 969 0098
clem@thecolumbogroup.com
www.theparadise.co.uk
Rail/Tube: Kensal Green

The Bridge House
This popular Little Venice spot is ideal for an al fresco drink in summer and a fireside meal in winter. Next door is the Canal Café Theatre if you fancy taking in a show.
13 Westbourne Terrace Road W2 6NG
+44 (0)207 266 4326
enquiry@
thebridgehouselittlevenice.co.uk
thebridgehouselittlevenice.co.uk
Tube: Royal Oak

Café Laville
With a perfect vantage point overlooking the water, this café is ideal for a coffee and a rustic Italian lunch.
453 Edgware Road W2 1TH
+44 (0)207 706 2620
Cafelaville.fr@gmail.com
www.cafelaville.co.uk
Tube: Warwick Avenue

Dock Kitchen and Tom Dixon Shop
Found inside a resplendent Victorian wharf, The Dock Kitchen overlooks the Grand Union Canal. The menu is experimental and served to the backdrop of a fully kitted-out Tom Dixon interior. Below the restaurant is the Tom Dixon shop itself, where the British designer's furniture is sold, alongside that of other international designers.
Portobello Docks, 344/342 Ladbroke Grove, Kensal Road W10 5BU
+44 (0)208 962 1610
reception@dockkitchen.co.uk
www.dockkitchen.co.uk
Rail/Tube: Kensal Green

Notting Hill and Shepherd's Bush
Idyllic cobblestoned streets, a penchant for design and antiques, plus a healthy dose of Victorian townhouses and exclusive mewses, make this a much-loved part of town. There's more of a feeling of life on the streets than in other parts of the city, particularly given the energetic Portobello Market and the annual Notting Hill Carnival. Most of the time, however, there's an artsy and dream-like vibe to Notting Hill, making it a haven for creative types who can afford the rents. Shepherd's Bush is a more urban, fast-paced part of town, well-known for its huge Westfield shopping centre and the O2 Shepherd's Bush Empire music venue.

Where the locals recommend:

Golborne Road
This iconic Notting Hill street is a place to wander to experience the melting pot of cultures and local pastimes of the neighbourhood. Golborne Road Market is known for its international food stalls and vintage wares. Permanent eateries include the trendy Pizza East and Café O'Porto, loved by the local Portuguese community. Golborne Road is also home to the Ernö Goldfinger designed Trellick Tower, a cult London landmark that appears in many films.
Golborne Road W10 5NR
www.golbornelife.co.uk
Tube: Westbourne Park

Shepherd's Bush Market
This historical market site combines traditional market stalls with stands that meet the modern demands for trendiness too. Find everything from bric a brac and niche international ingredients to summer pop-up food stands.
Shepherd's Bush Market W12
myshepherdsbushmarket.com
Tube: Shepherd's Bush Market or Goldhawk Road

Museum of Brands, Packaging & Advertising
This treasure trove of retro design takes a creative look at brands and packaging through the ages.
111-117 Lancaster Road W11 1QT
+44 (0)207 908 0880
info@museumofbrands.com
www.museumofbrands.com
Tube: Ladbroke Grove

The Ledbury

The two Michelin star restaurant is one of the most talked-about eateries in London and attracts foodies from far and wide.

127 Ledbury Road W11 2AQ
+44 (0)207 792 9090
info@theledbury.com
www.theledbury.com
Tube: Ladbroke Grove

Holland Park

In the discerning residential locality of the same name, Holland Park's actual park is a jungle-like green space surrounding a Jacobean mansion. It's peaceful, romantic and the perfect London spot to get lost in.

Ilchester Place W8 6LU
Tube: Holland Park

Events and key dates

An outline of national holidays, popular events and quirky annual festivals in London.

January

1st: National holiday

New Year's Day Parade
A street parade travelling through the streets of central London to welcome the start of the year.
www.lnydp.com

London Boat Show
A revered show for sailing enthusiasts, boating lovers and general fans of the great outdoors.
www.londonboatshow.co.uk

February

London Fashion Week
The first of London's bi-annual fashion weeks, where global designers flock to show their Spring/Summer collections.
www.londonfashionweek.co.uk

Chinese New Year
Parades and festivities take place in London's Chinatown and Trafalgar Square to mark the occasion.
www.chinatownlondon.org

League Cup Final
One of the most important events of the annual football calendar, join droves of football fans at Wembley Stadium.
www.capitalonecup.co.uk

March

St Patrick's Day
An Irish day of celebration, green hats, drinking Guinness in Irish bars and the St Patrick's Day parade from Green Park to Trafalgar Square is the order of the day in London.

Ideal Home Show
A popular show with Londoners looking for inspiration for the interiors of their homes.
www.idealhomeshow.co.uk

April

Good Friday and Easter Monday: National holidays

London Marathon
One of the world's greatest marathons takes over the streets of London for a day.
virginmoneylondonmarathon.com

The Boat Race
A competition between Oxford University Boat Club and Cambridge University Boat Club, the four mile race runs from Putney to Mortlake.
www.theboatraces.org

May

First Monday of the month: National holiday ('Early May bank holiday')

Last Monday of the month: National holiday ('Spring bank holiday')

Chelsea Flower Show
Every horticulturalist's delight, this flower show attracts keen gardeners from across the world to view rare flowers and innovative landscape garden installations.
www.rhs.org.uk

Grand Designs Live
Popular with architecture buffs, designers and dreamers, this annual event is a spin-off of a popular TV programme about designing architecturally impressive homes.
www.granddesignslive.com

Scrap Club
An annual event to smash old objects up in the name of de-stressing, with a sprinkling of anti-consumerist tendencies. Artists convert the debris into works of art.
www.scrapclub.co.uk

Rugby Union Final
The biggest club rugby final takes place at Twickenham Stadium at the end of May each year — a spirited day out with sport-loving Londoners.
www.premiershiprugby.com/final

Land of Kings
A music and arts festival in the grungy neighbourhood of Dalston.
www.landofkings.co.uk

MCM London Comic Con
A pop culture show for gaming, comic and anime enthusiasts.
www.mcmcomiccon.com/london

June

Holland Park Opera
An annual summertime occurrence of several opera productions taking place in this well-to-do west London neighbourhood.
www.operahollandpark.com

Trooping the Colour
This royal spectacle celebrating the Queen's birthday starts at Buckingham Palace and ends at the Horse Guards Parade.
www.royal.gov.uk

Field Day
An outdoor east London music festival known for pulling in a trendy line-up.
www.fielddayfestivals.com

City of London Festival
This annual programme of artistic events includes everything from live debates and interesting talks, to performance arts and comedy sketches.
www.colf.org

Pride in London
A huge event coined as one of the world's largest LGBT+ celebrations, the Pride in London weekend includes a parade, festival and live entertainment.
www.prideinlondon.org

Wimbledon Tennis
The world's most prestigious tennis tournament takes place in the leafy locale of Wimbledon for two weeks each year.
www.wimbledon.com

July

Wireless Festival
One of London's many outdoor music festivals, the Wireless Festival takes place in Hyde Park over a weekend in early July.
www.wirelessfestival.co.uk

Calling Festival
London's classic rock festival found in one of London's huge parks.
www.callingfestival.co.uk

Summer Series at Somerset House
A ten-day line-up of established and emerging music acts performing at the iconic London landmark of Somerset House.
www.somersethouse.org.uk/music

London Film and Comic Con
An opportunity to meet stars from TV, comics and films in panel interviews and fun events.
londonfilmandcomiccon.com

August

Last Monday of August: National holiday ('Summer bank holiday')

The Proms
A globally famous festival of classical music with more than 100 classical performances taking place at the prestigious Royal Albert Hall and a handful of other venues.
www.bbc.co.uk/proms

Carnaval de Pueblo
The largest outdoor Latin American event in Europe, this festival involves floats, processions, music and food from across Latin America. It takes place in the Elephant and Castle neighbourhood, home to a large Latin American community.
www.carnavaldelpueblo.com

Great British Beer Festival
An annual celebration of one of Britain's best friends: beer. It's a place to enjoy a range of beers and ales to suit all palates.
www.gbbf.org.uk

Notting Hill Carnival
This Afro-Caribbean street festival celebrating London's multiculturalism attracts a million people over the bank holiday weekend every year.
www.thenottinghillcarnival.com

London Mela
A huge celebration of Asian culture, with market stalls to music stages.
www.londonmela.org

The Camden Fringe
An annual performing arts festival taking place in the artsy/grungy area of Camden during most of August. From operas and musicals to stand-up comedy and cabaret, there are events in Camden venues to suit all tastes.
www.camdenfringe.com

Film4 Frightfest
This festival for horror fans sees horror movies being shown in a Leicester Square cinema over five days.
www.frightfest.co.uk

London Triathlon
The world's largest triathlon with 13,000 competitors and plenty of cheering spots to spur the triathletes on.
www.thelondontriathlon.com

Summer in the City
A huge YouTube convention bringing together well-known vloggers and social media fans.
www.sitc-event.co.uk

September

Totally Thames
This month-long event brings the River Thames to life with river races, market stalls, live theatre and other entertainment.
www.totallythames.org

London Fashion Week
The second of London's bi-annual fashion weeks, where fashion designers show their Autumn/Winter collections.
www.londonfashionweek.co.uk

London Open House
A weekend where usually private buildings of historical, cultural and architectural importance open their doors to the public.
www.openhouselondon.org.uk

Portobello Film Festival

An annual festival with showings of hundreds of films in this leafy west London neighbourhood.

www.portobellofilmfestival.com

October

London Restaurant Festival

This month-long celebration of food sees hundreds of restaurants putting on special menus for foodies to indulge in.

www.londonrestaurantfestival.com

London Film Festival

The annual festival for film buffs, this is your opportunity to watch new films for the first time across an array of London venues, plus get involved in special events with filmmakers and screenwriting experts.

www.bfi.org.uk/lff

Diwali on the Square

An annual outdoor celebration in Trafalgar Square, popular with Londoners of Indian descent keen to celebrate the festival of lights.

November

Bonfire Night

Firework displays take place across London on 5 November to mark the date when Guy Fawkes attempted to blow up the Houses of Parliament in 1605.

Remembrance Day

A day to remember those lost in wars since 1914, a number of events happen in London and across the UK. Expect to see many Londoners wearing remembrance poppies on their clothing to mark the occasion, and many public places holding two minutes' silence at 11:00.

www.britishlegion.org.uk

ATP World Tour Finals

The annual end of the tennis season happens at London's O2 Arena, where the world's eight best male singles and doubles players battle it out for the last title of the season.

barclaysatpworldtourfinals.com

London to Brighton Veteran Car Run

This quirky motoring event has been happening since the 1890s, and sees vintage cars travelling through London and onwards to Brighton on the south coast.

www.veterancarrun.com

The Lord Mayor's Show

Dating back to 1215, the Lord Mayor of London and three miles worth of floats pass through the City of London in this throwback occasion of times past.

www.lordmayorsshow.london

London Jazz Festival

Internationally-renowned jazz musicians play at venues across London for this ten-day annual celebration of jazz.

www.efglondonjazzfestival.org.uk

London International Horse Show

A prestigious indoor championships of everything from show jumping to the Shetland Pony Grand National.

www.olympiahorseshow.com

Royal Variety Performance

An annual gala of the best of British entertainment and performance, alternating between London and regional British venues.

www.eabf.org.uk/royal-variety-performance

December

Christmas Day and Boxing Day: National holidays

Winterville

While the huge Winter Wonderland Christmas market and fairground in Hyde Park packs in large crowds wanting to celebrate during the festive season, Winterville is a little more low key and off the beaten track.

www.winterville.co.uk

Peter Pan Cup

Serpentine Swimming Club swimmers head out to the Hyde Park lake on Christmas Day to brave the elements to try to win the annual swimming cup.

www.serpentineswimmingclub/our-special-races

New Year's Eve fireworks

The city's famous fireworks display takes place on the River Thames around Embankment. Beware: there are usually heavy crowds, cordoned-off roads to prevent overcrowding and changes to public transport schedules.

A lot can happen in a year.

Useful websites to find more London events

London Town
www.londontown.com/events
Time Out London
www.timeout.com/london
Visit London
visitlondon.com/things-to-do

Venues hosting London events

Business Design Centre
www.businessdesigncentre.
co.uk/events
ExCeL London
www.excel-london.co.uk/whats-on
Olympia London
www.olympia.co.uk/whatson
Southbank Centre
www.southbankcentre.co.uk
The O2
www.theo2.co.uk/events

See also: London work-related events and conferences, starting on page 158

London is the design centre of the world.

I have absolutely no doubt about that.

Nathalie Rozencwajg
Architect

Introduce yourself.
I'm the co-director of RARE Architecture. We work on projects across the
world based out of the main London office. I've had a relationship with
London for 20 years now. I grew up in Brussels and then studied in London
for my architectural degree. Having attended the European School in
Brussels, I was in a very international environment, and a lot of my peers
were intending to continue their studies in London. Despite this, London
wasn't really on my trajectory in those days, but when I was offered a place at
the Architectural Association (AA) School of Architecture it opened my eyes
to London. It's a very famous school. That decision to move to London ended
up being a life changer. After I graduated I moved to Paris but I've been
commuting back and forth between the two cities ever since. That makes
me quite a modern day urban worker, although I meet a lot of people who
live between two cities in Europe. As well as working for my architectural
practice I also teach in London at the AA School of Architecture.

You sound like an urban nomad in action — how does that influence
your relationship with London?
London seems to be a city in which many people live and work for a few
days a week. I know a lot of people who live across two cities on a weekly
basis and I think it's becoming more of a lifestyle choice for urban dwellers
today. London is geared up for this kind of lifestyle, especially with the
prevalence of co-working spaces. So it's definitely a city that allows you to
live like this without feeling different to other people. You never feel like
an outsider in London. I mostly spend a few weekdays in London and I
spend weekends with my family in Paris. I also organise my travels to be in
London for longer at key moments in the design world, such as the London
Design Festival, and Clerkenwell Design Week. I feel like I need to squeeze
in the best of London while I'm in the city, and although it's busy in terms
of work, I also make use of the time I have free in the evenings.

You've received a lot of accolades in recent years — which ones are
you most proud of?
In 2012 I was commended as Architects' Journal's Emerging Woman
Architect of the Year and in 2014 I was named by The Guardian as one of
ten women to watch in architecture. Having more women in architecture
has been a recurrent interest in the profession in the last few years. I think
it's very good, but I try not to make gender a factor in my work because

it shouldn't be an issue. That said, I do notice that when I tell people I'm an architect, I very often get a second question asking if I work in interior design. My male business partner never gets asked that second question! So there is still very much this idea that women do interiors. But it's good there's awareness about gender imbalance in architecture and that people are talking about it.

Are there more women in the classes you teach?
There's a fairly even split between men and women studying architecture. But the profession becomes very male focused very early on in people's careers. In London I think this is partly due to the cost of childcare. I've recently become a mum and I really realise the impact this has. Speaking of people around me, that's the main reason women stop working or work part time, because they can't afford childcare. I think it's much more of an issue in London than in other cities in Europe.

What kind of projects do you take on in London?
One of our most famous projects in London is the Town Hall Hotel in Bethnal Green. Since then we've had a number of projects such as hotel refurbishments, new build hotels and a lot of residential work. Our work has a touch of the remarkable about it. People call us when they want something bespoke that deals with the local and historical aspects of a site, but in a contemporary way. We work in a range of different areas and styles in London, but our designs always have a relationship to something already existing in the London fabric. Working with hotels in the city is a dream because you create a story and a world within a world, which both the neighbourhood you develop in and the hotel guests get to benefit from.

The Town Hall Hotel has become something of a landmark in London — tell us more about it.
The project involved the conversion of an old Town Hall into a hotel. The building itself was listed, so it was immediately a very delicate environment to work with. We proposed a contemporary extension on the roof and on the side of the building, which was economically needed for the viability of the project. The juxtaposition of something very new in relation to something old actually created a landmark in London. We won several awards for it, including a Royal Institute of British Architects (RIBA) award and Royal Institute of Chartered Surveyors (RICS) awards. We were also published in the Japanese architecture journal a+u, who listed the building as a top landmark to visit. We're proud as we created something new on the landscape and implemented a style between the old and the new. It's not a vestige of the old at all: it's contemporary and it creates a dialogue. The pattern was created by a laser cut 'skin' of aluminium and the pattern is derived from an old ornamental ventilation grille we found in the original building.

What was the most surprising thing about the Town Hall Hotel project?
The building is really iconic in the London film industry. In the decade
or so between the building being sold by the council and falling into our
hands, it was used for shooting films. A lot of very famous London based
movies were filmed there, including some Guy Ritchie films. We weren't
sure whether some of the features we discovered in the building were film-
related décor or the original aspects of the building! It was an interesting
play between stage set and actual historical features. It was a fun building
to work with.

How does the feeling of a neighbourhood influence the designs you
create?
It plays a huge part. When we built the Town Hall Hotel, the local area
was going through a big change. It has a very traditional East End history
and is now becoming gentrified and popular with design communities.
On the other end of the spectrum, we worked on a high-end residential
new build in a conservation area in Westminster. It's a really different
setting because it's 500 metres away from Buckingham Palace, making it
a much more conservative area and a very different type of development.
The project involved a contemporary reinterpretation of the bow window,
which is a recurrent feature in the area. In Europe, London is definitely the
most cosmopolitan city. There are so many different communities living
in London and as architects, we live through and with these communities
during the course of our projects. It's very rare to find a city with such
richness, with a very conservative historic side, to the other extreme of
being very contemporary.

Why is it important for you to have a base in London?
It's the design centre of the world; I have absolutely no doubt about that.
So many people come to London from all over the world to look for
creative talents and design. The opportunities for development in London
are immense; it's definitely a place where you feel things are constantly
happening. The only downside is that the planning process is very long
in London, so we're often in funny situations where buildings we design
in South East Asia are built already while we're still waiting for planning
permission for London projects we started around the same time. So
there's a lot going on in London but there's also still quite a conservative
process in the city.

Where is RARE Architecture's London office?
Shoreditch. We're quite a small, boutique firm of just eight people. It's
small, especially compared to the size of some of the firms in London, but
as directors we like to be very involved in the projects we take on. We like
to keep to a size that allows us to do that.

What is the London aesthetic?

It's eclectic. It's very interesting because you get such a variety of things happening around the city and you find areas that are more conservative and areas that are developing in very different and very contemporary directions. The various building styles and high rises mean there are many different worlds within one city. We think it's important to always have a strong relationship with the context of London, but also to interpret something into a building style that's very contemporary. Building in London is a continuous process and the city continues to grow outwards and in all different directions.

Do you think architects experience the city in a different way from other Londoners?

The areas where a lot of architects have practices are less centred on the tourist areas of London, both for reasons of budget as well as the types of communities architects want to be in. Architects in young practices especially tend to live by a different map of London. We like to work from design-led, fringe and creative localities that are still in the making and so are not yet 'complete'. When new buildings and projects come up and areas get regenerated, architects have a reason to go and discover new areas. London is a fabulous city, but you never see all of it and you never see it in full. For all the years I've spent in the city, there are still areas I'm waiting to discover. There's always a part that's new, there's always a part that's just been finished and there's always another side that suddenly pops up. It's just huge.

Which neighbourhoods feel most like home when you're in London?

There are two centres in London for me. King's Cross St Pancras is one of my hubs because I commute to and from Paris and the Eurostar terminal is in St Pancras station. The AA where I teach is nearby on Bedford Square too. So the area from Fitzrovia to St Pancras is one I'm very familiar with and spend a lot of time in. The other place that feels like home is Shoreditch, where the RARE Architecture office is. Of course, it's always nice to visit other areas too, like going to Chelsea on a lovely summer evening to do something completely different.

Can you describe the feeling in Shoreditch and King's Cross St Pancras?

St Pancras, for me, is a huge surprise. The area has changed so much: it's a neighbourhood that's really in the process of defining itself and is surprisingly bold with its identity. In the last five years it's become an area that's really on the map of London, whereas before you wouldn't really hang around there. I think it's partly because of the success of the architectural developments happening in the area, such as Central Saint Martin's, which has a beautiful building and is a great place to wander around.

Shoreditch is probably one of the only areas in London where you don't have the regular chain shops that you see everywhere else. There are very unique restaurants and one-off cafés. I think that's the great thing about the area. One disappointment in Europe today is that wherever you travel, you tend to see the same things. The same chains, the same shops, the same restaurants. It's actually hard to find uniqueness in a city, and Shoreditch really has that. Of course, this is almost old news now in Shoreditch, as these more unique London localities are pushing out to other areas further east. But Shoreditch still has uniqueness and this great feeling of having a lot of creative industries around.

Are there any other neighbourhoods you like in London?
I like the stretch of the city when you take the bus from Shoreditch to the West End, through Clerkenwell. You see the gradual change of more to less corporate. Clerkenwell itself is a great area. It's slightly more expensive than Shoreditch, so you have a different type of crowd, but you also get great quality design shops, design practices and street food.

Where do you like to eat out in London?
One thing I find special about London that I don't find in other European cities is the Asian food. You get great Asian food in the city, especially the low-key Vietnamese restaurants around Kingsland Road. My favourites in that area are Sông Quê Café and Que Viet. Recently there have been some really good Vietnamese sandwich shops opening up in Shoreditch, as well as some South Korean street food stands. Banh Mi Bay and On The Bab are on the top of my list and they're great for lunch. Another excellent lunch spot is Ruby, a tiny Italian restaurant for delicious pasta. On my teaching days, I like eating at Gail's Kitchen off Bedford Square. It serves very special food. For more of a treat, I love going to The Wolseley. I always find it to be a very nice British experience and it's great for afternoon tea, dinner or just a drink. It's a unique place.

Where do you like to go for coffee in London?
There are quite a few really good cafés around Shoreditch and Hoxton Square, such as Old Shoreditch Station, Fix 126 on Curtain Road, and Slate. When I'm teaching, I like to go to Store Street Espresso. It's a really simple café, but with very good coffee and it's a good place for a meeting or to come with a laptop to do some work. I also like TAP Coffee on Rathbone Place. The coffee culture in London is great: you get very good coffee and some nice places to sit, where you can work and isolate yourself for a while.

What's the difference between the coffee culture in London and Paris?
You definitely don't have so many plug sockets for your laptop in cafés in Paris! And in Paris you don't have so many different choices of coffee, like lattes and cappuccinos. The Parisians are more into old-fashioned, bistro

style places. Londoners are more into coffee shops with these spaces you can really use as working areas for a while. Parisians also hold many work meetings in cafés, but London has truly adopted the Australian art of good coffee culture.

Where is your favourite place to work in London?
I love working in London taxis! You get your own private space within the city and an opportunity to hold a meeting, do some work, or make phone calls while you're commuting. Not a lot of cities offer that type of space!

Where do you stay when you're in London?
In an ideal world I would stay in the Town Hall Hotel every time! But it's not always possible. I love staying there. Not because we designed it as such, but because it feels very familiar. The service and personnel are great and your hotel room is actually an apartment, so you get this feeling of being in a world of your own. The restaurants are great, the swimming pool is a bonus, and you can generally enjoy the space. Sometimes when I'm in London on a very short visit, I go to a Tune Hotel. Their hotels are convenient for a quick trip in and out of the city, they've got everything you need, and they have some good locations across the city. I also have family in London; it's definitely nice to stay with family when you travel too.

What do you do during free evenings in London?
There are a few places I like in the King's Cross area. If I want a very quiet evening, I go to the lobby space in the St Pancras Renaissance Hotel because it's nice and calm. I like the Gilbert Scott bar for its beautiful décor and generally nice atmosphere. The Great Northern Hotel has a great restaurant as well.

Around Shoreditch there are loads of places that are great for dinner, like The Clove Club in Shoreditch Town Hall and HIX at The Tramshed. Even though it's a chain, I also like Busaba Eathai, as it has good food and great décor. I also love eating at The Corner Room at the Town Hall Hotel. The menu changes all the time so every time you go it's a new surprise, but the food is always delicious. You can eat very, very well in London.

How do you soak up the latest of London's culture and design worlds?
It's impossible for me to come to London without taking in some of the cultural scene in the city. Taking time out for galleries and exhibitions is partly work, partly leisure time. I get invited to many openings and launches of galleries, which I try to go to when I'm in London. Exhibitions in general are so high profile, with a focus towards contemporary art. London has really put itself on the global design map in recent years. Obviously there's competition from places like Paris and Milan, but London design events are really interesting.

Which galleries and venues do you like to visit in particular?
In the East End, the galleries around Vyner Street are interesting to see; I especially like the Wilkinson Gallery. Many former East End galleries have opened in Fitzrovia; I often go to Edel Assanti and Alison Jacques Gallery. I also like the Contemporary Applied Arts in Southwark for interesting ceramic and jewellery pieces. And finally, I also love seeing the antique shops along Ebury Street. It's not a very long stretch of road but you always find beautiful things there.

Where do you go shopping in the city?
Topshop is one special place that I still haven't found the equivalent of in Paris. The variety and the newness of fashions you have there is great. I usually go shopping in between making my way from one meeting to another and I look for shops and brands I can't find in Paris, such as REISS and Whistles. Kate Kanzier near Hatton Garden is great for cheap but original shoes, and I also really like the Paul Smith shop in Mayfair. I think the fact that the shops open late every Thursday evening is great. For architectural publications, I go to the AA book shop, and I visit the Central Saint Martin's store to check out the work of emerging designers. Paperchase sells really unique paper products, and the large store on Tottenham Court Road is a great place to spend some time.

Name an experience every Londoner has had at least once in their lives.
Oxford Street the weekend before Christmas! You can barely move and it becomes your idea of the absolute London punishment when you've experienced it once. Even when it's not Christmas, I'm always amazed when you sit on the top deck of a double decker bus through Oxford Street and you just look down on the number of people walking.

Where inspires you in London?
The River Thames. The riverside is constantly changing and when you haven't been there for a while, you notice how the skyline of London is always evolving. The scale of the river gives you a sense of the scale of the city too.

What are your favourite buildings and structures in London?
I love the RIBA building on Portland Place for its beautiful art deco façade and interiors. The aviary and penguin pool in London Zoo are also wonderful pieces of design.

What do you do to relax in the city?
I take a walk through a park. I like to walk through St James's Park to get from the south to the West End. It's great to have a feeling of being outside the city while you're in the centre of it. Alternatively, an evening at the Town Hall Hotel with a swim followed by a drink at the bar is really relaxing.

What song would be on your London playlist?
Virtual Insanity by Jamiroquai.

What smell do you associate with London?
The rubber smell of the Tube! Something quite amazing happens when I get off the Eurostar in London too, when my mind automatically sets itself to look the other way when crossing the street, since people drive on the left in London. I don't even have to think about it and I'm sure it has something to do with the smell and sense of the city that makes my mind realise I'm there!

What is London's best quality?
Its energy. That can also be what is tiring about it, but overall people are friendly and everything is done with a form of politeness and friendliness.

What would you change about London if you could?
A few years ago I would have said the food, but that's definitely not the case anymore! I would change how expensive London is as a city. Through our work, we're noticing how the people who can afford to live in central London are not Londoners or locals, but people coming in from abroad with a lot of money. With that comes a risk that the city centre becomes permanently out of reach for Londoners.

How can visitors to the city blend in with Londoners?
You can easily blend into London because it's so multicultural. The pace that people walk at can be a culture shock; if in doubt, walk fast! I'd also advise people to try to live for a while in one neighbourhood. It's not a city you can take in as a whole in a few days, so rather than trying that, try to stay in one locality and understand what its rhythms are. Then you can stay in a different neighbourhood next time. I think you'll get more out of it that way rather than trying to do too much.

How can people 'get lost' and explore London for themselves?
London is so vast, so it's not too difficult to get lost. The city is very big and it's difficult to walk from one place to another, but there are areas that you can walk to, and it's a great way of experiencing the city. Walking from the West End to South Kensington is beautiful and you can stroll through Hyde Park. Places are often overlooked in the city because it's so big and the default is that you take the Tube.

Is there anything you'll never understand about London?
I'll never know how some girls wear sandals in January!

<u>What do you find surprising about London?</u>
You have the most out-of-the-ordinary juxtapositions in the city that happen alongside each other as if they were normal. One element of this is the mix of fashions. In most other cities and definitely in Paris, you have a strong dress code and identical fashions. In London, it's not like that. There are so many different types of fashions and they all somehow go together. These juxtapositions are just amazing.

Nathalie's London

Places to visit

Alison Jacques Gallery
16-18 Berners Street W1T 3LN
+44 (0)207 631 4720
info@alisonjacquesgallery.com
www.alisonjacquesgallery.com
Tube: Tottenham Court Road

Architectural Association (AA) book shop
36 Bedford Square WC1B 3ES
+44 (0)207 887 4041
bookshop@aabookshop.net
www.aabookshop.net
Tube: Tottenham Court Road
Central St. Martin's

Granary Building
1 Granary Square N1C 4AA
+44 (0)207 514 7023
www.arts.ac.uk/csm
Rail/Tube: King's Cross

Clerkenwell Design Week
www.clerkenwelldesignweek.com

Contemporary Applied Arts
89 Southwark Street SE1 0HX
+44 (0)207 620 0086
sales@caa.org.uk
www.caa.org.uk
Tube: Southwark

Ebury Street
Tube: Sloane Square

Edel Assanti
74a Newman Street W1T 3DB
+44 (0)207 637 8537
art@edelassanti.com
www.edelassanti.com
Tube: Tottenham Court Road

Kate Kanzier
67-69 Leather Lane EC1N 7TJ
+44 (0)207 242 7232
info@katekanzier.com
www.katekanzier.com
Rail/Tube: Farringdon

London Design Festival
www.londondesignfestival.com

London Zoo
Regent's Park NW1 4RY
+44 (0)207 449 6200
info@zsl.org
www.zsl.org/zsl-london-zoo
Tube: Camden Town

Paperchase
213-215 Tottenham Court Road
W1T 7PS
+44 (0)207 467 6200
www.paperchase.co.uk
Tube: Goodge Street

Paul Smith (Mayfair)
9 Albemarle Street W1S 4HH
+44 (0)207 493 4565
www.paulsmith.co.uk
Tube: Green Park

REISS
www.reiss.com

RIBA
66 Portland Place W1B 1AD
+44 (0)207 580 5533
info@riba.org
www.architecture.com
Tube: Regent's Park

St James's Park
Birdcage Walk SW1A 2BJ
+44 (0)300 061 2350
stjames@royalparks.gsi.gov.uk
www.royalparks.org.uk/parks/st-jamess-park
Tube: St James's Park

St Pancras Renaissance Hotel
St Pancras International, Euston
Road NW1 2AR
+44 (0)207 841 3540
www.stpancras.com/hotel
Rail/Tube: King's Cross

The Great Northern Hotel
King's Cross Station, Pancras
Road N1C 4TB
+44 (0)203 388 0800
www.gnhlondon.com
Rail/Tube: King's Cross

Topshop
www.topshop.com

Town Hall Hotel
Patriot Square E2 9NF
+44 (0)207 871 0460
reservations@townhallhotel.com
www.townhallhotel.com
Tube: Bethnal Green
Rail: Cambridge Heath

Tune Hotels
www.tunehotels.com/gb

Whistles
www.whistles.com

Wilkinson Gallery
50-58 Vyner Street E2 9DQ
+44 (0)208 980 2662
info@wilkinsongallery.com
www.wilkinsongallery.com
Rail: Cambridge Heath

Eating and drinking

Banh Mi Bay
www.banhmibay.co.uk

Busaba Eathai
www.busaba.com

Fix 126
126 Curtain Road EC2A 3PJ
+44 (0)207 739 7829
www.fix-coffee.co.uk
Rail/Tube: Old Street

Gail's Kitchen
11-13 Bayley Street WC1B 3HD
+44 (0)207 323 9694
hello@gailskitchen.co.uk
www.gailskitchen.co.uk
Tube: Goodge Street

HIX at The Tramshed
32 Rivington Street EC2A 3LX
+44 (0)207 749 0478
www.chickenandsteak.co.uk
Rail/Tube: Old Street

Old Shoreditch Station
1 Kingsland Road E2 8DA
+44 (0)207 729 5188
www.jaguarshoes.com/cafebar/
the-old-shoreditch-station
Rail: Hoxton

On The Bab
www.onthebab.co.uk

Que Viet
102 Kingsland Road E2 8DP
+44 (0)207 033 0588
Rail: Hoxton

Ruby
8-9 Hoxton Square N1 6NU
+44 (0)203 487 0277
Rail/Tube: Old Street

Slate
96 Curtain Road EC2A 3AA
+44 (0)203 620 6980
www.slatecoffeelondon.co.uk
Rail: Shoreditch High Street

Sông Quê Café
134 Kingsland Road E2 8DY
+44 (0)207 613 3222
www.songque.co.uk
Rail: Hoxton

Store Street Espresso
40 Store Street WC1E 7DB
+44 (0)207 637 2623
info@storestespresso.co.uk
www.storestespresso.co.uk
Tube: Goodge Street

TAP Coffee
26 Rathbone Place W1T 1JD
+44 (0)207 580 2163
www.tapcoffee.co.uk
Tube: Tottenham Court Road

The Gilbert Scott
St Pancras Renaissance London
Hotel, St Pancras International,
Euston Road NW1 2AR
+44 (0)207 278 3888
enquiries@thegilbertscott.co.uk
www.thegilbertscott.co.uk/bar
Rail/Tube: King's Cross

The Clove Club
Shoreditch Town Hall, 380 Old
Street EC1V 9LT
+44 (0)207 729 6496
hello@thecloveclub.com
www.thecloveclub.com
Rail/Tube: Old Street

The Corner Room
Town Hall Hotel, Patriot Square
E2 9NF
+44 (0)207 871 0460
info@cornerroom.co.uk
www.townhallhotel.com/
cornerroom
Tube: Bethnal Green
Rail: Cambridge Heath

The Wolseley
160 Piccadilly W1J 9EB
+44 (0)207 499 6996
info@thewolseley.com
www.thewolseley.com
Tube: Green Park

Read more about Nathalie Rozencwajg
on the RARE Architecture website:
www.rarearchitecture.com

Photo: RARE Architecture

Photo: Impact Hub Islington

chapter 2

Work

*Find out where to rent office space or plug into
one of London's many co-working offices.*

Working in London
Global economic centre and start-up hub

There's no doubt that London is one of the best cities in the world to work. Hailed by Forbes and influential think-tanks as the world's leading city, London is widely recognised as being prosperous, powerful and increasingly creative and cutting-edge. London's inherently international workforce cut across all sectors, from the arts to accountancy. Londoners work hard and play harder, with work and social time often blurring at networking gatherings and a busy schedule of world-leading conferences, from London Design Festival to World Travel Market.

TECH CITY

In recent years, London has gained a global reputation for its thriving start-up scene. London is seen by many as being the gateway to European and US markets, and with a time zone in the middle of the world, it's easy to do business on a global scale from the city. This attracts entrepreneurs from all corners of the world to set-up business. Propelled by the UK government's commitment to invest heavily in the start-up scene, some commentators estimate there are currently 500,000 new start-ups setting up in the UK every year.

The UK start-up scene is centred heavily in and around 'Silicon Roundabout' — the roundabout in the Old Street area of east London. Spreading out towards Stratford with its centre in the trendy Shoreditch, London's start-up hub is also known as Tech City. There are an estimated 1,500 tech businesses located in the area, which is said to be the world's third largest technology start-up cluster after San Francisco and New York. Notable technology companies in the area include Facebook, TweetDeck, Google and Last.fm.

With more than 100 co-working spaces and dozens of incubators and accelerators, all occupied by an estimated 4,000 small and medium sized businesses at any one time, the conditions in London are ripe for collaboration and success.

Whether you've already made up your mind to up sticks and work in London, or are simply curious about what the working world is like in the city, this section covers everything from how to find work and where to set up your office in London, to finding free Wi-Fi and gaining funding for your start-up business.

Essentials

Find out a little bit more about the practicalities of moving to London to work or to set up a business.

Bank accounts

It is possible to open a UK bank account by going into a branch of a bank or building society. Opening a bank account requires a passport and proof of a UK address. If you are setting up a limited company, you are required to have a business bank account. Sole traders can either use their personal bank account or set up a business bank account. It is also possible to use your bank account from a different country, but fees incurred on foreign transactions may make this an expensive option.

Some of the major banks and building societies in London include:
Barclays:
www.barclays.co.uk
Co-operative Bank:
www.co-operativebank.co.uk
HSBC:
www.hsbc.co.uk
Lloyds Bank:
www.lloydsbank.com
Metro Bank:
www.metrobankonline.co.uk
TSB:
www.tsb.co.uk

Business insurance

Business insurance is available from most major banks in the UK as well as independent insurance providers. Business insurance can cover business assets, such as office equipment, and indemnity to protect you against mistakes your business may make. If you have employees, you are legally obligated to take out Employers' Liability insurance, in case an employee becomes injured at work. If you will come into contact with members of the public in your work, you are also required to take out Public Liability cover. There are a number of price comparison websites available to compare different business insurance options.

Moneysupermarket:
www.moneysupermarket.com/business-insurance
Confused.com:
www.confused.com/small-business-insurance

Business registration

Before setting up a business in the UK, you need to decide on the legal structure of the business. The UK government's setting up a business website provides advice on different business structures. Business owners must usually be living in the UK before being able to set up a business. Business registration requirements differ depending on which type of business you are setting up. Many new businesses are set up as limited companies, for which you need to have a name and address for the company, have at least one director and one shareholder and have articles of association (rules of how you'll run the company). You will also need to register the business with Companies House.

UK government setting up a business website:
www.gov.uk/set-up-business-uk/overview

Council tax and business rates

Residents in the UK have to pay council tax to the local council in which their home is located. The council tax rate is calculated by the council according to the size of the property, and each local council charges different rates. Council tax payments are usually paid in ten instalments over the course of the financial year. Businesses do not have to pay council tax, but instead have to pay business rates to the local council. The UK government's business rates website has an online tool to help you calculate your business rates bill.

UK government council tax website:
www.gov.uk/council-tax/working-out-your-council-tax
UK government business rates website:
www.gov.uk/introduction-to-business-rates

Directory enquiries

There are a number of telephone directory services that enable you to find out the phone number and other contact information of businesses across the UK. Be aware these services charge a fee for using the service, and an additional fee if you ask to be connected directly to the phone number. There are also online directories available to use free of charge.

Some directory enquiries services include:
118118:
Dial 118 118 or go to 118118.com
BT Directory Enquiries:
Dial 118 500 or go to www.bt118500.com
BT Phone Book:
www.thephonebook.bt.com
Whitepages:
www.whitepages.co.uk

Healthcare

For those entitled to live and work in the UK, healthcare is available free of charge via the National Health Service (NHS). You'll need to register with a General Practitioner (GP) close to where you are living. You can find local GPs using the NHS Choices website. In emergencies, the NHS also entitles you to go to Accident and Emergency departments at hospitals and NHS walk-in centres outside of GP hours. You can also search for local NHS services via the NHS website.

Find a GP:
www.nhs.uk/Service-Search/GP/
LocationSearch/4
NHS services:
www.nhs.uk/service-search

National Insurance

All employees and employers in the UK earning above a certain threshold are required to pay National Insurance (NI) contributions, which pays towards the cost of certain state benefits. If you work for an employer, NI contributions will be deducted automatically from your regular payslip. Business owners and those who are self-employed are asked to pay contributions directly. Everyone planning to work in the UK must have an NI number, which includes an interview as part of the application process. Some European Economic Area (EEA) countries have a social security agreement with the UK, meaning some EEA nationals may be exempt from paying NI.

UK National Insurance website:
www.gov.uk/national-insurance/
overview

Sim cards

All major mobile phone network providers in the UK sell sim cards which can be used in any compatible, unlocked mobile phone. Most offer free sim cards if you buy some credit straight away. You subsequently have the ability

to top-up your credit as and when you need to.

Some of the major mobile phone networks in the UK include:
3:
www.three.co.uk
EE:
www.ee.co.uk
O2:
www.o2.co.uk
Vodafone:
www.vodafone.co.uk

Tax

All employees in the UK must pay tax to HM Revenue and Customs (HMRC) from earnings. If you work for an employer, tax will be deducted automatically from your regular payslip. The amount of tax you pay depends on how much you earn. If you are self-employed (or a 'sole trader'), you must register yourself as being self-employed with HMRC and submit an annual tax return declaring how much you have earned in the previous financial year. You will subsequently pay any outstanding tax you owe. You have the option of appointing an accountant to submit the tax return on your behalf. If you're a business owner and planning on employing staff, you will have to register for corporation tax and as an official employer with HMRC. If you're planning on turning over more than £81,000 per year within the EU (as a business owner or sole trader), you also need to register for value added tax (VAT). This means 20% (the current VAT rate) of your business income goes to HMRC, but you can claim back any VAT you pay on items for your business, e.g. computers.

HMRC website:
www.gov.uk/government/
organisations/hm-revenue-
customs

Utilities and service connections

Gas and electricity

There are a number of companies that can supply homes and business premises with gas and electricity and you do not have to remain with the company the previous inhabitants used, unless otherwise stipulated by your landlord if you have a rental agreement. To decide which gas and electricity suppliers you would like to use, contact the major suppliers to find out the estimated costs involved or plans available, or use a price comparison website such as uSwitch. You can decide on how frequently you'd like to be billed. Taking regular meter readings and giving them to your chosen supplier helps ensure you pay for exactly what you use.

Major gas and electricity suppliers:
British Gas:
www.britishgas.co.uk
EDF Energy:
www.edfenergy.com
E.ON:
www.eonenergy.com
Npower:
www.npower.com
uSwitch (price comparison):
www.uswitch.com/gas-electricity

Internet connection

Several companies supply internet connection to homes and business premises and you do not have to remain with the company the previous inhabitants used, unless otherwise stipulated by your landlord if you have a rental agreement. Internet service providers offer different packages according to the internet speed you require and your expected internet usage. Most packages include a telephone line as standard, and you can add on other services such as television bundles too. All major providers have home and business deals available. Price comparison sites can help you identify the package that best suits your needs.

Major internet service providers:
BT:
www.bt.com
EE:
www.ee.co.uk
Moneysupermarket (price comparison):
www.moneysupermarket.com/broadband
Plusnet:
www.plus.net
Sky:
www.sky.com
TalkTalk:
www.talktalk.co.uk
uSwitch (price comparison):
www.uswitch.com/broadband
Virgin Media:
www.virginmedia.com

Telephone lines

A number of providers can supply landline telephone services to homes and business premises and you do not have to remain with the company the previous inhabitants used, unless otherwise stipulated by your landlord if you have a rental agreement. If you have selected an internet service provider, it's likely you will already have a landline as part of the package but it is also possible to buy landline-only packages. The major telephone line providers are the same as the major internet providers, and have home and business deals available.

TV licence

If you have a television in your home or business, you must have a TV licence. You can decide on your preferred method of payment and how frequently you wish to make payments.
TV Licensing:
www.tvlicensing.co.uk

Water

Water providers supply water and sewerage services to homes and business premises. When you move into a home or business premises, you must update the local water supplier with your details and payment information. You can decide which method of payment you prefer and how frequently you would like to make payments. There are a few suppliers serving the London area, the main one being Thames Water.

Major London water suppliers:
Affinity Water (north London and home counties):
www.affinitywater.co.uk
Thames Water:
www.thameswater.co.uk

Visas and work permits

Check the government's UK visas website before travelling to London to work: the website includes an online tool to check if you need a UK visa. Residents of Switzerland and European Economic Area (EEA) countries have the automatic right to work in the UK. People of other nationalities are advised on the visa options available via the UK government's visas website.
UK government visas website:
www.gov.uk/government/organisations/uk-visas-and-immigration

Useful resources

Setting up a company:
www.startups.co.uk/setting-up-a-company
Small business advice:
www.smallbusiness.co.uk
London & Partners:
www.invest.london

GOOD THINGS COME TO THOSE WHO WAIT

GOOD THINGS COME TO THOSE WHO WORK THEIR ASSES OFF AND NEVER GIVE UP

Find a job in London

While it's advisable to come to London with a job lined up and with some savings to help you find your feet, there are plenty of resources and an abundance of recruitment agencies in London to help you find employment. If you're not from the UK but have the right to work there, make this explicitly clear on your job applications. While including your photo in applications is the norm in some countries, this is not the case in the UK and would come across as being a little unusual. Londoners love LinkedIn, so make sure your LinkedIn profile is up-to-date too.

General job boards

Indeed
This is one of London's largest job websites, with thousands of jobs being advertised in London at any one time. You can also upload your curriculum vitae (CV) to help employers find you.
www.indeed.co.uk

Reed
Another of the largest job websites in the UK, Reed tends to have tens of thousands of jobs being advertised in London.
www.reed.co.uk

Jobsite
This large general jobs site has thousands of jobs in London and also has a section with advice and tips about gaining employment.
www.jobsite.co.uk

Other job boards:
www.londonjobs.co.uk
jobs.theguardian.com
www.gumtree.com/jobs/london

www.monster.co.uk
www.totaljobs.com
www.fish4.co.uk/london-and-home-counties
www.cityjobs.com/jobs/london

Start-up jobs

London Startup Jobs
This easy to use website has start-up jobs advertised requiring an array of skillsets, from tech, software, design and user experience (UX), to marketing, communications, sales and finance.
www.londonstartupjobs.co.uk

Work in Startups
A start-up jobs board with thousands of jobs advertised for people with a range of expertise and practical experience. It also has co-founder opportunities for those who want to go in right at the top of a start-up business.
www.workinstartups.com

UK Startup Jobs
This site advertises mostly technical and marketing opportunities in UK start-ups, with plenty of jobs available in London at any one time.
www.ukstartupjobs.com

Other start-up job boards:
www.angel.co/london/jobs
www.unicornhunt.io
www.techcityjobs.co.uk
www.builtinlondon.com/hiring
www.jobpage.com
www.startupdeveloperjobs.com

Creative jobs

Escape the City
A website for those wanting to move from unfulfilling corporate jobs to creative and entrepreneurial opportunities. Jobs are advertised from across the world, but there are always some going in London.
www.escapethecity.org

The Dots
This website has dozens of creative jobs advertised in London. It also helps you find creative workspaces and creative training courses.
www.the-dots.co.uk/jobs

The Drum
This large jobs board advertises opportunities in a range of creative sectors, from digital and design to brand management and e-commerce.
www.thedrum.com/jobs

Other creative jobs boards:
www.designjobsboard.com
jobs.designweek.co.uk
www.impact-london.com/jobs
creativeopportunities.arts.ac.uk
www.purple-consultancy.com
www.creativepool.com/jobs

Services

Job Centre
The UK government runs Job Centres across the country. Job Centres provide support to those looking for employment and have vacancies advertised in Job Centre locations as well as online.
www.gov.uk/browse/working/finding-job

Hiring staff

There's a huge amount of talent in London, but it can be tricky to find exactly the right person for the job you need done. Be as specific as you can in job adverts and if you're a start-up company, advertise on start-up specific jobs websites to target people who are already engaged in the start-up world. Most jobs websites listed on page III also give jobseekers the chance to upload their CV, so actively search for jobseekers as well as advertising and hoping they'll come to you. Make sure you educate yourself about the UK's minimum wage and look at similar job adverts to the role you want to recruit for, to ensure you're offering a fair and competitive wage.

www.gov.uk/national-minimum-wage-rates

Silicon Milkroundabout

This annual start-up jobs fair is an ideal forum for finding a workforce and comes recommended by London's Tech City. It brings tech start-ups and would-be employees together, allowing you to meet a lot of people in one go, helping you find the best talent for the job at hand.
www.siliconmilkroundabout.com

Salt

This specialist digital recruitment agency works closely with tech and other start-ups in London to find the right candidates for jobs in innovative fields.
www.welovesalt.com

Digital Gurus

This recruitment agency regularly works with start-ups to match candidates to start-up roles.
www.digitalgurus.co.uk

Recruitment Genius

This jobs website posts your job advert to multiple websites for a reasonable one-off fee.
www.recruitmentgenius.com

Twellow

If you want to be more hands-on with your talent scouting, this directory allows you to search for Twitter users in relevant business categories.
www.twellow.com

Other resources for hiring staff:
www.startups.co.uk/taking-on-staff
www.techcityuk.com/community-resources

Office space

Office space in London is famously expensive, not helped by the fact many offices in the city come with five or ten year leases, which is often too long a commitment for start-up companies. Narrowing down your search to short leases or 'fag-end' leases can be the way forward in this case. 'Fag-end' leases are where the remainder of another company's lease is available because they've gone bankrupt or moved to a larger office space. Appointing a commercial property advisor to handle negotiations with landlords can also be beneficial.

Office space portals

www.officegenie.co.uk
www.londonofficespace.com
www.rightmove.co.uk/commercial-property-to-let/London
officespace.techcitynews.com

Commercial estate agencies

Find a London Office

This agency is familiar with sourcing office space for companies with a variety of needs.
www.findalondonoffice.co.uk

Tower10

This site features office space in the Shoreditch area only and comes recommended by Tech City.
www.tower10.com

Currell

This estate agency focuses on office spaces in Clerkenwell, Hackney and Islington.
www.currell.com/commercial

Robert Irving Burns

This agency specialises in central London areas such as Soho, Mayfair and Oxford Circus.

www.rib.co.uk/commercial/commercial-lettings-london

Cheaper office space solutions

Hubble

A successful start-up company itself, Hubble is an online marketplace matching those looking for office space with providers who have space available. Offices are sourced with start-ups in mind.

www.hubblehq.com/office-space-london

London & Partners

As the Mayor of London's official business development company, London & Partners is able to support businesses in their search for office space in London. They also connect business owners with their network of commercial property agents and lawyers, and provide a free desk space for up to a year via its Touchdown London scheme.

www.invest.london/setting-up/setting-up-your-office

We Are Pop Up

For those looking for temporary retail space, We Are Pop Up has a variety of spaces that can be booked easily and at short notice. It's the perfect way for start-ups to dip their toe into the real world.

www.wearepopup.com

Appear Here

This website connects people who need retail space with empty spaces. Search by different neighbourhoods in London or by the 'feeling' of the place, e.g. 'bohemian', 'affluent' or 'trendy'.

www.appearhere.co.uk/destinations/london

Meanwhile Space

This company aims to put empty spaces back into use by finding businesses to occupy the buildings while they're otherwise unused. In partnership with the Cu-Cu app, business owners can view available properties, arrange viewings, apply for spaces and fast-track the legal process.

www.meanwhilespace.com
www.cu-cu.co

Morgan Pryce

This tenant acquisition agent has experience of identifying 'fag-end' leases for young businesses in London.

www.morganpryce.co.uk

London Office Space Finders

This company has experience of sourcing 'fag-end' leases for companies looking for shorter leases.

londonofficespacefinders.co.uk

Find government property

Government-owned property can be cheaper to lease or buy. The UK government's find government property website allows you to search for available properties.

www.gov.uk/find-government-property

Commercial property advisors

DeVono

This company of property advisors works on behalf of potential tenants rather than landlords to secure office space.

www.devono.com

GN2

A small commercial property advisory company based in London's West End.

www.gn2.uk.com

Barnes & Barnes

This company provides advice on all aspects of commercial property leases.

www.barnesandbarnes.london

What's so amazing in London is that so many museums are free.

Photo: Beth Evans www.bethevans.com

Graham Hollick
Creative Director

Tell us about your background.
I did my degree in textile design. After I graduated I went straight to Paris and I ended up working there in trend forecasting with Li Edelkoort. Through that, I also got into magazine styling and art direction. After 10 years in Paris, I was ready to come back to London, and I've been freelancing ever since. I work in styling for interiors, mainly for magazines, catalogues and advertising. I also do theatre design, but I only work with one company: Chicken Shed. I've been working with them for about 30 years. I went to Chicken Shed as a child and then when I graduated, I started to design for them. I've always designed their Christmas production, and sometimes other productions during the year.

What have you been getting involved in more recently?
For the last five years I've been working for an online trend prediction company called WGSN. It's a subscription trend company that's fashion based. I got involved because they were launching a separate website that dealt specifically with interiors. Since I've worked so much in interiors, I was asked to help them get it going. My job involves working on macro-trends twice a year; these are the big directional guiding trends. We then develop them into areas of home design, from tableware and soft furnishings, to kitchens and bathrooms. It's a process that starts off very creatively and then it filters down into commercial, realisable products.

How did you become a trend forecaster?
I sort of fell into it after I graduated. Trend forecasting is a trade: you learn to pick up on new things and think about where things are going next. It's about looking at what's becoming really big and interesting, and where the seeds are that will lead to the next thing. There's not a formula to it, but you learn the trade through doing it.

What are the trends in interiors at the moment?
The whole artisan, crafted and handmade idea has a massive buzz around it at the moment. We're looking at that to see how bigger industries and companies can develop those concepts. The other trend is almost the opposite to that: the people who want to opt out. There's an idea of going back to the minimalism that was very big in the nineties. It's almost a rejection of over-production. It's all about people wanting much calmer environments, people wanting less detail on things, and consumers wanting things that are really toned down and purified.

Which project are you currently most passionate about?
My collection of ethical home textiles called Stitch by Stitch. I work with artisans in Nepal and India, such as weavers and embroiderers. It started off when I was invited to work on a project with a group of female embroiderers from the Self Employed Women's Association (SEWA) in India. They had built a trade facilitation centre and wanted to run an event to show off all the different crafts going on there. I was asked to do a collection of garments which showed the traditional crafts in a new light. I loved it so much, I realised it was the perfect chance for me to launch my own collection of home textiles. Stitch by Stitch has a fair trade ethos and we've now shown three times at MAISON&OBJET in Paris, which is a big interiors trade fair. The interiors shop twentytwentyone stocks these beautiful felted rugs we make in Nepal too. In the last couple of years I've been joined by an old college friend Karen Sear Shimali and she's taken on the marketing and sales side of it, so we're trying to build it up.

What's the difference between the creative scene in London and Paris?
London has always had this powerful creative buzz. When I first went to Paris in the early nineties, it definitely didn't have a creative buzz. But it's changed a lot now and there's much more cross-fertilisation between London and Paris. I think the Eurostar had a really big influence on that; it's so easy to zip backwards and forwards by train. So I think Paris has a much healthier creative scene than it did when I first went there. London has always thrived on this idea of contrasts and people rebelling against the rules. That was what punk was all about, and I think in turn, that had a big connection with people's creativity.

What changes have you noticed in London's creative scene?
It just seems to be growing and growing. Young people seem to be so creative now. They all want to set up their own thing, and it's a feeling that seems to be getting stronger and stronger. There was a period in the early noughties when it felt like there wasn't so much going on. The fashion scene felt quite flat and people weren't really dressing creatively. That has definitely changed. High street shops in London are also so street savvy; they reflect whatever the latest trend is. When I was growing up, you couldn't go to a high street shop and buy the latest fashion in a very affordable way. The only options were the high end, designer scene that was very expensive, or you went to Camden and bought second hand things. Now, even shops like Primark and definitely Topshop cater to so many sub-cultures within their clothes. People can much more easily look more creative.

Where do you go shopping?

I'm really into vintage shopping. So on a Thursday, I go to the vintage market in Spitalfields and on Fridays I go to Portobello Market. For an insider choice of vintage goods, I regularly go to the Sunbury Antiques Market held at Kempton Park Racecourse, which is where all the buyers and stylists go. You have to get there really early, but it's a really fun trip to do. For fashion I go to places in the West End, like the department store Liberty and the little shops in Soho. Trunk is a menswear shop on Chiltern Street, opposite Chiltern Firehouse. That's very good. Since I have to research for trends, shopping is a big thing for me: I kind of keep my eye on everywhere. I find the way people dress is really inspiring. You can walk down the high street and see a lot of different fashions going on. I think a lot of English people are quite crazy in the way they dress and put outfits together!

How would you describe people working in creative industries in London?

I think creative people in London get very much into their little niche. We have yearly street parties on my road and at the last one, I invited my lovely neighbours who work in television into my flat. They were very enthusiastic and said my flat was like a museum and they loved all the creative elements to it. You'd think that everyone who's creative would be similar, but that's not really the case. There's so much going on in London that different types of creative people tap into. There are people who love vintage stuff. Then there's the whole artisan food scene, which is really creative. London has a very strong music scene too.

Which London neighbourhood do you live in?

I live in Dalston. When I came back from Paris in around the year 2000, I wanted to buy a flat in Islington, but I couldn't afford it. I grew up in the suburbs of north London, so I knew I wanted to be in the north somewhere, and eventually found my flat in Dalston. When I first moved to the area, I said I lived in Stoke Newington. Many people hadn't really heard of Dalston, and it also had a reputation for being a bit dangerous. Now it's completely changed and if anyone asks me where I live, I always say Dalston! I didn't choose it for the kind of lifestyle it offers now, because that simply didn't exist.

What's the vibe like in Dalston at the moment?

It's just changed so much over the last five years. Now it's a happening and creative area, which happened by chance, but I feel fortunate it did. There's a new café, restaurant or bar opening every few weeks. It's just been a treat to start trying out all the new places and working out which ones I like. So even though Dalston wasn't like this when I first moved there, it's become a

BREAKFAST
LUNCH
TEA

ROSE BAKERY

real advantage. The only place to go was the Turkish restaurant if I wanted to go out when I first moved to the area. Otherwise you'd go into the centre of town or into Islington. Now I go into the centre of town less.

Where do you like to eat out in London?
I like Primeur, which is closer to Islington. It's in a fantastic location with Mediterranean-style small plates. At the bottom of my road there's a lovely café called Fingers Crossed. They do great breakfasts and lunches, but they don't open in the evening. Off Mare Street near Hackney Town Hall is a restaurant called LARDO, and they've opened LARDO bebè just around the corner from me. They do delicious pizza, and they deliver too, which is handy. Further afield from Dalston, I like Barrafina, which has tapas bars in Soho and Covent Garden. There aren't any tables: all the seating is around the bar, but rather than being a drinks bar, it's actually the kitchen. Everything is prepared in front of you as you order. That's definitely one of my top London places.

Where do you like to go for a casual drink?
I like Dalston Superstore and a pub at the bottom of my road called Hand of Glory, which has the same people behind it who set up Dream Bags Jaguar Shoes in Shoreditch. They took over this old pub and they've made it into a place that feels like a country pub, but in a really hipster way. And obviously, it has craft beers and that kind of thing.

What's the most memorable cultural experience you've had in London?
I love unusual theatre. Punchdrunk does immersive theatre and I went to see this awe-inspiring performance by them called 'The Drowned Man' where they took over this whole building. There were people performing a story and by following different characters, you got to discover different parts of the story. I spent two hours in this huge building having this all-encompassing experience. I think that kind of thing is really interesting. There's another good venue called The Jetty in Greenwich which calls itself a temporary platform for immersive performance.

Where do you go for inspiration?
What's so amazing in London is that so many museums are free — you can just wander in — even if you're just passing and only have 20 minutes. You can go in and just soak it all up. The V&A (Victoria & Albert Museum) is my favourite museum. I often go into the V&A and discover something I've never seen before; London's museums are so big. I also love the Tate, especially Tate Britain which is a bit more sedate than Tate Modern.

Where is London's most original museum?
There are a lot of museums you don't even realise are there. Dennis Severs'

Photos: Beth Evans www.bethevans.com

House is in Shoreditch and it's one of the Huguenot silk-weavers houses from the 1700s. Dennis Severs bought it in the seventies and he tried to bring it back to how it was when it was built. After he passed away, the house was kept on by a group of friends and it's now a museum. It's designed as if a family's still living there, but they've just walked out of the room. So you'll see washing hanging up, slightly wilting fresh flowers, or fruit on the table. They only let a certain number of people in at a time, so it's never over-crowded. It's quite special.

Where else can you go to get a feeling of London from a different era?
Shepherd Market is an area in Mayfair that feels like a little village. It's definitely unexpected. I also used to love the old Routemaster [double-decker buses]. Especially on a dark winter's night, you'd sit on a Routemaster and London would have this timeless feel. It could have been the fifties or sixties; the design was exactly the same. The new one, the so called 'Boris Bus' [named after London Mayor Boris Johnson] designed by Thomas Heatherwick isn't quite the same.

What would you do during a perfect day out in London?
I'd start with a flea market early in the morning, then have brunch with friends. I love brunch. For a smarter brunch I like Bistrotheque in Hackney. It was there long before Hackney became trendy, and it's in a factory building where you don't see any evidence of what the restaurant is going to be like from the outside. When you do go in, it's got this very stark but really smart interior. In the afternoon, if it was winter, I'd go to an exhibition or a show. If it was summer, I'd go to hang out in a park. Victoria Park's great, as is Hampstead Heath. There are parts of Hampstead Heath where you feel like you're in the countryside, yet you can see the skyscrapers on the horizon. Alternatively, I'd walk from my flat to the Queen Elizabeth Olympic Park. It takes about an hour and you can walk right along the canal. In the evening I might go to the Rio Cinema in Dalston — they show the latest releases as well as some great independent films.

Do you go out to watch live music?
If I go to see live music I usually go to the Barbican or to the Roundhouse. I'm into world music, so if there's a really amazing person coming from Africa or India, I'm always keen to go and see them.

What music do you associate with London?
Definitely reggae. In certain parts of London like Notting Hill, or even around Dalston, I'll often hear really heavy roots reggae coming out of someone's window. Sometimes it's Bob Marley, sometimes it's reggae that's been produced in London, but it's a sound I really associate with the streets of London.

Is there a particular smell you associate with the city?
A breakfast fry up: eggs and bacon! Also, Tom Dixon did a scented candle of what he called the 'scent of London'. You can't really work out what it is, but the scent very much seems like London.

Have you got any exciting plans on the horizon?
I'm looking into buying a house in Italy with friends. That's my next big project. I love Italy! I love the food, the Italians and the weather. A photographer I used to work with bought a house in a village near the French border, not too far from Nice. It turns out there's a whole community of creative people who moved to this village. A couple of friends and I went down there and we found this amazing old house. It's an industrial building, it used to be an olive oil mill, and we're looking into buying it as a holiday home.

Would you ever leave London permanently?
Not yet! I think my long-term plan would be to downscale in London, but I would always keep a small studio in the city if I was living somewhere else. I've still got my studio flat in Paris, which I love. I rent it out on Airbnb, so if I ever want to go to Paris, I just block the dates out. I can imagine doing that in London as well, but not yet, not for another 10 or 20 years. You take it for granted when you live there, but London really is the most amazing city.

How would your friends describe you?
I think they'd probably say I'm creative, a good cook and that I like to travel.

Where's a good place to go people watching in London?
Dalston is a great place for people watching: you can just sit in a window seat in a bar or café and watch people walking by. Broadway Market on Saturdays is also great for that, you can just sit in a café and watch the market life.

What is London's best quality?
Acceptance of anyone and everyone. London is very open-minded and the people are welcoming.

What would you like to change about London?
I'd make it more compact. London is so sprawling, meaning that some places take a long time to get to. That's definitely a huge contrast with Paris: you can almost walk anywhere in Paris, or you can definitely jump on the metro and be there in 20 minutes. That's not the case in London.

How can visitors to London blend in and 'get lost' in the city?
People shouldn't plan too much and they should wander around without a map. Getting on a bus and seeing where it takes you is a great way to explore. By walking or cycling, you get to connect the dots and see places you'd completely miss if you took the Tube.

How do you get around the city?
I have a scooter, so I do nearly all my travelling around London on that. In the local area, I like to walk. It's just nice to wander and look at things, even people's houses: there are so many different styles of architecture.

What trends are there in London at the moment?
American food. It's just gone crazy. There's pulled pork and sloppy burgers everywhere. Beards are another trend, as is taking your laptop and working in a café.

What makes Londoners happy?
Days of glorious sunshine in London are rare. Coming out of your front door and going somewhere on an amazing sunny day always feels like a big treat. That definitely changes London: everybody seems to be really happy.

Graham's London

Places to visit

Barbican
Silk Street EC2Y 8DS
+44 (0)207 638 4141
tickets@barbican.org.uk
www.barbican.org.uk
Tube: Barbican

Broadway Market
Broadway Market E8 4QJ
www.broadwaymarket.co.uk
Rail: London Fields or Cambridge Heath

Chicken Shed
290 Chase Side N14 4PE
+44 (0)208 351 6161
info@chickenshed.org.uk
www.chickenshed.org.uk
Tube: Cockfosters

Dennis Severs' House
18 Folgate Street E1 6BX
info@dennissevershouse.co.uk
www.dennissevershouse.co.uk
Rail: Shoreditch High Street

Hampstead Heath
Rail: Hampstead Heath
Tube: Hampstead

Liberty
Regent Street W1B 5AH
+44 (0)207 734 1234
www.liberty.co.uk
Tube: Oxford Circus

Queen Elizabeth Olympic Park
Rail: Stratford International, Stratford or Hackney Wick
Tube: Stratford International or Stratford

Portobello Market
Portobello Road W11 2DY
www.portobelloroad.co.uk
Tube: Ladbroke Grove

Primark
www.primark.com

Punchdrunk
+44 (0)207 655 0940
punchdrunk@punchdrunk.org.uk
www.punchdrunk.org.uk

Rio Cinema
107 Kingsland High Street E8 2PB
+44 (0)207 241 9410
www.riocinema.org.uk
mail@riocinema.org.uk
Rail: Dalston Kingsland

Roundhouse
Chalk Farm Road NW1 8EH
+44 (0)300 678 9222
www.roundhouse.org.uk
Tube: Chalk Farm

Shepherd Market
Shepherd Market W1J 7QU
www.shepherdmarket.co.uk
Tube: Green Park

Spitalfields Market
Brushfield Street E1 6AA
www.spitalfields.co.uk
Rail/Tube: Liverpool Street

Sunbury Antiques Market
Kempton Park, Staines Road East, Sunbury on Thames TW16 5AQ
Kempton.thejockeyclub.co.uk/markets
Rail: Kempton Park

Tate Britain
Millbank SW1P 4RG
+44 (0)207 887 8888
visiting.britain@tate.org.uk
www.tate.org.uk
Tube: Pimlico

The Jetty
Greenwich Peninsula SE10 0FL
+44 (0)20 7183 0446
info@thejettygreenwich.co.uk
www.thejettygreenwich.co.uk
Tube: North Greenwich

Topshop
www.topshop.com

Trunk
8 Chiltern Street W1U 7PU
+44 (0)207 486 2357
info@trunkclothiers.com
www.trunkclothiers.com
Tube: Baker Street

V&A
Cromwell Road SW7 2RL
+44 (0)207 942 2000
contact@vam.ac.uk
www.vam.ac.uk
Tube: South Kensington

Victoria Park
Rail: Cambridge Heath or Hackney Wick

Eating and drinking

Barrafina
www.barrafina.co.uk
54 Frith Street W1D 4SL
Tube: Leicester Square
10 Adelaide Street WC2N 4HZ
Rail/Tube: Charing Cross

Bistrotheque
23-27 Wadeson Street E2 9DR
+44 (0)208 983 7900
reception@bistrotheque.com
www.bistrotheque.com
Rail: Cambridge Heath

Dalston Superstore
117 Kingsland High Street E8 2PB
+44 (0)207 254 2273
hello@dalstonsuperstore.com
www.dalstonsuperstore.com
Rail: Dalston Kingsland

Dream Bags Jaguar Shoes
32-36 Kingsland Road E2 8DA
+44 (0)207 683 0912
www.jaguarshoes.com
Rail: Hoxton

Fingers Crossed
247 Amhurst Road N16 7UN
Rail: Rectory Road

Hand of Glory
240 Amhurst Road E8 2BS
+44 (0)207 249 7455
www.jaguarshoes.com
Rail: Rectory Road

LARDO
197-201 Richmond Road E8 3NJ
+44 (0)208 985 2683
info@lardo.co.uk
www.lardo.co.uk
Rail: Hackney Central

LARDO bebè
Sandringham Rd E8 2AF
+44 (0)203 021 0747
info@lardobebe.com
www.lardobebe.com
Rail: Hackney Downs

Primeur
Barnes Motors, 116 Petherton
Road N5 2RT
www.primeurn5.co.uk
Rail: Canonbury

See also:

Stitch by Stitch
www.stitchbystitch.eu
Tom Dixon, Scent London
www.tomdixon.net
WGSN
www.wgsn.com

Find out more about Graham Hollick
at: www.grahamhollick.com

Photo: Beth Evans www.bethevans.com

Co-working

The expense of renting an office in London makes it an impossible proposition for many small and start-up businesses, but this isn't the only reason co-working spaces in London are so popular. With ready-made networks of entrepreneurs and freelancers working in related industries, many self-employed Londoners find co-working spaces give them business networks, a social circle and that elusive creative buzz to help propel their businesses forward.

There are more than 100 co-working spaces in London and this number has been rapidly rising since 2012, after the UK government started investing more in the start-up scene. As a result of the concentration of investment in the East London Tech City, there is an obvious cluster of co-working spaces in this area. That's not to say co-working spaces aren't available elsewhere in London, particularly since co-working is rapidly becoming a global trend that increasingly meets the needs of the self-employed and the ambitious.

The co-working scene in London is vibrant, and most co-working spaces come with much more than a desk and Wi-Fi. Most co-working spaces run networking and training events and come with extra perks such as free tea and coffee. A couple even throw in a membership with Zipcar, the car-sharing club, in case you need to make short trips in a car around town without having the hassle of actually owning a car. The most popular co-working spaces in London have carefully designed, and sometimes quirky, interiors. It's all part of co-workers taking pride in their work, and having a professional and impressive place to bring clients.

London's co-working spaces come in all shapes and sizes. Some are tech-only, while others thrive on diversity and have screening processes to ensure one industry or profession doesn't dominate the space. Some have quiet corners and cubby holes for a little more privacy, while others have wide open spaces to encourage the buzz that solo workers crave. In a city famed for being bustling but anonymous, co-working is a way of life that many workers find thrilling and stimulating. Most of all, co-working in London is about being part of a community and dreaming, big side by side with like-minded people.

Photos: TechHub

TechHub

This co-working space can be found in three east London locations, including one at the Google Campus. Its locations at the heart of east London's technology cluster position it well in the start-up scene, while the events calendar and networking opportunities are brimful. The #TechTuesday Demo night is great for telling others in the TechHub community about your ideas and getting their feedback. TechHub partners also run competitions every now and again for start-ups to win cash for their business. The co-working space has 24/7 access, free coffee and toast. Membership with a fixed desk in a shared space costs £330 per month, and also allows access to other TechHub locations.

london.techhub.com
hello@techhub.com

4-5 Bonhill Street EC2A 4BX (Google Campus)
+44 (0)207 256 6551
Tube: Old Street

207 Old Street EC1V 9NR
+44 (0)207 490 0764
Tube: Old Street

14-22 Elder Street E1 6BT
+44 (0)203 030 8402
Rail: Shoreditch High Street

Photos: Central Working

Central Working

A co-working space found in four central locations in London, Central Working is all about open airy spaces pocked with bright sofas, funky cushions and work benches to plug in and get on. Collaborating with other members is actively encouraged. Central Working clubs are accessible to members 24/7 and full time members pay £349 per month, although part-time options are available from £99 per month.

www.centralworking.com
hi@centralworking.com

4 Crown Place EC2A 4BT
+44 (0)203 095 6449
Tube: Liverpool Street or Moorgate
Rail: Liverpool Street

11-13 Bayley Street WC1B 3HD
+44 (0)203 095 6449
Tube: Tottenham Court Road or Goodge Street

6-8 Bonhill Street EC2A 4BX (Google Campus)
+44 (0)203 095 6449
Tube: Old Street

83-89 Mile End Road E1 4UJ
+44 (0)203 095 6449
Tube: Stepney Green

Photos: THE CUBE

THE CUBE

This co-working space is flooded with natural light from the huge windows in the old industrial building. Individuals are interviewed before being given membership to keep the co-workers truly diverse. As a result, members include everyone from photographers, space designers and surgeons to fashion stylists, business analysts and book publishers. Members receive free coffee and tea, free access to member events and a profile on THE CUBE's website. Full time membership is £300 per month, or part-time membership starts from £100 per month.

Studio 5 155 Commercial Street E1 6BJ
+44 (0)207 377 9279
hi@thecubelondon.com
www.thecubelondon.com
Rail: Shoreditch High Street

Photos: WeWork

WeWork

This international co-working space has three co-working locations in London and offers hotdesks as well as private offices for small companies. Trendy spaces filled with distressed wood, exposed brickwork and plush leather sofas make WeWork's London spaces both striking and affable. Membership includes a number of perks, including free beer, micro-roasted coffee, purified water, weekly events and private phone booths at a couple of the spaces. Full time hotdesking starts from £250 per month and £45 per month for part-time working.

www.wework.com
+44 (0)203 695 6990

Medius House, 2 Sheraton Street W1F 8BH
Tube: Tottenham Court Road or Oxford Circus

22 Upper Ground SE1 9PD
Tube: Waterloo or Southwark
Rail: Waterloo or Blackfriars

9 Devonshire Square EC2M 4YD
Tube: Liverpool Street, Aldgate or Aldgate East
Rail: Liverpool Street

Photos: Impact Hub Islington

Impact Hub

With four totally unique locations across London, Impact Hub describes itself as being 'part innovation lab, part incubator and part community centre.' Indeed, there is a real community spirit in Impact Hubs. The interiors each inspire creativity in their own ways, from the sleek and modern Brixton and Westminster spaces (complete with a greenhouse-style work room), to the industrial-trendiness of Islington and King's Cross. The Islington space is by far the most quirky, found in a converted warehouse with a high wooden roof with windows capturing the best of the London daylight. The opening hours and cost of full time desks varies depending on location, starting at £250 per month in Brixton to £475 per month in Westminster. Part-time working starts from £40 per month.

Impact Hub Islington, 4th Floor, 5 Torrens Street EC1V 1NQ
+44 (0)207 841 8900
islington.hosts@impacthub.net
islington.impacthub.net
Tube: Angel

Impact Hub King's Cross, 34b York Way N1 9AB
+44 (0)207 841 3450
kingscross.hosts@impacthub.net
kingscross.impacthub.net
Rail/Tube: King's Cross

Impact Hub Westminster, 1st Floor New Zealand House, 80 Haymarket SW1Y 4TE
+44 (0)207 148 6720
westminster.impacthub.net
Tube: Charing Cross or Piccadilly Circus

Impact Hub Brixton, Lambeth Town Hall, Brixton Hill SW2 1RW
+44 (0)207 926 3032
brixton.hosts@impacthub.net
brixton.impacthub.net
Tube: Brixton

Photos: Le Bureau

Le Bureau

This stylish south London co-working space comes with oak mocha desks, designer lamps and ergonomic chairs, giving a sense of privacy and elegance in open-plan spaces. With Skype pods, quiet rooms, a bean to cappuccino coffee machine, organic teas and boiling water taps, this is a chic space complemented by creature comforts.

Studio F7 & F8, Battersea
Studios, 80 Silverthorne Road
SW8 3HE
+44 (0)207 100 5666
info@lebu.co.uk
www.lebu.co.uk
Rail: Queenstown Road

Photos: Rainmaking Loft

Rainmaking Loft

A co-working space and start-up hub, Rainmaking Loft is a buzzing space designed to help start-ups collaborate and succeed. There are Wednesday breakfasts, Friday beers and a series of events to help entrepreneurs mingle and network. As well as desk space, there are break-out areas, meeting rooms, phone booths and an event space with beanbags and ping pong tables. The cost for full time workers is £419 per month.

International House, 1 St Katharine's Way E1W 1UN
+44 (0)203 432 3258
info@rainmakingloft.com
www.rainmakingloft.com
Tube: Tower Hill

More co-working locations

The Trampery London Fields

The Trampery runs four sites across London, each with a slightly different focus in terms of provision and industries served. The Trampery London Fields is ideal for desk-based designers looking for a desk or studio, or those in the fashion industry who also get access to professional equipment in The Fashion Lab on the first floor. The interior is a blend of vintage and modern furniture and art, giving an industrial yet artsy feel. Full time desks cost £240 per month.

125 - 127 Mare Street E8 3RH
+44 (0)203 111 9885
frontdoor@thetrampery.com
www.thetrampery.com
Rail: London Fields

Shoreditch Works

This co-working space specifically for tech start-ups offers 24/7 access and connections with like-minded developers and tech entrepreneurs. The space is peppered with large tables and small desks, with plenty of comfy chairs dotted around for good measure. Full time membership costs £354 per month.

32 - 38 Scrutton Street EC2A 4RQ
contact@shoreditchworks.com
www.shoreditchworks.com
Rail: Shoreditch High Street

The Soho Collective

This Soho co-working space attracts members from design, marketing, multimedia and other creative industries. The space is minimalist and working here is all about the location smack bang in the middle of London. Full time membership includes perks such as Zipcar membership, locker storage and free tea, coffee and sweet treats. Monthly full time membership is £410 per month, although it's also possible to rent a desk by the day for £35.

12 Moor Street W1D 5NG
+44 (0)7803 581 806
www.thesohocollective.com
Tube: Covent Garden, Leicester Square or Tottenham Court Road

ClubRoom Paddington

A little more corporate in feel compared to the east London co-working spaces, ClubRoom Paddington is accessible directly from Paddington Station and is inside a restored Grade 1 listed building dating back to the mid 1800s. A minimalist space with a Scandi-feeling, there are large tables and discrete booths to suit every co-worker's preference. It's ideal for those who like sleek comfort, great transport links and a little distance from the trendy east London scene. There is free tea, coffee and guest lounge access. There are other ClubRooms in locations across London too. Membership starts from £250 per month for access to one ClubRoom, or £300 per month for access to other ClubRooms as well.

19 Eastbourne Terrace W2 6LG
+44 (0)203 626 0100
paddington@theofficegroup.co.uk
www.theofficegroup.co.uk/locations/paddington
Rail/Tube: Paddington

Hampstead Design Hub

The leafy north London locale of Hampstead is home to this co-working space with 20 work desks up for grabs. Freelancers and creatives love it here, with its design-conscious interiors and woodpanelled relaxation areas with beanbags and sofas. Tea and coffee is free too. Full time workers pay £365 per month and a day pass costs £20.

39 Fairfax Road NW6 4EL
+44 (0)207 625 2727
www.hampsteaddesignhub.co.uk
Tube: Swiss Cottage
Rail: South Hampstead

Co-working portals and resources

NearDesk:
www.neardesk.com
CoWorkingLondon:
www.coworkinglondon.com
ShareDesk:
www.sharedesk.net
London Open Workspaces
http://bit.ly/YLA27k
GoCoWo:
www.gocowo.com

I can't, but we can.

Free Wi-Fi

If you enjoy the buzz of cafés or public spaces to do your work, you'll be pleased to know that free Wi-Fi can be found in an abundance of locations across London.

Here are our top tips for connecting to Wi-Fi for free in London:

Cloud Wi-Fi

Sign-up to this free cloud service and download the FastConnect app to make sure you can sign-in to Cloud Wi-Fi at hotspots across the city. A huge number of businesses have an agreement with Cloud Wi-Fi, meaning you can connect to Wi-Fi for free whenever you're in one of the participating businesses, which include many cafés, stations and shopping centres. Cloud Wi-Fi's website also has a hotspot finder so you can identify the exact participating locations.
www.thecloud.net

O2 Wi-Fi

O2 is another provider that has free Wi-Fi spots across London. Just search for available Wi-Fi networks on your mobile phone and if an O2 Wi-Fi spot appears, connect for free. O2 Wi-Fi's website also has a hotspot finder so you can see exactly where the hotspots are.
www.o2wifi.co.uk

Southbank Centre

London's world famous arts centre in the middle of the action on the River Thames has five floors of open spaces peppered with tables and sofas, some with fabulous views over London. Wi-Fi is free here, making it an ideal place to spend an afternoon on the laptop.
www.southbankcentre.co.uk

British Library

As the UK's library and the largest library in the world, the British Library is an inspiring location filled with the most famous books on the globe. Given this and the free Wi-Fi available, it's also a place where a lot of people love to camp out to do a day's work. Expect an eclectic mix of fellow workers, from internationally-renowned researchers and students from the nearby universities in Bloomsbury, to creative types enjoying the inspiration from their surroundings.
www.bl.uk

Wi-Fi at Tube stations

Wi-Fi is now available via Virgin Media at 150 Tube stations across London. It's free if you're a customer of one of the UK's major mobile phone service providers. Non-customers can purchase daily, weekly or monthly Virgin Media Wi-Fi Passes.
tfl.gov.uk/campaign/station-wifi

Photo: deathtothestockphoto.com

Working lunch
Business lunch etiquette

Business lunches are common in London, providing a slightly less formal environment to discuss business and build rapport with those you are working with, or hope to work with. It's important to remember business etiquette can vary drastically from country to country. Don't trip up by not knowing the protocol!

Professional/formal lunches
For those who work in professional services, such as banking, finance and sometimes marketing and PR, formal business lunches are common. If you invite someone to a business lunch, it's expected you will book a table and pay at the end. Lunch is typically served between midday and 14:30 in London and it's most appropriate to meet in a mid to high end restaurant or gastropub. It's always safest to choose a venue with a range of 'classic' food options. Business lunches in someone's home are extremely rare. Confirm the lunch appointment a few days before by email. Wear business attire unless you're certain your business associates will be dressed casually.

Punctuality is important to Brits. Leave extra time to get to a lunch meeting in case there are delays on public transport, or in case of heavy traffic. Greet your business associate with a brief handshake and a polite greeting; Brits don't tend to be back-slappers or cheek kissers. Start off with an informal general topic to break the ice, and if in doubt, talk about the favourite subject matter of the British: the weather! Go on to discuss business matters, although business lunches are often seen as a general opportunity to build rapport too, so further informal conversation is usually fine. If in doubt, take the lead from your business associate. British people value general politeness, so don't interrupt others when they're speaking and ensure your mobile phone is on silent.

It's usually acceptable to order a glass of wine or beer with your meal, but don't order anything stronger and don't get drunk. Demonstrate your good manners by keeping your elbows off the table, being polite with the waiting staff and leaving a tip (10-15%). Write a prompt thank you email to your business associates afterwards and take the opportunity to note down any actions you agreed on.

Creative

Working in creative industries such as art, design and technology often means business lunches are less formal. The focus tends to be on building a good relationship and discussing business ventures both parties are passionate about. The dress code is typically smart-casual rather than formal business attire, and you might choose a restaurant with a charismatic interior or cool architecture rather than selecting a formal fine dining establishment. Breakfast meetings are becoming a little more common in these industries and there are various breakfast networking events, which are also great for meeting business associates you strive to work with. A lot of co-working spaces have cafés or stylish meeting rooms where you could order lunch in.

While these business lunches are less formal than those in other industries, it still pays to be polite and punctual, and the rule still applies to pay for the lunch if you extended the lunch invitation. It's also becoming increasingly common to have business catch ups over a drink in the evening, such as at events run by co-working spaces.

Working lunch

Here are our top tips for business lunch options to suit different occasions.

Professional lunches

Balthazar

This NYC-French brasserie-styled restaurant was one of the most anticipated restaurant openings in London in 2013. The interior has just the right blend of intimate comfort and chic elegance, making it ripe for a working lunch that's professional but not too stuffy. Lunch can be as grand or as laid back as you like it, with menu items ranging from steak sandwiches to seafood platters.
4-6 Russell Street WC2B 5HZ
+44(0)203 301 1155
info@balthazarlondon.com
www.balthazarlondon.com
Tube: Covent Garden

Brigade Bar & Bistro

Based inside an old fire station dating back to 1879, Brigade is now a restaurant and social enterprise; the kitchen staff are previously homeless people who have been offered catering apprenticeships on-site. The menu focuses on good quality British ingredients with some European influence and there are plenty of options for a business lunch, including the two or three course 'quick fire' lunch which can be served within one hour.
The Fire Station, 139 Tooley Street SE1 2HZ
+44 (0)844 346 1225
www.thebrigade.co.uk
info@thebrigade.co.uk
Rail/Tube: London Bridge

Oblix

If you're looking to impress your business associates, dining in this restaurant in Europe's tallest building is a must. Oblix is found on the 32nd floor of The Shard and specialises in modern grilled dishes, from dover sole to organic pork chops. The interior is slick, urban and the ideal spot for a bird's eye view over the city.
Level 32, The Shard, 31 St. Thomas Street SE1 9RY
+44 (0)207 268 6700
www.oblixrestaurant.com
Rail/Tube: London Bridge

Brasserie Zédel

This grand Parisian brasserie with an impressive art deco interior is ideal for a business lunch designed to impress without breaking the bank. The menu is full of French classics, but plats du jour or two to three course prix fixe menus are ideal for lunch; all of them are less than £15 per person.
20 Sherwood Street W1F 7ED
+44 (0)207 734 4888
reservations@brasseriezedel.com
www.brasseriezedel.com
Tube: Piccadilly Circus

Creative lunches

Rochelle Canteen

This airy eatery is housed inside an old bike shed and attracts local creatives in droves. There's indoor and outdoor seating and a refreshingly to-the-point seasonal menu. It's ideal for an unstuffy business lunch that offers an understated backdrop ideal for exploring creative ideas.
Rochelle School, Arnold Circus E2 7ES
+44 (0)207 729 5677
info@arnoldandhenderson.com
www.arnoldandhenderson.com/4-rochelle_canteen
Rail: Shoreditch High Street

The Modern Pantry

This Clerkenwell spot is part-café, part airy brasserie. White furniture and copper light fittings give it a modern veneer. A working lunch in the relaxed ground-floor café offers an informal but professional backdrop, while the upstairs dining rooms can be booked for larger groups. The menu is internationally inspired with options to suit all palates, accompanied by an impressive selection of tea, coffee and cocktails.
47-48 St John's Square EC1V 4JJ
+44 (0)207 553 9210
enquiries@themodernpantry.co.uk
www.themodernpantry.co.uk
Rail: Clerkenwell

Merchants Tavern

Found inside an old Victorian warehouse and former apothecary, Merchants Tavern is in the heart of east London's Tech City and sits among world renowned creative and design businesses. Given its location and industrial chic décor, Merchants Tavern attracts a stealthy mix of start-up investors and entrepreneurs. Run by renowned British chef Angela Hartnett MBE, the food is certainly up to scratch too, with seasonal small plates and mains infused with modern British style.
36 Charlotte Road EC2A 3PG
+44 (0)207 060 5335
booking@merchantstavern.co.uk
www.merchantstavern.co.uk
Rail/Tube: Old Street

Dabbous

If you're looking for highly-acclaimed food in a design conscious interior for your business lunch, Dabbous is the place to go. The on-trend industrial aesthetic reigns supreme here, with exposed beams and plenty of metal and leather thrown in for good measure. The modern British menu is impeccably executed and the four course lunch menu offers an opportunity to taste the chef's genius for a reasonable price.

39 Whitfield Street W1T 2SF
+44 (0)207 323 1544
info@dabbous.co.uk
www.dabbous.co.uk
Tube: Goodge Street

Order-in

Deliveroo

This company works with some of the most popular restaurants in London to deliver to your door. Restaurants include well-loved chains and independently owned eateries, meaning you can have the best of London's dining scene in your meeting room.
www.deliveroo.co.uk

Lunch BXD

This young company is run by a pair of chefs who deliver fresh and nutritious meals to workplaces. Plenty of London's workforce already order their daily lunch from Lunch BXD, but they can also cater for group meetings. The food is tasty, nutritious and a far cry from the limp sandwich lunches so frequently found in corporate meetings.
www.lunchbxd.com

City Pantry

This company brings together food offerings from London's street food vendors, pop-ups, chefs and restaurants, allowing you to pick and choose the right order-in business lunch for your meeting. The participating vendors have catering packages displayed on the City Pantry website, including the price per head, making it easy to compare like for like.
www.citypantry.com

itsu

This Asian-inspired London chain is a favourite with the city's workforce for nutritious meals, from high-protein low-carb salads to sushi trays and miso broths. itsu also offers free delivery for orders over £20, making it an ideal lunch option for self-hosted lunch meetings.
www.itsu.com

Order tasty, nutritious food at Lunch BXD

Photos: LunchBXD

London simply has that kudos for design.

Photo: Lee Thornley

Lee Thornley
Design entrepreneur and director of Bert & May

Tell us your story.

My wife and I both originally lived in London. I was a barrister, but unfortunately I became seriously ill and so moved to Spain to recuperate. We decided we wanted to live in the Spanish countryside so we bought a field and ended up building a boutique hotel, Casa la Siesta, made almost entirely of reclaimed materials. It became one of Tatler's top 101 hotels in the world. I realised the beauty of the hotel was its materials: the design itself was pretty simplistic, so I decided to set up a business based on that idea. After living in Spain for six years, we decided we wanted to educate our children back in the UK, so we came back. We set up Bert & May as an online business to begin with, and later opened the physical showroom in our current location in Vyner Street in Bethnal Green, London.

What is Bert & May's focus?

Bert & May now has two divisions, Bert & May Materials and Bert & May Spaces. Bert & May Materials sells reclaimed wood, tiles and terracottas. All of our tiles are designed by the in-house team, handmade in Spain and then shipped to our Yorkshire salvage yard. It was only when I realised that we were selling these beautiful materials to people to make great spaces with that I thought we should be doing the same. So we are building on our 'Spaces' side of the business, which is our take on modular homes. We make three different sizes of 'boxes', which can be used for people to have on their rooftops or in their gardens as a home office or an extra bedroom. We do kitchens, and we also do barges; we're looking at alternative ways of living. The good thing is they are unique spaces in their own right, but you can also put them all together and create a flexible and mobile home from it. Every project is a collaboration. We have a lot of ideas on the drawing board and want to look into developing the ultimate garden shed, and perhaps even a camper van and treehouses at some point in the future. Ultimately we're trying to give people unique living spaces. The business has been going from strength-to-strength and has been growing year-on-year for the last four years. So it's been a really exciting and a busy time for the whole Bert & May team. We are hoping to roll out the business in New York and Australia in the coming years too.

Talking about barges, we heard a rumour you live on one of Bert & May's barges?
I live in London during the week and in Yorkshire at the weekends. Bert & May is located right by the canal and has a mooring that's attached to our building that wasn't being used, so it seemed like a very logical thing to live on one of the barges. I occasionally use the office as my dining room in the evening and it's a great space for entertaining large numbers of people. It's great having the barge so close to the office because it's a great showcase of a Bert & May Space. We're doing two types of barge: the city barge and the country barge. The city barge is very urban, slick and minimalist. Some people might say it's quite cold, yet stylish; this is the one I live on in London. The country barge is a two bedroom, more family orientated pad for people who can't afford to have second homes outside the city, but want to have an affordable second home. It costs £150,000 for a barge, but it could give you a two bedroom space in the Cotswolds, which is cheaper in comparison to what a house would cost there.

Why does a business like yours work so well in London?
In Europe, London — and maybe Berlin — are the only two places we would ever consider having a Bert & May Materials shop at the moment. The German market is very interesting because the economy's booming and they're very design savvy. But London is the hub of the creative industry and events like London Design Festival are massive. We've exhibited at other London events like Design Junction, Clerkenwell Design Week and Décorex; which all make total sense for us. London is the ideal place to have a head office because internationally renowned designers are always coming to the city. London simply has that kudos for design. People are very design savvy and they're prepared to pay for it.

What kind of people are Bert & May's customers?
I'd say around 90% of our customers are London-based. We work with a lot of trade clients — architects and interior designers who are working on restaurants, hotels, shop fittings and commercial projects. We also work on mid-to-high end residential projects. Our aesthetic is quite raw and rustic. Rustic is a bit of an overused word, but our designs are a bit rough around the edges.

How did you decide which neighbourhood to locate Bert & May in?
We were very quickly drawn to Hackney because it feels like such a creative hub. We're so, so lucky to be located on Vyner Street. It's got a great community with lots of art galleries and the First Thursdays of the month, where all of the galleries and stores are open late; it creates a fantastic buzz around the whole area. We are so lucky to share the street with galleries like HADA Contemporary, the first East Asian art gallery on Vyner Street, and DegreeArt, which supports artists of the future.

<u>Has the local area changed in the last few years?</u>
It has changed as it's become a bit more gentrified, and galleries have been replaced with apartment blocks, but I still think it's a very creative place to live, work and visit. It isn't full of cheese and olive shops that you might find in places like Peckham now, and it hasn't become a residential-only area. Thankfully we've still got all of those wonderful creative places that keep the street alive with interest.

<u>Tell us more about Hackney; what's the vibe?</u>
What I like most about the area is the fact new businesses are always emerging. And as a foodie, I love that I can get great produce and interesting cuisines so locally. I think Hackney is one of those few areas that still feels like it's true to its roots, and walking through Broadway and Netil markets, you really get a feel for this community. While it's becoming wealthier and property prices are going up, it still feels like the East End. It still feels like an interesting place to be.

<u>What's the benefit of splitting your time between London and Yorkshire?</u>
I love it. Some people are surprised I do such a commute, but for me it's perfect. During the week in London, I get to go to great restaurants, see a lot of people and do lots of work. I love London because everything's on tap. You can decide to go to wherever you want at the drop of a hat: an independent French cinema screening might be on the cards one evening, or dropping in at a debating society the next. London is the political centre of the UK, it's the economic centre, and it's arguably the cultural centre. So if you're British and you love being in Britain, it feels important to have a strong link to London. Then at the weekends, I go and spend time with my family in the countryside: enjoying the fresh air and open space. And actually, getting to Yorkshire takes me less than two hours, so it's really easy.

<u>How would your friends describe you?</u>
A family-man. Ambitious. A foodie. Bossy!

<u>What is London's best quality?</u>
The diversity of people. I passionately believe that it's such a great city because of its multiculturalism and because of the fact such a tolerant society lives here.

<u>Is there anything you'd change about London if you had the power?</u>
The public transport system works really well, but if there were more pedestrian zones and more cycle zones, it would force people out of taxis and cars. That would only be a good thing, because it would benefit more people than it would punish.

What's the best thing about being a design entrepreneur in London?
Getting invited to all the cool new openings! Béton Brut was one of my
favourite openings. It's a modern design store and gallery space in east
London. Sophie and Augustus are the owners and they have a genuine
passion for modernist architect-led design pieces. We actually used some of
their furniture in our first barge.

Where are your favourite places to eat out in the Hackney area?
One of my favourite places is Mission, which is at the end of Bethnal Green
Road under the railway arches. It's a California-inspired restaurant, and it's
really good. The other place I really like is The Corner Room, which is in the
Town Hall Hotel. All of the ingredients in their dishes are sourced from the
UK and the food is really affordable — you can have two courses for £19.

And where do you eat when you go further afield in London?
I go to Andina on Shoreditch High Street, which is a very good ceviche
restaurant. There's a place on Upper Street called The Afghan Kitchen,
which is a great place to go with friends so you can share dishes. A good
curry on Brick Lane is a must; Sheba is one of my favourites and was voted
best curry house in the UK in 2013. I also really like No 32 in Clapham Old
Town — they serve delicious craft beers which are great on a hot summer's
day. Finally, I like Trio in Peckham, which also uses its space to host
creative workshops.

Where do you like to go for drinks?
There are a couple of pubs right near the office on Broadway Market. The
Cat & Mutton is a great example of a traditional east London pub serving
delicious food; it's just on the corner of London Fields and Broadway
Market. I also like the Peg + Patriot for cocktails, which is opposite the
Town Hall Hotel. It has a great stripped back, industrial finish with nice
homely touches and interesting design features.

Where do you like to go shopping?
I really like BOXPARK: it's a shopping strip made entirely of shipping
containers dedicated to pop-ups and there are always interesting things
to find there. In terms of where I spend most time shopping, it's probably
Kempton Market, which is an antiques market at Kempton racecourse in
west London. That's a definite favourite. Redchurch Street has some great
shops too: the collection at Labour and Wait is always evolving which
means there is something new to explore every time I visit.

What do you do for soaking up culture in London?
There is so much choice in London. I would definitely recommend heading
to Greenwich Park; it's one of London's eight royal parks and at the top

of the hill there are incredible views out across London. For another great view over the city, I like to visit the new 'Walkie-Talkie' building at 20 Fenchurch Street: it has landscaped gardens that span three floors and is an example of how new modern architecture is changing London's skyline. For colour inspiration, I like to head to Columbia Road Flower Market on a Sunday, which is transformed into an oasis of fragrance and foliage. For experiencing the real London, I like Brixton Market for its open restaurants and street food, and Herne Hill for its bustling market; these should both be on any visitor's must-visit list. To the west of London I would recommend Petersham Nurseries: you can take a boat down the River Thames from central London to Richmond; it's a great way to see how London changes. The petting zoo in Vauxhall is a favourite with my children as well as Battersea Park, where you can go on a boat out around the lake, and Crystal Palace Park to see the dinosaurs, which have been there since the 1850s. If I find myself at a loose end I will try and squeeze in a visit to the Open Air Theatre in Regent's Park: it only goes on for three months in the summer, but it is definitely one of my favourites. I like the theatre generally; I try to go to see the more independent performances. The last one I went to was the Porgy and Bess Opera; that was great.

What else do you like to do with your free time in London?
I love going to watch my football team, Arsenal. And I love Wimbledon; I go to watch the tennis every year. I also love to cycle so I always take part in the Ride London event which happens in August. You get to cycle around traffic free roads in London, with thousands of other cycling enthusiasts, which is a great experience. As a foodie I am also a huge fan of Street Feast which happens in three locations across London.

You obviously know a thing or two about hotels since you built your own one in Spain. Can you recommend any hotels in London?
I am a member of Soho House and would definitely recommend it. It was set up in 1995 as a home from home for people in the creative industries. I also go to Shoreditch House quite a lot, I love the fact it's in a converted warehouse and I like to sit by the swimming pool on the roof and watch the world go by! In terms of other hotels in London, I think Firmdale Hotels, who are behind the likes of the Charlotte Street Hotel, have a great brand and really make you feel welcome and at home.

What would your perfect day in London consist of?
I'd go out early in the morning: it's the best time to see London before the crowds start to form. I love rummaging round at fairs and markets for antique finds and the earlier you get there the better. After that I would go for breakfast somewhere like Honey & Co, who serve a delicious Middle Eastern inspired big breakfast. Then I would pop to Borough Market to

stock up on some fresh produce before packing a picnic and heading to Victoria Park for a couple of hours; it's one of London's most historic parks. After a couple of hours I would head to the London Fields Lido for a quick swim in the open air.

What's the most bizarre thing that's happened to you in London?
One thing did happen to me which is something you really wouldn't expect in London. One particular day, I was in a taxi and I was having a really hard day. The traffic was really slow moving and I started telling this female cab driver my entire life story, because it's like therapy and you know you're never going to see them again. We stopped at some traffic lights, and the cab driver jumped out and got into the back of the taxi with me, gave me a kiss, and then got back in front. Ha ha! And I thought, 'I wasn't expecting that'!

Do you have a chill out place in the city?
The mooring at the back of our office is the best place to escape from things. You can just close the door to the office and sit by the canal.

Where's the best place to go for an adrenalin rush in London?
I like climbing so I go to the climbing wall in Mile End. I first got into it at that very climbing wall, so now when I'm in Yorkshire I go and do real climbs too. Climbing at the Mile End centre is really fun: they've got automatic lifts, so you basically have to jump off the top and hope the machine catches you. So that's quite an adrenalin rush. The climbing community at the centre is really good. Since it's very near the city, it's full of young like-minded people. We all go out drinking after we've been climbing and the centre runs loads of trips to other climbing centres and out of London to do real climbs. It's really fun. If you don't want to be constantly eating as a form of socialising, it's a great thing to do in London.

What is the current fad in London?
Pop-ups are a fad. There are a lot of good things about pop-ups, but there are also bad things. It legitimises businesses that have no real sense to them. For example, you sometimes see trustafarians at BOXPARK who have been given a bit too much money and want to sell their hand-knitted scarf that's £97million per scarf! Of course, there's no business sense behind it. That's not to say I wouldn't do a Bert & May pop-up, because it allows you to take the brand to a new area with a new captive audience, so in that sense sometimes it can make good business sense. Everyone now believes that the coolest thing in the world is to go to a pop-up bar. It's just a bar! It doesn't make it cool because it's only going to be there for a week.

How would you advise visitors to London to blend in and become 'citizens' of the city for the duration of their stay?
I would recommend visiting the Meetup website: it's a great website where you can find groups of like-minded people who arrange activities and events, which is a great way to meet people and to immerse yourself in London life. If you are staying in London for a longer period of time I'd suggest joining as many clubs and societies as possible. I'm quite into politics, so I go to certain political groups within London and I'm part of the climbing club. People make the mistake of thinking that going to a bar is the right way to meet people. People in London are quite friendly, but we're not very good as a nation at standing at a bar and chatting to others. It's a bit like sitting on the Tube: you talk to someone and they think you're weird! So I think you've really got to surround yourself with people who are like-minded, and I think the only way of doing that is via clubs and societies.

How would you encourage people to 'get lost' in London?
I would suggest picking up a map and just randomly selecting an area from it. Then visit The Nudge website to find out what is going on in that area: it lists all of the pop-ups, events and places to eat in each locality.

Lee's London

Places to visit

Arsenal Football Club
Emirates Stadium N5 1BU
+44 (0)207 619 5003
www.arsenal.com
Tube: Arsenal

Battersea Park
Rail: Battersea Park
Béton Brut
Unit 2, 30 Felstead Street E9
5LG
info@betonbrut.co.uk
www.betonbrut.co.uk
Rail: Hackney Wick

Bert's Barge
www.airbnb.com

BOXPARK
2 Bethnal Green Road E1 6GY
+44 (0)207 033 2899
info@boxpark.co.uk
www.boxpark.co.uk
Rail: Shoreditch High Street

Bert & May
67 Vyner Street E2 9DQ
+44 (0)203 673 4264
info@bertandmay.com
www.bertandmay.com
Tube: Bethnal Green

Brixton Market
Rail/Tube: Brixton

Broadway Market
Broadway Market E8 4QJ
www.broadwaymarket.co.uk
Rail: London Fields or Cambridge
Heath

Clerkenwell Design Week
clerkenwelldesignweek.com

Columbia Road Flower Market
Columbia Road E2 7RG
info@columbiaroad.info
www.columbiaroad.info
Rail: Hoxton

Crystal Palace Park
Rail: Crystal Palace

Décorex
www.décorex.com

DegreeArt
12 Vyner Street E2 9DG
+44 (0)208 980 0395
Info@DegreeArt.com
www.degreeart.com
Tube: Bethnal Green

Design Junction
www.thedesignjunction.co.uk

Firmdale Hotels
www.firmdalehotels.com

First Thursdays
www.whitechapelgallery.org/
first-thursdays

Greenwich Park
Rail/Tube: Greenwich

HADA Contemporary
21 Vyner Street E2 9DG
+44 (0)208 983 7700
info@hadacontemporary.com
www.hadacontemporary.com
Tube: Bethnal Green

Herne Hill Market
Railton Road SE24 0JN
+44 (0)208 302 9010
www.weareccfm.com/locations/
herne-hill
Rail: Herne Hill

Kempton Market
Kempton Park, Staines Road
East, Sunbury on Thames TW16
5AQ
Kempton.thejockeyclub.co.uk/
markets
Rail: Kempton Park

Labour and Wait
85 Redchurch Street E2 7DJ
+44 (0)207 729 6253
info@labourandwait.co.uk
www.labourandwait.co.uk
Rail: Shoreditch High Street

London Design Festival
www.londondesignfestival.com

London Fields Lido
London Fields West Side E8 3EU
+44 (0)207 254 9038
www.better.org.uk/leisure/
london-fields-lido
Rail: London Fields

Netil Market
23 Westgate Street E8
+44 (0)203 095 9718
market@
creativenetworkpartners.com
netilmarket.tumblr.com
Rail: London Fields

Open Air Theatre, Regent's Park
Inner Circle, Westminster NW1
4NU
www.openairtheatre.com
Tube: Baker Street

Petersham Nurseries
Church Lane, Petersham Road
TW10 7AB
+44 (0)208 940 5230
info@petershamnurseries.com
www.petershamnurseries.com
Rail/Tube: Richmond

Ride London
www.prudentialridelondon.co.uk

Sky Garden at 20 Fenchurch Street ('Walkie –Talkie' building)
20 Fenchurch Street EC3M 3BY
+44 (0)33 3772 0020
info@skygarden.london
www.skygarden.london
Tube: Monument

Soho House Group
www.sohohouse.com

Vauxhall City Farm
165 Tyers Street SE11 5HS
+44 (0)207 582 4204
www.vauxhallcityfarm.org
Rail/Tube: Vauxhall

Victoria Park
Rail: Cambridge Heath or
Hackney Wick

Mile End Climbing Wall
Haverfield Road E3 5BE
enquiries@mileendwall.org.uk
www.mileendwall.org.uk
+44 (0)208 980 0289
Tube: Mile End

Wimbledon Championships
Church Road, Wimbledon SW19
5AE
www.wimbledon.com
Tube: Southfields or Wimbledon
Rail: Wimbledon

Eating and drinking

Andina
1 Redchurch Street E2 7DJ
+44 (0)207 920 6499
welcome@andinalondon.com
www.andinalondon.com
Rail: Shoreditch High Street

Borough Market
8 Southwark Street SE1 1TL
www.boroughmarket.org.uk
Rail/Tube: London Bridge

Cat & Mutton
76 Broadway Market E8 4QJ
+44 (0)207 249 6555
info@catandmutton.com
www.catandmutton.com
Rail: Cambridge Heath or
London Fields

Honey & Co
25a Warren Street W1T 5LZ
+44 (0)207 388 6175
enquiries@honeyandco.co.uk
www.honeyandco.co.uk
Tube: Warren Street

Mission
Arch 250 Paradise Row E2 9LE
+44 (0)207 613 0478
hello@missione2.com
www.missione2.com
Tube: Bethnal Green

No 32 The Old Town
32 The Pavement SW4 0JE
+44 (0)203 535 0910
reservations@no32theoldtown.
co.uk
www.no32theoldtown.co.uk
Tube: Clapham Common

Peg + Patriot
Patriot Square E2 9NF
+44 (0)207 871 0460
hi@pegandpatriot.com
www.pegandpatriot.com
Rail: Cambridge Heath
Tube: Bethnal Green

Sheba
136 Brick Lane E1 6RU
+44 (0)207 247 7824
www.shebabricklane.com
Rail: Shoreditch High Street

Street Feast
260-264 Kingsland Road E8
4DG
www.streetfeastlondon.com
Rail: Haggerston

The Afghan Kitchen
35 Islington Green N1 8DU
+44 (0)207 359 8019
Tube: Angel

The Corner Room
Town Hall Hotel, Patriot Square
E2 9NF
+44 (0)207 871 0460
info@cornerroom.co.uk
www.townhallhotel.com/
cornerroom
Tube: Bethnal Green
Rail: Cambridge Heath

Trio
182 Bellenden Road SE15 4BW
hello@triobellendenroad.co.uk
www.triobellendenroad.co.uk
Rail: Peckham Rye

See also
www.meetup.com
www.thenudge.com

Find out more about Lee Thornley and
Bert & May at www.bertandmay.com
or on Twitter @bertandmay

Funding for start-ups

Having a start-up dream is one thing, but transforming it into reality takes dedication, professionalism and of course, money. As one of the world's global economic centres and with the UK government being particularly focused on supporting start-up businesses at the moment, there are various different options for gaining funding and investment for businesses in the city. To have the best chance of securing the right deal for your business, it's prudent to have your affairs in order before approaching the various sources of capital. This means having a great idea, a solid business plan and a professional as well as creative approach.

Advice about funding

Department for Business, Innovation & Skills (BIS)
This UK government department focuses on economic growth and is the UK's hub for people to find out more about starting a business, including what grants, loans and other business support is on offer. The BIS website has an online tool to help you identify some of the places where finance is available.
www.gov.uk/bis
www.gov.uk/business-finance-support-finder

j4bGrants
This portal provides funding information for small businesses currently in the UK, or businesses looking to move to the UK.
www.j4bgrants.co.uk

Small Business Centre
This organisation helps small businesses identify opportunities for funding, as well as providing general support on common business matters.
www.smallbusinesscentre.org.uk

National Enterprise Network
This website lists National Enterprise Network members across the UK who can provide advice to small and start-up businesses. There are several listings under each of London's boroughs.
nationalenterprisenetwork.org

Grants

The Pitch
This annual competition is for small businesses less than three years old. The prize is a package of business-related goodies, from free phone lines, business advice and central London office space for four months, to £10,000 worth of online advertising and lifetime membership of UK Business Forums.
www.thepitch.uk

Shell LiveWIRE Smarter Future Programme
This programme is for entrepreneurs aged between 16 and 30 with a business idea that addresses the UK's future transport, energy, or natural resource challenges. There's £5,000 up for grabs on a monthly basis plus the opportunity to be entered into the annual £25,000 Shell LiveWIRE Young Entrepreneur of the Year Award.
www.shell-livewire.org/awards/smarter-future-programme

UnLtd
This not-for-profit organisation invites social entrepreneurs to apply for their various awards three times a year. Awards include cash as well as other support from UnLtd staff and are available for people at different stages of their social entrepreneurship journey, from the ideas stage to those looking to quickly scale up a business.
www.unltd.org.uk

European Commission
The European Commission provides funding to businesses who have been successful in response to invitations to tender advertised on its website.
ec.europa.eu/contracts_grants

GRANTfinder
GRANTfinder and Grantnet.com provide information about thousands of funding opportunities.
www.grantfinder.co.uk
www.grantnet.com

Grants Online
Opportunities for grants available in the UK are available via subscription to this website.
www.grantsonline.org.uk

Lottery Good Causes
This website helps identify funding options for those involved in businesses and projects that support the community.
www.lotterygoodcauses.org.uk/funding-finder

Investment

Seed Enterprise Investment Scheme (SEIS)
This government-backed scheme gives better tax rates to those investing in small and start-up businesses. Entrepreneurs and business owners can apply to be showcased on the SEIS website so they can connect with potential investors.
www.seis.co.uk

Funding London
This independent organisation channels funding available from UK and Europe towards start-up applicants. They also manage the London Co-Investment Fund set up by the Mayor of London for tech and science start-ups.
www.fundinglondon.co.uk

#1seed
This early stage tech start-up investor provides seed funding of between £50,000 and £300,000.
www.1seed.co.uk

EC1 Capital
This company invests mostly in mobile and web-based start-up businesses.
www.ec1capital.com

Entrepreneurs Fund
This investment company looks for life-science and technology businesses to invest in.
www.entrepreneursfund.com

Loans

Community Development Finance Association (CDFA)
The CDFA works with finance providers who have a commitment to community or economic development within disadvantaged communities, or within markets not adequately served by mainstream financial providers. Start-ups can apply for loans, which come with added perks such as a virtual office for six months and reduced PayPal fees.
www.cdfa.org.uk

Start Up Loans
This government-funded scheme offers loans of up to £25,000 to start-up companies that have been trading for less than two years, with a fixed interest rate of 6% per annum.
www.gov.uk/start-up-loans
www.startuploans.co.uk

The majority of banks in the UK have schemes for small business loans. See a list of some of the UK's major banks on page 108.

Learn or improve English

If you're moving to London and want to improve your English, or if you want to focus in on the English vocabulary and skills you will need in business situations, London is full of language schools offering different types of courses. Many offer evening business courses, helping you fit this into your schedule if you're also working full time. Visit the British Council's website for a comprehensive list of accredited language course providers:
www.britishcouncil.org/education/accreditation/centres

Incubators and accelerators

Incubators and accelerators help young companies grow by providing finance, mentoring, or access to new customers and markets. Some provide all three. Incubators typically help entrepreneurs get their start-up company off the ground, and although they don't tend to invest directly in the companies, they may help attract funding through their networks. Accelerators are all about fostering growth in a young company and tend to invest in the new company in exchange for equity.

London has been hailed as the European capital of start-up incubators and accelerators. Research shows that start-ups who gain a place in an incubator or accelerator programme have a survival rate of 92% after two years, compared to a 75% survival rate for those who don't get onto one of the programmes. Given this, the number of incubators and accelerators in London is increasing at a steady pace, giving start-up owners a choice of programmes to apply for that best meet their needs.

Here's a selection of incubators and accelerators in London:

Incubators

Kitchenette
This incubator in London Fields works with food entrepreneurs to help their start-up food businesses flourish. Support includes access to mentors, street food and pop-up residencies and introductions to investors.
www.wearekitchenette.com

Centre for Fashion Enterprise
This fashion business incubator offers different tiers of support depending on how far along you are in your business and what you want to achieve. Advice is available on everything from financial and legal matters to manufacturing and marketing.
www.fashion-enterprise.com

Accelerator
Despite its name, Accelerator describes itself as being more of an incubator than an accelerator. The Shoreditch based organisation provides pre-start-up and start-up support to businesses focusing on information and communications technology (ICT) and digital media. Services offered include affordable desk space, business support and training.
www.accelerator-london.com

MeWe360
This incubator for creative entrepreneurs offers business support, desk space and opportunities to pitch for investment from MeWe360's £1million investment fund.
www.mewe360.com

Accelerators

Level39
This Canada Square technology accelerator space works with young companies in finance, cyber-securities, retail and future cities. Start-ups work with experienced entrepreneurs, technology investors and industry experts to accelerate growth. Desk space, access to an iPad coffee machine and cookies at 3pm every day are also thrown in for good measure.
www.level39.co

Microsoft Ventures Accelerator
This accelerator offers a three to six month programme to start-ups working in cloud, internet and mobile businesses. They offer deskspace, access to Microsoft's networks and routes to market; they take zero equity.
www.microsoftventures.com/locations/london

Entrepreneur First
This accelerator for technology start-ups offers an intensive six month programme to get start-ups off the ground. You don't necessarily have to have a team together or even an idea before applying to Entrepreneur First, as they select people they believe have the right talent. Those who are successful go on to spend six months developing a business and making it grow as quickly as possible.
www.joinef.com

Oxygen Accelerator
This established tech accelerator runs intensive 13 week programmes designed to make tech start-ups with big ideas a success. Support includes an initial investment from Oxygen, access to more than 150 mentors, collaborative office space and a demo day for you to present your business to a group of handpicked investors.
www.oxygenaccelerator.com

Wayra
Telefónica's start-up accelerator, Wayra offers initial funding to start-ups and provides mentors, desk space and the opportunity to work with Telefónica's global businesses. They focus on digital start-ups that have the

capability to have a positive impact on society.
www.wayra.co/uk

Seedcamp

This accelerator provides a variety of support and masterclasses, desk space at the Google Campus and access to a Founder's Pack in exchange for 3% equity in your business.
www.seedcamp.com

Photo: *deathtothestockphoto.com*

Networking

Business clubs

The Hospital Club

Inside a renovated Covent Garden hospital, The Hospital Club is a members club attracting creatives and entrepreneurs. As well as providing cool spaces to set yourself up with a laptop, there are regular members-only networking and social events, an online platform to meet and message other members and access to equally trendy reciprocal clubs in locations across the world.
www.thehospitalclub.com

B.Hive

This business club for women has regular networking and wellbeing events and access to stylish B.Hive lounges, iMacs and a peaceful courtyard.
www.bhiveclub.com

The Oyster Club

This club runs different types of networking events depending on your interests, from networking dinners and breakfast meetings to workshops.
www.theoysterclub.co.uk

Business Junction

This large club registers whole companies as clients, meaning any member of a company can attend the hundreds of networking events, breakfasts and lunches put on every year.
www.businessjunction.co.uk

Century Club

More of a social club than a business club, this Shaftesbury Avenue private members venue is frequented by those working in the media and in the performing arts. There are bars, a restaurant, a games room and a roof terrace.
www.centuryclub.co.uk

Institute of Directors

This high-end business club is one of London's most famed. Benefits include a number of networking opportunities, access to airport lounges in the UK and access to meeting rooms and working spaces in hundreds of worldwide locations.
www.iod.com

London Chamber of Commerce (LCC)

Joining the LCC gives members access to business support services, a members lounge and a busy calendar of networking events.
www.londonchamber.co.uk

The Supper Club

This exclusive private member club is for CEOs and founders of businesses with more than £1million turnover. Members regularly meet over supper or at social events to network and exchange ideas.
www.preludegroup.co.uk/what-we-do/the-supper-club

Networking gatherings

Silicon Drinkabout

This weekly meeting for start-ups is all about getting like-minded people together to relax at the end of the working week. It also has connections with a larger global movement.
www.silicondrinkabout.com

MiniBar

Held on the last Friday of every month, a huge crowd of web and tech entrepreneurs gather to drink beer, chat and watch showcase presentations by a handful of new start-ups.
www.meetup.com/minibar

London OpenCoffee Meetup

This group of entrepreneurs meets every Thursday morning for an informal catch-up. The group's mailing list also helps members keep in touch with news from the community.
www.meetup.com/londonocc

London Social Media

This monthly Friday morning meeting with free coffee is for Londoners interested in social media. Participants range from entrepreneurs and freelancers to marketing executives and senior managers.
www.socialmediacafe.co.uk

O2 Workshop

This store on Tottenham Court Road is no ordinary O2 mobile phone shop. As well as running weekly seminars and networking events, the O2 Workshop also offers drop-in workstations for flexibly working entrepreneurs.
www.o2.co.uk/business/tottenhamcourtroad

Google Campus events

As London's centre for all things start-up, Google Campus has a packed events calendar, with events on most nights of the week accompanied by free beer and soft drinks.
www.campus.co/london

Startup Digest

The London edition of this online platform has a regularly updated calendar of events aimed at start-up companies. You can also sign-up for a weekly email about the latest events.
www.startupdigest.com/digests/london

ThinkingBob

www.thinkingbob.co.uk

Photo: TechHub

Working in London: Events

With a number of large expo spaces and an international reputation for business, London has an impressive events calendar for those wanting to network, discuss new business initiatives and learn from established entrepreneurs and companies.

January

LeanCamp
This 'unconference' is all about lean methodology and strikes a balance between a conference and a gathering of like-minded people, with even the conference agenda being crowdsourced.
www.leancamp.co

February

Finovate
The London edition of this conference takes place every winter and is ideal for tech and financial start-ups.
www.finovate.com

The Franchise Show
An exhibition and series of seminars with franchising opportunities and advice on how to fund dream businesses.
www.thefranchiseshow.co.uk

March

The Guardian Changing Media Summit
A conference for anyone working in or with the media, run by the UK's most influential newspaper in the world of media.
www.theguardian.com/media-network/changing-media-summit

Fast Growth Forum
An annual conference to help start-ups grow, with impressive line-ups of successful founders and facilitated one-to-one meetings with experts and peers.
www.fastgrowthforum.com

QCon
A conference for developers and software innovators.
www.qconlondon.com

Startup Weekend London
This is global entrepreneurship movement powered by Google for Entrepreneurs, where you develop your business idea over a weekend with a team of experts. There are usually a few London events per year.
www.up.co/communities/uk/london/startup-weekend/events

April

London Book Fair
A trade fair for those in the world of publishing, where hundreds of deals for rights and distribution are struck every year.
www.londonbookfair.co.uk

FailCon
A conference designed to help technology entrepreneurs lose the fear of failure.
europe.thefailcon.com

Big Data Week
This global event has events in London including hackathons, debates and networking functions about data in the commercial, financial, social and technological sectors.
www.bigdataweek.com

Property Investor and Homebuyer Show
A long-running conference for those interested in investing in property.
www.propertyinvestor.co.uk

Natural and Organic Products Show
The largest trade-only show in Europe for those looking to source or supply natural or organic food and health products.
www.naturalproducts.co.uk

Marketing Week Live
The show for marketing professionals and those wanting to find out more about the latest trends in marketing.
www.marketingweeklive.co.uk

May

Business Startup Show
A large show of exhibits, masterclasses and networking opportunities with entrepreneurs at all stages of their journey.
www.bstartup.com

Decoded Fashion London: summit and hackathon
This annual event is about bringing together the best tech innovations from around the world and applying it to the worlds of fashion, beauty and retail. Start-ups in related industries can also apply to be showcased at the event.
www.decodedfashion.com

Digital Shoreditch
A festival for tech, creative and entrepreneurial talent in the hip start-up neighbourhood of Shoreditch.
www.digitalshoreditch.com

Going Global
An exhibition for those looking to expand their businesses overseas.
www.goinggloballive.co.uk

June

London Festival of Architecture

This month-long celebration of architectural experimentation brings together cultural and academic institutions, professionals and students for installations, exhibitions, talks and debates. It's the ideal stomping ground for those looking to network with industry movers and shakers.
londonfestivalofarchitecture.org

London Technology Week

A week of events across the city from workshops and face-to-face investor meetings, to pitching competitions and hackathons.
www.londontechnologyweek.co.uk

July

Electronic Visualisation and the Arts (EVA)

EVA London is for people interested in new technologies to network and discuss ideas on the application of visualisation technologies, particularly in art, music and dance.
www.eva-london.org

August

Computational Intelligence Unconference (CCIUK)

This unconference, an informal non-profit self-organising event, is all about evolutionary algorithms and other techniques which give machines capabilities similar to humans.
www.ciunconference.org

Nine Worlds Geekfest

This annual conference about gaming, fandom and geek culture includes opportunities to learn how to code for free.
www.nineworlds.co.uk

September

London Design Festival

An annual show for those who live, breathe and work the world of design, usually accompanied by some impressive installations.
www.londondesignfestival.com

London Startup Week

A free, five day celebration of entrepreneurship, with talks and events led by local entrepreneurs across the city.
london.startupweek.co

Photo: London Book Fair

Over the Air

A celebration of technology and creativity and a 'festival of all things hackable', this two day event involves lightning talks, workshops and 36 hours of hacking. Great for mobile and tech start-ups, and those who want to learn more about technology trends.
www.overtheair.org

The Food Entrepreneur Show

A conference and exhibition for those who have innovative foodie ideas they want to bring into fruition.
www.foodentrepreneurshow.co.uk

100% Design

The UK's largest design trade event, with installations, seminars and product showcases.
www.100percentdesign.co.uk

October

WIRED

Hosting a series of events throughout the year, culminating in an annual summit, WIRED is all about identifying the newest ideas and trends. It's a place where innovators, inventors and entrepreneurs come together, and there are usually big name speakers in the line-up.
www.wiredevent.co.uk

IP Expo Europe

The show for those who want to explore cloud and IT infrastructure for their business.
www.ipexpoeurope.com

November

World Travel Market

The place to be for travel professionals, attended by 50,000 people in related industries and generating £2.5billion in new business every year.
www.wtmlondon.com

Social Media Week

This global conference has its London outing every September and is ideal for social media start-ups and any business looking to make more of current social media trends.
www.socialmediaweek.org/london

NOAH London

This notable conference for later stage start-ups connects entrepreneurs with potential funding opportunities and ideas for business growth.
www.noah-conference.com

Apps World

A conference for app developers and entrepreneurs.
www.apps-world.net/europe

Silicon Valley Comes to the UK (SV2UK)

An annual series of events in London and other UK cities to bring together early stage investors and entrepreneurs with Silicon Valley experts to discuss creating and funding the most innovative new technologies. There is also a 'Scale Up Club' for CEOs who are looking to broaden their businesses.
www.svc2uk.com

December

Lean Startup Machine

A three-day workshop on building a successful business, the event organisers also run regular events throughout the year.
www.qconlondon.com

See also: London key dates for non-work events, starting on page 86

Many co-working spaces run regular events; find out more about co-working spaces in London from page 126

Just go out there and do what you have to do.

I just pick a Tube stop I like
the sound of, get off
and see what's there.

Jess Williamson
Director at Techstars

Tell us about your background.
I'm originally from California. I spent a few years in Chicago for university, then studied in Edinburgh. While I was living in Edinburgh, I fell in love with the UK. I had to go back to the US to finish my degree, but I ultimately decided to move back over to Scotland, doing a master's degree as a way of getting a work visa to stay in the country. I lived in Scotland for a few more years and joined a few different start-ups there, before getting convinced to move to Cambridge to run an accelerator called Springboard. I wound up moving to London after Springboard merged with Techstars, and I'm currently the director for one of our Techstars programmes, focused on financial technologies, and partnered with Barclays.

What drew you towards working with start-ups?
Coming from California, people often assume I got involved in Silicon Valley in some way, but this isn't the case at all. My Dad was involved in running a software company, which I thought was really boring when I was little — sorry Dad! All I knew was that I wanted to do something totally different, and then I accidentally fell into the start-up world when I was in Edinburgh. There was a society at the university called iCUE offering a subsidised trip to Brussels, and since I love to travel and it would cost me just £35 to go to Belgium, I decided to join the group. It turned out to be a group of people focused on starting their own businesses and junior enterprises at the university. So I have to credit iCUE for drawing me into the start-up scene. I guess I should be careful who offers me the next subsidised trip and what that leads to in my life! Together with the people at iCUE I started a couple of student businesses, including a textbook marketplace and a little catering company called Party Pizzas. After I finished my master's, I decided to join a start-up straight away, which was developing a new medical device to help women check themselves for breast cancer. I realised people in other start-ups were just making it up as they went along. When it came to building relationships there weren't as many right ways and things to be educated on as I expected. So I thought I would make it up as I went along too, as quickly as possible and using common sense.

Tell us about your role at Techstars.
I'm currently focused on our FinTech accelerator: Barclays Accelerator powered by Techstars. We're a small team, so my role includes a mix of

everything, from helping line up the start-up selection process and meeting with a lot of start-ups that want to enter the programme, through to structuring the three month accelerator programme and helping manage the relationship with Barclays, ensuring they're involved in the process in the best ways possible. I also work with our managing director and programme manager to run the accelerator programme smoothly. We basically work together to find any way we can to help our start-ups move forward as quickly as they can. It involves a lot of coffees, a lot of emails and a lot of late nights. Sometimes I feel like I'm living under a rock, because I love it and I get very obsessed with doing whatever I can to help the start-ups. That also means it can be hard to break away from work to do anything else, but it's not a terrible problem to have.

How does the corporate nature of an organisation like Barclays work alongside the creative spirit of start-ups?
To be perfectly honest, working with a big corporate was something I was nervous about to start with. I wasn't sure it was the best fit with my background and personality. In fact, I've been so amazed. Barclays has been a fantastic partner for us, and we are just really lucky there have been key individuals within the company who have had the right mentality for working with start-ups, which has been contagious to the people we need help from within the organisation. I used to imagine that partnerships or relationships between companies existed between actual entities, and I realise now the relationship is actually about a few human beings on one side interacting with a few human beings on the other side. We're lucky we get along very well: that helps facilitate the relationships for the start-ups, who get a tremendous amount of access into Barclays, meaning they're able to get more things done in the time they're with us.

How would you describe the people in the start-up world?
The people I work with are the best! Everybody in this industry is crazy in one way or another; I don't think any of us pretend to be normal or play by all the rules or work in boxes. We have a lot of fun together and if we didn't, I don't think the drama and the late nights would be worthwhile. We're all on the same page about that, so it's good we have a great dynamic, enjoy working with each other and enjoy solving problems together. Being around start-ups where everyone is trying to build up an interesting company, make an impact on the industry and make an impact on the world is addicting. If I don't surround myself with people like that constantly, then I feel withdrawal, wondering 'where are my interesting people doing crazy things and not worrying about what people think of them?' It's a fun environment and I feel really lucky to be there.

<u>How does the start-up lifestyle differ from the existence of other Londoners?</u>

When you're outside the start-up scene, it's very easy to think it doesn't exist or to think it's just this group of young, hipster techies. A lot of people's worlds don't touch it. When you're in the start-up scene, I think it becomes hard to remember that anything else exists. We're such a large community in our big bubble, it's difficult to remember what normal people are like. You don't come across so many people who leave the office at a predictable time, people who don't take an interest in what phone you have, or people who don't get emotional about new Gmail features, or join in a Skype vs Hangout vs new video conferencing system debate. I do think it's easy to get obsessed with all these new things that sometimes don't make a big impact on your life, so I try to be careful to focus on the big picture and realise what's actually meaningful. But when you're in the start-up scene, you don't see a lot else. People get sucked in and then don't remember what prior life was like.

<u>Why is London's tech start-up scene so successful?</u>

I think London is strong across technical skills, business skills and design skills. Over the last two years I have gotten hugely sucked in to the FinTech side of things and I've realised start-ups across financial services are so broad. I originally thought of FinTech as being one small piece of the London ecosystem, but now I think it's one giant piece with extremely blurry edges; it's not exactly clear cut where FinTech ends and where other industries begin. FinTech can overlap with social, gaming, a lot of consumer businesses, a variety of B2B software and even the construction industry, for example. I think London is special for having both the banks the FinTech companies need as customers, but also having regulatory bodies and key government organisations who care, listen and want to continue to make London and the UK successful on a global scale. So whenever start-ups encounter problems with bureaucracy or regulation, at least people are willing to listen and figure out how to change things to trigger success. It's rare to find a city that has so many of these elements all in one place. At the same time, when I lived in the Edinburgh start-up community, I was amazed and really obsessed with the strength of the start-ups and the talent in the city. Cambridge is fantastic too for people looking at hardware and the Internet of Things, and great companies are coming out of places like Newcastle, Manchester and Glasgow. So while London is my home now, I don't want to be so obsessed that I forget all the other places in the UK. I don't want to become one of the folks in the London bubble that people can resent when they're living outside of it.

<u>Is there an innovation you're particularly excited about at the moment?</u>
Something people don't always appreciate is how companies based in London are able to have a huge impact on other parts of the world. A good demonstration of this is a company we invested in called DoPay, which is focusing on countries where the economy is highly cash based and a very high percentage of residents are unbanked, without access to traditional financial services. DoPay is banking the unbanked, creating ways to bring people out of that cash cycle and giving them access to financial services for the first time. The company is starting in Egypt, where the vast majority of the population has jobs but no bank account. Rather than paying everyone each month or each week in envelopes full of cash, they're intervening at the point of payroll, and helping companies transition to issuing pre-paid debit cards with employees' salaries paid onto those debit cards. People can then withdraw money from an ATM in cash when they need it, or they have the ability to purchase things online. Ultimately, they're storing money on their debit card rather than storing cash under a mattress. This all really helps move the economy forward, it reduces fraud and theft, and it mitigates the high overheads involved in managing a payroll that's super cash based. I think it will be really exciting to see where DoPay winds up a year or two from now. There are so many companies we've worked with that are based in London and are demonstrating the huge opportunities there are for making global impact. It's really exciting.

<u>Where is your favourite place to work in London?</u>
My favourite place at the moment — and I'm quite fickle — is our Barclays accelerator office in Whitechapel. We have tonnes of space so we're really lucky, but it's mostly because of the energy I get from seeing people when I walk in the front door. The office entrance is through the hip café — Foxcroft & Ginger — downstairs, so it's great being able to order a flat white and a muffin or croissant as I walk through the door, then walking into the office and being greeted by tonnes of people. Saying hi to everyone, getting morning hugs, seeing smiles all round, getting people's news, hearing updates on progress and giving high fives: it's just very energising. While I do love to work from cafés, I don't get the same energy and buzz as I do walking into a room of people I like. We're like a tight-knit family. I might spend a day a month working somewhere else for peace and quiet, but our office is definitely my favourite place to work.

<u>Any exciting career plans in the pipeline?</u>
Yes, but you'll have to stay tuned! I'm definitely staying with Techstars and FinTech, but there might be more news soon…

<u>What made you choose the UK when you first moved there as a student?</u>
I often say I picked Edinburgh out of a hat. I knew I wanted to go somewhere far away. My Spanish wasn't good enough to think about going to a Spanish speaking country and I was afraid I wouldn't make real friends with people if I couldn't communicate authentically as myself, so I decided I wanted an English speaking country. My older sister had studied in Australia which was great, but as the younger sister, I wanted a country of my own! When I was 11 I'd been on a family trip to London, so I felt like London had already been 'done' and it wouldn't be my own city. I heard people mention this place called Scotland, and people had reported having good experiences. I knew absolutely nothing about the place before I went. I also found out one of my grandparents I hadn't met had been Scottish. In no way did I go to Scotland to find my roots, but as I was already leaning towards Scotland, it felt like a nice coincidence to have a family connection. I still remember the taxi ride from the airport to my dorm and I remember feeling like I was in a medieval city: all the buildings were so old. I'd imagined there would be one old building once in a while mixed into the city; I had no appreciation for the fact Edinburgh is so well preserved and so beautiful. It just felt magical living in a place like that.

<u>How did you adapt to London life?</u>
I was very resistant about moving to London. I thought it was too big a city and I didn't think I would like it there. I'm more used to being in smaller cities and having access to major centres like London. I danced in and out of London from Cambridge for a while, spending three months at a time in the city when we were running accelerator programmes. I tested living in a few different areas of London for those chunks of time, and each one really sucked! So I ruled out London for a while, deciding to stay in Cambridge for as long as possible, commuting to London — even if it was a little over two hours each way — or sleeping on friends' couches from Monday to Friday for several weeks at a time. Now I've realised life in London really depends on which part of the city you call your home and which part you call your office, and I've found an area to live in that works really well for me. Now I'm a London person; I've embraced the city and I'm happy.

<u>Tell us about the area you work in.</u>
I typically tell people Whitechapel is up-and-coming, with an emphasis on the 'coming'! It's a fun place because it's in transition. Ever since we've opened our doors early in 2014, we've seen the neighbourhood change. We used to call Fridays 'Dirty Burger Fridays' because we were so excited there was a new restaurant called Dirty Burger / Chicken Shop, so we would go for cheeseburgers and onion rings whenever we had time on a Friday. It's not the healthiest habit or routine to establish, but it was good for a while.

To be honest, I don't often leave the office for lunch, but I'm trying to get better at going outside. One of the guys I work with pointed out the other day there are two new coffee shops. Two new coffee shops in Whitechapel — this is gentrification in action! Traditionally, however, the area has a high immigrant population, particularly Bangladeshi. So if anyone's looking to live or work from the area, I sure hope they like samosas and biryani. You can have all the South Asian food you like in Whitechapel. I was so excited to see a Mexican restaurant spring up in the area, but Mexican Grille is definitely run by a South Asian family, and all the Mexican food has an Asian spice somehow infused into it. I think it's hilarious and quite a cool combination, but other people expecting authentic Mexican food aren't as amazed by it as I am!

Which London neighbourhoods have you lived in before settling into your current home?
Whenever I moved my life temporarily to London from Cambridge, I would have to find affordable — in other words cheap — short-term accommodation. Anyone who's lived in London knows that finding a three to four month contract on the cheap doesn't always go so well! My first experience of this was in Mile End. I helped our start-ups find housing and threw myself in with them into our Mile End property, but unfortunately we had some unwanted tenants in the form of cockroaches; a battle we never managed to win with our landlord. For the next accelerator programme, I found temporary accommodation in Drayton Park, near Arsenal. The area itself was fine, but the flat was pretty nondescript and there were no local restaurants, bars and cafés that I wanted to go and enjoy spending time in. Then I lived, amazingly, really centrally by Holborn station in a five person place with four randoms, who were actually great. We had no communal living space, so while the location was much improved, I realised having a community space was much more important to me than I originally expected. And the landlord kept inviting me on holiday with him and turning up unannounced, trying to get social dates in the calendar. Having a creepy landlord was really stressful...

Oh no! What happened next?
I discovered Islington! Now I live halfway between Angel and Highbury & Islington. It's just the best. For me it was like finding a miniature Cambridge or a small version of Edinburgh within London. I realised these neighbourhoods do exist; you just have to find the one that's right for you. I can't say enough good things about the area. I have four housemates who are fantastic, I live by more restaurants than I could probably eat at in my lifetime, and there are endless cafés that I would happily spend afternoons in. I just think Islington is the answer for everyone! Even though I know in reality everyone has different criteria for the kind of neighbourhood they're looking for.

Where do you go out in your spare time?

Most of the time, I just wander aimlessly and see where I wind up. I go out my front door and my housemates ask me where I'm going. Usually I have no idea! All I know is that I'm going out the front door and then I'll figure the rest out from there. The only place where I've repeatedly ended up is Camden Passage. It was so magical when I first discovered it. It's a little pedestrianised area full of restaurants and cafés and there are usually hanging flowers that are in bloom. You feel transported into a picture perfect world out of somebody's painting. I felt like I'd gotten off the plane and found myself on a little street in France or some other European country. I couldn't believe it was only five minutes away from where I live.

Where do you rate for food in the area?

The Elk in the Woods does delicious brunches and if it's warm outside, I just love sitting at the tables outdoors because you can people-watch all day long, whether you're with friends or by yourself. If I can't get a table there then right across the street is an Austrian place called Kipferl. You can get delicious coffee and croissants, or a breakfast fry-up with eggs, potatoes and sausages. I've kind of ignored The Breakfast Club, which is further up the road. There's usually a giant queue for The Breakfast Club and I just don't understand why people don't go to The Elk in the Woods instead. I think that's how I first discovered it; we were waiting in line for The Breakfast Club and I was getting impatient thinking there must be somewhere else around here. Then I saw this menu that offered things like blueberry pancakes with maple syrup, pear and bacon; everything just sounded irresistible. Apart from there, I don't have a lot of go-to places; I just try to get myself out the front door and wander around until I find somewhere I want to spend some time.

What advice do you have for people who want to wander aimlessly but don't know where to start?

When I lived in Chicago, every week or two my friends and I used to pick a different train stop to get off at, then we'd just wander around until we found a restaurant that we were excited about. It led to so many good adventures that I've transferred that way of life to my London outings. I don't have a specific group of friends that I do this with, but I just pick a Tube stop I like the sound of, get off and see what's there. I did that once with Elephant & Castle; it sounds a bit grander than it is in real life, so that's probably not the best place to start! But it's about not being afraid to have an unplanned exploration. The worst case scenario is that you pick a place you don't like, so you get back on the train and pick another one. Maybe if you've read up a bit more and have picked out a place you want to eat at, then don't just keep your adventures to that restaurant or that café. Put your map away, have a look around afterwards and just see what happens. As long as you've got the Citymapper app to ultimately get you back to where you need to go at the end of the night, it's fine. I think too many people feel a social pressure to have a concrete answer when somebody asks where they're going. I just say: "I don't know — where should I go?" I think I've always been a bit resistant to having a plan!

Where do you go during free evenings?

My local pub is The Bull. I haven't gone there often enough, but sometimes when I just feel like going out — even if none of my housemates are coming with me — I'll just go to The Bull by myself to feel like I've had a little adventure. I also love going to comedy shows, and there's a pub not too far away — The Camden Head — that does free comedy every single night at 8pm. I don't make tonnes of commitments with friends during the week, as I'm always nervous I'm going to end up working late and I don't want to disappoint people. So my plans are usually last minute: if I'm out of the office and the sun's still up, I'll decide to go and do something. I really like seeing new places more than I like revisiting the same ones over and over. The only exception is a pub near our office called Blind Beggar, which becomes a gathering place for us if we're going out after work on a Friday evening. I'd happily go somewhere new, but they do a great hotdog and chips there, so I've gotten hooked.

Where's the most bizarre place you've come across in London?

The strangest thing I've experienced in London is a nightclub called The Box in Soho. Anyone who's been to The Box will understand. Anyone who hasn't been probably doesn't need to go! It's very chichi and hard to get into, but I had a last-minute invitation and decided to go. Some friends picked me up in a taxi at a petrol station while I was eating fried chicken and chips, then whisked me away to this club. It was a very funny experience because I'm sure we were dancing on chairs and drinking the most expensive bottles of champagne I've had in my life, but the acts on stage are meant to shock you and make you feel uncomfortable. They were definitely successful!

Where do you find inspiration for making the most of London's many offerings?

Anyone who lives in London will know what it's like on Tuesdays, when people are trying to stuff this magazine in your face. I always used to say "No thank you!" But I've recently resolved to develop some hobbies and have more of a personal life. I realised this magazine coming out on Tuesdays is Time Out London, and that it's full of awesome things happening in the city, from restaurant openings to festivals and events. So I've started saying "yes, thank you" instead. For me, it's a mix of taking recommendations from what Time Out says and just generally feeling more inspired to keep my eyes open to all the cool things happening in town. In particular, I'm a fan of dim sum, so sometimes I'll just wander through Chinatown and pick different restaurants where I can get dumplings. I think that's my main consistent calling. Other than that, I'm open to whatever funky new things are happening.

What would your perfect weekend in London entail?
I'd wake up before noon; I always congratulate myself if I wake up before noon on the weekend! It would be sunny, of course, on my perfect day. I'd head out by myself and have an unplanned and unstructured wander. I'd find somewhere for a coffee; it has to be a café with a nice barista because I think service makes such a difference. I just love brunch, so I'd go and meet some friends for brunch: somewhere new that I've never been to before and that's got an interesting vibe to it. I love places that are converted: maybe we'll check out one of the converted toilets that's now a café, like the Attendant or WC. I would probably have no plans for the rest of the day, but at brunch one of my friends would have an awesome suggestion of a festival or event to go to for the afternoon. Then we'd have a delicious dinner on the go from a street vendor and then hit a comedy show at night. My favourite nightclub, which I'm definitely not supposed to confess, is Infernos in Clapham. I've been twice. People had set my expectations really low, but I loved it both times and I'm dying to go back, but nobody will accept my invitation! But on my perfect day, my friends would humour me and we'd go to Infernos, followed by the classic getting-a-kebab-at-3am thing, because everywhere else is closed at that time. Then we'd magically get home by night bus or a cheap Uber taxi.

What is London's best quality?
There's always somewhere new to explore. Always. Each neighbourhood is a bit different, and there are always new activities, events, pop-ups and festivals. If you enjoy new things, random adventures, and wandering, you'll have a blast and you'll never stop discovering new places.

Is there anything you'd change about London?
I wish we'd talk to each other a bit more on the underground: I know each of us has the power to influence change like that. I wish rush hour wasn't quite so cramped. And I wish there was something interesting to look at while you're stuck squished on the Tube smelling someone's armpit and counting down until you get to your station. I don't know what that would be, but we could probably improve the quality of at least half an hour in everyone's day, if we figured out how to improve that user journey in some way that doesn't involve people playing Candy Crush.

Have you developed any tactics for coping with public transport during rush hour?
I have made a conscious effort recently to listen to more music, and I've realised I'm in a much better mood if I spend more of my day listening to music generally. So I've started putting on my headphones as I'm travelling into the office and pressing random, which plays a combination of Now 60 to Now 70 albums, and all the other cheesy pop music that I've acquired over the years! I've definitely enjoyed having more music in my life.

What sound do you associate with London?
The sound of construction. There's construction everywhere you go. I'm grateful there's no annoying noise by my flat or near my office, but everywhere in between seems to have the sound of construction. I'm a bit more oblivious to it with my headphones on nowadays!

What smell do you associate with London?
The general pub aroma of beer mixed with hot warm winter comfort food — things like steak and ale pie, fish and chips, and shepherd's pie — is a familiar London smell for me.

Have you had any random but 'totally London' experiences?
Londoners love going to summertime festivals, whether they're in a city park or somewhere outside London. On a whim I accepted an invitation to join some friends at Wilderness Festival, near Oxford. I was travelling there by myself and on the train I overheard a woman saying she didn't have tent because she was going to sleep under the stars on her mattress. There was a guy giving her a hard time, saying he'd been to Wilderness before and that he didn't think it was good idea. She responded that she didn't have a tent, so she had no choice. Randomly and without having spoken to her before, I told her I had a tent and if she needed somewhere to stay, she could stay with me. So she wound up staying with me in my little tent for three nights and we had such a blast! There were endless weird and wonderful things at Wilderness Festival, which I think anyone going to a festival can attest to. It mostly involves glitter and sequins and costumes that don't make sense. Everyone suddenly feels like part of the same family, and you end up doing things like listening to talks by people describing their experience of becoming cult leaders. I had a wonderful time there; it felt like a suspended reality. It was the first time I'd given this British festival tradition a try, and it was great.

What is the current trend in London?
The 'hipster' word gets thrown around a lot. There is a trend towards things that feel genuinely funky, hip, cool, underground, a bit warehousey and a bit dingy, but at the same time that don't look like they're trying too

hard. If it looks like they're trying too hard, then they get labelled 'hipster' in a bad way. If they get it just right, where they're accidentally just really cool and funky, then they're 'hip' in a good way. There's definitely a trend in London towards experiences that feel authentically hip. Even if things are highly engineered in the background — the walls are painted to look cracked or the floors are damaged to look grungy — I still think there are more experiences being created that are of this vibe. As long as it doesn't feel try-hard, it's ok. I'm guilty; I like it and I generally don't mind the whole hipster thing.

What's the latest achievement you're most proud of?
I recently turned 30, and once upon a time I created a list of 30 things to do before I reached that age. I wasn't making a huge amount of progress with completing the list, so my best friend's gift to me was to project manage my completion of the list. One of my favourite things was my guitar lesson. I just wanted to make a start and learn four chords; who knows what's next, maybe the triangle!

How would your friends describe you?
Probably the first thing they'd tell you is that I'm obsessed with the colour blue. I don't really know why I like blue so much, but even my Twitter handle is @jessinblue. They would probably say I have an insane amount of energy. It's usually true, but I do get tired as well; they probably just don't see me when I'm too exhausted to meet up. They might say I'm horrible with directions and that I seem to just go exploring. Having said that out loud, my aimless wandering is probably a technique I've developed to compensate for the fact I suck with directions! And they might tell you that I'm fairly spontaneous and unplanned, but that I tend to come back at the end of it with quite funny stories. I like to have adventures that are worthy of laughing at later: stories for the very hypothetical grandchildren!

Jess's London

Places to visit

Camden Passage
N1 8EA
camdenpassageislington.co.uk
Tube: Angel

Wilderness Festival
www.wildernessfestival.com

Eating and drinking

Attendant
27a Foley Street W1W 6DY
+44 (0)207 637 3794
info@the-attendant.com
www.the-attendant.com
Tube: Goodge Street

Chinatown
Gerrard Street W1D
www.chinatownlondon.org
Tube: Leicester Square

Dirty Burger/Chicken Shop
27a Mile End Road E1 4TP
+44 (0)203 727 6165
www.eatdirtyburger.com/
whitechapel
www.chickenshop.com/
whitechapel
Rail: Whitechapel

Foxcroft & Ginger
Whitechapel
69-79 Mile End Road E1 4TT
www.foxcroftandginger.co.uk
Tube: Stepney Green

Infernos
146 Clapham High Street SW4
7UH
+44 (0)207 720 7633
www.infernos.co.uk
Tube: Clapham Common

Kipferl Islington
20 Camden Passage N1 8ED
+44 (0)207 704 1555
www.kipferl.co.uk
Tube: Angel

Mexican Grille
194 Mile End Rd E1 4LJ
+44 (0)203 638 0799
info@mexicangrille.co.uk
www.mexicangrille.co.uk
Tube: Stepney Green

The Box
11-12 Walker's Court W1F 0SD
+44 (0)207 434 4374
www.theboxsoho.com
Tube: Piccadilly Circus

The Bull
100 Upper Street N1 0NP
+44 (0)207 354 9174
www.thebullislington.co.uk
Tube: Angel

The Camden Head
2 Camden Walk N1 8DY
+44 (0)207 359 0851
camden.head.5101@
spiritpubcompany.com
www.camden-head.co.uk
Tube: Angel

The Elk in the Woods
37-39 Camden Passage N1 8EA
+44 (0)207 226 3535
info@the-elk-in-the-woods.co.uk
www.the-elk-in-the-woods.co.uk
Tube: Angel

WC
Clapham Common South Side
SW4 7AA
+44 (0)207 622 5502
info@wcclapham.co.uk
www.wcclapham.co.uk
Tube: Clapham Common

See also:
Citymapper app
www.citymapper.com
**Time Out London (free
magazine out every Tuesday)**
www.timeout.com/london
Uber app
www.uber.com

Find out more about Jess Williamson
at www.techstars.com or on Twitter
@JessinBlue

Having a drink at The Hoxton hotel in Shoreditch

Photo: The Hoxton

chapter 3

Live

*Retailers with flair,
a haven for artists
and some nice pillows
to put your head on.*

Live in London

Life in London is all about working hard and playing harder. There's no doubt the pressure is on in this global city and international centre for trade and politics. But where there's business, there are the amenities to serve the working population, and in London you're truly spoiled for choice. You can't go far without finding a traditional pub, a design conscious café, or a hotel with creative flair. And that's just for starters.

In fact, Brits have a love affair with eating out, and an estimated 19 million people eat out at least once a week in the UK. London itself has around 150 new restaurant openings every year. One of the things Londoners love about the city is the combination of cultures living there, and there are more than 300 languages spoken in the city. This multiculturalism that Londoners adore is also reflected in London's thriving ethnic food industry and the local pockets in London that have been synonymous with specific cultures, from the Turkish food in Harringay's Green Lanes, to Latin American flavours in Elephant & Castle and Indian food in Tooting. Long gone are the days of bland fish and chips or daily meat and three veg dinners!

London's newest amenities are styled in the industrial-chic genre, appealing to those into current trends and unpolished textures. From hanging pendant lights in hotel lobbies to pop-up shops in shipping containers, keeping things a little rough around the edges signifies London's modish vibe and ultimately, the city's prevalent creativity that's constantly demanding to be seen against the dominance of the corporate world.

This chapter is all about eating, drinking, shopping, sleeping and generally living in London. We take you to some of the city's greatest places to stay, from the most elegant hotels to the quirkiest boutique crash pads. If you want your London visit to become a more permanent thing, we also help you navigate the world of finding the perfect apartment or flat share. When you're hungry, we help you find a meal for every occasion, whether you want a coffee and cake while stroking a cat, or a meal in a secret pop-up location. If you want to shop til you drop, London is definitely the place for you, and we steer you in the direction of locally loved boutiques and creative havens for those working in the arts.

Breakfast

The Breakfast Club

This 80s-inspired hangout is a little retro and most certainly trendy; it's become such a hit with Londoners, there are now several branches across the city. Although The Breakfast Club serves food throughout the day, the breakfasts of its namesake are especially epic, with traditional British fry-ups found in several formations, huge stacks of pancakes and breakfast burritos.

www.thebreakfastclubcafes.com

NOPI

One of the newest additions to the London dining scene by celebrated chef Yotam Ottolenghi, NOPI is another triumph of Ottolenghi's Middle Eastern upbringing and his fresher than fresh style. Breakfasts at NOPI can be as simple as pastries and granola, or as exotic as the black rice with coconut milk or the shakshuka (braised eggs, tomato sauce and smoked labneh).

21-22 Warwick Street W1B 5NE
+44 (0)207 494 9584
contact@nopi-restaurant.com
www.nopi-restaurant.com
Tube: Piccadilly Circus

Kopapa

Meaning 'gathering place' in Maori, Kopapa's name is a nod to New Zealander chef Peter Gordon's Maori heritage. Breakfasts and brunches at Kopapa are fusion events, with everything from Turkish eggs to spiced banana French toast on the menu.

32-34 Monmouth Street WC2H 9HA
+44 (0)207 240 6076
www.kopapa.co.uk
Tube: Covent Garden

Habanera

Serving a weekday breakfast and a weekend brunch, all of Habanera's ingredients are sourced from local suppliers, making it a true neighbourhood gem. Breakfast items are typically Mexican and a little inventive, including breakfast tacos, Mexican fish and chips and the option for bottomless mimosas at the weekend.

280 Uxbridge Road W12 7JA
+44 (0)208 001 4887
hola@habanera.co.uk
www.habanera.co.uk
Tube: Shepherd's Bush Market

Parlour

In this hidden-away corner of north west London, Parlour has a trendy but low-key neighbourhood vibe. Chill-out with a morning tea and toast or a full-on plate of breakfast staples; the choice is yours.

5 Regent Street NW10 5LG
+44 (0)208 969 2184
www.parlourkensal.com
Rail/Tube: Kensal Green

Arabica

Tucked away near Borough Market, Arabica started out as a food stand in the foodie haven of the market itself, before getting a permanent base nearby. Serving breakfast Thursday to Saturday, Arabica offers the sun splashed flavours of Jordan and Lebanon, with spiced porridge and flatbread with mudammas gracing the menu.

3 Rochester Walk SE1 9AF
+44 (0)203 011 5151
reserve@arabicabarandkitchen.com
www.arabicabarandkitchen.com
Rail/Tube: London Bridge

Plateau

This glass-fronted restaurant in the heart of Canary Wharf has impressive views over London's corporate skyline and is an inspiring place to visit any day of the week. The Saturday brunch, however, is something quite remarkable, when a French-inspired three course meal is served alongside free flowing Prosecco for a price just shy of £40.

4th Floor, Canada Place E14 5ER
+44 (0)207 715 7100
plateaureservations@danddlondon.com
www.plateau-restaurant.co.uk
Tube: Canary Wharf

Breakfast at NOPI

Photo: NOPI

179

Lunch

Indian YMCA

This site has been welcoming Indian students to the UK for more than 60 years. The canteen-style restaurant serves some of London's best north Indian flavours at bargain prices. It's a local favourite among office workers and Londoners who enjoy being part of one of the city's secrets.

41 Fitzroy Square W1T 6AQ
+44 (0)207 387 0411
enquiries@indianymca.org
indianymca.org
Tube: Warren Street

Geales

This Notting Hill fish and chip restaurant has been in business since 1939 and it's been a favourite with the locals ever since. The menu is a little more upscale than traditional London fish and chip joints, making it an ideal choice for a sit-down meal. The two or three course lunch menu is especially reasonably priced.

2 Farmer Street W8 7SN
+44 (0)207 727 7528
info@geales.com
www.geales.com
Tube: Notting Hill Gate

Bao

This Taiwanese eatery specialises in steamed buns made with milk, filled with gorgeous braised pork or other soy marinated meats. The prices are cheap, service is fast, and a compelling selection of teas and other beverages make it more than just a place for a super-quick bite.

53 Lexington Street W1F 9AS
www.baolondon.com
Tube: Oxford Circus

tibits

This elegantly styled vegetarian restaurant is found in a pedestrianised street off Regent Street just a stone's throw from the Ice Bar. Help yourself to a mix of hot and cold dishes from the central bank: the selection on offer is as appealing to non-veggies. The deal is that you weigh your plate after filling it up so you only pay for what you want to eat.

12-14 Heddon Street W1B 4DA
+44 (0)207 758 4112
info@tibits.co.uk
www.tibits.co.uk
Tube: Piccadilly Circus

Franco Manca

These sourdough pizza makers use slow rising sourdough and wood burning brick ovens crafted by artisans in Napoli. Franco Manca has won over so many Londoners since humble beginnings in Brixton Market, they've now opened up branches across London. The flavoursome toppings include pecorino, buffalo ricotta, home-cured ham and organic chorizo.

www.francomanca.co.uk

Camino

This King's Cross tapas bar is hidden away in a courtyard, transporting diners away from the sometimes too-busy main drag. The quality of the tapas is top-notch, with the likes of exquisitely prepared manchego with huevos con calabaza, creamy croquetas and patatas bravas making for a delicious sharer meal. There are sister restaurants in Blackfriars and Monument too.

3 Varnishers Yard, The Regent's Quarter N1 9FD
+44 (0)207 841 7330
www.camino.uk.com
Rail/Tube: King's Cross

The Marmaris

This may look like a bog standard kebab shop, but look beyond the nondescript shop front and discover some of the best Turkish flavours in south London. A small sit-down restaurant at the back allows for a more leisurely meal. Favourites include the warm hummus and toasty pitta bread, grilled halloumi with rice and salad, and the yoghurt chicken shish. If you want to go in the evening, you can bring your own booze (BYOB).

3 Bedford Hill SW12 9ET
+44 (0)208 675 6556
Tube: Balham

SUSHISAMBA

The London edition of this Japanese-Peruvian-Brazilian restaurant is found in London's Heron Tower, offering outstanding views over London as well as impeccable cuisine. A selection of small plates makes for an ideal lunch, with dishes such as wagyu gyoza and suzuki usuzukuri (seabass sashimi) on the menu. In the evening, SUSHISAMBA turns into a swanky bar and dining room, with a range of inventive cocktails on offer.

Heron Tower, 110 Bishopsgate EC2N 4AY
+44 (0)203 640 7330
reservationslondon@sushisamba.com
www.sushisamba.com/location/london
Rail/Tube: Liverpool Street

Franco Manca's favorite sourdough pizza.

Photo: Alessandra Spairani

Dinner

Bubbledogs
Probably the only champagne and hotdog bar in London, Bubbledogs serves hotdogs in every way imaginable, along with a classy champagne and sparkling wine list. Try the Mac Daddy (with macaroni and cheese, crispy onions and bacon bits) or the Horny Dog (with corn breading, served on a stick) to experience the true range of the Bubbledogs repertoire.
70 Charlotte Street W1T 4QG
+44 (0)207 637 7770
info@bubbledogs.co.uk
www.bubbledogs.co.uk
Tube: Goodge Street

Red Dog Saloon
Barbecue is in an era of popularity in London, and our favourite is one of the more established restaurants on the scene. Found in trendy Hoxton, Red Dog Saloon specialises in ribs, pulled pork and brisket, with meats being smoked for up to 16 hours. For those with a larger than life appetite, The Devastator comes with an 18oz steak, pulled pork, bacon and cheese.
37 Hoxton Square N1 6NN
+44 (0)203 551 8014
info@reddogsaloon.co.uk
www.reddogsaloon.co.uk
Rail/Tube: Old Street

Onam
The south London neighbourhood of Tooting is well-known for its authentic and well-priced curry houses. In Onam, the furnishings are basic and there's just a smattering of tables, but the food is some of the best in the area. The cuisine is specifically from Kerala, southern India, with the Malabar chicken, masala dosa and mango lassi being among the firm favourites of the regular customers.
219 Tooting High Street SW17 0SZ
+44 (0)208 767 7655
info@onamrestaurant.co.uk
www.onamrestaurant.co.uk
Tube: Tooting Broadway

Polpo Soho
This Venetian bacaro is all about simple flavours and local wines, and it has an outstanding reputation among London's foodies. Favourites on the menu include arancini, crostini and inventively flavoured meatballs, such as spicy pork and fennel.
41 Beak Street W1F 9SB
+44 (0)207 734 4479
www.polpo.co.uk
Tube: Oxford Circus

Photos: Polpo

Pizarro

José Pizarro is practically the king of trendy Bermondsey Street, given that he always seems to be in his tapas bar, José, or his restaurant, Pizarro. While José is a tapas bar in the truest sense of the word, perfect for a snack and a drink over a sherry barrel, Pizarro at the other end of the street is ideal for sit-down dining. The menu is full of the chef's Extremadura genius, filled with the likes of acorn-fed Jamón Ibérico, salt cod and Castilian lamb.

194 Bermondsey Street SE1 3UB
+44 (0)207 378 9455
reservations@pizarrorestaurant.com
www.pizarrorestaurant.com
Rail/Tube: London Bridge

Gökyüzü

Found in London's largest Turkish community in Harringay, Gökyüzü is locally revered and is thus constantly full. Portions are huge and prices cheap, and the menu comes packed with all the expected Turkish staples, from a cacophony of mezze dishes and Turkish pizzas, to deliciously grilled meats and perfectly seasoned stews.

26-27 Grand Parade, Green Lanes N4 1LG
+44 (0)208 211 8406
info@gokyuzurestaurant.co.uk
www.gokyuzurestaurant.co.uk
Rail: Harringay Green Lanes

Viet Grill

Affectionately known by locals as the Pho Mile, Kingsland Road is the place to go for a great Vietnamese meal. Viet Grill is one of the Pho Mile's stalwarts and is a little more polished in décor than some of the other eateries in the area. The menu is filled with Vietnamese classics, from summer rolls to a huge range of pho and noodle soups.

58 Kingsland Road E2 8DP
+44 (0)207 739 6686
reservations@vietgrill.co.uk
www.vietgrill.co.uk
Rail: Hoxton

Kateh

This Persian restaurant tucked away on an elegant west London street serves some of the most raved about Iranian flavours in the city. The atmosphere is cosy and vibrant with chatter, while the food includes the likes of chargrilled meats, flavoursome stews and a range of salad and yoghurt accompaniments.

5 Warwick Place London W9 2PX
+44 (0)207 289 3393
info@katehrestaurant.co.uk
www.katehrestaurant.co.uk
Tube: Warwick Avenue

Bodo's Schloss

This wooden-clad, alpine-themed Kensington celebrity haunt is fun-loving and gimmicky in a way that people just seem to adore. The food menu comes straight from an Austrian ski resort, with staples such as schnitzel and 'The Slope Warmer' burger on offer. The brightly coloured cocktails are especially popular and become more so as the evening meal turns into a night out.

2a Kensington High Street W8 4PT
+44 (0)207 937 5506
reservations@bodosschloss.com
www.bodosschloss.com
Tube: High Street Kensington

Flesh and Buns

This Japanese restaurant with a penchant for rock and roll music is a sociable eatery where food is served fast. The specialities are the freshly steamed buns served with your choice of meats and pickled vegetables.

41 Earlham St WC2H 9LX
+44 (0)207 632 9500
www.bonedaddies.com/flesh-and-buns
Tube: Covent Garden

The Seagrass

Found inside a traditional marketside pie and mash shop, this eatery transforms into an evening restaurant from Wednesday to Saturday. Both the interior and the menu offer a slice of classical London, including dishes such as crab bisque, pigeon breast, sea bream and venison. Three courses cost just £30 and you can bring your own booze (BYOB).

Manzes, 74 Chapel Market N1 9ER
+44 (0)7902 015 200
www.theseagrassrestaurant.com
Tube: Angel

The Wild Food Café

This vegan and vegetarian café found in a tiny courtyard off the tourist tracks of Covent Garden is laid back and has a little of the free spirited feeling of the 70s. The menu is filled with organic salads, inventive burgers and pizzas, as well as fresh juices and organic and biodynamic wines and beers.

1st Floor, 14 Neal's Yard WC2H 9DP
+44 (0)207 419 2014
info@wildfoodcafe.com
www.wildfoodcafe.com
Tube: Covent Garden

Splash out

Dinner by Heston Blumenthal

This two Michelin star restaurant in Hyde Park's Mandarin Oriental is run by one of Britain's most celebrated chefs. Heston Blumenthal's use of science in his cooking has given him honorary degrees and fellowships at multiple universities and he was awarded an Order of the British Empire (OBE) in 2006 for his services to British gastronomy. A meal at Dinner is guaranteed to be an unpredictable assault on all the senses, with Blumenthal creations such as porridge with frog's legs and powdered duck breast on the menu.

Mandarin Oriental Hyde Park, 66 Knightsbridge SW1X 7LA
+44 (0)207 201 3833
molon-dinnerhb@mohg.com
www.dinnerbyheston.com
Tube: Knightsbridge

The Ivy. Photo: David Griffen

Hawksmoor

Probably the most revered steak restaurant in London, Hawksmoor painstakingly sources its meat from the best British farmers. Cuts available range from the chateaubriand to the 55-day aged D-rump, and all the expected accompaniments are on offer, from béarnaise sauce to grilled bone marrow. Hawksmoor is a favourite hangout for the suited and booted city types, but attracts meat-lovers from all walks of life. Given its popularity, there are now a few Hawksmoor restaurants across the city.

www.thehawksmoor.com

The Ivy

This newly renovated, old London institution is a favourite of those in the public eye and blends traditional elegance with modern tastes. The seasonal menu combines British favourites with international influences, with dishes such as shepherd's pie and shellfish bisque on the menu. Steeped in tradition, The Ivy is the place to go in London for time-honoured foodie traditions.

1- 5 West Street WC2H 9NQ
+44 (0)207 836 4751
www.the-ivy.co.uk
Tube: Leicester Square

Chiltern Firehouse

A relatively new favourite among London celebrities and public figures, this hotel and restaurant is found inside a former Marylebone fire station. The kitchen is headed up by the Michelin-starred Nuno Mendes and the menu is all-at-once laid back and vibrant, with dishes like Welsh lamb and monkfish cooked over pine on the menu. The restaurant area itself spills out into a secluded courtyard, making it a relaxed place to spend an evening, if you can get a table.

1 Chiltern Street W1U 7PA
+44 (0)207 073 7676
www.chilternfirehouse.com
Tube: Baker Street

La Porte des Indes

Found inside a former Edwardian ballroom, La Porte des Indes is an unexpected historical discovery in the heart of London. Opulence is the name of the game when it comes to the décor, with a huge waterfall and marble staircases found among the large jungle-like plants and Indian artefacts. The menu matches up to the interior, with an array of Pondicherry-inspired dishes on the menu such as parsee fish in banana leaves and home style goat curry.

32 Bryanston Street W1H 7EG
+44 (0)207 224 0055
www.laportedesindes.com
Tube: Marble Arch

Aqua Kyoto

Go through a moodily-lit, nightclub-esque entrance on Argyll Street and take the lift to be transported into this renowned Hong Kong group's restaurant and rooftop terrace. It feels exclusive, and indeed, the venue regularly plays host to private star-studded events. The Japanese menu is immense and offers some of the most perfectly concocted dishes in London, with the black cod and imaginative sushi rolls being firm favourites among regulars.

5th Floor, 240 Regent Street (entrance 30 Argyll Street) W1B 3BR
+44 (0)207 478 0540
www.aquakyoto.co.uk
Tube: Oxford Circus

The Ivy is the place to go in London for time-honoured foodie traditions.

The Ivy. Photo: David Griffen

Snack

Honest Burgers

The original Brixton branch of this eatery has a Bohemian vibe and some of the best burgers in town. The 35-day dry-aged steak that forms the basis of the burgers comes from well-known London butchers Ginger Pig, while there are toppings galore to suit every craving. The rosemary salted chips are almost as good as the burgers.
Unit 12, Brixton Village SW9 8PR
+44 (0)207 733 7963
www.honestburgers.co.uk
Rail/Tube: Brixton

Pizza Union

This glass-fronted Spitalfields eatery with an industrial vibe is all about the love of the pizza. Order at the counter and watch it made fresh before your eyes in record time. Reasonably priced and fresher than fresh, this is a cool spot to hang out or grab a pizza and go. If you're feeling indulgent, the Nutella and mascarpone filled pizza rings are a real treat. There's now a King's Cross branch of Pizza Union too.
25 Sandy's Row E1 7HW
info@pizzaunion.com
www.pizzaunion.com
Rail/Tube: Liverpool Street

Meat Liquor

Many flock to Meat Liquor for the burgers (who can't resist ordering the 'Dead Hippie' burger?) but this eatery has more strings to its bow. The chilli dog, mac and cheese and chicken wings are all firm favourites for a quick snack too. This place has a loyal following and there's often a queue on the pavement outside.
74 Welbeck Street W1G 0BA
info@meatliquor.com
www.meatliquor.com/london
Tube: Bond Street

E Pellicci

You can't visit London without checking out a 'greasy spoon' — those no-frills cafés serving British fry-ups. E Pellicci is an east London institution, made better by the fact it's found inside a Grade II listed building with an art deco inspired interior. Stop off any time of day for an English breakfast, fish and chips or the daily Italian specials.
332 Bethnal Green Road E2 0AG
+44 (0)207 739 4873
Tube: Bethnal Green

The 'Dead Hippie' burger at Meat Liquor is a real favorite.

Photo: Meat Liquor

Cafés

Lady Dinah's Cat Emporium

This truly original east London café is designed especially for cat lovers. The resident cats hang around and do their thing alongside patrons, who enjoy a furry cuddle or just the homely cat-crazy atmosphere. It's always best to book in advance and time slots come in 90 minute increments. The menu is full of teas, cakes and light snacks.

152-154 Bethnal Green Road, Shoreditch, London, E2 6DG
+44 (0) 2077290953
www.ladydinahs.com
Rail: Shoreditch High Street

Department of Coffee and Social Affairs

Antipodean coffee is all the rage in London and the inaugural Leather Lane branch of this small coffee chain is a great place to start. The trendy interior of exposed brickwork and reclaimed wood provides a cool setting for the carefully crafted coffee menu. The window seats are perfect for people watching on Leather Lane Market.

14-16 Leather Lane EC1N 7SU
www.departmentofcoffee.com
Tube: Chancery Lane

Flotsam & Jetsam

Found in leafy Wandsworth Common, this café has built a reputation for the eclectic brunches that accompany the coffee. Brunch items include the likes of brioche French toast topped with blood orange and dark chocolate cheesecake, and pork belly eggs benedict. The interior is styled like a foodie version of the boutiques in this well-to-do part of town, and has quickly gained a devoted following of locals.

4 Bellevue Parade SW17 7EQ
www.flotsamandjetsamcafe.co.uk
Rail: Wandsworth Common

Ginger & White

This villagey Hampstead café spills out with tables on the pavement in a European fashion, while the communal table inside is favoured by those working on laptops. Open trays of cakes and snacks on the counter give it a farmhouse feel, and various prints of the Union Jack indicate Ginger & White is proudly British. A couple of other branches have sprung up in the city given its popularity.

4a-5a Perrins Court NW3 1QS
+44 (0)207 431 9098
www.gingerandwhite.com
Tube: Hampstead

Made By Jason - Lisa Jane Photography

Afternoon tea

Sketch

This Mayfair restaurant is a whimsical affair, with different rooms proffering weird and wonderful flights of fancy. The Gallery, with plush pink chairs and humorous artwork by Turner Prize winner David Shrigley, is where the Sketch afternoon tea takes place. Delicate sandwiches come with exquisite touches, such as a fried quail's egg placed neatly on top, while scones and cakes are enticing and a little avant-garde. Be sure to visit the facilities before you leave, and prepare to have your mind blown.

9 Conduit Street W1S 2XG
+44 (0) 20 7659 4500
reservations@sketch.london
www.sketch.london
Tube: Oxford Circus

Bea's of Bloomsbury

The afternoon tea at Bea's is a low key affair in a bright, bustling café. Famed for its enticing selection of gateaux and occasion cakes, Londoners love to go for a cup of tea and a chat, or for a full blown afternoon tea on special occasions. The selection of sandwiches, scones, cupcakes and brownies is enough for a whole meal, so remember to go hungry. While the original Bea's is in Bloomsbury, there are now branches across London.

www.beasofbloomsbury.com

Mr Fogg's

This eccentric afternoon tea is an immersive experience inside the imaginary home of globetrotting hero Phileas Fogg. There's a hot air balloon, cocktails served in tea cups and other fanciful details just waiting to be discovered. The name, Mr Fogg's Tipsy Tea, gives a clue of the festivities to come. Compared to other afternoon teas, there's more of a focus on alcohol instead of tea accompanying the food, with options for bottomless tea cups of champagne or gin tea. This is a place where whole afternoons disappear in the blink of an eye.

15 Bruton Lane W1J 6JD
+44 (0)207 036 0608
greetings@mr-foggs.com
www.mr-foggs.com
Tube: Green Park

The Wolseley

This London institution dates back to the 1920s, when it was first constructed as a grand car showroom with stately Venetian and Florentine touches. Today, it's a restaurant on the hit-list of those seeking a palatial dining experience, with the afternoon tea being especially famed. Afternoon tea platters over three tiers come decked with sumptuously prepared treats, served alongside an assortment of leaf teas.

160 Piccadilly W1J 9EB
+44 (0)207 499 6996
info@thewolseley.com
www.thewolseley.com
Tube: Green Park

Photo: David Loftus

Pub food

The Clissold Arms

There's nothing quite like having a simple meal in a good old London pub. North London's Clissold Arms is proud of the fact The Kinks played their first gig there in the 1960s, and there's a room named after the band to celebrate the fact. The pub garden with fairy lights makes for a true sanctuary, while the pub plays host to many fun-packed themed evenings. On normal days, the British menu includes gastropub classics like steak and chips and chicken salads, as well as traditional roast dinners on Sundays.

105 Fortis Green N2 9HR
+44 (0)208 444 4224
info@clissoldarms.co.uk
www.clissoldarms.co.uk
Tube: East Finchley

The Albion

This Georgian pub in Islington has old English charm and a tucked-away, residential feel in the walled beer garden. The menu offers plenty of options for big or small meals, from plates of cheese and scotch eggs to pie with mash and rib eye steak.

10 Thornhill Road N1 1HW
+44 (0)207 607 7450
bookings@the-albion.co.uk
www.the-albion.co.uk
Rail: Caledonian Road & Barnsbury

The Castle

This Tooting pub has been there since the 1830s, although the large beer garden with faux grass and wooden seating coves are a much more recent addition. It's the perfect spot to spend a summer evening, and the food menu has all the usual gastropub fare, from burgers to fish and chips and roast dinners.

38 Tooting High Street SW17 0RG
+44 (0)208 672 7018
castletooting@youngs.co.uk
www.castletooting.com
Tube: Tooting Broadway

The Avalon

This Clapham pub serves real ale and has a wide spectrum of indoor and outdoor seating areas, including the decked backed garden, which also has its own bar. All the usual pub foods grace The Avalon's menu, although you can sit in their more classy restaurant area if you want a less casual meal.

16 Balham Hill SW12 9EB
+44 (0)208 675 8613
info@theavalonlondon.com
www.theavalonlondon.com
Tube: Clapham South

The Gun

This sensitively restored pub in the London Docklands has a traditional but polished interior and views over the water. The menu consists of lovingly prepared British staples, from the pricier dinner menu items like cider braised pork belly, to the more casual pub menu items like fish finger sandwiches.

27 Coldharbour Docklands E14 9NS
+44 (0)207 515 5222
info@thegundocklands.com
www.thegundocklands.com
Tube: Canary Wharf

Princess Victoria

This west London neighbourhood pub was originally a Victorian Gin Palace. Beautifully restored, it attracts everyone from morning coffee drinkers and wine connoisseurs (there's a 30 page wine list!) to cigar lovers, who choose from the Princess Victoria's Cuban range and smoke in the walled herb garden. When it comes to food, the menu has rave reviews, with its combination of pub classics and Mediterranean inspired small plates.

217 Uxbridge Road W12 9DH
+44 (0)208 749 5886
info@princessvictoria.co.uk
www.princessvictoria.co.uk
Tube: Shepherd's Bush

Cow

This slightly offbeat pub has a laid back pub area and a more formal restaurant area, both of which you can eat in. The food is well-liked by neighbourhood locals and those coming from further afield, and although the menu has all the pub staples, its focus is on fish, with an indulgent seafood platter on offer for those who love flavours of the sea.

89 Westbourne Park Road W2 5QH
+44 (0)207 221 0021
www.thecowlondon.co.uk
Tube: Royal Oak

Supper clubs

The Underground Restaurant by MsMarmiteLover

MsMarmiteLover set up her underground restaurant in 2009 and is said to have started off the trend of supper clubs in the UK. She runs a calendar of themed meals and foodie events from her north London home. Secure tickets through her website, bring your own booze (BYOB) and she'll provide instructions on how to find her.
www.msmarmitelover.com

The Art of Dining

The chef and set designing duo behind The Art of Dining create multi-sensory dining experiences in intriguing venues. Previous themes include Gone Camping, Abigail's Party and the Chicken and the Egg.
www.theartofdining.co.uk

Hemsley + Hemsley

The Hemsley sisters have taken the London food scene by storm for their healthy, nutrient-dense recipes and clean-eating lifestyle recommendations. Their occasional supper clubs include food, inspiring chats and plenty of spiralised vegetables.
www.hemsleyandhemsley.com

Gingerline

These clandestine dining adventurers create design, art and food experiences in unusual spaces at locations near stations along London's rail network. After booking tickets, you typically find out which station to travel to an hour before the event starts, then follow clues to the final destination. The evening typically involves a welcome drink, a three course meal and some performance art thrown in for good measure.
www.gingerline.co.uk

Resources:
Find a supper club:
supperclubfangroup.ning.com

Photo: The Art of Dining

Street food

Street Feast

This street food organiser typically runs street food events during the spring and summer months, often in retro-trendy locations. Some of London's best loved foodie purveyors set up stands at Street Food events, from BOOM Burger and Capish to Dosa Deli and Le Swine.

www.streetfeastlondon.com

Real Food Market

This Wednesday to Friday afternoon market at King's Cross has an array of artisan food purveyors, including Bad Brownie and Casa Canoli. You can often find beers from London's local Greenwich Meantime Brewery too.

King's Cross Square, Euston Road N1 9AP

realfoodfestival.co.uk

Rail/Tube: King's Cross

Urban Food Fest

Found in a car park in Shoreditch every Saturday is the Urban Food Fest street food party. There's food and drinks to suit all tastes, while the crowd consists of the hipster and artsy types who like to hang around the Shoreditch area.

Euro Car Parks, 162-167 Shoreditch High Street E1 6HU

www.urbanfoodfest.com

Rail: Shoreditch High Street

Dalston Food Market

This east London food market has an array of locally produced food, coffees, craft beers and live music every Sunday.

The Petchey Academy E8 2EY

www.dalstonfoodmarket.com

Rail: Dalston Kingsland

Photo: Borough Market

Borough Market

One of the most popular foodie destinations in London, the daytime Borough Market sells fresh fruit and veg to cook at home, as well as freshly cooked treats ideal for lunchtime. There's a true blend of the best of British cuisine and internationally inspired flavours. Try Bread Ahead Bakery for doughy heaven, Brindisa for Spanish meats and cheeses, and Cartwright Brothers for English and international wines to wash it down with.

8 Southwark Street SE1 1TL

+44 (0)207 407 1002

info@boroughmarket.org.uk

www.boroughmarket.org.uk

Rail/Tube: London Bridge

Pop Brixton

Found inside shipping containers, this organisation helps foodie and other start-ups get established. While there are also non-foodie outlets such as vintage clothes shops, Pop Brixton is quickly becoming a destination for hungry Londoners, who especially love Zoe's Ghana Kitchen and Miss P's BBQ.

53 Brixton Station Road SW9 8PQ

+44 (0)207 274 2902

www.popbrixton.org

Rail/Tube: Brixton

Resources

London Street Foodie:

www.londonstreetfoodie.co.uk

Drinks

Mayor of Scaredy Cat Town

This speakeasy is hidden away in the basement of a restaurant and involves entering through the door of a Smeg fridge. The bar menu consists of fragrant cocktails and a few bar snacks to munch on, while the interior is all about exposed brick walls and reclaimed wood peppered with witty messages.

12-16 Artillery Lane E1 7LS
+44 (0)207 078 9639
henri@
themayorofscaredycattown.com
themayorofscaredycattown.com
Rail/Tube: Liverpool Street

Frank's Campari Bar

Found atop a multi-storey car park in Peckham, Frank's is the brainchild of a local architecture firm and opens every summer. It's a place where people while away warm evenings with refreshing drinks and small plates. The view of London from this south eastern spot is impressive.

10th floor, Peckham multi-storey car park, 95a Rye Lane SE15 4GT
info@frankscafe.org.uk
www.frankscafe.org.uk
Rail: Peckham Rye

Bounce

Apparently the largest purpose-built social ping pong club in Europe, Bounce is located on the site where ping pong was invented and patented in 1901. It's a place people love to go to play a few games and have a few drinks. Beware of stray ping pong balls, although dedicated staff are on hand to scoop them up as soon as they hit the floor.

21 Holborn EC1N 2TD
+44 (0)203 657 6525
www.bouncepingpong.com
Tube: Chancery Lane

The Old Ship W6

This pub was recorded on the census as long ago as 1722, making it a truly historic drinking hole. The pub occupies one of the prettiest hidden-away spots in London, overlooking the River Thames between Hammersmith and Chiswick. The pub has a decent selection of beers on draught and there's plenty of indoor and outdoor space to sit and enjoy the surroundings.

25 Upper Mall W6 9TD
+44 (0)208 748 2593
oldshipw6@youngs.co.uk
www.oldshipw6.co.uk
Tube: Ravenscourt Park

Antidote

This wine bar in the charming backstreets of Carnaby serves only biodynamic and organic wine from small, mostly French, producers. The selection is enough to thrill any wine aficionado. For those who want to make an evening of it, the food is equally impressive.

12a Newburgh Street W1F 7RR
+44 (0)207 287 8488
contact@antidotewinebar.com
www.antidotewinebar.com
Tube: Oxford Circus

BYOC

Bring a bottle of your favourite spirit, pay a cover charge and be mesmerised for the next two hours as the resident mixologists concoct amazing cocktails for you. The interiors are in a cosy speakeasy style and there are now London locations in the West End and Camden.

www.byoc.co.uk
28 Bedfordbury WC2N 4BJ
+44 (0)203 441 2424
westend@byoc.co.uk
Tube: Leicester Square
9-11 Basement NW1 7JE
+44 (0)203 441 2424
camden@byoc.co.uk
Tube: Mornington Crescent

The Nightjar

This bar in the heart of east London's Tech City serves innovative cocktails coined as pre-prohibition, prohibition or post-war in temperament. Drinking takes place to the backdrop of live jazz most evenings.

129 City Road EC1V 1JB
+44 (0)207 253 4101
info@barnightjar.com
www.barnightjar.com
Rail/Tube: Old Street

Cellar Door

This cocktail and cabaret bar can be found inside a previous public toilet. Intimate and quirky, evenings in Cellar Door are memorable and lively.

Zero Aldwych WC2E 7DN
+44 (0)207 240 8848
www.cellardoor.biz
Tube: Covent Garden

BrewDog Shoreditch

Even though the small brewery of BrewDog has gained a huge mainstream and international following, the brand still retains an independent flair. At this London bar you can try all their creations, from Punk IPA to Dead Pony Pale Ale. It attracts craft beer lovers from far and wide, as well as local hipsters who love to drink and snack on the Japanese street food served alongside the beer. Below BrewDog Shoreditch is one of London's favourite secret bars: UnderDog, which serves beer cocktails in a subterranean sanctum.

51-55 Bethnal Green Road E1 6LA
+44 (0)207 729 8476
shoreditchbar@brewdog.com
www.brewdog.com
Rail: Shoreditch High Street

Baranis

This bar, open weekdays only, transports you straight to Provence as soon as you step inside, with its chic yet sunny vibe and a cocktail list that makes many other London bars pale in comparison. There's a focus on pastis and absinthe drinks, with no less than 15 kinds of pastis on offer. A menu of snacks perfectly complements the drinks, with the likes of Provençal charcuterie selections and pizzetas on offer. The location inside the old vaulted cellars of a Chancery Lane auction house gives it a historic yet warm atmosphere. There's even an indoor pétanque court for those who like a little competition with their cocktail.

115 Chancery Lane WC2A 1PP
+44 (0)207 242 8373
bookings@baranis.co.uk
www.baranis.co.uk
Tube: Chancery Lane

Photos: Baranis

We moved to London because it's the best.
It's where the world's your oyster and anything goes.

Alice Hodge and Ellen Parr

Owners of The Art of Dining

Where are you from and why did you move to London?
Alice: We're both from the south west of England. Ellen's from Bristol and I'm from Stroud. We went to university up in Glasgow, and then moved to London.
Ellen: We moved to London because it's the best. It's exciting and when you're not there, you feel like you're missing out. It's quite a difficult place not to be in. If you're interested in art and food and all the things we love the most, then it's definitely the most exciting place to be in Britain.
Alice: I think we both came to a point in our jobs and wanted a change. We thought that if we were going to make that change, start our own business and be entrepreneurs, we'd better do it in London. It's where the world's your oyster and anything goes. And luckily, the wave carried us.

Tell us about your background.
Ellen: I'm a chef and started working in cafés when I was a teenager. I was lucky enough to get a trial at the Exmouth Market restaurant Moro in 2008. I had a brilliant time working there and they ended up giving me a full time job. I really got trained on how to be a serious chef there. I still occasionally do shifts at Moro to keep my hand in the kitchen. I've worked with a few other places too, such as Rochelle's Canteen and I've tried a bit of the St. JOHN style of food, which is classic British style with lots of delicious, unusual and often offal-based flavours. I've travelled a lot too and I always try to learn as much as I can when travelling around. I spent a bit of time in this amazing restaurant in Thailand called Nahm. I basically love to eat, cook and travel.
Alice: I'm a set designer and studied art at university. I became an art teacher before getting into set design. Throughout the years I've created everything from forests and deserts, to Women's Institute markets and Victorian parlours. Ellen and I met in Glasgow and we've been friends for a number of years. Our skills fit together really organically: to create a good experience you need to have good food and cool surroundings. So we decided to start working together on creative pop-up experiences, calling ourselves The Art of Dining. We never set out with a business plan; we never imagined it would become anything more than one event. It was just

a classic case of a snowball effect. There's a big pop-up scene, particularly in London, that we weren't even really aware of when we started. Suddenly we were in it and we just kept on planning the next event and the next event. Almost out of nowhere we found that we had built a business.

What is London's pop-up scene like?

Alice: Pop-ups are one-off experiences that people can be a part of, then they'll pop-down and won't happen again. At the beginning we thought pop-ups were just a flash in the pan, but they just keep on going. There are more and more pop-ups and they're getting better and better. They're becoming more theatrical too. Pop-ups are also a great way for brands to get new products out there. The term 'pop-up' can now mean something happening for one day only, but there are also pop-ups in London that are there for four years, such as BOXPARK in Shoreditch. That's really stretching the definition of a pop-up, though.

Ellen: That's not a pop-up in the traditional sense of the word. But pop-ups are definitely getting more extreme and more immersive.

Alice: I don't see pop-ups — the word or the actual events — disappearing. The whole nature of them is that they're one-off events, so you never know if they might just stop happening. Hopefully not!

What happens at pop-up events by The Art of Dining?

Alice: We combine theatre, food, music and design, all under one roof. It's not just about going out for a meal, it's much more than that, so people find it good value for money when you look at it in those terms. Every time we pop-up we have a different theme and we're in a different location. We'll run each event for anywhere between a week and a month. We've got a strong following of people who will come back time and time again because our pop-ups are completely different every time. A really wide mix of people come to our events. Some people turn up in suits and ties after a day's work in the City, and others turn up with a skateboard under their arm.

What has been your favourite event so far?

Ellen: We both really enjoyed our 'Abigail's Party' themed event. Alice made this amazing set like a weird suburban living room from the 1970s and everyone dressed up. We played music from the era and we had fun food ideas, such as a Vietnamese version of a prawn cocktail and cheese and pineapple cheesecake. We had a lot of funny props like hostess trollies, which made for quite a hilarious dining experience. Every single pop-up we do has good points and bad points. We face so many millions of challenges along the way because each venue presents itself with unexpected situations. But overcoming them is all part of the process and it's fun confronting the challenges and figuring out how to make an event work.

Alice: Our events are so different it's really hard to compare them. Some might be a real nightmare out the back because there's a tiny kitchen and only a couple of power outlets, although the diners will never realise. Some might be slap bang in central London, others might be further out. They're all so different, it's nuts. That's sort of what keeps us going too.
Ellen: We definitely like the change; it's like travelling in your job. It's quite nice that you can make your job change so much from one event to the next, which keeps it fresh. And our style can be so different, from a kitsch seventies house to a Tudor feast in the oldest house in Hackney!

How do you find inspiration for each pop-up?
Alice: We don't really have set rules, but we do tend to find the venue first. Once we've found a really cool venue, we think about what theme really fits within those walls. We've worked in collaboration with the National Trust for a few years, which means we can find out a lot about the history of a location and work out a theme from that history. Other times, we might have had an idea of a theme for a number of years and we're just waiting for the right venue to come along. Every pop-up is different; we reinvent the wheel every time. I go to museums before each pop-up such as the V&A (Victoria & Albert Museum), the Hunterian Museum, The National Gallery and Sir Winston Churchill's War Rooms. London has a huge variety of museums, so I usually visit some first to collect ideas.
Ellen: I get to go to restaurants to gain my inspiration!
Alice: Yes, I think Ellen gets the better deal! But we definitely like to get inspiration in person and not on a computer, and London's great for that.

What is it about London that makes a pop-up like yours work?
Ellen: It's a really foodie city and it's definitely got one of the most exciting food scenes in the world at the moment, so I think that really helps. The scope of the venues in London is immense too, which means the themes of our pop-ups can be diverse. We've been on a rooftop, in a basement, inside four National Trust properties, in an old seventies style community centre, and in an old school house, to name but a few.
Alice: London has a really open-minded crowd. At our pop-ups, people don't know where they're going to go, who they're going to sit next to and what they're going to eat. There's a real scene and buzz for that in London at the moment, where people want to have an all-consuming experience as a night out.

Where is your favourite place to work in the city?
Ellen: Allpress is a slick spot in Shoreditch with delicious sandwiches and great coffee. It's a good option if you want to do a day without the internet. Now we've got our studio we spend a lot more time there too.
Alice: I love the interior in Sketch so I try to orchestrate meetings to happen

in there. If we're having a meeting, we tend to coincide it with a mealtime. Getting to visit nice places within the working day is a great benefit of working for yourself.

What's the best compliment you've had about your pop-ups?
Alice: The nicest bit of the whole pop-up is when people are leaving and they want to know when the next one will be. People also ask for recipes on the way out. Sometimes people won't go home and we have to chuck them out! It can be tiring as we know we need the energy to do the pop-up again the next evening, but it's definitely a compliment when people don't want to leave.

What has been the most surprising thing that's happened at an Art of Dining event?
Ellen: Someone came from Germany for one event; she caught three buses to get there. That was when we did an event with my Dad, the photographer Martin Parr, and she was a mega fan of his. It was a very arty, bizarre, immersive and experimental pop-up that we've also done in Germany and Tokyo. It's called 'Say Cheese' and we used my Dad's photographs combined with set design, so you saw elements in his photographs from around the room. Each course of the menu had a photograph taken of it by him too, and on the night we recreated each plate of food according to each photo. The level of detail was insane, and Alice hand-painted 100 blue and white plates to make them look like each photograph! People were taking pictures of their food next to the photographs on the wall. So that was why this person came all the way from Germany.
Alice: At the end of the night she told us she'd come to London especially for our event. It was crazy! 'Give her another drink' I said! I introduced her to everyone in the kitchen.

Will you ever be a pop-up that goes permanent?
Alice: I'd never say never, but I don't think we want that. We like the full-on then full-off cycle of running a pop-up. We like reinventing ourselves and going to new places. I think it suits the way we work and who we are, and we prefer it to doing the same thing every day and having a permanent place. Even though that would be a lot easier on a lot of levels.
Ellen: We enjoy taking people to beautiful venues and unusual places they haven't been to before. But it is getting harder and harder to find venues and it's getting more expensive too. So you never know if we'll change our mind!
Alice: We rely on word of mouth to find new venues and we run competitions to get people to tell us about cool places they've come across. Usually what leads us to a new venue is a friend of a friend of a friend whose sister got married in some secret place, or something equally random. You have to hunt out the gems.

Are there any other pop-ups you rate highly?

Alice: Yes, we go to check them all out and lots of our friends are doing pop-ups as well. We're friends with the Gingerline; they also do immersive dining experiences.

Ellen: A few of my chef friends do pop-ups; they're mostly people I've met throughout the years at Moro. And they're always delicious, but it's not their permanent job, so you often have to know the people to know about the pop-ups, which is quite nice for us.

What does the future hold for The Art of Dining?

Ellen: We're always planning for the future. We're always on the lookout for cool venues to host the next pop-up.

Alice: We recently had a really big foodie opportunity to do a festival for the first time, so we may do more of those. It was Jamie Oliver's Big Feastival in the Cotswolds and we did a 'Gone Camping' pop-up. It's all tongue in cheek, but it had things like campsite safety workshops in between courses, a campfire song and a ghost story. Everyone got a whistle and we held a whistle-blowing workshop in the middle, which was chaotic.

Where in London do you work and live?

Ellen: Our studio is in between Seven Sisters and Tottenham in a small industrial estate with a lot of creative businesses in it. We both live in easy travelling distance of our studio. I live in Stamford Hill, very near Stoke Newington, which is full of nice bars and cafés.

Alice: I live in Hackney. Hackney is a vibrant place to live with loads of variety, from great restaurants to beautiful parks and old-school pubs. I've recently dug up a tiny garden — it's rare to have any outside space in London. I've been growing all this veg and spending my weekends gardening. The problem is that you're waiting for everything to grow for months, and then everything's ready at the same time and you've got to eat 14 cabbages!

Ellen: We could do a pop-up and give everyone half a leaf each!

Alice: I'd go round telling every single person they're eating food from my garden!

What's the area like near your studio?

Alice: Tottenham is totally unique and it's really on the cusp of improving. We see it changing every day. You'll find fly-tipping and litter, but also cool new businesses opening.

Ellen: There are definitely a lot of new things happening in the area. Our friends run an interactive theatre company called RIFT around the corner, and Alice helped them build the set. There's also a bar called The Fountain on Seven Sisters Road. It used to be quite a dive, but they play really fun music and it's starting to get quite trendy. We're seeing the classic signs of gentrification in the area.

Where do you like to hang out in London?

Alice: There's loads going on in east London. There are a lot of events and so many websites where you can find out what's going on, like It's Nice That and The Nudge. The nightlife in east London is great.

Ellen: There are so many exciting places to visit. The area around Victoria Park is so pleasant: that would be a dreamy place to live. London Fields is great; it's kind of the younger version of Victoria Park. I also like the area from Kingsland Road to Dalston. Dalston's getting almost annoyingly trendy these days, but every time you walk along the road there are new things opening. There are so many interesting places to eat in the area too. Most of the things I do in my social life revolve around eating and discovering the latest eateries. Clapton is great; there are a lot of exciting food things happening around there such as Sodo Pizza. Some of my best friends live in Borough, and it's super nice to go to the market and wander around there.

Alice: Equally, we still really like going into Soho and central London, because there are loads of great food happenings around there too. South London's got loads going on as well. There have been some great pop-ups there. There are also lots of galleries in south London: great independent places such as Gasworks and Drawing Room.

Where are your favourite places to eat out in London?

Ellen: We're lucky in London because you can eat incredibly delicious meals for cheap prices. You can spend hundreds of pounds very easily too, but you don't need to in order to have a great meal. My new favourite is Bao on Lexington Street in Soho. It's delicious. Most people like it for the steamed milk buns, but for me it's all about the side dishes. You do have to be prepared to queue to get in though. Som Saa, which pops up in places like Climpson's Arch, is run by a friend of ours and is really great. They serve really spicy and fragrant Thai food. Trangallan is this great tapas bar in Newington Green. It's really small and understated, but it's got a great following and the food is really delicious.

Alice: J Sheekey is great for an old-school meal out. The food is delicious and there's a doorman so it feels like you've stepped back into London from a previous era. For great baked goods, we always go to The Dusty Knuckle in Dalston. It's run by our friends and is inside a shipping container. It's a social enterprise too, as they employ ex-gang kids. We often get our baked good from them for our pop-ups.

Where do you like to go for drinks in the city?

Alice: There's a big drinks scene in London, with loads of cool cocktail bars and rooftop bars that we like going to and discovering Ruby's in Dalston is a firm favourite. It's a good winter cocktail bar because it's underground and it's got nice décor. I love the chilli apple Martini. But as soon as the sun comes out everyone's on the nearest rooftop. Our favourites are Frank's or Dalston Roof Park.

Ellen: We're friends with the people who run Background Bars; they set up bars in festivals and always have something exciting going on in the Red Gallery. It's always good to see what their latest project is. The Palm Tree in Mile End is a really cosy pub. You feel like you're in the countryside, but in fact it's on the canal by Victoria Park.

What else do you do in your spare time?

Alice: Food and theatre really; that's what we spend our money on. And if we can get the two in the same place, all the better. We go to Punchdrunk productions that are really immersive theatre experiences, where you can open every drawer and every cupboard. They create beautifully inspiring productions.

Ellen: One of my favourite things to do in London is swimming in the Ladies Ponds in Hampstead. It's amazing.

What are your friends like?

Ellen: We have a lot of freelance friends and we know a lot of people who live and work near our studio. They're quite a varied group of artists, food writers and actors. The people we hang out with have hundreds of different jobs, but everyone's open-minded and creative.

Alice: People definitely go to support other people's projects. There's a good after-work social scene, but when your work is creative, the lines often blur and they become the same thing. We go to loads of other people's pop-ups which is partly social and partly work for us.

Where do you recommend for culture in London?

Ellen: I always like to go to the Wellcome Collection at the Wellcome Trust. It's home to many of the curiosities of London and there are loads of pickled things.

Alice: Our collaboration with the National Trust took us to all the amazing National Trust properties in London. They're even more special to us because we've popped up in some of them. They have amazing houses dotted around the city filled with history, beautiful artefacts, lovely gardens and weird little tea shops. It's unusual for a city to have these kinds of places, but it's a cool sort of British institution.

Ellen: Our favourite National Trust property is our local one: Sutton House. It's tiny; it's the oldest house in Hackney and it's really sweet. It's made of wood and has open fireplaces. It feels like an untouched gem that you've just discovered. We do pop-ups in their main hall.

What is London's best quality?

Ellen: The diversity. I love how many different types of people live in the city and how accepting it is. You can go for a swim in the ponds at Hampstead Heath, then get the train to Whitechapel and feel like you're in Bangladesh. You can whizz around on a bicycle and have completely different experiences. There are so many wonderful parks and the variation in buildings is just incredible. London has got so many different parts to it.

Alice: I agree, the variety and spontaneity of London is great. You can go out without an agenda and pretty much stumble across something. I love wondering what I'll do that evening and knowing I will find something really cool to do.

Ellen: Food has also completely boomed in the last few years in London. It's become so fashionable. There are all these young foodie people setting up tiny little places, and loads of street food stalls. You can eat such good food in this city. I went to Istanbul a couple of years ago and I remember thinking the Turkish food in Dalston was better than half the food I was eating there. London pulls together so many styles and cultures.

Is there anything you'd change about London if you could?

Ellen: I'd like the house prices to be cheaper. A lot of people want to live in London but they just can't afford to. It's a shame as this can be alienating for some people. But the general cost of living other than housing is fairly reasonable in London.

Alice: Sitting in London traffic can be hell! We use public transport whenever possible and it's great, but as soon as you get in a car, London is a different city. We have to drive around a lot finding venues, picking up props and buying food. But these are fairly standard gripes I think; London has all the fundamentals right.

Where do you buy your props?

Alice: I've got a few firm favourites; the main one is Wimbledon Car Boot Sale on Wednesdays, Saturdays and Sundays. I go on a Wednesday because it opens at 10:30 so you don't have to get up at the crack of dawn. It's a real hidden gem of London and there are amazing things to be found. The guys selling there have been trading for generations. I also love finding things in charity and second hand shops. There are prop houses, but I tend not to use them: the fun bit is finding things yourself.

How do you get an adrenalin rush in London?

Alice: We both ride bicycles so that can be an adrenalin rush. And we both drink way too much coffee!

Where's the best coffee in London?

Ellen: Craving Coffee.

Alice: Craving Coffee is our local café based in the same block as our studio. We walk through it every morning and every night, and the coffee is great. They also have a cart they park outside Tube stations, so more people can access a caffeine-fuelled adrenalin rush!

How would you encourage people to 'get lost' in London?

Alice: The Victoria line is brilliant because it's so fast and you literally slice through the middle of London. There's an amazing food market in Brixton — Brixton Village — with loads of little cafés and great, great food. Then you could get off at Oxford Street, go shopping in Soho, and then come all the way up to us in Tottenham, where the artists are hunkering down.

Ellen: I always say I'm going to go to every Tube stop, especially in zones one and two, and just get out and wander around for a bit. I haven't done it yet, but there are so many different experiences to have in London. Even Londoners can have such different perceptions of the city depending on their experiences. I don't know much about west London, for example. I just know our London. It's such a huge place, but that makes it perfect for getting lost in, even if you're a Londoner.

Alice: Cycling or walking along the canals is another great way to get lost. Hackney Wick is a really cool area to bike around. There are lots of really industrial but amazing creative things going on in nightclubs and cafés in the area, such as Crate Brewery, which has great pizza and good DJs.

Ellen: There's a cool buzz around the canals and they're a peaceful way to see the city. You could cycle from Islington to London Fields and Victoria Park. You can go to Little Venice and all the way to Greenwich.

How can visitors to London blend in with the locals?

Ellen: My top thing to do is definitely to swim in Hampstead. I think it's a real secret no tourist seems to know about as you only ever seem to see Londoners there. I love it. I think going to pop-ups is a really great way of meeting Londoners. Then you'll sit next to Londoners and you can ask them what they like doing. London Pop-ups is a website that lists every pop-up happening that week.

What does your ideal day off in London look like?

Ellen: I'd go for breakfast in the Troubadour Café in Earl's Court. It's full of eccentric props and it's great for eggs benedict and a Bloody Mary. Then I'd go to an exhibition and have lunch in Bao, followed by a trip to Hampstead Heath for a long swim and a picnic. In the evening I'd go to some pubs in the Hampstead area, such as the Southampton Arms, which is an amazing old ale pub. Or The Bull and Last does great scotch eggs. Then I'd go out and dance loads at The Glory or Dalston Superstore.

Alice: I'd go for brunch at Allpress because of the great coffee and I love avocado! Then I'd go for a bike ride around the canals in east London, followed by a visit to one of London's great art galleries. I love the Whitechapel Gallery and the Hayward Gallery. Brewer Street Car Park has some excellent exhibitions too. Then I'd go for dinner in Soho at Polpo. If it was a perfect day I'd go to see a play too, ideally in an unusual venue. Then I'd go to a cocktail bar until very late and take advantage of London's amazing mixologists who do really interesting things with all sorts of berries and smoke and squirty things. Satan's Whiskers is great for this.
Ellen: Another good tip is that the bar at Duck & Waffle is open 24 hours a day. It's quite hard to get a booking, but if you're not dressed too scruffily and go after midnight on a week night, you can eat something and get a bottle of wine. It's not cheap but the views are amazing. Dining at the sky bars or restaurants inside London's skyscrapers is a great way of seeing the views over London.

What's your favourite random fact about London?
Alice: The luxury department store Harrods sold cocaine until 1916!

What is the current trend in London?
Alice: Interactive experiences. There are lots of themed bars where you can dress up, like Cahoots, which is Second World War themed. People are up for immersive experiences in London at the moment: anything that's new, exciting and challenges you, even if you're not quite sure what it's going to be like.
Ellen: More and more influence is creeping in from New York City too, which is really exciting.

What smell makes you think of London?
Alice: The smell of rain! We have such varying weather from minute to minute in London, so I always think of seeing hot dry tarmac and then suddenly being in the middle of a downpour, and that lovely smell of rain that follows.

Alice and Ellen's London

Places to visit

BOXPARK
2-10 Bethnal Green Road E1
6GY, UK
+44 (0)207 033 2899
info@boxpark.co.uk
www.boxpark.co.uk
Rail/Tube: Shoreditch High Street

Brewer Street Car Park
Brewer Street W1F 0LA
hello@thevinylfactory.com
www.brewerstreetcarpark.com
Tube: Piccadilly Circus

Drawing Room
Tannery Arts, 12 Rich Estate,
Crimscott Street SE1 5TE
+44 (0)207 394 5657
mail@drawingroom.org.uk
www.drawingroom.org.uk
Tube: Bermondsey

Gasworks
155 Vauxhall Street SE11 5RH
+44 (0)207 587 5202
info@gasworks.org.uk
www.gasworks.org.uk
Rail/Tube: Vauxhall

Hampstead Heath ponds
Rail: Hampstead Heath
Tube: Hampstead

Hayward Gallery
Southbank Centre, Belvedere
Road SE1 8XX
+44 (0)207 960 4200
www.southbankcentre.co.uk/
venues/hayward-gallery
Rail/Tube: Waterloo

Hunterian Museum
35-43 Lincoln's Inn Fields WC2A
3PE
+44 (0)207 869 6560
www.hunterianmuseum.org
Tube: Holborn

Kingsland Road
Rail: Haggerston or Hoxton

London Fields
Rail: London Fields

Punchdrunk
+44 (0)207 655 0940
punchdrunk@punchdrunk.org.uk
www.punchdrunk.org.uk

Red Gallery
1-3 Rivington Street EC2A 3DT
+44 (0)207 613 3620
www.redgallerylondon.com
Rail/Tube: Old Street

RIFT
5 Ashley Road N17 9LJ
info@r-ft.co.uk
www.r-ft.co.uk
Rail/Tube: Tottenham Hale

Sir Winston Churchill's War Rooms
Clive Steps, King Charles Street
SW1A 2AQ
+44 (0)207 930 6961
www.iwm.org.uk/visits/churchill-war-rooms
Tube: Westminster

Sutton House
2-4 Homerton High Street E9 6JQ
+44 (0)208 986 2264
suttonhouse@nationaltrust.org.uk
www.nationaltrust.org.uk/sutton-house/
Rail: Hackney Central

The National Gallery
Trafalgar Square WC2N 5DN
+44 (0)207 747 2885
information@ng-london.org.uk
www.nationalgallery.org.uk
Rail/Tube: Charing Cross

V&A
Cromwell Road SW7 2RL
+44 (0)207 942 2000
contact@vam.ac.uk
www.vam.ac.uk
Tube: South Kensington

Victoria Park
Rail: Cambridge Heath or
Hackney Wick

Wellcome Collection
183 Euston Road NW1 2BE
+44 (0)207 611 2222
info@wellcomecollection.org
www.wellcomecollection.org
Tube: Euston Square

Whitechapel Gallery
77-82 Whitechapel High Street
E1 7QX
+44 (0)207 522 7888
info@whitechapelgallery.org
www.whitechapelgallery.org
Tube: Aldgate East

Wimbledon Car Boot Sale
Wimbledon Stadium, Plough
Lane SW17 0BL
Rail: Haydons Road

Eating and drinking

Allpress Shoreditch
58 Redchurch Street E2 7DP
uk.allpressespresso.com
Rail: Shoreditch High Street

Background Bars
www.backgroundbars.com

Bao
53 Lexington Street W1F 9AS
www.baolondon.com
Tube: Oxford Circus

Borough Market
8 Southwark Street SE1 1TL
www.boroughmarket.org.uk
Rail/Tube: London Bridge

Brixton Village
Market Row, Coldharbour Lane
SW9 8LB
+44 (0)207 274 2990
info@brixtonmarket.net
www.brixtonmarket.net/brixton-village
Rail/Tube: Brixton

Cahoots
13 Kingly Street W1B 5PG
+44 (0)207 352 6200
www.cahoots-london.com
Tube: Oxford Circus

Crate Brewery
The White Building Unit 7,
Queen's Yard, White Post Lane
E9 5EN
mail@spacestudios.org.uk
www.thewhitebuilding.org.uk/
crate-brewery-pizza
Rail: Hackney Wick

Craving Coffee
Gaunson House, Markfield Road
N15 4QQ
cravingcoffeeuk@gmail.com
www.cravingcoffee.co.uk
+44 (0)208 808 3178
Tube: Seven Sisters

Dalston Roof Park
The Print House, 18-22 Ashwin
Street E8 3DL
+44 (0)207 275 0825
www.bootstrapcompany.co.uk/
community-event-spaces/
dalston-roof-park
Rail: Dalston Junction

Dalston Superstore
117 Kingsland High Street E8 2PB
+44 (0)207 254 2273
hello@dalstonsuperstore.com
www.dalstonsuperstore.com
Rail: Dalston Kingsland

Duck & Waffle
Heron Tower, The Heron Tower,
110 Bishopsgate EC2N 4AY
+44 (0)203 640 7310
londonreservations@
duckandwaffle.com
www.duckandwaffle.com
Rail/Tube: Liverpool Street

Frank's
10th floor, Peckham multi-storey
car park, 95a Rye Lane SE15 4GT
info@frankscafe.org.uk
www.frankscafe.org.uk
Rail: Peckham Rye

Gingerline
www.gingerline.co.uk

J Sheekey
28-32 St Martin's Court WC2N 4AL
+44 (0)207 240 2565
www.j-sheekey.co.uk
Tube: Leicester Square

Moro
34-36 Exmouth Market EC1R 4QE
+44 (0)207 833 8336
info@moro.co.uk
www.moro.co.uk
Rail/Tube: Farringdon

Polpo Soho
41 Beak Street W1F 9SB
+44 (0)207 734 4479
www.polpo.co.uk
Tube: Oxford Circus

Rochelle's Canteen
Rochelle School, Arnold Circus
E2 7ES
+44 (0)207 729 5677
info@arnoldandhenderson.com
www.arnoldandhenderson.
com/4-rochelle_canteen
Rail: Shoreditch High Street

Ruby's
76 Stoke Newington Road N16
7XB
+44 (0)208 211 8690
hello@rubysdalston.com
www.rubysdalston.com
Rail: Dalston Kingsland

Satan's Whiskers
343 Cambridge Heath Road
E2 9RA
+44 (0)207 739 8362
satanswhiskersblr.tumblr.com
Tube: Bethnal Green

Sketch
9 Conduit Street W1S 2XG
+44 (0) 20 7659 4500
reservations@sketch.london
www.sketch.london
Tube: Oxford Circus

Sodo Pizza
Upper Clapton Road E5 9JY
+44 (0)208 806 5626
www.sodopizza.co.uk
Rail: Clapton

Som Saa
@somsaa_london

St. JOHN
www.stjohngroup.uk.com

The Art of Dining
www.theartofdining.co.uk

The Bull and Last
168 Highgate Road NW5 1QS
+44 (0)207 267 3641
info@thebullandlast.co.uk
www.thebullandlast.co.uk
Rail: Gospel Oak

The Dusty Knuckle
Abbot Street Car Park, off
Kingsland High Street E8 2JP
www.thedustyknuckle.com
Rail: Dalston Kingsland

The Fountain
125 Westgreen Road N15 5DE
+44 (0)208 802 0433
fountain_hotel@btconnect.com
www.fountainhotellondon.com
Rail/Tube: Seven Sisters

The Glory
281 Kingsland Road E2 8AS
+44 (0)207 684 0794
www.theglory.co
Rail: Haggerston

The Palm Tree
127 Grove Road E3 5BH
+44 (0)208 980 2918
Tube: Mile End

The Southampton Arms
139 Highgate Road NW5 1LE
+44 (0)7958 780073
www.thesouthamptonarms.co.uk
Rail: Gospel Oak

Trangallan
61 Newington Green N16 9PX
+44 (0)207 359 4988
info@trangallan.com
www.trangallan.com
Rail: Canonbury

Troubadour Café
265 Old Brompton Road SW5
9JA
+44 (0)207 370 1434
info@troubadour.co.uk
www.troubadour.co.uk
Rail/Tube: West Brompton

See also:
It's Nice That
www.itsnicethat.com
London Pop-ups
www.londonpopups.com
The Nudge
www.thenudge.com

Find out more about
The Art of Dining at:
www.theartofdining.co.uk
or on Twitter @ArtofDiningLdn

4
Dinner...
Thai style BBQ with
potato and aubergine
salad and grilled gem

2
Breakfast...
Moroccan style eggs
with date and cumin
flatbreads

5
Bedtime...
Hazelnut marshmallow
and caramelised banana
with hot chocolate

3
Lunch...
Flageolet bean, sweet
herb and avocado salad
with Mojama

Shopping

General

BOXPARK

Based in the heart of trendy Shoreditch, this pop-up mall is housed in shipping containers, and is designed to give new businesses a place to start-up. It's a spot to pick up a range of the latest creations and inventions, with everything on sale from new fashions to intriguing giftware.

2-10 Bethnal Green Road E1 6GY, UK
+44 (0)207 033 2899
info@boxpark.co.uk
www.boxpark.co.uk
Rail/Tube: Shoreditch High Street

Liberty

This luxury department store was founded in 1875 and is smaller and quirkier than others in the city such as Harrods. Liberty is especially known for its graphic prints, original homeware and gifts. The store also sells luxury fashions, fragrances and jewellery.

Regent Street W1B 5AH
+44 (0)207 734 1234
www.liberty.co.uk
Tube: Oxford Circus

Westfield Stratford City

Found on the site of the 2012 Olympics, this Westfield branch has hundreds of shops and dozens of restaurants. It's a large shopping centre, but it has some cool touches, including outdoor areas, food trucks and deck chairs in the summer, as well as some independently-run restaurants and the All Star bowling lanes.

Westfield Avenue E20 1EL
+44 (0)208 221 7300
uk.westfield.com/stratfordcity
Rail/Tube: Stratford

Selfridges

This department store sells a little bit of everything with mid to high end prices. It's a place people love to explore and there are always new innovations to discover too. Selfridges' rooftop sometimes plays host to launch parties and special events.

400 Oxford Street W1A 1AB
0800 123 400
www.selfridges.com
Tube: Bond Street

One New Change

As a newer addition to London's shopping scene, One New Change hosts a range of independent and chain shops in a city centre location, frequently visited by the high weekday working population. That means One New Change is pretty chilled out on the weekends and is a far cry from the crowds of Oxford Street. There are some truly decent eateries too, including Gordon Ramsay's Bread Street Kitchen.

1 New Change EC4M 9AF
+44 (0)207 002 8900
enquiries@onenewchange.com
www.onenewchange.com
Tube: St Paul's

Markets

Camden Market

A stalwart on the London market scene, Camden Market has hundreds of stalls sprawling around the lock, selling everything from handmade fashions to trinkets for the home. Wandering around is a great way to experience Camden's unique vibe too, with an eclectic mix of sub-cultures congregating in the area.

56-56 Camden Lock Place NW1 8AF
+44 (0)203 763 9999
support@camdenmarket.com
www.camdenmarket.com
Tube: Camden Town

Spitalfields Market E1

Inside restored Victorian market buildings, Spitalfields Market E1 is a popular hangout in a relatively recently gentrified area of London. Market stalls sell everything from fashion to art, and some food stands make for an ideal lunch stop. The Saturday Style Market is a favourite for fashion lovers looking for clothes from new designers.

Brushfield Street E1 6AA
www.spitalfields.co.uk
Rail/Tube: Liverpool Street

Cabbages & Frocks Market

This retro market in Marylebone sells vintage clothing and hand-made goods by artisans. There's also a focus on food, with olive oils, breads and cheeses for sale, and Bedouin food and a hog roast available to eat there and then.

St Marylebone Parish Church grounds, Marylebone High Street W1U 5BA
info@cabbagesandfrocks.co.uk
www.cabbagesandfrocks.co.uk
Tube: Baker Street

Portobello Road Market

This well-known antiques and vintage market is home to more than 1,000 stallholders. As well as the wares on offer, it's a stimulating place to enjoy street life on one of London's best loved streets.

Portobello Road W11 2DY
www.portobelloroad.co.uk
Tube: Ladbroke Grove

Greenwich Market

An eclectic market in villagey Greenwich, find everything for sale here from antiques and old books, to quirky bag designs and small crafts. Greenwich Market dates back to 1700 and is a World Heritage Site, so it's an ideal

place to soak up some of London's history too.

5b Greenwich Market SE10 9HZ
+44 (0)208 269 5096
greenwichmarketlondon.com
Rail: Cutty Sark

Fashion

Beyond Retro

This vintage store sells second-hand clothes from a range of labels and eras. As well as selling these trendy once-loved fashions, Beyond Retro also sells its own vintage-style accessories, while the on-site café has vintage tea sets.

92-100 Stoke Newington Road N16 7XB
www.beyondretro.com
Rail: Dalston Kingsland

The Hackney Shop

This not-for-profit enterprise gives Hackney creatives and collectives the opportunity to produce a pop-up shop free of charge. As a result, it's a great place to find the latest fashions from east London designers.

99 Morning Lane E9 6ND
info@thehackneyshop.com
www.thehackneyshop.com
Rail: Hackney Central

Universal Works

This branch of the menswear designer is a success story of a UK start-up gone global while retaining local and small-scale integrity. The brand blends British heritage with contemporary design, and the owners collaborate with artists and designers on a regular basis.

40 Berwick Street W1F 8RX
+44 (0)203 581 1501
info@universalworks.co.uk
www.universalworks.co.uk
Tube: Tottenham Court Road

Wolf & Badger

This store promotes independent fashion, jewellery, accessories and interior design brands, making it a great place to find designer labels and some of the latest creative outputs from the fashion industry.

46 Ledbury Road W11 2AB
+44 (0)207 229 5698
www.wolfandbadger.com
Tube: Notting Hill Gate

The Goodhood Store

This shop brings together hundreds of high end fashion brands, attracting people looking for chic clothing for men and women.

41 Coronet Street N1 6HD
+44 (0)207 729 3600
www.goodhoodstore.com
Tube: Old Street

Specialist

Cass Art

As the largest store of this small UK chain serving London's creative community, this Islington shop is an architectural triumph set over three floors. It sells well-priced art materials and offers inspiration even for casual browsers.

66-67 Colebrooke Row N1 8AB
+44 (0)207 354 2999
www.cassart.co.uk
Tube: Angel

Daunt Books

London's much-loved bookstore specialising in travel books, Daunt Books is a place to explore and be inspired. The Marylebone branch is found inside a former Edwardian book shop with oak galleries and huge skylights.

83 Marylebone High Street W1U 4QW
+44 (0)207 224 2295
orders@dauntbooks.co.uk
www.dauntbooks.co.uk
Tube: Baker Street

Design Museum Shop

The Design Museum is much-loved by creatives and entrepreneurs, and as a result, the Design Museum Shop is one of the best places in London to pick up lifestyle goods embodying the latest designs, as well as innovative office technology and homeware.

Design Museum, 28 Shad Thames SE1 2YD
+44 (0)207 940 8775
www.designmuseumshop.com
Tube: Tower Hill

Circus

This quirky shop specialises in clothing items by young designers and vintage finds. Find everything from affordable art and home accessories, to handmade poetry books and modern ceramics.

Brixton Village SW9 8PS
info@circusbrixton.com
www.circusbrixton.com
Tube: Brixton

Rough Trade East

This music store with an array of vinyl releases aims to shorten the distance between artists and audiences. As a result, it's a treasure trove for music-lovers looking to unearth artistic talent.

Old Truman Brewery, 91 Brick Lane E1 6QL
+44 (0)207 392 7788
www.roughtrade.com
Tube: Aldgate East

Boutique

The Zetter
Found inside an old Victorian warehouse in Clerkenwell, The Zetter was one of London's first boutique hotels that helped make the area around Exmouth Market trendy. Suites have a contemporary feel with vibrant splashes of colour, while communal areas have playful touches of chintz. Quirky touches include vending machines on each floor dispensing everything from deodorant to champagne, and spring water sourced from The Zetter's own borehole. The Zetter's restaurant, Grain Store Unleashed, is a popular destination for foodie Londoners. Across the road is The Zetter's little sister, The Zetter Townhouse, which has fewer rooms and greater eccentricities in terms of style.
St John's Square, 86-88
Clerkenwell Road EC1M 5RJ
+44 (0)207 324 4444
info@thezetter.com
www.thezetter.com
Rail/Tube: Farringdon

Ten Manchester Street
Hidden away along an elegant Marylebone street and around the corner from celebrity haunt Chiltern Firehouse, Ten Manchester Street offers modern and graceful suites. Rooms are cosy with sumptuous bedding and designer furniture. The on-site restaurant Dieci is another firm favourite with the London set, but the real pièce de résistance of the hotel is the indoor-outdoor cigar terrace, ideal for supping cocktails and smoking Cuban cigars that can be purchased from the adjoining humidor.
10 Manchester Street W1U 4DG
+44 (0)207 317 5924
reservations@
tenmanchesterstreethotel.com
www.tenmanchesterstreethotel.com
Tube: Baker Street or Bond Street

A deluxe king twin room in The Zetter

Photo: The Zetter

Design

citizenM London Bankside

This Dutch hotel group is all about shirking the things people dislike about hotels and embracing technology and great design. It takes one minute to check in or out via screens at the entrance, there are free movies in rooms as well as international plug sockets. Moodpads control the temperature, window blinds, television and wake-up alarms in each soundproofed room. The design of the huge 'living-room' lobby is as astutely crafted as the suites, with huge windows bringing shedloads of natural light into the iconic Vitra furniture adorned spaces.

20 Lavington Street SE1 0NZ
www.citizenm.com/destinations/london
Tube: Southwark

Ace Hotel

This Shoreditch hotel embodies a playful minimalist design with creative touches imbued in the interiors, contributed to by a number of London artists and creatives. Vintage furniture sits alongside original artwork, and some rooms even have turntables with vinyl and acoustic guitars. The hotel makes for a hip hangout joint, attracting the entrepreneurs of east London as well as passing travellers to enjoy the calendar of music events and the much-loved Hoi Polloi restaurant.

100 Shoreditch High Street E1 6JQ
+44 (0)207 613 9800
enquire.ldn@acehotel.com
www.acehotel.com
Rail: Shoreditch High Street

A playful minimalist room in the ACE hotel

Photo: Andrew Meredith - ACE hotel

Luxury

Covent Garden Hotel

London is full of big-name, globally recognised hotels allowing guests to live in the lap of luxury. The Covent Garden Hotel is one of the more toned down of these high-end hotels, despite its central location in the heart of the West End. This old-established gem — a favourite haunt of public figures because of its well-known discretion — is all about impeccable but homely service. Suites are décorated in a traditional British countryside style, but with all the mod cons. With its own film screening room, the occasional exhibition and an intimate bar serving gorgeous cocktails or cream teas, the comfort of the Covent Garden Hotel signifies understated luxury, blended with on-site cultural and social pursuits. For those who prefer a more modern and vivacious décor, The Soho Hotel nearby is a sister hotel to the Covent Garden Hotel.

10 Monmouth Street WC2H 9HB
+44 (0)207 806 1000
covent@firmdale.com
www.firmdalehotels.com/hotels/
london/covent-garden-hotel
Tube: Covent Garden

Blakes Hotel

Although this hotel dates back to 1970s London, the style is far from the bold and brash characteristics of this era. Designed by the globally famous Anouska Hempel, Blakes draws inspiration from a number of Asian regions, concocting an exotic and opulent interior in its tucked-away South Kensington location. Some suites take the Asian inspiration to new heights, while others are about clean, modern lines; while all have Bang & Olufsen gadgets. The hotel's Corfu Suite even won a 'Sexiest Bedroom' award from Mr & Mrs Smith a couple of years ago.

33 Roland Gardens SW7 3PF
+44 (0)207 370 6701
reservations@blakeshotels.com
www.blakeshotels.com
Tube: South Kensington

City apartments

Europa House

These apartments found inside an elegant townhouse amid the tranquil canals of Little Venice offer residential living in the heart of London. Kitchens are impeccably kitted out, while the rooms themselves feel elegant and homely. The apartments embody understated luxury and come with one, two or three bedrooms. The icing on the cake is the access guests get to the largest private garden square nearby.

79a Randolph Avenue W9 1DW
+44 (0)207 724 5924
sales@europahouseapartments.
com
www.living-rooms.co.uk/hotel/
europa-house
Tube: Maida Vale

Town Hall Hotel

In the previous location of Bethnal Green's town hall, this lovingly restored pinnacle of the local community now offers trendy hotel rooms and fully fitted studio apartments. The studios are open plan with vintage furniture, benefitting from international plug sockets and the hotel's turndown service. The winner of dozens of architecture and preservation awards, the Town Hall Hotel makes for a crash pad with a little wow factor in this east London neighbourhood.

Patriot Square E2 9NF
+44 (0)207 871 0460
reservations@townhallhotel.com
www.townhallhotel.com
Tube: Bethnal Green

Quirky

The Bush Houseboat

This impeccably furnished houseboat on the River Thames, near the leafy neighbourhood of Kew, is a truly original accommodation option. Flooded with natural light and with beautiful river views, guests become part of the Thames's riverboat community for the duration of their stay. There are no compromises on comfort, with a dishwasher, washing machine and three bedrooms to spread out in.

River Thames, near Kew Bridge
+44 (0)208 892 7241
www.bushhouseboat.co.uk
Rail: Kew Bridge

Batty Langley's

Previously a Spitalfields office building and car park, Batty Langley's was transformed over a number of years into what looks like an eighteenth century inn, finally opening in 2015. Painstakingly put together, period furniture and trimmings were sourced from across the UK to get the look just right. There's no hotel signage on the outside either, giving it a feeling of a secret club when you do eventually find your way inside. Modern conveniences are either hidden away in suites or sympathetically styled so the centuries-old feeling isn't lost.

12 Folgate Street E1 6BX
+44(0)207 377 4390
reservations@battylangleys.co.uk
www.battylangleys.com
Rail: Shoreditch High Street

A Room for London

This one bedroom architectural installation has been a hit with quirky accommodation lovers since it was placed above the Queen Elizabeth Hall on the South Bank in 2012. A location like no other, the boat-like structure looks out over the River Thames and beyond. After guests climb aboard, they're invited to fill in the boat's logbook about their experience. With self-catering facilities and the best rooftop terrace in London on the upper deck, A Room for London has to be the quirkiest place to stay in the city. Would-be guests can only secure a space by entering a ballot.

Queen Elizabeth Hall SE1 8XX
www.living-architecture.com/
aroomforlondon
Rail/Tube: Waterloo

Church Street Hotel

This Central American inspired hotel is décorated with hand-painted Mexican tiles and is peppered with Cuban cigar cases (with chocolate treats hidden inside) and Hispanic religious art. Havana Club rum bottles make fun flower vases, while the on-site Havana lounge has free organic teas, coffees and an honesty bar. The owners even make their own hot sauce, which gets rave reviews from visiting foodies. A surprising and vibrant find in the middle of the unassuming London neighbourhood of Camberwell, Church Street Hotel offers a kitsch take on Latin American style.

29-33 Camberwell Church Street
SE5 8TR
+44 (0)207 703 5984
info@churchstreethotel.com
www.churchstreethotel.com
Rail: Denmark Hill

A Room for London has to be the quirkiest place to stay in the city.

Photo: William Eckersley

40Winks
London's most charming
boutique hotel.

More hotels

40 Winks

This Stepney Green hotel has just two bedrooms, making it more like a homestay. An enchanting home straight from a fairytale, the décor is part-grandiose, part-flamboyant. Luxury comes in the form of creature comforts rather than whizzy technology, and occasional events include Bedtime Story nights, where everyone must come dressed in pyjamas.
109 Mile End Road E1 4UJ
+44 (0)207 790 0259
reservations@40winks.org
www.40winks.org
Tube: Stepney Green

Artist Residence London

This homely and slightly eccentric hotel in south London has just eight hotel rooms, a cocktail lounge and a restaurant. Found inside a former public house dating back to the 1850s, the building has been restored and original artwork subsequently sourced to give it an original feel. Exposed brickwork, wooden floors and furniture from all eras make for a comfortable and design conscious stay.
52 Cambridge Street, London, UK, SW1V 4QQ
+44 (0)207 931 8946
london@artistresidence.co.uk
www.artistresidencelondon.co.uk
Tube: Pimlico

Ham Yard Hotel

This Soho hotel has a modern British style and lots of added extras, from its own 1950s style bowling alley and theatre, to a rooftop terrace and tree-filled garden. It's the best of British in the centre of the city.
1 Ham Yard W1D 7DT
T: +44 (0)20 3642 2000
E: hamyard@firmdale.com
www.firmdalehotels.com/hotels/london/ham-yard-hotel
Tube: Piccadilly Circus

Megaro

This vibrant boutique hotel has surprisingly spacious rooms and a penchant for oak. The velveteen Megaro Bar downstairs feels a little like an old Hollywood film set and is the ideal place to settle in with a cocktail or two.
Belgrove Street WC1H 8AB
+44 (0)207 843 2222
reservations@hotelmegaro.co.uk
www.hotelmegaro.co.uk
Rail/Tube: King's Cross

Rough Luxe

A boutique hotel by architect and interior designer Rabih Hage, Rough Luxe has juxtaposing styles of urban shabby chic vs. classic English luxury. With nine rooms only, the staff are attentive but laid-back. King's Cross isn't the prettiest part of London, but the location is ultra convenient for getting around town.
1 Birkenhead Street WC1H 8BA
www.roughluxehotel.co.uk
Rail/Tube: King's Cross

The Grazing Goat

With just a handful of airy, country-style rooms above the well-liked gastropub of the same name, The Grazing Goat has a village-like feeling, despite its prime location between the bustle of Oxford Street and the charm of Marylebone. Guest

40Winks

Photo: 40Winks

ales and beers make the pub downstairs a contender on the laidback London drinking scene.

6 New Quebec Street W1H 7RQ
+44 (0)207 724 7243
reservations@thegrazinggoat.co.uk
www.thegrazinggoat.co.uk
Tube: Marble Arch

The Hoxton Hotel, Shoreditch

This 'anti-hotel' hates the 'rip-off policies' of other hotels, so there are no expensive mini-bars or high rate phone calls here. Think open fireplaces, exposed brick and leather chairs in the heart of trendy east London. A free 'bag drop' consisting of a light breakfast is delivered every morning. If you want a hotel with the same vibe, The Hoxton Holborn is one of the brand's newest siblings, found in a more corporate part of town.

81 Great Eastern Street EC2A 3HU
+44 (0)207 550 1000
www.thehoxton.com/london/shoreditch
Rail/Tube: Old Street

The London EDITION

This slick, swanky and relatively new addition to London's high end hotel scene has a nightclub and free gin and mixers in Junior Suites. It's a place to see and be seen, and the hotel's restaurant Berners Tavern gets incredibly busy, given the fact it's run by Michelin star chef Jason Atherton.

10 Berners Street W1T 3NP
+44 (0)207 781 0000
www.editionhotels.com/london
Tube: Tottenham Court Road

The Pavilion

This wacky looking hotel is part ode to music and part fashion tribute. Rooms come with hare-brained names, from Honky Tonk Afro and Three's Company, to Better Red Than Dead and Funky Zebra. The clinquant interior has provided the backdrop to many a fashion shoot, while patrons from the fashion, music and media industries tend to dominate the guest list.

34-36 Sussex Gardens W2 1UL
+44 (0)207 262 0905
info@pavilionhoteluk.com
www.pavilionhoteluk.com
Tube: Edgware Road

Qbic London

This affordable design hotel in hip Shoreditch offers soundproofed rooms with blackout curtains to ensure the perfect night's sleep. Each room tends to have a startling oversized image of a person or animal keeping watch over the bed.

42 Adler Street E1 1EE
+44 (0)203 021 3300
reservationslcy@qbichotels.com
london.qbichotels.com
Tube: Aldgate East

The Hoxton Shoreditch

Photo: The Hoxton

Longer term accommodation

If you want to bite the bullet and stay for a while in London, it makes better financial sense to opt for a longer term accommodation rental.

Apartment portals

Some accommodation portals have apartments or rooms to rent to either short term visitors or those who want to stay for a few months. The following providers always have a great selection of London accommodation options:

Airbnb:
www.airbnb.co.uk
Oh-London:
www.oh-london.com
onefinestay:
www.onefinestay.com
Roomorama:
www.roomorama.co.uk/london
SilverDoor:
www.silverdoor.co.uk/city-of-london

Flat shares

A lot of London's new residents opt for a flat share to start off with, to meet new people and save money in those early days of making the big move. Beware — competition can be fierce and existing flat mates tend to look for people they think will 'fit in' — so be quick off the mark if you see a room you like and be prepared for an informal 'interview'. In some cases, all bills are included, while in other instances, bills such as electricity and water will be on top of the rental price, so remember to check first before committing. Some of the most popular websites to find a flat share are:

Gumtree

This is one of the most widely used websites in London for advertising available rooms in house and flat shares. There are typically thousands of adverts for flat shares on the site at any one time and it's possible to refine results depending on the size of room you want (e.g. single or double) or if you know which London neighbourhood you'd prefer to live in. The prices advertised are typically per week, with the very cheapest flat shares starting from around £120 per week.
www.gumtree.com/flatshare/london

Easy Roommate

This website allows you to search for available rooms in London, as well as advertise the fact you're looking for a room, helping you find like-minded people to share with. There are typically a few thousand rooms on offer at any one time and you can easily refine your search to very specific neighbourhoods and localities. Prices are posted per calendar month.
uk.easyroommate.com

SpareRoom

This website allows you to search for available rooms, advertise the fact you want a room, or search for 'buddy ups' —in other words, look for like-minded people who you can start a new flat share with. SpareRoom also runs 'speedflatmating' events to help people find their perfect flatmate. Some Londoners only want a room for the weekdays, and SpareRoom also offers plenty of these opportunities. In total, there are usually several thousand room adverts out there at any one time.
www.spareroom.co.uk/london

RoomHunters

This website helps flat share seekers search for available rooms in London according to different criteria, such as locations in specific London travel zones or near Tube stations. Enter in the amount you can afford to spend monthly and you'll get a list of appropriate results. The website also has useful information about tenants' rights.
www.roomhunters.co.uk

Longer term rentals

If you know you're going to be staying in London for a while and want the freedom of renting your own apartment, there are plenty of websites and companies out there to help. Be aware of the British system involved in renting an apartment, however. Tenants are often required to pay a deposit up front, which is at least the value of one month of rent, and can be more. This has to be placed by the landlord into a government-backed tenancy deposit scheme (TDP), which helps protect your money. If you go via an estate agent, you will also have to pay an estate agency fee. Apartments come either furnished or unfurnished, although unfurnished flats tend to come with 'white goods' in the kitchen, e.g. a fridge and a washing machine. While the landlord will take care of buildings insurance, tenants must purchase contents insurance to cover the value of their own items inside the home.

As well as searching on websites for available rental properties, it's a good idea to register with estate agents in localities you're interested in moving to. Rental properties can get snapped up quickly; if you're on the books of estate agencies, they may phone you before something is advertised more widely online.

Here are some of the most popular websites advertising longer term rentals in London:

Rightmove

This is one of the most popular websites in the UK for finding homes to rent or buy. It's possible to refine your search by specific criteria, such as within a certain mileage of a public transport hub, number of bedrooms you want and whether you want a flat or a house.
www.rightmove.co.uk

Zoopla

Another of the UK's most popular property sites, Zoopla has tens of thousands of rental properties available in London at any given time, and it's possible to search by specific criteria. It also shows useful statistics such as when a property was first listed and how many people have viewed the listing, giving you an indication of the level of interest in the property.
www.zoopla.co.uk/to-rent/property/london

PrimeLocation

This handy website allows you to search through thousands of rental properties according to several sets of criteria. Results show the square footage of properties available as well as key information like proximity to transport hubs and nearby amenities.
www.primelocation.com/to-rent/property/london

In Malta, there's a church on every corner; in London, there's a pub on every corner.

Marama Corlett
Actress

Tell us about yourself and why you moved to London.
I'm from Malta originally: my father's from New Zealand and my mother's
Maltese. I came to London initially because I wanted to further my studies
in classical ballet, having been dancing for a ballet company in Malta, Ballet
Russ de Malt. I eventually took a change of direction into acting but stayed
on in London. It's quite different from ballet, but still very much the arts,
which really is my passion. I got my first role working with New Zealand
director Lee Tamahori in 'The Devil's Double' and it went from there. I now
have an agent in London and two of my sisters live in the city too: one's a
ballet dancer and the other works in costume design for television and film.
We're a very artistic family!

**Which London neighbourhood do you live in and where in London
do you hang out?**
I've been in London for a while now. I lived in Lewisham and Honor Oak
Park in the south east for the first five years. I then moved to west London,
where I live now. I don't hang around there very much, but tend to go to
Soho a lot, partly because my work meetings happen around there, but I
also just love the atmosphere. I'm the kind of person who doesn't mind
being alone in places, but I also love having people around. That's why I
love Soho I think; there's always noise. I love the noise of people in the
street outside the pubs having a drink. I wouldn't mind living in Soho if I
could; watching people go by and listening to music from restaurants.

**What's the difference between Lewisham and west London as a place
to live?**
They're completely different. A lot of people in the arts seem to live in west
or north London. I like the Notting Hill Arts Club but there's also MODE
club near Portobello Road. An actor friend of mine who is also known as
DJ Lonyo puts on some great throwback tunes on Fridays for anyone who
loves to dance. I also like Portobello Road Market, where they sell a lot of
antiques; the best day to go is early on Saturday mornings.

Lewisham has changed a whole lot and is quite up-and-coming now. Lots
of families are moving there and although it feels more urban than west
London, Blackheath and Greenwich Park are close by, both of which are
really beautiful. The café I loved most in Lewisham was called Maggie's. It's
a bit random, but if you live in Lewisham, you know where Maggie's is! It's

an old Irish, breakfast sort of place; they do lunch as well, but you mainly go there for a big traditional breakfast. The price is really reasonable and Maggie and her family run the show. There are free tea and coffee top ups: not an empty mug in sight!

Are you ever tempted to relocate for your career?
London is a good place to live as an actress and there's a lot of work there. I'd say it's up there with Los Angeles and New York. These days, you hear about American projects anyway wherever you're located and you can have initial contact with casting directors over the internet. I find it quite convenient to be based in London and then travel to wherever filming is happening. I recently finished a TV series for NBC called 'A.D – The Bible Continues' and a feature film called 'Desert Dancer' both filmed in Morocco. Sometimes my job takes me back home to Malta, once for a series called 'Sinbad' and another time for 'The Dovekeepers'. My most recent feature film is called 'The Goob' which took me to Norfolk. It's a wonderful job as although I'm based in London, I do get to travel extensively, which I love.

Which one of your London projects are you proudest of?
I'm not sure to be honest; I care about all of them. I played Betty Parris in The Crucible at The Old Vic theatre for a good chunk of 2014. It was such an honour to perform in such a prestigious venue with so much history; and especially in a project produced by Kevin Spacey, who was running it at the time. Every night we had audiences from all over the world; it was brilliant.

Do people in your profession experience the city differently from other Londoners?
If you're filming in London you get to film on location, so you sometimes visit really interesting places you wouldn't get to see otherwise. Sometimes they'll rent out galleries or old buildings of historical importance that are privately owned.

Is London a good place to live for people who are in the public eye?
There are a lot of places that cater for people who are in the public eye, like private members clubs. They have privacy and you don't have to worry about people bothering you there. I'm lucky because I'm not in a situation where people are running after me, but I do know people who are, and it can be quite hard. My lifestyle in London is ideal because there's so much to explore — I spend a lot of time walking around. I rarely get people recognising me, but when they do it's always lovely. I don't have to hide from too much attention by any means, which is perfect for me!

What kind of Londoners do you hang around with?

In London the great thing is that everyone's doing so many different things, and in my line of work, that helps you stay sane. It's easy to get into this mode where you're constantly working, thinking about work, or always with people who are talking about work. I really love my job and I wouldn't change it for the world, but I think it's healthy to spend time with people with other interests and experiences. I'm always hanging out with different people of all ages.

What are the main differences you have noticed between Malta and London, and do you miss anything from home?

In Malta, there's a church on every corner; in London, there's a pub on every corner. I love it! The main thing I miss about home, though, is my family, and the close knit Maltese culture. In London, I find it can sometimes be quite lonely if you don't have the right friends. I think it's because everyone is so independent and constantly busy. I also have some of my family in London, which is great.

Have you got a favourite place to work in London?

There are a couple of places I go to in Soho to read scripts, learn lines or prepare for casting calls, since all the casting directors are in Soho. Maison Bertaux, a tea and cake shop which is more than 100 years old, is one of my favourite places. It's the oldest patisserie in Soho and by far the best. During the day it's mostly quiet, although there can be an occasional rush of tourists. When people find out about the place, they really do love it. Their chocolate éclairs are heaven. It's just so quirky and is still really authentic to Soho.

Another place at the top of my list is a place called Cotton Café on Berwick Street. It's a tiny café with only five tables. It's my favourite for beans, bacon and cheese jacket potatoes. How very English! It's also well-known for its avocado melt toasties and huge mugs of tea. It's all reasonably priced too. Mr Andrew Cotton, who runs the joint (naturally, it's named after him) and his friend Patrick are really lovely people and have a great energy about them, which makes the place extra special. They constantly have to remind me that they are closed on Sundays; I'm always forgetting! If it was up to me I'd turn Cotton Café into a 24/7 café. Soho is full of film and TV production houses, so you'll find a lot of people in the industry go to Cotton Café for a quick lunch.

Do you have favourite cafés elsewhere in London?

I adore England's Lane in Belsize Park, there are lots of cute little coffee shops. I like Ginger & White for their fish finger sandwiches, flat whites and banana bread. I go to Chamomile Café for their apple strudel, tarts and

1. Maison Bertaux
2. Highgate cemetery
3. In Soho with friends
4. At Maison Bertaux with friends.
5. Cotton Café
6. Tea with friends

full English breakfast, and Black Truffle for perfect sausage rolls and fresh juices: it's also a little shop. Belsize Park has some wonderful traditional pubs, one of which is Sir Richard Steele on Haverstock Hill: it's perfectly cosy in the winter time but it also has a great outdoors section for summer.

Do you know any quiet corners in London where you can have a wander?
Highgate Cemetery is a really beautiful place to go. It sounds a bit morbid, but it's so gorgeous there. It's one of what's known as the 'Magnificent Seven' cemeteries in London. It's so old — the tombs are sinking in some places — but there's just something magical about the place. There are guided tours, but I prefer to go when there's nothing on — even on a rainy day.

Do you go out to enjoy any of London's cultural offerings?
We're lucky, because many galleries are free in London. I like the Photographer's Gallery; there are always really good exhibitions on. I went to see David Lynch's exhibition and Warhol's exhibition there recently. I also love the National Portrait Gallery, especially the section on the monarchy with paintings of people like Henry V and Elizabeth I. All those paintings are really special. Going to see a play in London is a great thing to do too; a lot of visitors come and see the musicals only. They're great, but there's a lot more on offer in the city. Physical theatre companies such as Punchdrunk and Complicite always have really quirky and immersive theatre, where the audience are actually participants.

Are you into nightlife?
I did quite a lot of clubbing when I first got to London, but now I prefer to go out for a chilled drink and a chat. I love Gordon's Wine Bar: it's a tiny, Dickensian style place from 1890. I go there for port, cheese and to enjoy the authenticity. I also love cigars and whisky; the Whisky Exchange in Borough Market is fun. Milroy's of Soho has a great whisky selection and a little secret door through a bookcase leads to a cocktail bar called The Vaults, which is just under Greek Street. Floridita in Soho is great if you want to smoke a cigar indoors in Casa, their cigar lounge.

Do you like live music?
Yes I do. Ronnie Scott's hosts famous musicians from all over the world but they also have up-and-coming bands upstairs. There are so many live gigs in London it's ridiculous. Bands come here from all over and we're just so lucky that live music is so accessible!

What music do you associate with London?
It depends on the mood, but when I think of London, I think of jazz. I'm not sure why, maybe there's something about it that gives me butterflies and the feeling of discovering new things. Miles Davis's 'Blue in Green' is my London soundtrack.

Which restaurants do you like to eat at?
In Soho I like a casual Italian restaurant called Princi; the lasagne and the breaded chicken are to die for. I like Quo Vadis on Dean Street for the best British cooking traditions, and Sushi Eatery on Frith Street for Japanese. Also in Soho, I like Andrew Edmunds on Lexington Street. La Bodega Negra is great for Mexican food. It looks like a sex shop from the outside so it's the kind of place you should take someone who hasn't heard about it — just for the look on their face as you enter! The food there is amazing and the bar is great for a quick drink too. Simpsons Tavern close to Bank station is one of London's oldest restaurants and is a good one for pies. For a quick salt beef bagel and tea, there is no place like the Beigel Shop on Brick Lane.

What's the most surprising thing you've seen in London?
I once saw a man walking down a street in Soho wearing only a pair of see-through tights and holding a pineapple. Ha ha! The freedom around Soho is just brilliant; it's about being who you are — no-one's judging.

What would you change about London if you could?
I'd protect areas in London from being bought by rich foreign investors and companies. There's a campaign called Save Soho with celebrities like Stephen Fry and Benedict Cumberbatch behind it. All these really special, historical places in Soho are closing down and they're building fancy apartments and shopping malls instead. It's sad because if it continues it will completely change the place and it'll lose its authenticity. Soho should become a heritage site.

What's your favourite London discovery?
On a traffic island on Old Compton Street there's a street grate. You look down through the grate and you can literally see a hidden street!! The street was once Little Compton Street and its original path has since been blocked by construction in the area. It's something quite extraordinary.

What unusual thing do you like about London?
I like pigeons. I know a lot of people hate them but I think they're great. They're so funny, hanging about all the time. And London really wouldn't be the same without pigeons; they're iconic!

Is there a smell you associate with London?
Pubs in London have a very particular smell. It's kind of like an old cigar smell, even though smoking is banned in London pubs, it's embedded in the walls and carpets from past times. I think the London streets smell like a mixture of pigeons, cigars, beer and coffee!

What would you do on your perfect day out in London?
I love Hyde Park and it's beautiful to walk around. I'd then get a coffee in one of my favourite cafés and pop to the cinema in the afternoon. I love going to the cinema and I often go during the day because it's quiet; even if I'm the only one in there!

Where do you like to go shopping in London?
Second hand shops are great because you can find some really interesting little treasures. There are some very good ones in Hampstead and Belsize Park just across the street from the stations. There's also a cool place in Brick Lane called the Vintage Emporium on Bacon Street. It's a very cute vintage shop run by a lovely couple and doubles as a café. You can only pay in cash though, because they have an old-fashioned cash register. I love it. Brick Lane on Sundays is absolutely filled with vintage wear and knick-knacks in every corner, with people selling items on the street stalls and pop-up shops.

Where do you go to get away from it all?
The cinema. It takes you away to another world. I go to the cinema alone a lot. I love the Prince Charles Cinema; they show a lot of indie and old school films. The Curzon Soho also shows really great films. I love that feeling after a film finishes, when you're just taking it all in. I actually used to work in a cinema in Leicester Square, so I feel I know the real cinema: the life behind the popcorn, so to speak. My favourite job was cleaning the screens after the performance! There's that feeling when no one is in the cinema: the lights are back on and there's popcorn everywhere. I used to love that.

How would you encourage visitors to London to live like locals for the duration of their stay?
Get an Oyster card and take the bus, especially the night bus. That's an experience in itself for anyone coming to London: you'll see London for real. People don't usually talk on the bus and Tube, but people let loose at night. I'd also encourage people to walk around London; you get to see some beautiful and unexpected places if you travel by foot. And finally, I would encourage people not to stay in hotels and live with real Londoners instead. Everyone has their own secret place they love to go to, and everyone has a great local pub. You'll only discover these hidden gems by hanging out with Londoners. Visitors shouldn't be scared of talking to people either; London is such a cosmopolitan place where you can meet such interesting people — I talk to everyone! Just through talking to someone you can learn something new.

<u>What is the current trend in London?</u>
Selfie sticks.

<u>What is London's best quality?</u>
Artistic expression and the freedom to be yourself. Londoners are open to anything. What I loved when I first moved to London was that you could go to the supermarket in your pyjamas— no one cares. Do that in Malta and you'll probably end up in the newspaper! I just love how free you can be. You can be yourself and find yourself in this city.

Marama's London

Places to visit

Blackheath
Rail: Blackheath

Brick Lane
Rail: Shoreditch High Street

Complicite
+44 (0)207 485 7700
www.complicite.org

Curzon Soho
99 Shaftesbury Avenue W1D 5DY
+44 (0)330 500 1331
www.curzoncinemas.co.uk/soho
Tube: Leicester Square
Greenwich Park
Rail: Greenwich

Highgate Cemetery
Swain's Ln N6 6PJ
+44 (0)208 340 1834
info@highgate-cemetery.org
www.highgatecemetery.org
Tube: Archway

Hyde Park
Tube: Hyde Park Corner,
Knightsbridge, Lancaster Gate or
Queensway

Little Compton Street
Traffic island on Old Compton
Street
Tube: Leicester Square

MODE
12 Acklam Rd W10 5QZ
+44 (0)208 354 3864
reservations@modecollective.com
www.modecollective.com
Tube: Westbourne Park

National Portrait Gallery
St. Martin's Place WC2H 0HE
+44 (0)207 306 0055
www.npg.org.uk
Tube: Charing Cross or Leicester
Square
Rail: Charing Cross

Notting Hill Arts Club
21 Notting Hill Gate W11 3JQ
+44 (0)207 460 4459
www.nottinghillartsclub.com
Tube: Notting Hill Gate

Photographer's Gallery
16-18 Ramillies Street W1F 7LW
+44 (0)207 087 9300
info@tpg.org.uk
thephotographersgallery.org.uk
Tube: Oxford Circus

Portobello Road Market
Portobello Road W11 2DY
www.portobelloroad.co.uk
Tube: Ladbroke Grove

Prince Charles Cinema
7 Leicester Place WC2H 7BY
+44 (0)207 494 3654
www.princecharlescinema.com
Tube: Leicester Square

Punchdrunk
+44 (0)207 655 0940
punchdrunk@punchdrunk.org.uk
www.punchdrunk.org.uk

The Old Vic
The Cut SE1 8NB
+44 (0)844 871 7628
www.oldvictheatre.com
Rail/Tube: Waterloo

Vintage Emporium
14 Bacon Street E1 6LF
+44 (0)207 739 0799

Food and drink

Andrew Edmunds
46 Lexington Street W1F 0LP
+44 (0)207 437 5708
www.andrewedmunds.com
Tube: Oxford Circus

Beigel Shop
155 Brick Lane E1 6SB
+44 (0)207 729 0826
Rail: Shoreditch High Street

Black Truffle
41 England's Lane NW3 4YD
+44 (0)207 483 1623
enquiries@blacktruffledeli.com
www.blacktruffledeli.com
Tube: Belsize Park

Ginger & White
2 England's Lane NW3 4TG
+44 (0)207 722 4TG
www.gingerandwhite.com
Tube: Belsize Park

Chamomile Café
45 England's Lane NW3 4YD
+44 (0)207 586 4580
www.chamomilecafe.co.uk
Tube: Belsize Park or Chalk Farm

Cotton Café
82 Berwick Street W1F 8TP
+44 (0)207 287 3200
Tube: Oxford Circus or
Tottenham Court Road

Floridita/Casa
100 Wardour Street W1F 0TN
+44 (0)207 314 4000
info@floriditalondon.com
www.floriditalondon.com
Tube: Leicester Square

Gordon's Wine Bar
47 Villiers Street WC2N 6NE
+44 (0)207 930 1408
info@gordonswinebar.com
www.gordonswinebar.com
Tube: Embankment or Charing
Cross
Rail: Charing Cross

La Bodega Negra
16 Moor Street W1D 5NH
+44 (0)207 758 4100
www.labodeganegra.com
Tube: Leicester Square

Maggie's
320-322 Lewisham Road SE13
7PA
+44 (0)208 244 0339
info@maggiesrestaurant.co.uk
www.maggiesrestaurant.co.uk
Rail: Lewisham

Maison Bertaux
28 Greek Street W1D 5DQ
+44 (0)207 437 6007
www.maisonbertaux.com
Tube: Leicester Square

Milroy's of Soho (and The Vault)
3 Greek Street W1D 4NX
+44 (0)207 734 2277
info@milroys.co.uk
www.milroys.co.uk
Tube: Tottenham Court Road

Princi
135 Wardour Street W1F 0UT
+44 (0)207 478 8888
info@princi.com
www.princi.com
Tube: Leicester Square

Simpsons Tavern
Ball Court, 38½ Cornhill EC3V 9DR
+44 (0)207 626 9985
manager@simpsonstavern.co.uk
www.simpsonstavern.co.uk
Tube: Bank

Sushi Eatery
40 Frith Street W1D 5LN
+44 (0)207 734 9688
Tube: Leicester Square

Quo Vadis
26-29 Dean Street W1D 3LL
+44 (0)207 437 9585
info@quovadissoho.co.uk
www.quovadissoho.co.uk
Tube: Tottenham Court Road

Ronnie Scott's
47 Frith Street W1D 4HT
+44 (0)207 439 0747
www.ronniescotts.co.uk
Tube: Leicester Square

Sir Richard Steele
97 Haverstock Hill NW3 4RL
+44 (0)207 483 1261
sirrichardsteele@faucetinn.com
www.faucetinn.com/
sirrichardsteele
Tube: Chalk Farm

Follow Marama Corlett on
Twitter @maramacorlett

The Whisky Exchange @ Vinopolis
1 Bank End SE1 9BU
+44 (0)207 403 8688
vinopolis@thewhiskyexchange.com
www.thewhiskyexchange.com
Rail/Tube: London Bridge

See also
Save Soho
www.savesoho.com

Photo: Richard Harris - *deathtothestockphoto.com*

chapter 4

Getting away
and getting lost

*Wandering aimlessly without a plan
sometimes brings unexpected inspiration.*

Away for a day

Get away from the bustle of London for the day and experience quirky and creative hotspots outside the city.

Brighton

This southern seaside town has been a stalwart getaway spot for Londoners for decades, and with a train journey of less than an hour, there's a thriving community of London workers who live in Brighton and enjoy the best of both worlds. Enjoy a brisk walk along the pebbly sea-front, join the throngs in the carnival atmosphere of the pier and spot the last mystical remnants of the old West Pier. Design and vintage lovers should explore the bohemian hub of North Laine. Grab a coffee at The Witchez Photo Design Café, taste some traditional fish and chips at Bardsley's and partake in a drink at The Brighton Beer Dispensary. Also Brighton has a thriving LBGTQ community and an exciting nightlife.

www.visitbrighton.com

Transport: Regular train service from London Victoria to Brighton

Margate

This south-eastern coastal town less than two hours by train from London used to be anything but hip, but with recent design-conscious openings and a smattering of eccentricities, Londoners are travelling there in droves to enjoy a slice of the action. The recent re-opening of the Dreamland amusement park has definitely added to the town's appeal. Britain's oldest surviving amusement park has a good helping of vintage jocularity in its design, matched with nostalgic rides and a calendar of wacky events. Elsewhere, the Mad Hatter tea shop (only open on Saturdays) is full of over-the-top gaudy British memorabilia, the tidal pool is great for an open-air swim, and the Turner Contemporary Gallery is ideal for art buffs.

www.visitthanet.co.uk

www.dreamland.co.uk

Transport: Regular train services from London Pancras International or London Victoria

Bear Grylls Survival Academy

The well-known British adventurer Bear Grylls runs outdoor survival courses in locations across the UK and further afield. Just a stone's throw from London is the Surrey Hills centre, where 24-hour bush-craft courses teach you everything from learning how to forage and making safety harnesses to navigating river crossings. You'll also practice emergency shelter building, survival knife skills and fire lighting. There's no better way to escape the urban jungle of London than by getting back-to-basics in the not-too-jungle-like county of Surrey, less than an hour away from the city centre.

www.beargryllssurvivalacademy.com

Transport: Regular trains run from London Waterloo to Gomshall via Guildford

Away for a weekend

Discover more of what the UK has to offer by taking a weekend trip away from London.

Sawday's Canopy & Stars

Embrace the Londoner's love of all things quirky outside the city in one of the getaway properties advertised on the Sawday's website. Places to stay include treehouses, yurts, houseboats and water-borne cabins that can only be reached by rowing boat. Our favourite is The Big Green Bus, a bright green double-decker bus adorned with all the mod cons. It's found in the Sussex countryside, a county within striking distance of white-cliffed coastlines, the South Downs National Park and your pick of cosy pubs.

www.canopyandstars.co.uk

Gower Peninsula

Enjoy the beauty of this southern Wales beauty spot for the weekend, within four hours' travelling distance from London. With stunning bays, beaches and coves, The Gower is ideal for cosy camping trips and rugged coastal walks. Find a small campsite with beach views or beach access from Cool Camping, where you can enjoy daytime swimming, beachcombing, and evening campfires. Rhossili is home to an artsy community and the three-mile long sandy beach — a designated Area of Outstanding Beauty — or visit the lesser known Three Cliffs beach and its unusual tidal pools. Dine in the beachside 19th century restaurant, The Coalhouse, or check out the twinkly lights and live music at The Kitchen Table in Mumbles.

www.visitswanseabay.com
www.coolcamping.co.uk/campsites/uk/wales/the-gower
Transport: Trains run every 90 minutes from London Paddington to Swansea; catch local buses and trains to The Gower from there. Hire a car from various car hire companies in London (see page 39)

Isle of Wight

England's 'garden isle' off the southern coast is popular with outdoorsy people. Famous for the stack load of dinosaur fossils discovered there, numerous walking trails and a growing festival scene — with the annual Isle of Wight Festival, Bestival and Ventnor Fringe — the island has proven to be a welcome retreat for many-a-Londoner over the years. And it only takes three hours to get there from the city by public transport. Accommodation is in cottages or cool houseboats and apartments in the Golden Hill Fort. Take the almost vertical chairlift down to Alum Bay, have a coffee or beer at The Dairyman's Daughter inside a converted stable, and paint pottery while eating a very British cream tea at Chesell Pottery.

www.visitisleofwight.co.uk
Transport: Catch the train from London to Portsmouth, Southampton or Lymington, then catch a ferry to the Isle of Wight. Ferries also carry cars if you'd prefer to hire a car (see page 39)

Away forever

*Samuel Johnson famously said "if you're tired of London, you're tired of life". But sometimes it's time to
say goodbye. Here are some other destinations London-lovers like to travel to next.*

Manchester

Home to Tech North, the second start-up hub in the UK, those attracted
to London's start-up scene may feel equally at home in Manchester. If you
come from London, you may have to put up with a little 'southern softie'
banter, but with the cheaper cost of living and a thriving food and drinks
scene, Manchester is still an attractive proposition for many. Entrepreneurs
should find a funky desk at SpacePortX or hunker down in a small office in
a shipping container at The Sharp Project. Hang out with creative types in
the Northern Quarter, enjoy coffee and baked goods at the vintagey Sugar
Junction, and relish a slap-up Chinese meal at the much raved about Tattu.
Manchester has a famously good nightlife scene too: be sure to check out live
and world music at Band on the Wall, visit the laidback Soup Kitchen and
check out the arts venue and club, Islington Mill.

Amsterdam

Fans of London looking for a smaller city and better work-life balance
love to make that hop across the water to Amsterdam. The canal-adorned
Dutch capital has placed itself as a serious contender in the creative sector
and is now considered an established city for start-ups. During the working
week, grab a desk at funky co-working spaces such as The Thinking Hut
inside a previous horse stable, or at Open Coop with its ethical/collective
mantra and experimental energy drink lab. In between the coffee shops
galore, enjoy beers at Brouwerij 't IJ, a brewery in a windmill, or at the
17th century Hanneke's Boom on one of Amsterdam's islands. Try out
eclectic Dutch-Indonesian food at Café Kadijk or enjoy visionary vegetarian
inventions at de culinaire werkplaats. And when the sun cracks a ray, join
Amsterdammers on their canal boats or for picnics in Vondelpark.

Tel Aviv

Hailed as one of the hottest start-up hubs in Europe at the moment, Tel
Aviv has a painfully cool tech culture and an open attitude to business that
entrepreneurs love. The mind-set has been described as entrepreneurial
'chutzpah', a Yiddish term for an almost cheeky confidence. Despite the
population being a fraction of the size of London's, there's still a strong
pool of creative talent enjoying a much cheaper cost of living and a
friendlier way of doing business. Grab a desk at a co-working space such
as the traveller-friendly Mindspace, the industrial-styled SOSA or Google

Campus Tel Aviv, which also hosts a string of events. During downtime, take advantage of the ten miles of seafront the city offers and join the Israelis with a beer by the beach after work, or get stuck into the locally loved pastime of people-watching with a coffee: the Rothschild coffee kiosk and the artsy Casino San Remo are perfect for this. With a vibrant arts scene and spirited nightlife options, this Israeli city by the Mediterranean has tonnes going for it.

Sydney
Brits have been flocking to Australia for decades, entranced by the promise of a similar culture with an important climatic difference, since the country basks in sunshine for much of the year. As Sydney starts to makes waves on the start-up scene, moving here could be a real option for London-living entrepreneurs too, although the cost of living is on a par in both cities. With a couple of thousand active tech start-ups in the city and increasing commitment from angel investors, Sydney is a progressively vibrant spot to set up shop. Grab a desk at a co-working spot by the beach at Berrins, or follow in the footsteps of many Sydney start-up success stories at Tank Stream Labs. On weekends off, join the locals at hole-in-the-wall bars and get in plenty of beach time. Enjoy fish and chips — Sydney style — at North Bondi Fish, grab a cocktail at the kitsch Grandma's, and take advantage of a mostly free calendar of arts at The Gallery of NSW. It certainly does sound a lot like a sunnier version of London.

Getting lost

Wandering without having a destination in mind is becoming a lost art in cities today. Paying no attention to street names and directions, the ticking of time and 'having a plan', is a liberating way to authentically experience a locality and a moment in time.

'Getting lost' is not a new concept. Flâneurs — idle strollers — were first talked about in the 16th century. A concept with no true exact English translation, flânerie is all about aimless wandering, losing yourself and urban exploration.

We urge you to get lost in the urban jungle of London to experience the rhythm of the city without thought or direction. Our suggestions in this section are simply starting points for the adventures you'll create in the city. Whether you decide to jump on a bus and travel six stops, or make a beeline for something that looks interesting before sitting down and observing your surroundings, that's up to you.

Wandering aimlessly without a plan sometimes bring unexpected inspiration. We challenge you to give it a try.

Getting lost

Wandering aimlessly can bring some of the best discoveries in London. Here's some inspiration for how to 'get lost' in the city:

1. Thames Path
2. London's big business centres after dark on the weekend: Canary Wharf and Bank
3. Watch a local cricket match during the summer, such as at Burton Court Pavilion by the Saatchi Gallery or Kew Green
4. Chiswick House and Gardens
5. Hop on and off the Tube to discover new localities
6. Hurlingham Park
7. Emirates Air Line: Go outside rush hour, get a cabin to yourself and see London from a different perspective
8. Get off the main roads and duck into side streets, such as this one in Greenwich
9. Immerse yourself in London's beauty with an artistic pursuit
10. Canalside life
11. Camden Passage near Angel
12. St. Martin's Courtyard — a haven in the middle of tourist land
13. The area around Bank and Monument at the weekend
14. Neasden temple
15. Richmond Park
16. Geffrye Museum
17. Book stand under the bridge on the South Bank
18. The Crypt Gallery
19. Tinderbox Café, hidden away in Paperchase on Tottenham Court Road

Flâneur, from the French noun flâneur, means "stroller", "lounger", "saunterer", or "loafer". Flânerie refers to the act of strolling, with all of its accompanying associations.

Notes

Carl's friends

Brands, companies and people we like.

BERLIN **LONDON** COPENHAGEN AMSTERDAM PRAGUE
BRUSSELS BARCELONA MADRID HAMBURG VIENNA
STRASBOURG ROME LEIPZIG WROCLAW ISTANBUL
PARIS EDINBURGH MUNICH ANTWERP AND MORE

PANORAMA
STREETLINE

Panoramastreetline
PanoramaStreetline:
more city to view.
Linearised streets and
cityscapes from all over
Europe. Prints, licenses
and assignments via
panoramastreetline.com

Zoku

Zoku is a new category in the hotel industry: a flexible home/ office hybrid, also suitable for long stays, with the services of a hotel and the social buzz of a thriving neighbourhood. Zoku opens in Amsterdam early 2016.

www.livezoku.com

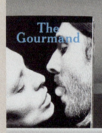

About Carl Goes

Travel guides for curious and creative people

Whether you travel to a city for three days, three weeks or three months, we know it's increasingly important to you to become part of the fabric of the city you visit. As a result, we see it as our job to give you an insight into how residents live, work and play in the city, with cherry-picked recommendations from locals of where you can find collaborative workspaces and homely city crash pads, or where you can meet up with like-minded people and find places you can visit to get away from the crowds. Perhaps you want to stay for longer than the length of a vacation or work trip, or want dream about the possibilities at least, in which case you might be curious to find out how to hire office space or gain work as a freelancer, where you can learn the language, and which neighbourhood would suit you best to live in.

Carl Goes wants you to become a citizen of the cities you visit

This is why we think *Carl Goes* is different from other travel guides. It's not about highlighting the well-trodden backpacker trails and tourist sites everyone already knows about, nor is it about featuring the most visually impressive sites of a city without any substance behind it. You want to know about the river barge doubling as a spa, the art gallery hiding away in a concrete car park on the edge of town, and how to discover the city for yourself. You want to know how local residents experience the city, where you can take your laptop to work for a day among like-minded professionals or creatives, and where you can sample cuisines prepared by trailblazing chefs.

Wandering aimlessly without a plan sometimes brings unexpected inspiration

Carl Goes guides are about presenting cities from local viewpoints: our guides are driven by insights from the people who actually live in a city. Juxtaposing our hand-picked recommendations of things to do and places to go with interviews giving the spotlight to a range of the city's residents, *Carl Goes* helps you become part of the city scene. Whether you're travelling for three days, three weeks or three months, a *Carl Goes* guide makes a destination a place to call home.

If you have any questions, ideas or suggestions then please e-mail us at info@carlgoes.com